FALL
TO
DOMUM

CASTLE SERIES, BOOK I

J. H. WEAR

ONE

Relax *And Take The Bus*. The words chiselled in the sign haunted Robert Jon McKinney as he peered out of the bus window. Jon squeezed his bulk across the hard seats in an attempt to find comfort on the cracked green vinyl; the seat in front of him forced him to sit slightly sideways. He ran his hand back through his short dark hair, attempting to smooth it down. His girlfriend, Nadine Newman, described his hair like that of a dandelion ready to explode. He really didn't think that it was an accurate assessment or a particularly funny one. Nadine's comments didn't stop just at his hair and occasionally she indicated his weight was on the high side as well. More than just indicate, and it made him wonder why she dated him. Jon was a big man and not soft, but he didn't scare anyone when he entered a room.

The sign, he recalled, was done on chipped paint on the side of a brick wall of a building he saw on the cab ride over from the airport. That should have given Jon a hint of things to come when he boarded the bus.

He felt apprehension about the final leg of his journey when the driver, a heavyset man approaching the age of retirement, yawned as Jon stepped past him. The bus, which had its best years behind it, was less than half full and Jon was able to have a bench seat for himself.

An hour after lurching through stop signs and traffic lights, the bus made its way into the countryside. Jon slouched in his seat and stared out of the window.

———

Two weeks previously he sat in a lawyer's office with Nadine to receive an inheritance from his Uncle Gordon Miller. He recalled meeting his uncle only once as a young boy, when the tall, distinguished man visited the family in Boston. Jon didn't talk much with him, at nine years old he didn't have a lot to say that grown-ups were interested in, but it seemed his mother's brother took a liking to him anyway. At first, he thought it was odd that he was left anything at all but Uncle Gordon often asked about him in his letters and paid for a sizable portion of his college tuition.

The rumours of his uncle's hidden riches made her excited as they exited the elevator on the twenty-fifth floor of the First National Bank Building. Nadine, a short, small boned blonde with her hair tied tight in a bun on her head, preceded Jon into the office. They had to wait several minutes past their two o'clock appointment time and Jon took in the thick carpet, the dark oak walls and the original paintings on the wall. He felt a bit intimidated wearing just a golf shirt and black jeans. A woman came from around the opening in the reception area and beckoned them to follow her.

"Mr. Van der Velde will see you now."

Unlike the receptionist, Van der Velde seemed pleased to see them and apologized for their wait. He stood up at his desk and opened his hand toward the chairs sitting in front. Van der Velde, a tall sixty-year-old on a slim frame, had retained most of his silver-white hair.

"First, Mr. McKinney, I need your signature on these documents… and these…and these." Van der Velde slid a small stack of paper across his desk to Jon.

Jon signed several legal documents as Mr. Van der Velde carefully explained the reason for each piece of the fourteen-inch paper.

"Now you may think the requirements of the will are a bit peculiar but rest assured that many wills have special conditions attached to them before they can be fulfilled."

Van der Velde paused and peered at them from the top of his bi-focal glasses. They nodded as they leaned forward in the soft leather chairs.

"First, he has bestowed upon you the legal possession of the Miller Castle, its land and any contents inside."

He paused as Jon sat upright and Nadine gasped as she covered her mouth with her hand. Van der Velde slid over the desk a set of papers folded together.

"There is also an item of some import inside this sealed envelope."

He lifted up a bulging envelope.

"The instructions in the will stipulate that you may not open this envelope until you have read and agreed to the terms of this final document inside this other envelope."

He held up a second envelope, this one flat.

"The final stipulation of the will states that you read this document alone, that it is for your eyes only, within twenty-four hours of accepting the legal document giving you possession of the Miller Castle."

He looked at his watch.

"The time is now fourteen minutes after two o'clock. If you wish you may read the document in a room we have for consultations. I would advise you do this as I can then verify that you have met all legal requirements of the will and will be able to attest to that fact if the need should arise."

Jon nodded. "Perhaps I better do that now."

Van der Velde escorted Jon to another office through an adjoining door. The next office was larger, with ten chairs around a rectangular oak table and had a second door that Jon believed led to a hallway. He sat at one of the chairs, opening the envelope after Van der Velde closed the door. The paper inside was plain white, with carefully hand-written words in blue ink. Jon smoothed out the folded paper with reverence and read his uncle's final instructions to him.

Robert—his Uncle Gordon had not known Jon had switched over to using his middle name—*I can only ask that you follow these final instructions, as I have no way of enforcing them. I can only trust your own good judgment on these conditions.*

1) Take particular care of the necklace; it is not valuable in a monetary sense but rather as a symbol and conveyance of power.

2) Visit and claim possession of the castle as soon as possible, hopefully within a few days of reading this document. Please don't delay this request.

When you arrive at the castle, and it is best you do so alone, you will probably soon discover the secret that I cannot reveal now. I have left you additional information in a desk located in a small study on the main floor.

I also ask you not to reveal the contents of this letter to anyone. In good conscience I must warn you that there is a degree of danger for you. There are forces out there that will stop at nothing to gain what you now have. Be careful whom you trust; they may not be what they appear. I wish I could tell you more, but I doubt you would believe the truth. Besides, as I have learned over the years, the truth is an elusive commodity.

I understand if you think of me as a bit of a madman, but I have given these items to you because of all my relatives and acquaintances, you alone seem to possess the character and intellect for the task that may come to you.

Sincerely,
Uncle Gordon

Jon sat alone in the office the lawyer had provided and reread the letter. Uncle Gordon was known as an eccentric in the family. Well off, but a bit odd.

———

Jon considered it fortunate that he was able to fly to Ireland in the middle of summer. He would be able to see the castle and return home and not miss any of his final year of college. Nadine saw him off at the airport, along with his parents and older sister. They stood purposely apart from each other, although they were polite to each other. Nadine was upset he wouldn't reveal the letter contents to her, however when he told her, "It's a promise and condition," she seemed to accept that explanation. She wanted him to postpone his flight for a few weeks, so she could arrange time off work but he denied her request on that as well, stating the letter requested he visit the castle soon. It made it an awkward goodbye.

Despite Nadine's anger at him for leaving on the first available flight, or perhaps because of it, Jon relaxed as he sat back on his seat.

At the Shannon Airport in southwest Ireland, he walked around while waiting for his next flight, making use of a pay phone to call Nadine's apartment. He was surprised that he could only leave a message on her answering machine, after she had told him to phone when he arrived in England.

Slightly peeved he phoned his parents' house, surprised when his sister answered.

"Hi there. Mom and Dad are out in the back. We're here for dinner." Sandra was referring to her husband, Martin and their son Jason. "How's the weather there?"

"Don't know, I haven't left the terminal yet. Did Nadine tell you where she was going to be later today? I tried her place, but she wasn't home."

She sighed. "No, she doesn't like to talk to the rest of the family, remember?"

He remembered all right. He remembered both sides giving him their opinion of each other. His sister once called her an anorexic witch to him, a comment that caused him to chastise her. He felt uncomfortable telling off his older sister but considered this time she had crossed the line. And as he pointed out at the time, although she was small framed, she certainly had an appetite. In fact, her love for rare steak was a bit startling when he saw her eat.

"Yeah, but I thought she may have said something in passing."

"Sorry, as soon as you walked through that gate, she was gone. Don't fret, I'm sure you'll hear from her soon enough. Hey, do you want to talk to Mom?"

He talked to his mother for a couple of minutes, purchased a magazine and waited. Another hour passed and he boarded the plane for the final flight, which was shorter than his wait time at the airport. From the terminal he took a bus to his last destination.

The bus was determined to make sure he didn't get any more rest. It jostled down the uneven streets, made hard stops, and turned frequently enough that Jon lost his sense of direction. He still wasn't able to get a hold of Nadine, and his anger for her not responding began to turn into concern. He stared out at the moving countryside. As the afternoon sun began to drop lower, the glass gave an odd reflection of the interior of the bus imposed on the outside. It looked like two different worlds fighting for the same space.

———

The bus completed its last stop, the town of Ballymiller. The driver announced the stop without joy, adding a comment in a flat voice that Jon wasn't sure if he was joking.

"Eighty-five hundred souls, eighty-six if ye count the ones without bodies."

Jon checked in the Demister Hotel across the street from the bus stop. The room was small, although comfortable and used dark colours on the walls and furniture. An air freshener made the air smell of decaying flowers. The TV received only the local channels and after trying the two stations, he decided the local pub would be a better place to spend the remaining hours of the evening.

The Demister Pub was located next door in the same building as the hotel, though for reasons unexplained to him he had to go outside of the hotel to gain access to it. The bar was quite full and lively, which he found surprising for a Wednesday night. He ordered a pint of beer and a sandwich from an energetic young blonde woman from behind the bar. He carried his beer to a table, and watched part of a darts tournament, eyeing some of the surrounding people.

The bartender, Charlene, introduced herself a bit more formally by shaking his hand when she brought him the sandwich, chatting with him for a moment before running off to do some more work.

As he neared the bottom of his glass, a pair of women at a neighbouring table struck up a conversation with him. Intrigued with his American accent, they invited him to join their table, consisting of several members of a darts team. Jon, though not used to being the centre of attention, slid his chair to their table. He enjoyed listening to the banter and the jokes but was reserved in adding his own thoughts.

The barmaid swung by the table, and as she stood by Jon, rested a hand on his shoulder. "Well then, are we having another round?" She squeezed his shoulder a bit. "Who'd be buying?"

The hint worked on Jon.

"That would be me."

Everyone at the table grinned happily at the news. Apparently, he passed some sort of test with the four male darts players and the two women.

They soon found the reason why he was visiting their Ballymiller, to claim ownership of the Miller Castle.

"So, do you know the story behind the Miller Castle? Or the whole town for that matter?"

Tori had short, almond-coloured hair and a medium-sized frame. She wore clothes as though she were a size smaller.

"No. Uncle Gordon was known as being a little eccentric but I can't say anything beyond that."

"Well then, I can tell you the castle and the area is haunted and not just by human ghosts either."

Thomas chimed in, "Tis true. I myself saw a demon there with me own eyes. Ganky thing. Disappeared in a blink of an eye."

Jon was told of other strange happenings around the castle that included leprechauns, goblins and other assorted creatures. The common denominator seemed to be the ability of the creatures to vanish a moment later, and for most of the sightings to be around the castle itself.

"Well, that all sounds interesting. Did Uncle Gordon ever talk about them?"

Travis laughed.

"Himself? I can't say your uncle ever talked about them or anything else for that matter."

Liz shushed him.

"Your uncle was a private man, that's all. I talked to himself a couple of times and he was always nice."

She rested a hand on his knee. Liz tossed her long, blonde hair behind her head. She was average height with a nice figure that was obvious under her loose T-shirt and blue jeans. Jon was momentarily taken back by her touch. Back in Boston, young ladies rarely seemed to find him interesting enough to flirt with him.

"Where did you talk to him?"

"That would be at the café where I work. He'd stop in from time to time for lunch. We didn't talk about those creatures, just stuff like the weather."

"Oh. How did he die? I was never told exactly, just that he was missing and presumed dead."

"Well, I'm sorry to say he was presumed drowned. Your uncle fished from a pier near the castle. His fishing stuff was found at the end of the dock. But your uncle had disappeared."

"Never found the body," Travis pointed out as he took a long drink. He didn't look too keen on Liz cozying up with Jon.

"Yeah, but the lake is deep, more like a loch." Liz turned her attention on Jon, twisting in her chair. "They hoped his body was going to show up after a bit. Sorry, I didn't mean to sound crude."

"That's okay. I only met him once when I was young. But the

police figure that was the only explanation, that he fell off the dock and then drowned?"

"You'll have to see the dock. You can see it's pretty old and slopes down at a grand angle. It was chilly the morning he disappeared and would have been wearing heavy clothing. The cold water would have soaked into the clothing and pulled him down fast."

"I'll have to take a look. I'm going to get the keys and location of the castle tomorrow morning."

"'Tis not hard to find, far end of town."

She got up and put on her coat.

"I best be heading out. I have to work in the morning." She looked at Jon. "Care to walk me home?"

His eyes opened wide at the possibility. "Oh, for sure."

He quickly put on his own coat, bid everyone goodbye and followed Liz out the door. She lived only a short distance away, but they managed to squeeze a fair amount of conversation in that time. She found out he had played football.

"You must be good, you're so big and strong."

He told her he was studying to be a computer network analyst.

"You must be really smart," she said, which made him feel on top of the world.

She gave him a quick kiss on the cheek at her house, quietly, because she didn't want to wake her parents, and received a promise from him to call her.

Halfway back to his hotel he remembered Nadine and the rush of guilt feelings. In his bed he thought of Nadine again and wondered why he couldn't get a hold of her. Then, finally, he reflected on Liz and how good she made him feel about himself. How odd, he contemplated, that he had to travel across the ocean to get a compliment.

The following day he rose early. His biological clock still hadn't adjusted to Europe. He sat in bed and watched the news, knowing it was too early for breakfast. The leading story on the local politics baffled him. *Isn't that supposed be a good thing that they're going to pave a road?* After the news, he returned to where he had been the night before, leaving his suitcase at the hotel. After devouring the food and tea, he made his way to the lawyer's office in town that held the keys to the Miller Castle.

The white-haired gentleman acting as a lawyer had him sign some papers and gave him a collection of keys, including a rusty skeleton key. By the time he left the office, it was warm enough for him to take off his jacket, carrying it as he made his way to the iron gate of the Miller Castle.

The first key opened the padlock securing the chain that went through the bars of the gate. He walked along the curved, gravelled roadway to the two massive front doors. Jon hesitated before carefully slipping the skeleton key in the lock. The right door quietly and slowly opened to his push, until near the end of its journey when it gave out a squeak. Jon stood at the door, facing the gloom of grey stone walls as cool air blew past him, causing goose bumps to appear on his arms. A shiver raced down his back.

Jon took a deep breath and boldly stepped inside, leaving the door open so more light could enter the dim interior. Not, he told himself, that he was concerned about any ghosts or demons.

The main room that adjoined the entrance hall rose two stories high with a staircase located at the rear wall. A gaudy, red and gold short pile rug covered the marble floor where several oversized chairs sat around a coffee table. A thin layer of dust covered the table and other horizontal surfaces. Along a wall, a large fireplace sat with half-burnt logs inside the hearth and a stack of chopped wood sitting next to it. Jon took in the huge chandelier marking the centre of the room, the large rectangular windows high above, the large paintings and the large everything in the room. Some parts of the room were well lit from the sunlight that poured through the windows but there were still dark shadows that hid other areas.

Jon noticed a lamp cord going to an outlet at the wall, with a metal conduit running from it before disappearing around a corner. It looked like the modern convenience of electricity was added to the castle.

He tried the lamp but didn't get a response. Jon tried to inspect other rooms but wasn't willing to do too much exploring without light. He did find the study, a dark room with a single small window and located next to the kitchen. Another key opened the desk drawer and he found a large yellow envelope with his name on it, 'Robert McKinney'.

He carried the envelope to the front hall when he heard a scampering sound in the kitchen. Jon didn't investigate what caused it, be it a mouse or a ghost. He quickly left the castle and locked the front door behind him.

Jon released his breath. *I can't let those stories of ghosts get me to overreact.*

As his heart rate slowed, he walked around the outside of the castle, fighting the overgrown plants encroaching on the stone path to the backyard.

The yard extended toward the lake and Jon saw the pier that was slowly sinking at the far end into the water, one side dropping more than the other. A large tackle box sat at the edge. He decided fishing on the edge there could be a hazard. He stared out toward the lake, watching the water lap toward the shore and thought it looked rather peaceful. Jon suddenly felt a tickling at the back of his neck, causing him to turn around quickly. He saw a shadow disappear at the edge of the castle and that was enough for Jon to call a retreat. He hurried back along the path to the front, retied the chain and locked the gate.

Damn stories of ghosts last night are working on my mind.

He shook his head, slightly annoyed with himself. *I can't start jumping at every shadow I see. I need to get something to eat and read what's in this envelope.* He looked up and down the street, deciding to turn left and see if there was a place to eat. He came across Aunty Lena's Bar and stepped inside. The place was busy and he found a table near a window.

In an afterthought he supposed it wasn't much of a coincidence; it was close to the castle and there could not have been too many cafes and bars in Ballymiller. However, it was a pleasant surprise to find Liz there and she was happy to see him.

"Hey, fancy seeing you here. Were you at the Miller Castle?"

"Yeah, but it was pretty dark in there. They'd shut off the electricity."

"You didn't bump into any ghosts now, did you?"

He gave a nervous laugh. "No, I think they were all in hiding."

"When are you heading back there?"

"Well, I'm not sure. I guess I'll have to get the power back on or use a flashlight."

"If you like, I'll go with you. I'd love to see what's inside that castle. Me parents have some torches we can use."

He readily agreed. Some company going into that castle would be welcome, especially with someone like Liz. He actually made two dates with her, one at the pub for later that night and a second one for tomorrow to return to the castle after she finished work.

During his lunch he opened the envelope and read a second letter from his uncle.

Robert;

I trust you will take this information with an open mind. You may find it bizarre but allow me to tell you of my own investigation.

If one does even a cursory examination of the tales of fabled creatures such as goblins, leprechauns, ogres, fairies or ghouls, it becomes apparent that these myths must have had some basis for their being. It is easy to reduce these creatures to mere superstition and imagination, but that doesn't explain the persistence of these myths over time and different locations.

If you, like myself at one time, still scoff at suggestions there may be something behind these tales, then do what I did and ask people in Ballymiller if they have seen any strange creatures. Their answers are not lacking in conviction and their insistence that the best place to see them was at the castle inspired me to renovate the castle and live here.

Previously, I was an absentee landlord of the castle but I moved in to prove or disprove an existence of the creatures. Robert, without a word of a lie I have found that the castle appears to be a gateway to another world! How, I do not know, but I have had enough interaction with various creatures to know this is true. My plan is to find a means in which I can cross over from where they came.

The necklace with the crystal is very old and has been handed down through generations. It was willed to me as one of a pair. Where the other one is, I cannot say. The crystal is a key of some sort and is much sought after in the other world (or the Alternative World as I've come to call it).

A final note: I have learned some of these Alternative World beings may be living among us in disguise, or at least hiding very well. Be wary of those who take too much interest in what you are here for.

Sincerely,
Uncle Gordon

Jon carefully placed the letter back in the envelope and finished his lunch. The walk back to the hotel was slow as he contemplated the contents of the letter. The desk clerk was a young man with jet-black hair and a weak growth of hair on his chin, who displayed a nervous energy. He grabbed the register book when Jon announced he would be staying at least another night and handed him a message written in a barely legible scrawl of a name and phone number.

"Uh, your sister called, sir. Early this morning. Just after you left." The clerk added the last statement with an anxious smile.

Jon thanked him and climbed the stairs to his room. He used the old phone on the antique table to call his sister. He left the paper on the table, not needing it to call the memorized number.

"Hey, sis, you called."

"Yeah, I did. Everything going okay down there? Have you been to the castle?"

"Everything's fine. I went to the castle but without any power or lights it was hard to see anything. I'm going to try again when I can get some lights."

"I guess there's no hurry since the castle has been there a few hundred years." She paused before continuing. "Look, I phoned Nadine at her apartment but didn't get any answer, so I phoned her at work. That place with the weird name, DeltaBio. She was a bit curt with me that I phoned her there but she calmed down when I told her you had been trying to reach her. She did ask if you were okay and I said as far as I knew you were. Anyway, the gist of it was she got an emergency call at work and that's where she's been pretty much the past couple of days."

"Thanks, I was getting a bit concerned."

"It wouldn't have hurt her to call you and let you know what she was doing. What do you see in her? She must be real good in bed."

"Sandra! That's none…"

"Relax, I'm just joking. You know me, no tact at all."

"Yeah, I know. Must make you a good lawyer though."

"Thanks, I think. How's Ireland?"

"Nice. I'm enjoying it. They have some nice pubs here."

"That's a surprise, Mr. Social Butterfly. Are you just sightseeing or are you meeting new people?"

"Uh, a little of both."

"Well, well, well. Some of them female, I hope?"

"They're just being friendly."

"I'll bet."

They ended the conversation with Jon wondering how Sandra always could put him on the defensive. He thought about Nadine and despite the time they spent together, they had not yet been really intimate. He did find that a little perplexing, but she claimed she needed time to get used to him. Her own history of being raised as a foster child made it understandable; it would take time for her to lower her barriers, although it was odd that she had been the aggressor when they first met.

He phoned Nadine but only had the answering machine to talk to. He gave her a short description of his day at the castle and left the hotel's phone number. He did bring his mobile but so far had kept it off to avoid the roaming expenses while in Europe.

He washed up before heading to the pub to meet Liz, feeling guilty that he was cheating on Nadine. He finished his dinner at the pub, currently quiet of people and noise. He nursed his beer and chatted with Charlene. The conversation drifted about Liz when he told her he was meeting her.

"Nice lass. She's back here for the summer university. She had trouble keeping the local lads in line though, as they all wanted to be the one keeping her company. So, she refused to date any of them so there wouldn't be any problems. All the same I don't think she's had to buy a drink yet this summer." She laughed and added, "I should have her problem. And speak of the devil," she nodded toward the door.

Liz bounced in wearing a short top and tight jeans. Jon took a deep breath and waved at her. He glanced at the clock in the bar as they made their way to a table near the back. She was right on time at half-past six. Nadine usually kept him waiting, and he found it annoying she rarely bothered to apologize or explain her tardiness. They drank and talked. She asked him several questions about Boston and was pleased to hear he loved the Boston Celtics.

"Grand Irish name. Do you have many girlfriends back home? Anyone special?"

He froze as he raised his glass to take a drink.

"Uh, no, I don't have a lot of girlfriends. Just one, she's, that is, she's the one I'm going out with."

Liz laughed and patted his arm.

"It's okay. You won't be breaking me heart when you head back to Boston. I'm here just for a good time too, so let's just try to have some fun."

They continued to talk and he started to get hungry again. He checked his watch. The time approached nine o'clock, surprising him how fast the time went by.

"Hey, are you hungry? Want to order some food?"

She laughed. "I bet you can eat all the time. But the pubs here don't serve grub much past dinner time. You're out of luck."

Jon shrugged his shoulders, mentally translating what she said. Her way of speaking with an accent made him aware that she probably had trouble understanding him too. Still, he did enjoy listening to her speak with a lilt in her voice. "Well I guess I have enough body weight to hold me for a while longer."

They chatted a bit longer when Liz glanced at the clock on the wall behind the bar. "It's getting to closing time. We best leave before they kick us out."

As they walked down the street, they slipped arms around each other's waist. Just before they reached the next street, he took a gamble and turned her to kiss her. He kissed her gently on the lips but she wrapped her an arm around his neck, pulling him closer. The kiss became much more forceful.

She grinned. "First American I ever kissed."

"First Irish girl I ever kissed."

She glanced at her mobile. "It's after eleven. I have to get up early even if you don't."

He continued to walk her home, holding her hand along the way.

"How come you picked the Demister?"

"It was right across from the bus stop and was cheap."

"Room okay?"

"Yeah, I suppose so. Would you like to see it sometime?"

"Shame on you. That was a bit forward." She laughed. "No, although the offer is tempting for when we know each a bit more."

He suddenly realized she thought he was offering something else and hadn't said no to another time. He hadn't meant it that way but now was elated she was hinting she was willing to. They stopped in front of her parent's house again, kissing once more. He tried to slip his hand under her shirt before she gently pushed him away.

"Me father would have a fit if he caught us necking out here. I'll see you tomorrow, alright?"

He stood at the front of her house until she closed the front door and walked out onto the deserted street.

———

The following day Jon finally was able to reach Nadine at her apartment. She sounded tired and spoke only briefly before complaining she needed to get some sleep.

"Things are going really bad at work. I'm tired and not feeling very good."

"You need some rest. Can't you take some time off from work?"

"Hardly. Crisis situation."

"Are you going to be able to fly down soon?"

It was such a long pause before she spoke, he almost started to repeat his question.

"Why? Do you miss me?" There was a hint of sarcasm in the voice. She paused, and continued, "I have to go. I have your number at the hotel. Be careful, there's danger at... never mind. Just be careful."

He hung up feeling rather perplexed. The 'Do you miss me' question hinted she knew about Liz and what did she mean 'be careful'? She seemed to know more than she was willing to say, and there was a suggestion of a particular place of danger as well. But he still felt more distant than ever from her.

TWO

Liz stopped to look out the front window, pushing the curtain aside enough to see the dark street outside. Jon walked slowly and suddenly took two quick steps, jumped while raising his arms above his head before yelling touchdown! She covered her mouth to stifle a laugh before going upstairs to bed.

She quietly went upstairs. The sight of Jon jumping up in the air so excited made her feel special. True, she told herself, he was just supposed to be visiting Ballymiller, but he had inherited the Miller Castle. This meant, she assumed, that he was likely to be around a bit longer. Unfortunately, she had to go back to university in the fall so that would put an abrupt end to any romance. *Likely. But you never know…*the unfinished thought drifted away.

Still, there was something about him that drew her to him, even on the first night when she nervously invited him to their table and flirt. Perhaps she reflected, it was due to not worryin' about how much dating she was pressured to do with the local boys. She didn't want a relationship with anyone destined to live their lives out in Ballymiller. An image of her cooking, cleaning and raising two kids while her man sat in the local pub didn't appeal to her at all. *Best stop any pretences of romance they may have with her right in the bud.* As far as Jon was concerned, it could because he was new and spoke with a strange accent but he had gotten under her skin.

The next morning she made her way to work, almost forgetting the torches they would need later to visit the castle. Business at the bar was slow but steady, with old Mr. Doherty being the usual pest in asking for endless cups of tea. Her shift ended at two, and she checked her watch several times. Jon finally arrived and she hurried over to his table to see how he was doing.

They chatted about their day and when he ordered a sandwich, she had an excuse to talk with him a bit more at his table.

They walked hand in hand after her shift down the partial concrete walks to the castle. Parts of the walk had never been paved and they used the sparsely travelled road to continue. She, like most people in Ballymiller, had never seen the inside of the Miller castle. She was anxious when he pushed open the front door.

The castle was cooler than the outside and her summer top and short skirt quickly caused her to feel a chill. She noticed Jon had enough weight to be able to absorb a few degrees of coolness without a problem.

After they left the main room, which had been converted to a living room, they had to use what he called flashlights to see into the other parts of the castle. It was unnerving and she stayed close to him as the beams danced ahead.

Liz thought her imagination was taking leaps into the unknown. Twice she thought her light caught something for a split second only for it to vanish. She felt eyes were watching her, taking a quick glance behind her looking for the source. "This is a bit spooky. I think the light is playing tricks with me. I swear I saw something move a couple of times."

"Yeah, I know what you mean. I think it's our brain trying to make up something that doesn't exist."

"Maybe. But I'm staying close to you just in case." She decided the flashlights made shadows appear to move as living creatures when the light slid over objects. Liz listened to Jon as he gave her a tour of the castle, although he was as unfamiliar with it as she was.

"It's a bit cold in here."

"Do you want to leave the rest of the upstairs for another time?"

"Yes, please. I want to warm up and leave the dark for another time." Liz had hoped the castle would be a romantic place for them to spend some time together but between the chill and the sensation of something else lurking about, she just wanted to leave.

Jon took her outside again, and the sun quickly warmed her up. They left via the front door to go to the back and she saw the path he had used the previous day. Liz guessed how the back yard looked like when it was still being cared for.

"Hey, there's the back door. It must lead to the kitchen or some-place like that."

He walked over and peered through the glass window, trying to make out was on the other side.

"Can't see nothing. But at least it's better than having to walk around the whole castle every time we want to go to the back."

It didn't escape Liz's attention he used the word 'we' and she was pleased at his unconscious inclusion of her. He rejoined her where she stood on the edge of the small brick patio.

"What's kept in there?"

She pointed with her free hand, the other wrapped around his waist. A small green wood garden shed stood partially hidden by a large oak tree. Thick black wires ran from it to the castle.

"I dunno. Tools I suppose."

They walked over the small wooden building and pulled open the unlocked door, a padlock hanging open at the latch.

"What's that? A motor of some kind?" Liz took in the orange metal object.

"It's a generator." A moment of realization crossed his face. "Uncle Gordon must have used this to provide power to the castle."

"How do you start this thing? Does it still work?"

Liz watched him walk around the dim interior with his flashlight. He tapped on a tank. "That's the gas tank and it's empty. We could put some gas in it and see if it'll start."

"Why don't we check that tomorrow? Let's go for a drink and a bite."

Jon seemed quite willing to give up on the project of starting the generator for a chance to eat. They made their way the Demister Hotel just as some regulars had sat down. Jon and Liz accepted the invitation to join them, with Jon buying a round for the table. Liz waited until Jon had eaten and rested a hand on his lap.

"'Hey, I've had enough to drink. How about showing me your hotel room?"

Jon almost spilled his beer but recovered in time to nod. He gulped down the rest of his drink.

The room was much like she expected. The older hotels had small rooms and the furniture close to being called antiques. Still, it was clean and reasonably well appointed. Jon was nervous and excused himself to go the washroom, where she heard him make use of his toothbrush. She sat on the edge of the bed and stared around before her eyes fell on the night table holding a small lamp with a folded piece of yellow memo paper lying by it side. She picked it up and looked at the scrawled message: *Sandra Draper, call as soon as possible.* A phone number was attached underneath.

"Well," she murmured to herself "at least I know the name of me competitor."

She carefully refolded the paper and replaced it.

He appeared composed when he entered the room again and she relaxed a bit more herself. Liz felt she was being a bit too forward and didn't want to appear anxious to go to bed with him. He sat down next to her and the small talk led to hand holding, then kisses and finally hands pushed under clothes. He left a trail of kisses from her mouth, down her neck and to her chest. She took a series of deep breaths as he pulled her top off, exposing her bra. Jon used his fingers to push the bra straps away from her shoulders.

Liz moaned as his hands reach under her back to try to undo the bra strap, and she lifted herself against him. She was relieved when he didn't fumble with the hooks and the bra slid away. Liz pulled off his shirt while he focused on her breasts. His hands carefully cupped each breast and his mouth took turns with each swollen nipple.

Jon responded to her moans and worked to free her of her skirt, and her panties.

"Hey, how come I'm naked and you still have your pants on?" she gasped out.

As he stared wide-eyed at her body, he took off the rest of his clothes, pulling his pants inside out in the process.

Liz licked her upper lip, wondering if she should slow down his eagerness. *He certainly is a big man everywhere.*

Jon climbed back on the bed, feeding her kisses. His hands touched her everywhere as he moved down on her. Liz found his weight restricted her own movements. She found it best to let him continue with his carpet of kisses and she responded the best she could, noticing he was fascinated with her breasts as he kept returning to them.

She softly cried out, encouraging him when he placed a hand

between her legs. Her hands pulled at his neck and he slid upward on her. She felt the press of his weight and wrapped her legs around him. She dug her fingers into his shoulders as she climaxed, dimly aware of the bed protesting their combined efforts at the end.

She considered he wasn't the most experienced lover she had been with but he was caring and kept her in his arms afterward. She relaxed against him and started asking him how long he was planning to stay in Ballymiller.

"Uh, I guess planning is the wrong word. My ticket is open ended. I figured I would take a month to check out the castle and the country. I can't afford to stay in this hotel too long. I'll check out other types of accommodation, even staying in the castle."

"A month. Hmm, I can do some checking for extra rooms in homes around here. There should be a few that would be willing to take someone in for a few weeks. And then there's the haunted castle."

She nudged him in the ribs and laughed.

"Thanks. I think I'll get the power up and running so I can look around better. As far as staying there, perhaps it's a little too rustic for my tastes."

She laughed and kissed his chest.

"Yeah, like old ghosts."

After exchanging a few more kisses she informed him she had to leave, explaining her parents would have a fit since she was already late returning home.

Reluctantly, he walked her home. She expressed relief that the lights were out in her parent's home, and they were not waiting up for her.

The next morning, she met up with him after breakfast and together they returned to the castle. Jon borrowed an old metal jerry can from a service station to pour gas back into the generator's tank.

Liz watched him study the controls for the generator and lift off a cover.

"Battery's dead. This generator uses a small electric motor to start it and that motor in turn uses a battery. I might be able to pull start the generator."

Liz trained the flashlight on where he grabbed a cord with a black rubber handle at the end and pulled. And pulled. And then pulled some more.

"Getting tired?"

"No, but my shoulder is complaining."

He fiddled with the top of the motor and he played with a couple the devices there, mumbling to himself about the 'choke' and 'prime the damn thing'. He replaced the covers and pulled again and this time the generator sputtered. Three more tries and the generator stayed on.

"You did it!"

He stood grinning.

Liz led the way back into the castle, entering through the back door this time. Once they were inside, they tried the various light switches. Most of the lights came on and for the first time they could see how the inside looked.

Liz noticed the paintings hanging on the stone walls were mostly scenes of medieval times. The colours in the paintings and the other furnishings were generally rich, as if Gordon Miller was trying to breathe life into the rooms despite the grey walls and floor. Liz started the fire in the fireplace. She was familiar with her parent's fireplace, pleased Jon didn't try to take over as most men were prone to do.

With the fire burning and the lights on, the castle didn't seem so fearful and Liz didn't get the sensation anyone or anything was watching them. She sat against him on the couch and heard his stomach growl.

"Getting hungry again, are we?"

"A little."

She took out her mobile.

"I'll see what I can do."

Why she did that she wasn't certain. She rarely had invited boys over before to meet her parents, let alone have them come over for supper. But before she knew it, she called her parents and asked if she could bring over a special friend from Boston.

"There, it's settled. You are invited to eat at my parent's place," she said and grinned happily at his puzzled face. "They won't bite, honest."

She then remembered she had told them he was a special friend and also recalled she hadn't come home until late the previous night. Her parents would put two and two together rather quickly on that one, she supposed. She doubted it would even be worth it to tell them she had stayed too long at her girlfriend's place. The lie would be too obvious.

———

Liz was pleased her parents didn't even frown when they arrived. In fact, they were great hosts, smiled nicely and asked only polite questions. Her father, Patrick, she thanked the Lord, didn't ask him what his future plans were and talked instead about American football and rugby. Her dad was a big man, almost as tall as Jon and about the same weight, and had played rugby in a senior league until a knee injury forced him to stop.

Liz wasn't surprised he enjoyed the dinner and complimented Margaret O'Doul several times as he ate. Margaret began to blush after the third compliment, the redness in her cheeks accenting her red hair. She was a small woman and managed to appear younger than her fifty-two years.

After dinner Liz helped her mother wash the dishes while Jon and her father retired to the living room with cans of Guinness.

"Your man is a pure nice, Lizzy."

"That he is."

A moment dragged on as she passed a plate over to be dried.

"You spent last night with him?"

To Liz her voice was casual, perhaps too casual. The question wasn't really a question; just a confirmation of what her mother already suspected.

"Aye."

She turned to watch her mother's face show a sign of disapproval, but her face continued to look relaxed.

"Your father would have a fit, you know." She passed over a glass. "He thinks you spent last night at Tori's."

"He doesn't have to know, does he?"

"Not from me he won't. You're old enough to make your own decisions on life. Just be careful."

"To be sure, I don't sleep around. Not in university, not here either. He, he's just someone I got close to real fast."

"I can understand why but don't fall too hard, Lizzy. Summer romances don't often last."

The rest of the evening went well but she decided to say goodnight to Jon at the door, rather than leave with him and raise her father's suspicion.

———

Jon told Liz he made a decision to move into the Miller Castle, telling her while most of the castle was dark, dusty and generally not very inviting, a large portion of the main floor was furnished and well lighted. That included living room, entrance hall, kitchen, study, bathroom and a bedroom converted from a drawing room.

Liz helped him repack his suitcases and did a final check of the room as he lugged the two bags through the door. She spotted the folded memo paper still on the nightstand.

"There's a paper on the table here. You want it?"

"Na, it's not important. I have the number memorized."

She picked up the paper and held it over the wastepaper basket, changed her mind, and slipped it into her jeans pocket.

Liz wasn't certain why Jon was determined to stay at the castle when he could have obtained other accommodation. She knew he was a bit nervous about the rather abundant stories he'd heard of ghosts, goblins and other creatures that were supposed to hang around the castle but he refused to be kept away.

Male ego or bravado, I suppose.

———

Liz continued to spend much of her free time with him and was tempted by his offer to spend her nights with him. She wanted to ease the possibility of moving in with him by her parents first and knew her father would be upset with her. Strange, she thought to herself, how a mature, university educated woman could be intimidated by her parents on what she did. And then there was the matter of the other girlfriend living in Boston. She wondered if he was still in contact with her on a regular basis and was curious what she looked like.

"How are things at the castle?" she asked when she met him for dinner at the Dockers Pub, "Spotted any more creatures?"

She referred to Jon's chance encounter with an odd-looking man standing less than three feet high. He wore brown pants, a green shirt under a black cape and covered his bearded head with a peak cap. Jon mentioned the small man was coming out of the kitchen while he sat in the living room. He saw Jon and ran back into the kitchen in slipper-like shoes. Jon hurried into the kitchen himself but found nothing, even after opening cupboards in a vain attempt to find where the man had disappeared.

"Yeah, another one like that small man, again in the kitchen. But I also saw this really strange thing in the back yard through the window last evening. Thin, about four, perhaps five feet high wearing dark clothing. Ugly face, though I couldn't see much detail. Ran away when I turned on the outside light, and man was it fast. Zip! And it was gonzo."

"You sure it's safe to be there? I could find you a place to stay, you know."

"I'll be fine. Hey, I found this really neat room upstairs on the third level, like a laboratory. Tools, equipment, textbooks, notebooks, the whole works. I don't know what it's supposed to do but Uncle Gordon wrote something about being able to investigate the Alternate World, whatever that meant. I'm going to read the notebooks some more to try to figure out what he was trying to discover."

"You'll have to show me that room."

She took a drink and casually asked what was on her mind. "What does your girlfriend back home say about this?"

He froze a moment, lifting a chip to his mouth and slowly eating it.

"I haven't been able to get a hold of her much. I spoke to her a couple of days ago but she's got some kind of emergency at work and is spending a lot of time there and when she's home she pretty much sleeps, so we haven't talked much." He spoke in a rush and quickly shoved another chip into his mouth.

"Jon, I don't want to put pressure on you but you've asked me to stay overnight with you. It would be awkward if she were to show up here. A summer fling is one thing but we're heading wee too fast if you've got someone else waiting for you. Understand?"

He rubbed his face with his hand.

"Liz, if you're asking me to choose between you and, and…her, then I'll do that. But I don't want to tell her it's goodbye over the phone or by an answering machine." He reached over and grabbed her hand. "I don't want this to be just a summer thing."

"Okay," *He indicated he's willing to drop her over me but wants to do that face to face. That's good. I don't care for people who dump others by texting them. And he avoided using her name.*

She squeezed his hand back letting him know she had finished 'we need to talk' conversation.

He walked her home and hinted on her staying at the castle with him. She gave a smile and a kiss in reply.

"We need to talk about that a wee more first."

―――――

After a week and a half of eating out and bringing in prepared food, she decided a change in diet was necessary for both of them. She brought over some groceries after work and decided she would attempt to cook dinner that night.

Attempt, she admitted to herself, *is the operative word.*

At university, the microwave and frozen were the two words she used most in preparing dinner. Still, she had watched and helped her mother often enough in making meals as she grew up to give her some confidence. She placed the groceries in the kitchen and a small overnight bag in the living room. Even though she decided to spend the night with Jon, she didn't want to appear too anxious by putting it in the bedroom where it would eventually end up.

Liz eventually had a talk with her parents about her relationship with Jon after dinner. As she expected, her mother was supportive on her decision. Her father was less so. His words were calm, even admitting she was a grown woman and could do what she wanted. His body language was opposite and indicated he was anything but calm on the inside. Liz ended up crying. She hugged her father, pleading with him not to be angry with her.

"Please. You and mom were married at my age. Jon is a good man. I want to be near him while I can."

Gradually her father began to soften his resistance, "Alright, I can't stand to see you cry. But I warn you, I'm too young to be a grandfather."

―――――

She ended up spending more than one night with him but the step of moving her belongings into the castle was one she was a bit hesitant about, not the least because of what her parents would think. Still, after she accepted a copy of the keys to the castle from Jon a few days ago, it was inevitable she would be moving in. She still wanted him to see the bag first and coax her into staying one more time, just to make her feel pursued a bit more. *After all, I did most of the flirting in the beginning when we met and now it is his turn to show how much he wants me.*

Liz called out to him but didn't get a reply. She did a quick check around the castle before looking out a window and saw a newly cut lawn out back. The small side door from the kitchen led her to the back yard where she spotted him standing on the dock. She called out, "Jon."

He was wearing a long sleeve grey shirt, worn jeans and sandals, looking a bit ragged. He was holding a can of pop and raised it in a salute to her. She noticed the rest of the yard had been cleaned up. She walked to where he stood and after giving him a kiss, followed his gaze along the shoreline.

"I almost expect to see him washed up to the shore." His voice sounded a bit strained when he added, "Never really knew him, but…"

"Jon, don't go there," she said and squeezed his hand. "Come on inside. I'll make you something to eat."

He nodded, staring at the dock with an oversized fishing tackle box sitting on the end.

"Hey, see that fishing box there?"

"Yeah?"

"It's nailed down to prevent it from sliding off the dock. If the police assumed he drowned because of the tackle box sitting there, they should know that it was always there. Could be there's another reason he disappeared."

"Like what?"

"I don't know. Maybe something to do with his experiments. I'll tell you later about them."

―――――

He sat in the kitchen while she made him a sandwich. He looked a bit worn from his labours outdoors and she had to listen how he cut this, mowed that, dug that and generally reformed the landscape of all of Ireland.

Liz sat across from him at the small table teasing him on what he considered hard work.

"A wee bit of hard work will do you good." She saw his open collar and asked, "What exactly is that thing around your neck? You told me you inherited it from your uncle, but what does it mean?"

He lifted out a crystal tied to a leather string.

"It's something my uncle said was a symbol of power or something like that. Kind of like a lucky charm."

A shadow of something caught her attention in the next room through the open doorway where the living room resided.

She stood up, pushing her chair back.

"I think I saw something in the other room."

Jon turned around as he followed the direction of her pointed finger. He stood and went to the living room with Liz close behind him.

At first Liz couldn't believe what she saw as she peered around Jon. He was perhaps four feet tall, with a full head of dark hair and beard. His garments were in slightly worse condition than Jon's work clothes but did have some colour to them, with red and yellow dominating. A gold chain hung around his neck that shimmered as he whirled around and snarled at them.

"Get 'way!"

He started to run, his short legs moving remarkably fast. In one hand he was holding a pale-yellow cloth with a white tag attached by a string, in the other a small knife. Jon froze for a moment as the dwarf ran through a doorway toward the staircase, and he started to chase him.

Liz took a quick glance in the room as she followed. Her overnight bag had been emptied on a chair, the contents spread out on the cushion and the floor. Liz considered the cloth the dwarf was clutching in one hand.

"My knickers! The bastard has stolen my knickers!"

Jon wasn't running too fast in his sandals and was barely gaining on his adversary, but the last comment caused him to turn around at her.

"Your what?"

"Underwear." She sounded exasperated. "He's stolen my under-wear from the bag."

Jon opened his mouth to say something but abruptly closed it, renewing his efforts with more vigour to chase after the dwarf up the stairs. Liz followed behind Jon as he trailed the dwarf to a room on the second level. The room's only light came from the open window showing off a dusty and mostly bare room. A wood table leaned against a wall, its four legs too weak to hold itself up on its own. A single grey metal fold up chair sat at its side. Liz watched the dwarf turned around and wave his knife at Jon and her.

"Get 'way! Get 'way!" he growled at them in a remarkably deep voice.

Jon stepped forward slowly, looking at the knife.

"Drop what you took and you can go."

"Tis mine! I finds it!"

Liz certainly didn't want Jon getting hurt for the sake of rescuing her underwear. She reached out her hand to pull at Jon's arm. The dwarf saw her restrain Jon and quickly sheathed his knife, pocketed her panties and now used his free hands to pull himself up the window ledge. He stood on the ledge and reached inside his shirt, producing two coloured glass-like lumps, blue and yellow. He began to press the blue coloured one to the yellow one when Jon pulled away from her grasp and charge him.

"Stays away, I say. Stays away!"

He pressed the two objects together and gave them a twist. A small but bright flash of green light appeared between the combined objects just as Jon reached him. Jon grabbed his arms and the two struggled at the window ledge, with the dwarf trying to pull away and Jon with one leg on the ledge.

"Let me go, yous stupid bastard! Yous don'ts know what yous doing."

Liz watched horrified as the two men struggled and seemed to be covered in a shimmering light. Jon had a death grip on the dwarf and didn't seem to be aware he was being dragged onto the window ledge. The dwarf apparently wanted to jump out of the window and was pushing hard with his legs as he stood on the outside of the ledge.

"Jon, let him go. You're going to fall out of the window too!"

Liz ran over to where they fought, wanting to grab him and pull him back. But in a nightmare moment, both men tumbled out of the window. She reached the two-foot wide ledge and looked down. Below her stood a small tree and the rocky surface of the ground. Jon and the dwarf were nowhere to be seen.

Her cries for Jon were unanswered. She ran out of the room and downstairs, bursting outside to where they may have fallen. Despite the fact they obviously had fallen to the ground from the window above, she couldn't find any sign of Jon, or any evidence of anything hitting the ground.

Later she phoned her parents, crying as she related the story. Her father drove over and helped her look for him but he too came up empty handed. She wanted to stay at the castle and wait to see if he returned, but her father insisted it wasn't safe for her to be there alone and took her home.

That evening her mother suggested that they try to contact his family if they could. At first Liz wasn't sure if there was a way of contacting him, other than the lawyer who handled the transfer of the Miller Castle's title. Then she remembered the yellow memo paper folded in her pocket.

"I might have a number of someone in Boston. I'll try that."

She went to her room to phone. *Lord, what's his girlfriend going to say when she hears the news from me, the woman with whom he's been sleeping with?*

She unfolded the paper and held it in her fingers, studying the numbers and name. She punched in the numbers, half hoping it would be too late for anyone to answer and she could just leave a message. The phone rang several times before a woman's sleepy voice answered.

"Hello?"

"Sandra Draper?"

"Speaking. Who is this? Do you know what time this is?"

"Uh, look, this is difficult. It's about Jon."

"Jon? What happened?"

"He's disappeared."

Liz felt a tear run down her cheek.

"Disappeared? How? Who is this?"

"He, he just fell, fell out of a window and then vanished."

"That doesn't make any sense. What's your name and how do know this?"

"Liz. Liz O'Doul. I was with him at the castle when it happened."

"You were with him? Just you?"

"Aye."

Here it comes, the blast from a wronged woman to the one who caused her man to stray.

"So, Jon and you are friends? More than that?"

"More than that. But he…"

"Well, at least that part is good news. But just how did he vanish?"

That part is good news? Did I miss something here? "It's tough to explain, but I was wondering how to get a hold of his family to let them know."

"His family? I'm his sister. Who did you think I was?"

"You're not his girlfriend?"

"I said I was his sister, didn't I? Please don't confuse me with that bitch. How exactly did Jon disappear?"

"He was fighting with another man. A dwarf, actually. And they fell out of a window in the castle. They both vanished."

"Look, I think it would be best if I flew over there."

Liz hung up after agreeing to Sandra's suggestion. It would be a relief to get some help in finding Jon and it was a bigger relief in not having to talk to Jon's girlfriend. And apparently not a very popular one with his family.

THREE

For Jon, it was a bewildering few seconds. He hadn't expected the dwarf to actually pull himself off the ledge. The dust and dirt on the marble floor caused him to lose his own footing. He tumbled out of the window while still holding on to the dwarf, banging his knee in the process. There was an odd shimmering around them with the air smelling like ozone. Liz's scream disappeared abruptly as the sky changed from mid-afternoon to night. A few seconds later he hit the top branches of a tree, causing him to release his grip on the intruder in the process. The ground was not quite as forgiving, but Jon landed with a roll and eventually stopped against another tree on an embankment.

The dwarf wasn't quite as fortunate and continued to roll past him and down the muddy slope. He moaned as he tried to dig his fingers into the soft ground.

Jon reacted quickly and dived head first, his arm extended toward the sliding dwarf. His fingers clutched at the shirt collar and held fast as he halted the downward progress. Jon looked up from his stomach to see an empty space beyond the dwarf's legs.

"It's okay. I got you."

He hauled the struggling man back to the tree, where the dwarf pounded his arm with his fist.

"Ye moron! Idiot! Imbecile! Looks what yous done!"

"Hey, I just saved your life for crying out loud." Jon took a step back from what he thought was a crazed individual.

"Stupid, that's what yous is!" The dwarf stopped his insults. "What yer mean yous saved me life?"

"Just that. I stopped you from falling down into the river or whatever is down there. I saved your bacon."

"I don'ts knows about that, you can't prove it," he said, without conviction.

"Bullshit, you ungrateful thief. I saved your life, and you didn't even say thanks," Jon found himself getting hot. "So, say thank you already, will ya?"

"Keeps yer loud mouth down, someone might hear us. Yous don'ts know for a fact yer saved me life, there's ain't no proof."

"Prove, why would I have to prove…"

"Do ya even have a clue what's going on here? Of course not! Let's just jumps out of a window and sees what happens. That's you. Oh, the fools I has to put up with. If ya want thanks, then thanks for nothing."

With that he flopped on the ground and covered his eyes with his right arm in a tragic pose.

"I, I don't understand. You…"

"Of course ye don'ts understand because yous an idiot. Why, oh why couldn't ye let me be?"

"You stole something from…"

The dwarf suddenly sat up. "Says who? I finds it there by itself. No one around. Tis mine now." He sighed, "Gotta think what to do, what to do. Big, big problem."

"What problem?"

Though by the fact it was now suddenly night time meant something had happened. He looked around and realized he didn't recognize the street in front of him and instead of the iron fence around the Miller Castle there stood a stone wall.

"Shut up, me trying to think."

The dwarf sat cross-legged, holding his chin with one hand.

By the time the dwarf jumped up and said, "I got it!" Jon had figured out he wasn't in Ballymiller anymore. Besides the stone wall around the castle, the tree was also bigger and the buildings across the street appeared to be something from another time. The structures were made from stone blocks with wooden framed windows, appearing as if they belonged in the middle ages.

"That's good to hear. My name is Jon McKinney, by the way."

The dwarf peered at him suspiciously as he replied, "Ye can call me Gilbert." Then with a snarl that Jon suspected was a semi-permanent feature on his face, he pointed across the street at one of the rough stone buildings. "Let's go to the tavern. I knows someone there who can help us."

At first, he had trouble figuring out which building was being pointed to by the short dirty finger, but the dwarf gestured again and shouted out in a rather thunderous voice for a small person.

"Idiot! The tallest one is the tavern, obviously. What else could the Cobbler Inn look like?"

Jon wanted to protest he didn't know that the tavern was part of the Cobbler Inn but thought that would only bring another round of insults. Jon glanced up and down the dark street, the stone blocks were damp and reflected the light from open windows. A horse with a rider covered by a dark cloak slumped on the saddle walked by, the hoofs making a clacking noise on the hard surface.

"Couldn't I just climb back up through the window? It's high but with a ladder I could…"

"No, don't be daft. It don'ts work like that. Now let's gets be going."

Cautiously, as he had no intention of being run over by a horse, Jon crossed the street with Gilbert, who continued scowling and muttering to himself. The road was made up of uneven flat stones cemented together that gave a durable surface. Perhaps it wasn't ideal for wheeled vehicles, but for horses it worked fine. The buildings were separated from the road by a wooden sidewalk that appeared to sit on top of the edge of the road.

Jon crossed the road with Gilbert close at his heels. A low rumbling cry sounded from high above, startling Jon to stop short and look up. He spotted a large bird shaped object glide above as Gilbert ploughed into the back of his legs, causing him to trip.

"Imbecile! What the hell did ya stop for?"

Jon picked himself off from the street, wiping his hands on his pants.

"Did you see that, that thing up there? It was huge…"

"No, I didn't, I was too busy running into your ass. Can we cross the road before we get runs over by a bloody horse?"

The tavern doors were well lacquered with black paint with a gold circle drawn inside a pentagon in the center of the right door. Jon stopped to inspect the twelve-inch symbol, but Gilbert wasn't in a mood for any inspection.

"Hurry up, hurry up. I don'ts want to stand out here all blooming night."

He turned the handle and pushed against the massive door, surprised to find it swung open fairly easily after the initial shove. It squeaked just a little, but that noise was subdued compared to the boisterous noise that roared from the tavern.

In front of them stood an old wooden counter where a heavyset, bald innkeeper looked up from his dinner plate. Gilbert gave him a toothy smile and flipped a coin with a hole in the center at him. The large man was quick as he caught the coin and favoured Gilbert with a smile.

"Ah, not big enough for a room so you're wanting something else instead."

"Me needs to see Council Madoc. Is he available?"

"I'm afraid to advise he's out at present."

"Then we'll wait in the tavern. Tell him we seek his wisdom."

This he said in a cordial voice and gave a small bow of his head. The innkeeper returned with a nod. Gilbert turned to open the door to the tavern. Jon followed, surprised that Gilbert could sound pleasant and well mannered.

The noise of men arguing loudly to prove an unknown point assaulted them as they made their way into the dimly lit tavern. Various tables, mostly rectangular but a couple of circular ones could be spotted as well, sat scattered about the dark grimy floor. The chairs were also of assorted sizes and shapes that more or less matched their occupants. Several turned to watch as they crossed the room.

Gilbert took the lead and a few of the odd-looking customers gave a short acknowledgement to the dwarf. Jon resisted the temptation of wrinkling up his nose at the reek of stale beer, cheap whisky, smoke and body odour as they moved to one of the corners and sat at one of the wobbly tables. The chairs at the table were of normal proportion so Gilbert dragged a taller chair from a neighbouring table to their own, grumbling as he did so. He climbed up on the chair, scowling for good measure.

"Kind of an unusual place."

"Compared to what? Ye don't get around much, do ya?"

"I meant it's unusual compared to the bars back home."

"Oh yeah, the land of the feeble and noise."

"The feeble and noise?"

Gilbert waved at a serving wench.

"Feeble, ye idiots have lost your ability to use magic. And the bloody noise, machines all over your damned world. And if that wasn't bad enough your ether is saturated with clatter from those infernal electrical devices. No wonder magic spells fall apart there."

"Magic? What are you talking…?"

"Hush up. We don'ts need anyone to knows that you're from the Other-side."

Jon was opening his mouth to ask about the Other-side when a dark-haired young woman stopped at the table. She gave Gilbert a shove at his shoulder and stood with her hands on her hips grinning at him.

"How's me short handle doing? Getting rich yet on stolen treasure?"

Gilbert appeared uncomfortable with her questions as Jon took in her grin that was missing a front tooth. She wore a long dark skirt that was split open along one side clear to her hip. Her yellow peasant blouse was cut low enough that Jon wondered if it would cause her problems with modesty as she leaned forward. The other item he noticed was she wore a leather collar with a metal ring around it. Jon thought it was a peculiar looking piece of jewellery.

"A couple of your best, Jessica. Clean mugs if you have them."

"Alright then. And who's your silent friend then?"

She turned to him with her unique smile and rested her hand on his arm.

"Jon. My name is Jon. Nice to meet you, Jessica."

She gave a big smile that might have been inviting if all her teeth were present. "Oh, you're the polite one now. Perhaps we can talk later."

She quickly turned away, yelling at another customer if he wanted another drink. Another of the dubious patrons gave her a slap on her rear as she stepped between two tables. She gave him a quick smile as she wagged her finger at him.

Jon tried to take in the rest of the tavern now that his eyes had adjusted to the dim interior. Besides the obvious size difference of the people, some also seem to exhibit definite battle scars on their face, including missing ears and part of their noses. Their dress was a mixture of colourful garments and armour. Several of the patrons had knives or swords along with protective plates on their bodies. Jon felt the scene would have been at home in medieval times.

Gilbert was inclined to sit with his arms crossed as he scanned about the room, nodding at a few of the other drinking men. His main interest lie toward the entrance of the tavern where a set of stairs from the hotel part of the establishment was located.

"Gilbert, why are we here? I mean this is as good a place as any but what exactly am I supposed to do? I don't have any money with me, by the way."

Jon's jeans had holes in the pockets and had been relegated to work only.

Gilbert waved an intolerant hand.

"Quiet, that's what you's supposed to do. It wouldn't do no good for these scum to know where yous from. I'm waiting for someone I know, a business associate of sorts. I needs to get some advice on how to handle this. And yours money no good here."

Jessica returned with two metal tankards, dropping them on the table as the dark brown ale slopped over their sides. She didn't appear to be concerned that it added to the growing mess of liquid and food bits on the table and floor. Gilbert passed a bronze coin to her, and she moved to the next table.

Jon tried the ale, finding it heavy, flat and with a yeast taste to it. Still, it was drinkable and since Gilbert wasn't in a talkative mood, there was little else to do but watch and drink.

Several new arrivals entered the tavern before Gilbert reacted to a tall, distinguished man dressed in a white shirt under a dark blue jacket and pants. A small beard and short, combed dark hair set his face apart from most of the others in the tavern. He didn't hesitate more than a moment as he passed through the doorway, heading straight to them.

He stopped just before their table, opening the palm of his right hand toward Gilbert.

"You desired to see me, Freeman Gilbert?"

"Yes, yes Council Madoc. I need some help on a rather peculiar problem."

"I see."

Council Madoc gave Jon a quick glance before pulling out one of the vacant chairs. He swept his hand across the seat before sitting down. Jessica hurried to their table and wiped the table portion in front of him with a grey rag. The contents were sent to the opposite end of the table, and Jon had to move quickly to avoid the debris that washed over the table edge.

"What can I getcha, sir?"

"Red wine, please."

As she turned away, he lightly touched her sleeve. She froze on the spot, looking back anxiously.

"Made sure it is of good quality and not cut."

"Oh, yes sir. Only the very best, I promise you."

Council Madoc turned to Jon.

"And who might you be, young sir?"

"Jon McKinney."

He turned his eyes on Gilbert. "Perhaps you can inform me of this situation that has presented itself on you."

Jessica reappeared with his wine causing Gilbert to stay silent until she left. He hooked his thumb in Jon's direction and spoke in a growl as he lowered his voice.

"This here followed me from the Other-side. I don't knows what to do about him."

Council Madoc raised his eyebrows. "Surely there is more to this tale than that. If I'm to assist you, I'll need more information." He turned toward Jon. "Perhaps you can enlighten me, Master McKinney."

He caught Gilbert's annoyed frown but decided Council Madoc offered him more hope of returning to his own place than Gilbert.

"Well, see, I inherited this old castle. And I was having lunch when I saw Gilbert. I thought he was trespassing..."

"Trespassing!! That castle belongs to..."

"Freeman Gilbert, please let him finish first. You may add to his story afterward." He gestured with his hand at him. "Please continue."

Jon explained to Council Madoc how he encountered Gilbert and how he came to be there.

"Is that essentially correct, Freeman Gilbert?"

"Yes, but..."

"A moment, if you please."

Madoc massaged his forehead and took a drink of his wine. He returned his gaze at the two of them.

"There are several problems here. First, Master McKinney is not here in our place with authority. I also suspect that you, Freeman Gilbert, did not have permission to seek fortune in the Other-side."

Gilbert pursed his lips together and nodded.

"There is also the delicate circumstance of Gilbert being in debt to Master McKinney for saving his life."

"But I didn't need him to do that!" Gilbert raised his voice in protest but as he caught Madoc's look, lowered his tone, "I would've survived."

"Possibly. But all that has to be accomplished in determining obligations is if Master McKinney truly believed he was saving your life. It is the intention that is the requirement, not possible outcomes if he didn't act."

"Oh, of all the curses of a dragon's nest," he snarled, slammed his fist on the table and then suddenly seemed worried. "Oh, pardon me, Council Madoc, I means no disrespect."

"None taken. This situation does have a resolution. If you, Freeman Gilbert, play an active role in returning Master McKinney to his own home, this will resolve your life debt to him. If you can accomplish this quietly, and discreetly, you may also avoid detection of your visit to the Other-side without proper authority."

"Ah, a way to get me off the hook."

Jon looked at Gilbert who was grinning away.

"I have a question. How do I get back home? I mean, Gilbert said I couldn't just climb back up through the way I came."

"Excellent, you have a keen mind for details. Yes, unfortunately, you just can't return the way you came in. Nor can you go the way Gilbert does. That only works for a very few people here. You do not possess, or rather control, enough magic to return home. What you must do is increase your magic by obtaining certain devices to amplify it. This is where Freeman Gilbert comes in. He must help you in your quest as payment of his debt. It won't be necessarily easy, but certainly can be done." Council Madoc stood. "I trust I have been of some assistance to both of you. Unfortunately, I have to arise early tomorrow and must now bid you goodnight. If either of you require my expertise, I will be available in this area for another fortnight."

Gilbert reached into his pouch, bringing out several gold coloured coins.

Council Madoc held up his hand.

"No need to pay, perhaps I can make use of your service in the future."

Jon asked Gilbert after Madoc had left.

"So how the heck do I increase my magic to get home?"

Gilbert gave him a withering look. "It'd be easier turning Jessica back into a virgin." He shook his head. "I need to get drunk." He proceeded to do just that.

As Jon watched Gilbert consume tankard after tankard of ale he reflected on several things. One, somehow, he had fallen into a rather strange world. Two, his way back home involved learning magic. And three, for a little guy, Gilbert could drink an enormous amount of ale.

———

Jon woke up on the floor with a thin blanket covering him. He tried to peer at his watch, noting that the time was 9:10. Whether that was supposed to be AM or PM he couldn't be sure. It certainly wasn't nine o'clock anything as far as he could tell. Only an overly bright moon, attesting it to being sometime in the middle of the night, lighted the darkness of the room. The room was warm and humid, even with the window open. He had taken off his shirt and jeans to try to cool down and used a brown blanket to shield his back from the hard floor.

Gilbert, meanwhile, was lying on the bed and kept up a steady stream of mutterings as he slept. Jon had more or less carried Gilbert up to the room after borrowing a few coins from the dwarf's pocket that he gave to the innkeeper. He even tried to haggle a bit with the innkeeper with the amount but without knowing what each coin's worth put at him a heavy disadvantage. Jon attempted to act drunk as well, so that that it didn't appear to be too suspicious that he couldn't count out six ferns. Now all he could do was wait for Gilbert to wake up, so he could start his quest to find his way home.

One thought that appeared suddenly was that Liz was probably wondering what happened to him. Another thought came to him that

Nadine would try the hotel and find he had left and was now living in the Miller Castle.

If she was to fly down and meet Liz…no, that couldn't happen.

He pondered that unpleasant possibility when there was a knock on the door.

FOUR

Adept Rwerge was old for a gnant at nearly sixty years old. Gnants resembled that of a bipedal monkey but with a flat face and without a tail. Their spine was curved that caused them to walk in a slow, stooped fashion which contrasted sharply with the lightning speed gnants attained when running, occasionally using all four limbs to propel them.

Adept Rwerge had become the spiritual leader to the Tyreel Followers, gnants bred to enhance their ability to fight humans. As she eased herself down on the wooden stool, she reflected she had overseen the period from when the Tyreel Followers were but a small portion of the population, to that of being the majority of gnants. But the final goal had still not been achieved of eliminating humans from Domum. The Tyreel hair blemish, a small streak of white hair on the left side of the head that contrasted with the normal black hair of most gnants, originated with Tyreel who lived several hundred years ago, one of the survivors from the human-gnant wars.

Hundreds of years ago, Adepts had pushed the boundaries of magic, crystals and their technology. They used magic to supplement a crystal's power and found a way to join non-identical crystals together to create new powers. A rift opened to another dimension and suddenly a gate opened that allowed a flow of species between two worlds—Earth and Domum.

The creatures that crossed to Earth did not fare well in the new world. Dragons, gnants, gargoyles and others found the climate too dry and extreme. Humans hunted and killed them as monsters. In less than a hundred years almost all had died out.

Humans and other creatures from Earth were more successful on Domum and soon conflicts arose between gnants and humans.

Unfortunately for the gnants, the humans had weapons the gnants never considered necessary, knives, swords, bow and arrows, spears, shields and finally horses. The humans also used battle strategies using large groups of men, while the gnants often attacked in small, undisciplined clusters. The near extermination of the gnants ended in a truce with the gnants allowed to live in a small land dominated by swamps and sulphur hot springs.

Tyreel was a small male gnant who had to survive by using his wits. He spent a good portion of his youth wandering about, thinking about the war and how the gnants lost to an enemy they outnumbered. Weapons, he decided, they could match or copy, but that had not helped them in the past. The critical factor he concluded was that humans could live and fight together in a common cause and follow a leader without question. His own race couldn't work, fight, or even hardly live together and in battle quickly fell into a group of disorganized individuals.

That conclusion led to Tyreel's First Insight; success in battle lies in tolerance of being together. As the years passed, he avoided other gnants that wanted to be left alone, not stepping within the other's personal zone. However, some gnants weren't so particular and the odd one he was able to share conversation and food. One gnant not only shared conversation but something else—Tyreel's hair blemish. It didn't take long for the two gnants to arrive at the same conclusion; the younger gnant was Tyreel's son. This led to Tyreel's Second Insight; characteristics can be bred into gnants that can change and improve behaviour.

The second insight was put into practice, leading to the movement of the Tyreel Followers.

Adepts continued to work at increasing their knowledge, looking for new spells and ways of using crystals to use against humans. Adept Rtal was fascinated with stolen human books on biology that had drawings of organs and cells. Rtal wondered how humans were able to decipher what the invisible cells were like, finally deciding they used mechanical means to see the cells rather than using magic. But it occurred to Rtal that humans and gnants were both made up of the very small and if one used the proper spells one might be able to change those small cells into something else. If the small cells could be changed, then the whole body could be changed. Rtal wondered if she could change a gnant into a human to use as a spy and began to experiment with crystals and spells.

Nadine Newman, Jon's girlfriend, thought back to the time when she was approached to be turned into a human to be used as a spy. She was told that afterward she would be returned to being a gnant and be rewarded for her bravery.

What she wasn't told was the first gnants died horribly during the transformation and that she herself would have to endure pain and nausea as her flesh and bones tried to re-conform to a new shape. Besides her body changing she found her mind saw the world differently, a human with gnant memories. The reinforcing spells became less and less frequent until the time came when Nadine almost thought herself as human except for her gnant memories.

The months passed slowly for Nadine when Rtal came to see her again at her simple lodging at the edge of Seilini. Rtal paced in the small living quarters while Nadine curled up in her wooden chair. Rtal spoke in the gnant's native tongue, knowing that while Nadine couldn't speak it with her human tongue, she could understand it.

"/Why do humans like music so much?\"

"I cannot say why. It is pleasant to hear."

"/Why do humans lie so much? Make up things that never could happen?\"

"They do not consider all of them lies. Some they call it fiction and use it to entertain. A human who lies is not regarded as honourable."

"/None of them are honourable. They are all evil. Ugly with their hairless skin.\" Rtal gave a small snarl, showing her contempt.

"I do not think humans think of themselves as ugly. Several male members have stared at me with lust."

"/Possible. But what is attractive about having two lumps of fat sitting on your chest?\"

"Does it matter why males find it attractive? Why do male gnants enjoy the scent of females? It is part of what preludes mating." She didn't add she found human males attractive, not wanting to try to explain that emotion as well.

"/You have been a disappointment so far. Perhaps not your fault; humans may be more complex than what I expected. However, you have an opportunity at redemption. The Adepts have decided to move you to Earth to see if you can give us a better knowledge. You will be transported tomorrow.\"

———

Nadine wrapped the blanket around her as she curled up on the couch of her apartment. She watched her cat jump on the coffee table to nibble on the remains of her meal.

"Rzet, if I were still a gnant you might be my dinner instead of that steak."

She had spent the past two years on Earth with Rtal supplying her with enough gold so she could live in an apartment and to lease a vacant building on the outskirts of the city.

"No," she said aloud to herself, though Rzet peered at her curiously, "I do not want to go back to Domum. I do not believe I would survive being changed back into a gnant."

Nadine picked up her cat and stroked her fur as it purred. She considered the news a few days ago that Jon had been seen in the company of another human female while visiting the town of Ballymiller. In a way she was relieved she didn't have to continue her courtship with him. She did like him; for a human he did exhibit some positive qualities but his size made her feel vulnerable.

Tomorrow she would have to go back to Deltabios and endure more questions about being human, endless questions she was starting to resent. But there were more than the questions bothering her. Rtal and the other Adepts were planning something. It was an odd sensation. Gnants depended on smell, in particular with their tongue, to detect the emotions of others. As a human she didn't have that ability but found she was using other clues to sense emotions. Perhaps it was

Rtal's body posture or facial features but something was not quite right at Deltabios.

————

When she arrived by taxi the following day to Deltabios, the place was empty. The score of gnants that normally were around the laboratory were gone with only Rtal waiting for her.

"What's happening? What's going on here?"

"/Not of your concern. We are going back to Domum. You are no longer effective on Earth.\"

Nadine stared at Rtal. "What about me? I am not a gnant any more. What am I to do?"

"/You come back with me. We will decide then what to do.\"

Nadine nodded. But she knew the Adepts must have already decided her fate on their return to Domum. The reason they hadn't told her, she assumed, was because it probably was best to eliminate her.

Rtal produced a crystal and it immediately began to glow with a soft yellow light. "/Stand close so we both go.\"

Nadine nodded. "Just a moment. I better lock the door to the laboratory. It's a human custom here if we are never coming back here."

That didn't surprise Rtal. Humans had so many strange customs and even more so on Earth. It didn't occur to her why Nadine had to lock the door if they weren't returning. She watched her walk over to the door, open it, and run out into the night before disappearing down the street.

Rtal considered what she should do. She decided it didn't matter if Nadine wished to stay on Earth; they were going to kill her on Domum where she wouldn't cause any problems. It was too risky chasing her down the streets and not likely to cause any problems in letting her live on Earth.

FIVE

At the sound of the knock, Jon sat up quickly, looking around the room before focusing his eyes on the door. Jon considered his options. Gilbert still slept and waking him likely wouldn't produce any desirable results. The knock repeated.

He debated keeping quiet in hope that the visitor might go away but then it might also be someone like Council Madoc with more information on how he might escape this middle age copy of Ireland. Jon ventured with a whispered, "Who is it?"

"Jessica."

He watched as the door latch lifted up and the door swung open a few inches. "Would you like some company?"

"Company? Gilbert's here as well."

"I knows." She pushed the door open, revealing herself dressed in a wrinkled, white nightgown, frayed on the bottom edges. His eyes were quickly drawn to the unlaced top that she held together with her left hand, while her right hand held a flickering lamp. She gave a nervous smile. "It be okay if he wakes up. I knows him."

Jon didn't want to hear her elaborate on that last statement and swallowed hard as he got up from the floor, clutching the blanket in his fists in front of him as he stood facing her. "Uh, well, I don't think..."

She released the top of her gown and Jon momentarily lost his train of thought of the reason for saying no. He stepped back and fell sitting on the bed, fortunately missing Gilbert. The dwarf continued to sleep on, though his mutterings increased in volume.

"Look, Jessica, I really would like to but I'm seeing someone else and it wouldn't be right and I really should get some sleep and I don't want to wake up Gilbert because, well, uh, you know." Hoping she would know because he wasn't sure he followed his own argument. He stared at her bare breasts.

Whether she did know was hard to say as she placed the candle-holder on the ledge that circled the walls. She retied her top and favoured him with a shy smile. "Perchance 'nother night when you're by yourself then?"

"Uh, yeah, sure. Goodnight."

"'Night and fair sleep, sir."

She quietly disappeared, leaving him to slide back down on the floor to find some sleep.

Some time later, he woke to the unpleasant sound of Gilbert moaning and cursing some unknown maker of the ale he had drunk last night. The room was barely lit from the partially risen sun and cast a yellowish light through the dirty glass window.

"Are you alright?"

"Do I sounds alright? Me heads about to explode."

"Can I get you anything?"

"Quiet. You cans get me quiet." After a minute of silence, Gilbert expanded on his request. "Go downstairs and get me some more of that ale and some burnt wood."

"What? I don't..."

"Go ask Jessica. She'll know what to do."

He went downstairs and found Jessica in the tavern, sweeping up the debris that lay on the floor. Trying to explain what Gilbert told him caused her to laugh. She walked to the back, returning with a half measure in the tankard of ale and pieces of burned wood chips. The wood had apparently come from the oven. Jon looked at the handful of charred bits, wondering what Gilbert wanted with them.

"Here ya go. I'll square with 'im later. You don't needs any do ya?"

"No. I don't even know what he wants them for."

She laughed again. "For his 'ead. Takes out the demon inside."

He wasn't sure if she was serious about the demon but he took the tankard and bits of black wood chips. He made his way back up to the room, noting the mixture of worn wood and stone as the building material. Gilbert groaned as he sat up. He grabbed the tankard and burned wood chips that resembled bits of charcoal.

"Is that really going to help?"

"Quiet. Please be quiet. Go and have breakfast. I'll be okay by then." He dropped back on the bed and closed his eyes. Gilbert placed his arm on his forehead, trying to block out the feeble light coming through the window.

Once more, Jon returned to the tavern. More light streamed through the windows and with the floors and tables cleaned, it appeared safe to eat breakfast. Jon sat at one of the tables near a window and looked outside, though the glass distorted the view and made the images go by in waves. Jon thought part of the heavy beer and whiskey smell had gone, either that or he was getting used to it. There were only two other patrons in the tavern, one was an old man dressed in torn clothing nursing his ale, and the other was a better-dressed gentleman finishing the last of his breakfast. The latter looked up as Jon made his way across the room to sit down but then resumed his occupation of his meal.

Jessica came to the table and surprised him by sitting down on the opposite side of the square table. "How're ya doing this mornin', sir?"

Jon couldn't resist but smile at her missing tooth grin. "Fine, just fine. I didn't drink that much last night."

"You talk funny. Where're ya from?"

"Quite far from here."

"I knows that." She pointed at his wristwatch. "That's an Other-side charm, ain't it?"

"Yeah, it is." He pulled down his sleeve to cover it. "I was told to keep that quiet by Gilbert. If you don't mind keeping it a secret…"

She brushed the air with her hand. "'Tisn't a big thing. Lots of people have Other-side charms. But I keep it to meself." She pushed her dark hair back with a hand, exposing a thin scar near her right ear. "Wouldcha like something to eat?"

"Yeah, what is there?"

"I'll make up something." She stood up. "Do you want ale or tea?"

"Tea. I've seen what that ale can do to a man."

She laughed and disappeared into the kitchen.

Jon checked the two other occupants in the tavern, but they didn't appear to notice him. He did wonder a bit about Jessica. She certainly seemed to have taken a liking to him but Gilbert also hinted that she wasn't that particular about whom she bedded. Today she wore the same open-sided skirt as last night, but her top was now a pink blouse underneath a partial buttoned up vest. Her clothes were worn and perhaps not entirely clean, but that was hard to tell under the weak light that came through the windows. It wasn't difficult to tell her hands had seen some hard work and overall she appeared to be part of the hard-working poor. Still, if he ignored the missing tooth, she had a friendly smile and was easy to talk to.

She returned with a plate of two large sausages, eggs, a slice of dark bread and to Jon's infinite surprise, an orange. To find fresh fruit in a place like Ireland that acted like the Middle Ages in many respects was puzzling. The meal was heavy with grease and he wasn't too keen on the sausages, wondering what was in their contents. Still, Jon wasn't sure how soon again he would be eating again and finished the breakfast, discovering the orange was fresh and sweet.

Jessica had been busy and had not stopped to talk to him until only the tea was left to drink. She wiped her hands on the front of her skirt and sat in front of him.

"Do ya need more tea?"

"No, no thank you."

She smiled. "You're so polite, like Council Madoc, or one of the King's gentlemen." She paused and looked around at the now only other patron. But the old man apparently had fallen asleep, his chin resting on his chest. Still she lowered her voice to an almost whisper. "Are ya from the Other-side?"

Jon knew he was supposed to be discreet, but Madoc already was aware of his predicament and to deny that he was from what they called the Other-side would mean he would have to invent a place where he did come from.

"No, just far away."

She studied him for a few seconds and grinned. "That really true? What's the name of this place you're from then?"

"You probably haven't heard of it. Boston."

"Boston? That's a strange name. Are you certain that's not on the Other-side?" She noticed Jon was looking away to the entrance of the bar. "That's alright, I can hold a secret. I'm just a wondering, that's all. Maybe 'nother time you can tell me abouts it." She stood up, disappearing to the far end of the tavern.

Jon sat quietly at his table. He felt guilty lying to her, although it was clear Jessica still believed he had come from the Other-side. All he could hope is that she wouldn't say anything to anyone about it. Jon also wished Gilbert would get up and give him some help in finding his way home. He really didn't have a clue where to start on his quest. As if answering his silent request, Gilbert appeared at the tavern entrance. He looked about and after spotting Jon, wandered over. Gilbert looked better and climbed up on a chair to sit without any apparent ill effects.

"Are you feeling okay, Gilbert?"

"Right as rain. Just needs some food and we cans gets started."

Jon was pleased by Gilbert's improved disposition. In fact, he was almost cheerful. Whatever the hangover cure was it seemed to have a marvellous effect on him.

When Jessica appeared, he ordered a large breakfast. He also ordered two tankards of ale, ignoring any plea from Jon that he didn't want to drink.

"It'll do you good, best thing there is to start the day."

Gilbert continued to talk as they waited for the breakfast, revealing some interesting stories about Council Madoc, who was an independent advisor to people in high positions.

Several times a year he traveled about, staying at some less than desirable places such as the Cobbler Inn to gather information. Who his sources were exactly and what other ways he obtained information wasn't well known but Council Madoc managed to make a tidy income on selling that information to those who could pay for his services. The fact that he was still alive and living comfortably showed he had rarely been wrong in his advice.

Gilbert gulped down his breakfast and ale, leaving Jon to wonder how someone could eat such a heavy, greasy breakfast with such gusto. Gilbert ordered two more ales and jumped down from his chair to, as he delicately put it, get rid of the water part of the ale. The Cobbler Inn was not on the high end of drinking establishments and the facilities for men were outside, specifically in the brush in the back. Women, for the few that ventured there, had the opportunity to use a small closet size room.

Jessica set the tankards on the table and though she was busy, stopped to chat. Jon mentioned Gilbert seemed to be in a rather good mood, especially considering how grumpy he was last night and the resulting hangover in the morning.

"Oh, his 'angover is gone now. But he's happy because he's found a way out of his problem, whatever that might be."

"Hmm, is that good or bad?"

She shrugged. "He's okay. Ya can trust him for the most part."

It wasn't exactly a ringing endorsement but Jon really didn't expect anything better. The long and the short of it was he didn't have much of a choice but to trust Gilbert.

An hour later, they left the Cobbler Inn and stepped outside to a warm, sunny day. Only a few small clouds broke up the blue sky.

Now that it was daytime, Jon could see the street much better. He saw that the buildings were made of brick or stone, standing separately from each other. The establishments left a narrow space between them and the shoulder-width space wasn't inviting to use as a shortcut. The street itself was made of stone that gave it a sense of permanency but didn't stay straight or level as it followed the natural fluctuations of the ground.

Across the street stood the huge stone structure designed much like the Miller castle that Gilbert and Jon dropped in from the previous night. Jon thought it was fortunate that they landed outside the stone walls and not inside the courtyard. The imposing front entrance included two armoured guards holding on a chain giant dog-like beasts that had claws like that of a lion. The creatures currently were lying down, but it was not hard to envision them springing to life to defend the property from intruders.

"What is that place? Does a king live there?"

"Naw. Rich guy, calls himself Lord Bennett. He was born rich, but also uses magic to keep himself powerful, such as those rogs at the front."

"Rogs? You mean those dog-like things?"

"Yeah. Some suspect those guards ain't human either but hard to tell with their helmets on."

Jon walked in silence for a few minutes with Gilbert, looking at the storefronts that displayed food, tools and other objects he couldn't fathom what their purpose was. What Gilbert said about magic and the rogs didn't take him aback. There was obviously something Gilbert did to cause them to arrive at this different world and perhaps that could be called magic. The other factor was that Gilbert was superstitious and blamed what he didn't understand on magic. "Gilbert, why did Council Madoc refer to you as Freeman and myself as Master?"

"Just a title. Master, 'cause he wasn't sure of your status yet. I'm a Freeman, meaning I don't belong to nobody."

"You mean some people are slaves or something?"

"Yeah. Like Jessica for instance. She belongs to the innkeeper. She'll work for him until she can pay for her freedom. That'll take about another ten years."

"That's awful."

"Not really. He's providing her with a roof over her head and food. Better than if she was living on the street which she was doing before she got caught."

"Got caught? By who?"

Gilbert sighed. "By the authorities, stupid. Everyone has to have means to support themselves and a place to live. If they don't, they're locked up. The lucky ones are bought and put to work by somebody until they can pay their debt. Jessica gots it easy. She don't have to do no whoring and rarely gets whipped."

Jon just shook his head. *I guess I shouldn't be surprised by what happens in this world.* The hot air was making him thirsty again, even for the heavy tasting ale. "Where are we going? I'm getting a bit thirsty."

"Not far, 'nother mile or so. Just a minute." He ducked into one of the stores and came out with a couple of large oranges, tossing him one of them. "This'll help until we get there. Lord Sussex will provide with refreshments later."

The orange was delicious, but that just raised another question. "Gilbert, where do they get the oranges from?"

He stared at Jon as if he were a fool. "From trees. You know, those big green things that have a trunk and limbs." He waved his hand in the general direction to his side. "They grow just outside of the town."

He held back from asking another question. *Orange trees growing in Ireland? Well, come to think of it, it is rather warm and humid here and not like the Ireland when I landed at the airport.*

The rest of the walk was uneventful, although they passed by a few poorly dressed individuals, horses with riders and pulling carts and two official looking soldiers. The approach of the lightly armoured soldiers caused Gilbert and Jon to step off the sidewalk and onto the road. After they marched by, Gilbert snarled.

"Arrogant buggers. Give thems a sword, and theys think theys better than us whos pay taxes."

"You have to pay taxes? To whom?"

"Neverminds. I pays what I needs to." Gilbert pointed at a tall grey-brown castle. "That be where we goes."

Lord Sussex lived in a stone castle where the back disappeared into a hill. The front was protected from visitors by a large hedge that turned out to be a maze. Gilbert had apparently been through it before and led the way without much of a problem to the front doors. They passed a large fountain spraying water over the white marble figures of four naked women with their limbs intertwined. The fountain was positioned just before a bed of flowers, which was the final barrier to the entrance.

The entrance consisted of a pair of large, imposing, dark wood doors. The hedge and the entrance appeared to have been designed to discourage visitors from approaching Lord Sussex without an invitation.

"Glad he hasn't changed the maze from last time. Hate to have to yell out for help." Gilbert pulled on a cord next to the large doors that disappeared into the house. "We needs his help, so lets me do the talking and just follow me lead."

It took several minutes but presently the right door swung open revealing a young woman dressed in a white wrap with a gold chain as a belt. The hem was uneven; below the knee on the right and nearly to the hip on the left. The loose top hung from the left shoulder and exposed her right breast.

Jon was startled by her appearance, though not so Gilbert.

"Hello, Patricia. Is Lord Sussex available?"

The long-haired blonde smiled warmly. "I believe he is, Gilbert. Would you be so kind as to wait in the drawing room?"

She led the way, padding barefoot to a room down a marble hallway. Jon took his eyes off her long enough to notice the high ceiling and the paintings that hung along the walls. On the far end of the hallway the head of some monstrous creature hung like a trophy. Two huge yellow eyes peered down from them from the crocodile like face and skin. Jon thought this would have been one humongous reptile. The jaws were partially open to reveal a double row of small pointed teeth, from which a forked pink tongue lopped to one side. He hoped this wasn't a real monster but rather one made up by some bizarre artist to impress visitors. Jon reminded himself this world might have some unusual creatures that lived here.

The drawing room itself held several chairs upholstered in red leather, wood tables, decorations and more paintings. Several paintings consisted of a knight rescuing a damsel from danger such as a dragon, the head of which looked similar to the beast mounted in the hallway. A set of candles gave off an aroma of flowers and spice.

"Want a drink?" Gilbert headed straight to a liquor cabinet and checked out the various selections.

"Just water."

Gilbert shook his head. "Good stuff here. There's water in that jug on the far table." He pointed to a gold metal pitcher with a finger.

The pitcher was wet from condensation and ice clattered against the spout as Jon poured a tumbler full of water, carrying it to where Gilbert was giving himself a generous amount of a gold coloured liquid.

"Just who is this Sussex guy?"

"Lord Sussex, he be connected with royalty. Just a business acquaintance, so to speak. But he does have some connections we can use."

Several minutes passed, and the door opened to a tall slim man, appearing to be in his mid-forties. He was well dressed in a long red cloak over a white shirt and slacks. In his right hand, Lord Sussex carried a silver and black cane that made a distinct clicking noise as he touched it on the floor. Behind him followed another young woman, dressed like Patricia, who carried a tray of fruit and sandwiches. She placed the tray on a table near where the liquor was kept and stood waiting.

"Gilbert, my old friend! What brings you around to see me? Ah, I see you have brought a guest with you." Lord Sussex gleamed at the two men.

"Hi, Troy." Gilbert tossed back his drink and nodded toward Jon. "This here is an acquaintance of mine, Sir Jon of McKinney."

"Pleased to meet you, Sir Jon." Sussex snapped his heels together and gave a short bow.

Sir Jon has need of a Voltaire Crystal. I was thinking that perhaps you might know how we might obtain one." Gilbert moved over to the tray and casually picked up a sandwich.

"A Voltaire Crystal? Those are not common my friend, no indeed. Of what importance might it be to him?"

"He's a collector, much like yourself. He's willing to trade for such an artefact. Are you able to help us?"

Lord Sussex spread out his arms. "Alas, I'm sorry to say I have none in my possession. I understand there are several specimens located at Cretal, near Paderno City."

Gilbert took another bite of his sandwich and appeared to be deep in thought. "Such a pity. I immediately thought of yous when this problem arose because of your well-known expertise on specialized goods." Gilbert inspected his glass. "Troy, did you say Cretal? Isn't that where Mood Figurines are made?"

Sussex raised his eyebrows. "Ah, you have a good memory, my friend, but they are actually made in Sevenor, a bit north of there." He pursed his lips. "I would like to have one for display here but circumstances have restrained my travels."

"It must be difficult for yous to longs for such an object d'art but unable to venture forth to retrieve one."

"True, if only there was a way...but there is no need for useless speculation."

"Perhaps, Sir Jon...no, no that wouldn't work." Gilbert shook his head and grabbed an apple.

"What wouldn't work?"

"Well, I was thinking it would be possible for Sir Jon to pick up a Mood Figurine if he was to travel to Cretal for the Voltaire Crystal. But I just remembered he's unprepared for such a journey. In fact, he isn't familiar with the route itself there. Otherwise, he just might be willing to accommodate your artistic needs."

Sussex looked crestfallen, but suddenly appeared to remember something. "Gilbert, Sir Jon. I believe I can see a method through our situation. Perhaps I can provide a guide to Cretal for Sir Jon so he can obtain his Voltaire Crystal. And if it wasn't too much trouble, perhaps he could pick up a Mood Figurine at the same time."

"An excellent suggestion, Troy. I think Sir Jon might be persuaded to do this. Though he be traveling light and it might be prudent to give him some working capital. Strictly for expenses, as he be accustomed to certain comforts."

Sussex waved his hand. "Say no more. I do understand the need of comforts myself. If Sir Jon agrees to such an undertaking, I can arrange a guide as well as some financial assistance."

They both turned their attention to Jon, who was a bit unprepared for the turn in conversation and could only nod with his mouth full of a turkey sandwich.

Lord Sussex looked pleased. "This is a most fortunate circumstance to meet you, Sir Jon. Gilbert, please go to Lord Perry and he will arrange for a guide, as well as funds for this journey. I will dispatch a messenger to Lord Perry to that effect."

Gilbert was about to take a drink when his hand froze. "Can't ye just give us the money? I'm sure I can hire a decent guide for Sir Jon and save the trouble of disturbing Lord Perry."

"Normally I would but I have an arrangement with Lord Perry to handle my financial requirements above normal living expenses. It is one of the penalties I must endure due to being cursed to live only in the confines of my property."

Gilbert was practically dancing as they headed back to the town. "I did it! I did it. And I got that fool to help." He laughed as his face turned red.

"I don't understand anything as to what just happened. And what was that Sir Jon of McKinney?"

"Don't matter. Sir Jon of McKinney, that was a stroke of genius. It mades you sounds more important than you is. Troy the boy likes to put on airs. He knew yous weren't no royal anything but helped him to play the game. That old goat wanted that Mood Figurine so badly but couldn't come out and say it. Hilarious." He laughed again.

"I don't understand."

"Obviously. Lord Sussex is two hundred and thirty something years old. He uses magic to keep his youth, but it only works within his property so he can't leave. He needs you to get his Mood Figurine, and he's willing to pay you to get it. You get the Voltaire Crystal and he gets his toy."

"What are those things?"

"The crystal is what you need to amplify magic so that yous can go back to the Other-side. The Mood Figurines are used to help put people, shall we say, in the horizontal bump frame of mind. Bad enough that he keeps all his ladies half undressed, but he wants them ready too. What a joker."

"People here keep talking about magic but I haven't seen any of it. I mean, I know I'm in a different place but so far all I've seen is this middle-ages scene."

"You want proof of magic? Shit, just look around. That ice water you drank at Lord Sussex's place had ice in it, right?"

"Yeah, so?"

"So where did the ice come from? Not from any of your mechanical contraptions, I'll tell you. That was a small magic spell."

Jon thought about it and though he wasn't convinced of the magic in it, he wondered where the ice did come from. He left that topic for now and decided to change subjects. "So, I'm going to be given money and a guide and then find these things in Cretal, or whatever you called it?"

"Yeah. It might be difficult but you can do it. When you come back, I'll help you use that crystal, no problem."

"You're not coming with me?"

"Na, I'll just be in the way. Come on, let's get drunk."

Jon didn't have a good feeling about what just transpired but so far he didn't have a lot of choice on what to do.

The tavern Gilbert chose was better than the Cobbler Inn. The ale was less bitter, the tavern much bigger and better lit, even though the clientele hadn't changed much. The tavern sported a bartender, several waitresses and a small, sinister looking manager who continually surveyed the goings on from his vantage point at the room's entrance. Their waitress, or serving wench, as Gilbert liked to call her, quickly brought their beer with a quick smile and a word to Gilbert to behave himself this time. Despite her warning, Gilbert gave her a quick pat on her ass.

"Gilbert!" She wagged a finger at him.

He merely grinned. "Sorry, Nicole, yous have a pretty behind."

Nicole walked away, not appearing upset with him. She was just a bit heavier than Jessica and at least sported all of her front teeth. Nicole wore a long skirt like Jessica, also split along the side. Instead of a blouse, she wore a brown leather vest tied at the front with string, leaving bare skin down her front chest.

Jon noticed a leather collar with a metal ring attached around her neck. "What is that collar around her neck? Is she a slave?"

Gilbert shrugged. "'tis a slave collar. The metal ring has marks on it showing who she belongs to. The leather just protects her skin."

The tavern was on the warm side and Jon saw as the evening progressed, Nicole's vest stringed front became more open. By that time Jon had gone past the point of remaining sober, having decided that if Gilbert could drink to excess, the third, fourth and so on tankards were just rewards for what he had been through. He decided after his second ale, Nicole was quite good looking. After his fourth tankard, Nicole became gorgeous.

Events of the evening became blurred for Jon. There was the occasion where Jon, copying the antics of some other inebriated patrons, grabbed Nicole and kissed her on the cheek and on an impulse, lowered his head to try to kiss between the parted halves of her vest. He wasn't sure what possessed him at that moment to try, but fortunately she laughed as she pulled him by his hair back to an upright position.

Later, it was with some effort that he tried to leave the tavern for the room that Gilbert had paid for earlier. Gilbert, who was none too steady on his feet himself, tried to provide some support for him. The result was knocked down chairs and spilled drinks, which led to shouts and curses. Fortunately, the barkeep, William, and Nicole were used to such discord, and they stepped in to prevent a drunken brawl that could have damaged the premises.

"Easy lads, easy. He'll pay for another round for you, not to worry."

"Th' hill I well!"

William ignored Gilbert's protests and pulled out a couple of coins from his pocket. "See lads, he's good for it." Jon continued to stagger out of the room with Gilbert offering minor support on the right.

After William determined that Gilbert had paid for a room, he told Nicole to help them upstairs, deciding he would prefer to tend the bar himself. Gilbert, usually when he planned to have a few drinks, obtained a room ahead of time. He didn't want to run the risk of being tossed out of the tavern drunk. There was a serious risk of being picked up by the King's patrol that would mean an unpleasant time in the holding cells. It could take several days and bribes to get out.

Jon leaned on Nicole as they made our way up the stairs while Gilbert hung on to the handrail and pulled himself up the stone steps. Nicole laughed at Jon's inability to step in a straight line.

Jon continued his awkward advance up the stairs and dropped his hand from her waist to her bottom. Nicole slid his hand back up to her waist, only to have him repeat the effort a few steps later.

"Now see here, keep your paws around my waist or you'll find yourself going downstairs real fast. Understood?"

"Sure, whatever you say." Part of Jon realized he was acting like a drunken jerk. "Sorry." They reached the second level, where she turned him around on the landing so that the three could journey on a wooden set of stairs up to the third level.

Gilbert complained that the steps were not made for those with his length of legs, but despite that and being intoxicated managed to keep ahead of Nicole and Jon.

The room fortunately was not far from the staircase and she eased Jon through the door before finally pushing him onto the bed, much to the annoyance of Gilbert.

"How comes he's in the bed? I's paying for the room, ain't I?"

She gave him an exasperated look. "Hey, I practically carried him up here without any bloody help from you, so I'll damn well dump him where I please. You want to roll him on the floor afterward that's your doing." She saw Jon was staring at her, or more precisely at where her vest had decided to part ways.

"Haven't you seen boobs before?" She pulled at the leather strings, drawing the halves back together.

"Sorry. I had to look."

Nicole appeared more amused than angry, so he gave her his best drunken smile.

"Cm'on, stay a while."

"As much as I would like to be spending time with gentlemen like you two, I have to go back to work." She paused to rearrange her vest and fix her skirt, returning her to some degree of modesty. "You," she pointed a finger at Jon "remind me of an American I once went out with. Like you, he had only one thing on his mind. He deserved a slap on the face too." She turned and walked out of the door.

Jon shut his eyes as the door closed. He made an effort to recall how he acted with her and decided he had acted like a real boor. "Hey Gilbert, remind me to apologize to her tomorrow."

But the dwarf was already asleep, sitting up against the foot of the bed on the floor with his chin resting on his chest.

Morning came, and Jon slowly lifted his head off the pillow. His mouth was dry and his head felt full of wet cotton, angry wet cotton that was giving him a headache. Gilbert wasn't anywhere to be seen and Jon decided he had to find some water to drink. He stumbled out of the hotel room and after looking up and down the hallway, found the stairs. His head throbbed with each step down but he made it to the main floor. The Magix Inn was a step up from the Cobbler Inn in more than one way, boasting of indoor facilities for men that Jon needed to use and he ducked through the wood door near the tavern entrance.

After he left the facilities, he made his way into the tavern. He spotted Gilbert in the nearly empty room, throwing back another tankard of ale. He walked slowly over to the table, grimacing at Gilbert's ability to drink. The odour of spilt drinks assaulted his senses as he dropped to the chair opposite of the dwarf.

"How're you doing?"

"Not so good. Headache. And my stomach's not so hot."

"Get something to eat. Make ya feel better."

"I don't think so." Jon pulled a face, sitting with his elbows on the table to support his head when he heard footsteps approaching, sounding thunderous in his present state. Turning he saw Nicole carrying a plate of food for Gilbert. He attempted to sit up straighter as he sought what he could say to excuse the way he behaved last night to her.

"Oh, you've managed to get up. How're you feeling?"

"Not so good."

She placed the food down for Gilbert, scrambled eggs, thick sausage and a hunk of cheese. Nicole turned her attention to Jon, her face hiding any emotion.

"It certainly looks like you're paying the price of too much drink."

"Uh, yeah. Not too smart last night." He closed his eyes for a moment to fight back the pounding in his head and to control a queasy stomach. "Look, I'm real sorry about my behavior last night. I don't normally drink so much and I…"

"That's okay, no harm done. Just don't get in a habit of it, okay? Would you like anything?"

"No, no thanks. Well, water would be good."

She laughed. "I'll get you something."

Gilbert shook his head at her retreating back. "I don't see why she's being nice to you. I hope she remembers to bring me another ale." He burped. "After breakfast we have to go visit a place where we have to get our money and guide."

Jon noticed he said 'our money' but decided against commenting on the change of ownership of the money. He wasn't in any mood to argue.

Nicole returned a few minutes later carrying a mug in one hand and a small plate in the other. She sat down on a chair next to Jon. "Okay, I think this will work. Do you trust me?"

"Uh, sure. What're you going to do?"

"She's going to try a bit of hocus-pocus on you to get rid of your hangover. Personally, I prefer a hair of the dog that bit me and some charcoal."

She glared over at Gilbert and put her finger in the small plate that contained a white paste. "Okay, I think I made this right."

Jon sat facing her as she used her finger to trace a pattern with the white paste on his forehead.

"What do you mean you think you made it right?"

"I take some magic lessons in my spare time. I'm actually pretty good at it." She handed him the mug. "Drink this in one gulp."

Jon looked at it dubiously and sniffed at the pale liquid inside. "What is it?" He had a sudden thought she had decided to poison him after all. He decided he couldn't really blame her if she did.

"Bunch of stuff. But it'll get rid of your hangover."

He lifted the mug hesitantly. "Promise?"

"Drink."

Jon drank the sweet tasting liquid as fast as he could. It wasn't too bad, tasting like coffee and oranges mixed together. Immediately after swallowing the potion his head began to feel hot and suddenly cool before returning to a hot feeling again. At the same time his stomach tightened up at the strange liquid and relaxed. Then in a blink of an eye his headache disappeared, along with the rest of the ills harbouring in his body.

"Well?"

"It's gone! My hangover is gone. I feel great!"

"It worked? That's fantastic! How about that?" She stood, looking quite pleased. "I'm going to have to remember that formula."

"You mean you didn't know that would work?"

She shrugged. "I never tried it before. But it was in my notes, so I thought it would."

Jon wanted to kiss her but considered that would have had serious repercussions after last night. Suddenly he was hungry, calling out after her retreating back. "Hey, could I get something to eat?"

Gilbert snarled. "She better remembers to bring me another ale or

I'll toss some not so nice magic at her. And wipe those stupid marks off your head."

Breakfast, while perhaps not the best in Irish cuisine, was filling and made Jon feel right with the world again. He even decided to have an ale before they left the tavern. Jon was glad he had made amends with Nicole but something still bothered him about her, something she said. The streets became narrower as they walked, the neighbourhoods showing more signs of disrepair. Brick and stone structures gave way to less durable ones made of wood. The people were dressed poorly as well, and they were of a mixed variety. Some inhabitants didn't seem quite human, too much hair on their faces including the women and children. One block consisted almost entirely of dwarfs and it was there Gilbert made a stop at a dwelling made of stone. The door was of normal size but the latch was located about a foot lower. A mark on the wooden door indicated where the original latch was located.

"You can come in if ye want. I won't be long."

"Is this where you live?"

"No, one of me cousins. He's away on, ah, business."

Jon entered into a small sitting room about nine feet square. The far wall led to another room that Gilbert continued onto, leaving him in a room with several smallish chairs to choose from. The walls were covered with small paintings, ornaments and decorated fabrics. He sat down on a simple wood chair with a worn cushion, amazed that so much junk could fit on the walls. The ceiling was about eight feet high and showed signs where water had come from the roof, turning the yellow covering a deeper shade.

Gilbert returned to the living room carrying a couple of objects that he handed over to Jon. "Here ye be. You'll be wanting them on your quest. Theys be wee bit tarnished but are still effective."

Jon looked on at the rusted short sword and the knife with a damaged wooden handle. "I'm going to need those? I've never used either one of those before."

"Nothin' to it. You just swing the sword or jab with it, depending on the situation. The knife is for general use but sometimes will help in a close fight."

"You're kidding, right? I mean, you never said I had to fight on this journey."

"I'm sure you won't need it. It's just in case someone attacks you. If you don't have a weapon, someone may take you for easy pickings."

Jon rather reluctantly took the offered weapons, wondering what he was getting into.

Gilbert took Jon along another side street and stopped at the corner where houses of different shapes and styles jostled along the uneven road.

"Wouldcha mind waiting here a couple of minutes? I've got to see a friend of mine. It won't take long."

Gilbert hurried off down the street and after knocking on a door, entered the dwelling. Jon leaned on the side of the building wondering how long Gilbert was going to be, and a few minutes later he saw Gilbert exit. A moment later a woman just slightly taller than Gilbert emerged as well, stopping long enough to give him a kiss. In her hand she held a yellow cloth.

When Gilbert returned to Jon, he seemed embarrassed, giving a quick wave as they disappeared around the corner.

"Gilbert, was that your girlfriend?"

"No, no. Well, yes, in a way. I've a lot of friends and she be just be one of them."

"I see. Was that, uh, Liz's underwear in her hand?"

Gilbert stayed quiet, walking as fast as he could down the street.

"Gilbert you gave her that underwear that you stole, didn't you?"

"Didn't steal nothin'. I finds it and gave it to Donna 'cause…she likes that kind of stuff."

"I'm sure she does. Maybe if she knew it was stolen, she wouldn't like it so much."

Gilbert stopped walking and pleaded with Jon. "Now don't be doing that. Please. It be her birthday present."

Jon sighed. *Oh, what the hell. What good would it do anyway to talk to him why stealing is wrong?*

Gilbert led the way to the next stop, talking little as they negotiated several blocks of the winding and haphazardly placed streets and roads. Eventually they came to a large castle sitting on an extended property. Other dwellings matched the style but not the size in the sprawling neighbourhood.

Permission to enter was ascertained by a guard standing at the gate in the stone wall that stood a hundred yards from the main house. The guard, an older man who was missing two fingers on his left hand, squinted at them.

Gilbert announced, "Freeman Gilbert and Sir McKinney here on official business to see Lord Perry at the request of Lord Sussex. Important business, that is."

"Alright. You can come through. Go straight to the house. Mind the droppings."

Jon wondered if the guard, who had trouble sitting back on his stool by the gate, could actually stop anyone. He was about to comment that opinion to Gilbert when he saw one of the droppings. A dozen or more flies buzzed around a mound of the dark pile, an amount perhaps left by a large horse. He looked around for a horse, spotting a black dog lying on its stomach instead. The beast was beyond big and almost the size of the horse Jon was looking for. It watched them carefully. On the other side of the pathway sat another of the dogs and it too monitored their progress. It was now easy to figure why one old guard was able to keep unwanted visitors out. He had rather good support nearby.

Gilbert pulled a cord at the doors of the castle and used his hands to clean off the dirt on his shirt.

A guard standing almost seven feet tall in his armour opened the large double doors. He was overweight even for his height, his gut straining the big belt that held his broadsword. His mouth was partially open and revealed gaps in his teeth, like a poorly kept picket fence. The giant of a man didn't say anything. The only sound from him was the deep drawing and expelling of air through his mouth. The sight of him caused Jon's hand to rest on the handle of his own inadequate sword that hung from his waist on a leather loop.

Off to his side, a manservant appeared in a black cloak, white shirt and black slacks. The creature's height fell between Gilbert and Jon and was on the slim side. Skinny might be more accurate. Rather disconcerting was the sinister appearance of him, dark beady eyes, a huge hooknose, elf like ears, slick black hair and yellow pointed teeth. He clutched his hands together in front of his chest as if he was about to plead; the long fingers boasted black nails that resembled claws. Jon thought he recognized the creature similar to one he saw in his back yard on Earth.

"Yesss?"

Jon winced. The creature didn't fall into his definition of human. Fortunately, Gilbert was not taken aback by the appearance of either of the creatures that stood by the front door.

"Freeman Gilbert and Sir Jon of McKinney to see Lord Perry."

The manservant took in the information for a moment, his eyes darting about, before speaking again. "I'm sssorry but he isss not to be disssdurbed."

"Not to be disturbed! Why you…" Gilbert fell silent and produced a coin that he gave to the servant. "Please check again with Lord Perry."

The servant fondled the coin while examining it. "Wait." The guard closed the door and they stood in silence, at least until Gilbert starting speaking.

"That damned snake stinks worse than the sulphur lake that he crawled up from! He and his kind…"

The cursing continued, using words Jon thought golfers would appreciate on a missed putt.

"If we can see Lord Perry, perhaps we can inform him what he was doing."

Gilbert gave him a strange look. "Inform him of what he was doing? Where in hell did you learn to talk like an idiot? Gnants are not to be trifled with. They're the devil's blight and are quite capable of putting a curse on you or me that's difficult to remove. They move like a shadow at night and suck the blood out of you while you're alone eating your lunch. No, I have no intention of getting into a pissing contest with him."

The door reopened and this time the servant beckoned them to follow him into the front hall, from there he led the way down a long hallway to a library. In Jon's experience, it was the most impressive library he had been in. High on a ladder, servants were replacing books in the two-story library that contained thousands of books. The library room was almost as big as a city block, with the second level open to the first save for a walkway that went around the perimeter. Several persons were working on papers on the tables that sat in the main floor.

Lord Perry sat in the corner, his desk littered with books and papers. The desk was L shaped and was impressive. Two assistants sat with him, passing him books and taking notes as he spoke. One was a young black man and the other was a middle-aged woman. She had tied her blonde hair back so that it wouldn't interfere with her work. Her quick bird-like movements gave the impression of concentration and intelligence.

Lord Perry himself looked like he could have been in his early fifties, a heavily built man who so far had retained a good portion of his mostly dark hair that hung down to his collar, which was balanced by a reddish grey beard. He wore a purple shirt under a light grey cloak and black pants, and was a rather imposing figure when he stood up, which was higher than Jon by a couple of inches.

Lord Perry waited for the gnant to introduce them in his hissing type of speech. He frowned but beckoned them to sit at his desk. He excused his two helpers and sent the gnant away to obtain refreshments.

"Now what is this nonsense about Lord Sussex sending a Sir Jon of McKinney on a business trip? Are you supposed to be this Sir Jon?" He pointed his finger at Jon.

He nodded yes. "I am…"

"Really now. That sounds like a lot of bullshit to me. Is this just a con game of some sort? If so, you better come clean now before you really get yourself in a heap of trouble."

Jon took a bit of a liking to the man who seemed a decent sort and despite his words he came off rather friendly. He heard Gilbert begin to try to talk his way out of the situation.

"Oh no, your Lordship. We would never try to deceive you, or Lord Sussex, on any matter at all."

Lord Perry sat and leaned forward. "One of my gnants can certainly find out if you are telling the truth."

Gilbert suddenly turned pale. Jon decided he better say something before Gilbert's story really got them in a mess.

"Lord Perry, my name really is Jon McKinney. The Sir part was added, perhaps wrongly, to give it a bit more flair. The business deal we worked out with Lord Sussex is simply that. An arrangement to obtain what he needs; in exchange he helps finance a trip for us." Jon began to elaborate a bit on what he wanted but Lord Perry waved his hand at him to be quiet.

"I'm sure I don't want to know all the sordid details. What Lord Sussex does to pass his time is of no interest to me. I am obligated to help him with his business affairs but that's where it ends. However, I suspect you're still holding back some information from me. Why do you need to make this journey? Certainly not because you are a collector of rare crystals."

A gnant, and Jon couldn't say if it was the same one as before, returned to bring a tray of drinks and fruit, giving him an opportunity to exchange quick and worried glances with Gilbert. The dwarf was sweating noticeably on his forehead and he quickly reached for a glass of orange juice.

Perry steepled his fingers together and leaned back in his chair, turning his eyes at Jon. "Tell me the truth, all of it and quickly. Or I will have my gnants extract it from both of you."

Jon lost his liking for Lord Perry at that moment but couldn't find fault with the threat of interrogation considering the circumstances. He took a deep breath, observing Gilbert was studying his orange juice glass with great care. "Well, you see, I'm actually from the Other-side and I came here accidentally and Gilbert is trying to help me get back. To do that, I guess I need a special crystal." Lord Perry raised his eyebrows when he mentioned Gilbert was helping.

"Really? And why would Gilbert desire to help you? I wasn't previously aware of this charitable side of him."

"Uh, well I guess it's because I saved his life."

Gilbert reacted by having a coughing spell.

Lord Perry shook his head. "Gilbert, Gilbert, Gilbert. You do have a penchant for getting yourself in situations, don't you?"

"It's not that way, Lord Perry…"

"Hush." He raised his hand. "There are substantial penalties for sneaking into the Other-side but let's not involve our discussion on that right now. I won't turn you over to the King's authorities this time but don't expect me to be so tolerant next time. Sir Jon, if that's what you like to be called, you are also here illegally but again I won't involve the King's agents. I believe you when you said you arrived here accidentally and let's leave the matter at that.

"I mentioned I'm responsible for Lord Sussex in financial affairs; it's one of many obligations that I'm burdened with. I'll advance the capital necessary for you to complete your assignment with Lord Sussex. However, I will not send fools to their death gladly."

Gilbert had taken a step back from the table, trying to appear smaller than he was. He looked embarrassed.

Lord Perry apparently noticed this. "Gilbert! Were you going to send this man by himself to obtain the crystal? Shame on you!"

"Uh, no, not exactly. I was going to obtain guides and equipment for him. I would go but I have busi…"

"Enough of that. You will go with him. And I suggest that you get the best guides and guards you can afford to help you. Better still, I will hand pick them. You two will be my guests here until everything is prepared for the journey in a day or two."

With that statement the meeting abruptly ended.

They were not guests exactly. House arrest would be a better term but at least Jon had a room to himself, including a bath and a shave.

After washing his only clothes and setting them at the open window to dry, he decided he might as well enjoy a bath. The big tub, made of marble with gold trim, had two levers to add water. He was surprised that the castle not only had running water but also hot. *Maybe it's that magic Gilbert was yapping about.*

The bathroom contained several soaps and oils for him to choose from and he selected a soap that didn't smell flowery. He also came across a razor, a slightly curved metal blade stored in a leather sleeve. He sat in the tub, massaged soap on his face and whiskers and bravely began to use the dangerous implement.

By the time he had finished his bath, his clothes were only damp, and he decided he needed to obtain food. Lord Perry's castle had several places where he could eat and drink, choosing one that had a view of the setting sun.

Jon decided the food was great, and he didn't mind house arrest at all, at least compared to living on the street with Gilbert. Jon hadn't seen Gilbert during his walks around the castle and he surmised he was embarrassed at being caught trying to get rid of him.

The third night he wandered down yet another hallway. Most of Lord Perry's castle-like home was made of stone, except for wood that was used to cover the walls. Jon walked by several closed doors when he came across an additional library. This one was a smaller library than the massive one where Lord Perry conducted his business, perhaps the size of his guest room. The wood shelves were about half filled with a collection of odd sized books and manuscripts. The door was open and there didn't appear to be any restrictions on where he could go unless there was a guard or gnant standing there in silent protection. Jon pulled a book down at random and opened it. The pages were hand printed, complete with diagrams and what appeared to be mathematical symbols. It wasn't something Jon normally would be interested in.

However, boredom can do strange things and he continued to open books and browse, finding that the material was complex and the math well over his head. The gist of it appeared to be solving problems with three-dimensional objects but to what end he couldn't say. The drawings were poorly done, cube and other objects were shown with too many lines and it was difficult to ascertain their true shape. Some manuscripts appeared to be old, their pages yellowed and stiff and used more text to describe figures and had less math to deal with. It appeared to attempt to describe the relationship between this world and the Other-side. Unfortunately, the argument or proof in it, was beyond his comprehension.

He continued to search in the small room and found a book that came from his own world, a rather forbidding book on Calabi-Yau mathematics. This was at least written in a form of English but the math was just as unreadable. With a sigh he returned the book to its place on the shelf, looked up and saw Lord Perry standing at the doorway. Jon almost dropped the book.

"Find anything interesting?"

"Uh, well, a little. Sorry, I didn't mean to be poking around. I thought…"

He waved off the apology. "Quite alright. The library was open. Do you understand what these books are about?" He gestured around the room.

"No, not really. The math is a bit above me. Some of it's on some problem solving on objects but I don't understand the question let alone the answer."

He chuckled. "You're not alone in that regard." He eyed Jon for a moment. "You see, I have been blessed in many ways. I have wealth, power, health and if you'll excuse my lack of modesty, a high intellect. For those reasons and others, I have devoted many years to the study of our two worlds and how they came to be. The more I studied them, the more fascinating the answer seemed to be, an answer tied up in some rather forbidding mathematics as you discovered here."

For one reason or another Jon found himself drawn to his voice, a deep resonating tone. He wanted to learn more what he had to say, like when he accidentally turned on PBS one evening and learned all about the ancient Mayans, even though he was never interested in them before. "Can you explain any of this to me?"

He looked pleased at the question. "Then you're one of the few if you are indeed interested. Follow me."

Jon wasn't about to contradict him and trailed after him down the hallway, took a turn down another hallway and shortly after that he disappeared into a room. Jon ventured in after him.

The room had more books and tables, plus a model that appeared to be made up by a train set hobbyist gone mad.

"I'm going to tell you something that will knock your socks off." Lord Perry grinned.

SIX

Liz met Sandra Draper at the bus stop two days later in the evening. She recognized her as soon as she stepped off the bus, sharing a family resemblance with Jon in face and height. Sandra, unlike her brother, was slim and kept her shoulder length dark hair neat.

Liz felt underdressed in her blue jeans and t-shirt compared to Sandra's tailored slacks, a fitted blouse, and a light jacket. Her shoes and purse also matched, causing Liz to want to hide her own worn running shoes.

The two women sat in the Demister Pub after Sandra checked in at the hotel. She had declined Liz's offer for accommodation at her parent's place or at one of the other town residences. The possibility of staying in the Miller Castle itself was not brought up.

Sandra took a sip of her gin and tonic and seemed to relax a bit more in her chair. "Well, thank you, Liz, for meeting me. I'd like to get an early start tomorrow, so perhaps you can fill me in with a few more details now."

"Of course." Liz pushed back her hair from her face. She had ordered a glass of wine instead of beer, hoping that it would lend her a small degree of sophistication in front of Jon's older sister. "There isn't much more to tell. I returned yesterday, and today but there wasn't any sign of him or the intruder, that miserable little man."

"Jon was chasing an intruder?"

"Yes, and we caught up with him upstairs. Jon wanted to get something back from him and they struggled by the open window before both falling out."

"I see. What was Jon trying to get back from this intruder that was so important?"

"Uh, that was the stupid part. This man, he was a dwarf, had taken one of me knickers. It was in my suitcase I had just brought over." She added the suitcase in case Sandra was wondering if Liz had her underwear just lying around. She was embarrassed in relating the tale, but there was no denying it was part of the reason Jon had vanished.

"Your knickers? Jon attacked a dwarf over your panties?"

"I know it sounds silly, but…"

"It does. Though I'd like to get myself a pair of those that can drive men crazy like that. Especially someone like Jon, who's too passive for his own good."

"Jon's too passive?" *And you hardly seem the type that would want to drive men crazy with underwear. There's more to her than meets the eye.*

Sandra looked at Liz before answering, as if wondering if Liz saw something in him that others didn't. "My brother, despite his size, is not known for being a fighter. I remember watching him play football. He was good, but he drove his coach crazy because he just never played mean enough. Occasionally, something would get him going, like when the other team took a cheap shot at one of his teammates. Then for a while he would be a terror out there, a one-man wrecking crew. If he only could show some of that fire more often. Apparently, you have ignited some of that passion."

Liz felt her face getting warm. "Maybe it's because he's in a different country, away from home."

"Yeah, but I doubt it." The silence lingered for a moment. "Nadine. Did Jon mention her?"

"No, only that he had a girlfriend back home."

"She's an odd duck. Skinny little thing, a bit antisocial. This coming from me. She, from what I can tell, pursued him. He was like a puppy when it came to her, waiting patiently for her to finish work, picking her up to drive her here and there. She didn't have a driver's licence, which was odd. The other thing was that she was an orphan and was without family or friends. Nadine was smart, hardworking, but she just didn't get along with anyone. She wouldn't have anything to do with our family or any of his old buddies. I honestly don't know what he sees in her."

"How did she respond to him disappearing?"

"Well, to give her credit, she did sound quite worried when I got a hold of her on the phone. And she did inquire how long the flight was to here from Boston. There were times when I thought she was just using him for her own needs, but I guess she does care about him. I was also under the impression she was considering flying down here."

"She's coming down here?"

"Relax, I doubt she can. She works at a high-tech biology lab. Rather secretive place and she, according to Jon, spends long hours there. Apparently, they're close to a breakthrough and she can't get away from there. I'm under the impression her own work is vital to their research."

"She must be smart."

"Yeah, she isn't totally without redeeming features. But enough about her. What else can you tell me about the castle?"

"It has electric lights and power, at least on the main floor. It's also partially furnished, and that's why Jon was staying there. Other than the spirits that live there it would be quite comfortable."

"Spirits?"

Liz described the stories of ghosts and creatures seen in town and, in particular, around the castle.

"So, you think this dwarf may have been one of those creatures?"

"Yeah, I think so. He at least looked human, but he sure doesn't live around here. This is a small town and there's no way he could live here or even arrive here without the word going out. So he must come from the same place those other creatures come from."

"I'd be worried to check under the stairs. Anything else about the castle I should know?"

"There's this laboratory on the third floor that Jon told me about. He made it sound like your Uncle Gordon was doing some research there."

"Like Dr. Frankenstein's laboratory? All we would need to see is Igor to complete the picture."

Liz finished her drink and bid Sandra goodnight, promising to meet her in the morning. She found her a bit intimidating. Tall, confident, and rather direct in her questions and opinions. Still, she was obviously intelligent and came across the ocean to help find Jon. For that she was grateful to have her help.

———

Liz met Sandra at the hotel in the early morning. They shared a small breakfast and walked to the castle. When they arrived, Liz first opened the iron gate and next the front door to the castle. She explained Jon had just given her a set of keys only the other day, feeling defensive in front of Sandra.

They turned on the lights as they entered rooms. Liz watched Sandra look carefully around in each room, memorizing details. Liz also found herself checking for signs of the dwarf or any other visitors as they entered each room, making her anxious as they investigated each part of the castle.

The rooms were all quiet and still, save for dust particles that floated in the light. They went upstairs, retracing the steps Jon and Liz took in chasing the intruder a few days ago. Sandra walked in the room carefully, surveying it as she made her way to the window. She looked down and back toward Liz.

"Actually, it's not that far down. The castle must be set on uneven ground with this side up higher. And that tree is close enough Jon could have landed on one of the limbs." She returned her gaze outside. "There isn't any sign of broken branches though. Still, if he missed the tree, the fall isn't that high. Let's go and check the ground."

They went back down the steps and out the front door, reaching the spot under the open window where Jon fell out. Liz stood back as Sandra examined the ground, walking around the area in smaller and smaller circles.

"There isn't any sign of impact or footprints on the ground. Has it rained here recently? Since Jon disappeared, I mean."

"A little. It always rains here a bit, though nothing heavy. There weren't any marks on the ground that day either. It's like he vanished in mid-air."

"Hmm, let's take a walk around the castle."

The journey around the castle didn't reveal any new information, and when they reached the tree again, they decided to check the third floor and the laboratory Jon had found.

The second floor was devoid of any power or lights, but on the third floor two rooms were given outlets and lights. One of the rooms, a squarish room approximately twelve feet on the side, was almost empty, consisting of a workbench and a few tools. A single fluorescent fixture hung above it from the low ceiling.

Sandra examined the tools and the bits of wood, metal and large chunks of glass like material that was left lying on the workbench.

Liz felt bored just standing at the doorway and walked around the room. She looked out the lone window and saw something move among the bushes that bordered the castle's property. It crossed her mind that it might have been a dog, or perhaps a rabbit. Then it stepped between the bushes moving carefully as it advanced.

"Sandra, come here quick." She whispered and beckoned with her hand.

Sandra walked over and followed Liz's pointed finger.

"There, by the bushes. Do you see it?"

Sandra saw it. A small woman, no more than thirty inches high was stepping closer to the castle. She was wearing a long brown skirt, a green shirt and a straw-coloured bonnet on her hair. Her age was hard to determine from the distance but appeared to be an adult. In one hand she clutched a small metal case, while the other held something partially transparent in her fingers as she twisted them about. Then suddenly she was gone.

"I don't believe what I just saw."

"It's one of those creatures I was speaking about last night. That one I would bet has taken something from someone. It's well known here that if you have something small and shiny, you better hide it, or they'll steal it."

"Legend of the leprechaun?"

"If that's what you want to call 'em. But there're other types as well, most of them bigger. They all like to steal stuff, however."

"Metal, jewellery?"

"For the most part. It has to be small, for one thing. Also, they prefer gold, silver and expensive metals. Never takes anything electrical or made of stainless steel."

"Odd. And they just pop in and out like that?"

"Only around the castle. They've been seen in other parts of town, usually at night but mostly here around the castle. I've heard of some guys chasing them, but they're quick, only to lose them as they run toward the castle."

"Then there must be something about the castle or where it sits that allows these creatures to come and go. It could explain how Jon disappeared."

"I hope so, because that means he can make it back as well."

"I would like to catch one of those things."

"No one has done that as I long as I've lived here. But my dad told me a story how two brothers once caught one and kept it in a wire cage for a rabbit. They had it for a day or so and the creature yelled and cursed them and would vanish right inside the cage. But they took a stick and could poke it through the cage even though they couldn't see it; apparently it could make itself invisible.

The two brothers kept the thing in the cage in their house and had friends come over to see it. If it did its vanishing thing, they would poke it until it reappeared. They thought they could get rich by selling it."

"Hmm, so they can be caught. What happened? Did they sell it?"

"No. Shortly afterward the two brothers were found dead in their house with their throats torn open. This happened over a hundred years ago so it's hard to say how true the story is. But me dad has pointed out the cemetery where they're buried.

"Quite a story."

"That it is. But dad got that one from his dad and he believes it. And they're other stories around as well. After you hear a few of them you begin to wonder, especially after seeing that small woman disappear like that."

"Good point. Jon may have vanished in the same place she did."

The next room was the laboratory that Jon spoke about. Whereas the first room was sparse with only the workbench in use, the second room was cluttered with apparatus, books, notes and several tables. There was only one chair, a five-legged wheeled office chair. A motion detector hung from the ceiling by its wires, apparently the result of someone deciding to stop it from operating.

This room also offered a low ceiling, only eight feet high, but was bigger. It had a twelve-foot width that was doubled along its length and contained three windows. Like the other rooms in the castle, the openings had been modified to accommodate a glass frame that also allowed the windows to swing open. One of the windows was open, and a breeze had caused a few papers to drift from the tabletops to the floor.

"Gee, could Uncle Gordon be a mad scientist? What in God's name is that thing?"

Liz studied the device that used three different tables to support it. One table contained what appeared to be a power generator with heavy cables going to and from it. A coil of half inch copper tubing circled the main tank, a three-foot cylinder was placed horizontally and aimed at the next table, all on a heavy wood platform that seemed strong enough to hold a car. Instead it held various glass or crystal objects in various positions by wood and rubber clamps.

A third table sat by the side of the other two, holding a complicated array of coils, wires, circuit boards, and small electrical devices. Wires ran from the tables and to each other and to the floor where a large electrical outlet supplied power.

"I couldn't hazard a guess. I hope there's an instruction book here somewhere."

"Let's take a look in these notes."

Liz and Sandra leafed through the papers, textbooks and notes around the room.

"You're a fast reader, Liz." Sandra observed her putting down another stapled set.

"University training. I read a lot to get through courses."

"What are you taking?"

"History, but it's just my first year. I think I'm going to go into archaeology instead."

"More reading for that." She gave Liz a smile that indicated she had been through a similar experience herself.

"How about you? I gather that you have a career now. Jon said you were a lawyer."

"Corporate law. And have to study the latest changes on a regular basis. So, the reading never really ends." She tossed a small binder to the side and picked up another. "The reading is almost as dull as this."

"Happy thought. Hey, take a look at this. This is some sort of diary or journal." She passed over a black cardboard bound book.

Day 22: I have realigned the mirrors, prisms and crystals according to calculations based on the 'alternative world' having three dimensions as our own, not the six as I first speculated. I have made an assumption here—both our universes share eleven dimensions and seven of them are curled up past our point of observation. However, this other universe is apparently able to use four (time is the fourth one) different dimensions other than our own. My notes on this and calculations can be found in my other journal titled 'Superstring, M theory.' In a few minutes I shall turn on the laser and see if these results are different from my other attempts.

Day23: My experiment of yesterday was inconclusive. I certainly was able to obtain an image of some sort but whether that was of our own universe or the 'alternative world' I cannot say. I believe the problem lies in trying to make my optical set up, the various crystals, prisms and mirrors, more stable.

A special note here. I have spotted at least three of these gnome-like creatures watching me as I work in my lab. Later, one ugly creature, like a human-size bat without wings, was actually looking at my apparatus when I came into the room. Startled, it jumped out the window and what happened to it after that I cannot say. It had vanished by the time I looked out the window.

Day26: I spent the previous days buying and setting up the optical system on the new table. The table is strong and will resist vibrations from other parts of the room. In addition, I have purchased more rubber clamps to hold devices on the table. I am now ready to test my viewer again.

Success! At first my image was only of my laboratory wall, which was slightly out of focus. Then I orientated the last mirror toward the window, and lo-and-behold I saw images that do not belong in our world! Odd-looking buildings and strange people moving about in a place that does not exist here. Much to my disappointment my laser could not sustain a beam any longer and, as happened before, I must now have the power supply repaired. The generator I used to power the castle does not have the capability to supply a high enough current.

Clearly what I must do is arrange for an independent examination of my claims. Before I can do this, I will have to get a stronger laser and a new power supply. Unfortunately, these items are not readily available and I will have to order these to be shipped here. The wait will be unbearable.

In the meantime, I will try to bide my time by going fishing and perhaps to eat a meal outside of the castle. I will not divulge what I have found to anyone yet, save for my letter to young Robert that I have placed in my will. I also have to set up a security system for the laboratory in case I have any more unwanted guests here.

"Last entry. Your Uncle Gordon appeared to be on the edge of a breakthrough. At least that's what he believed."

"Hmm, if so I wonder if his own disappearance is a coincidence. These creatures appeared too interested in what he was doing." She pointed at the broken motion detector. "Someone or something did that, and I'll bet it wasn't Uncle Gordon."

"His body was never found, you know. Maybe he disappeared like Jon did."

"Or we're jumping to conclusions. Still it might be prudent to be careful around here. I don't want to do the vanishing act myself."

———

Laquil watched carefully and slowly backed away from the room. The gnome-shaped individual wasn't sure why the information he gathered was important or why it was worth so much. Three bronze ferns was quite an incentive to take the risk in jumping to the Other-side and back without the opportunity of bringing back any charms. The thought of picking a small item or two crossed his mind but when one did business with gnants, it paid to follow the exact wording of the agreement. Misunderstandings could be fatal.

SEVEN

Lord Perry addressed Jon. "What have you noticed about this world compared to your own?"

Jon's first thought was that this world was backward and populated by strange people, but that was not obviously what Lord Perry was asking. "Well, a lack of machines for one. And it's warm here compared to the Ireland on the Other-side."

He frowned. "I suppose my question was a little vague. Yes, those are true but take, for instance, the Moon. Have you noticed how much larger it appears here? That's because it's closer here, despite actually being smaller."

He looked quite excited, so Jon responded with an "Oh?"

Lord Perry explained that the Earth belongs in a three-dimensional universe and so did the one Jon fell into. But not necessarily the same three dimensions, at least two of them extend in different directions than Jon's world. "That's why the two worlds can exist together without interfering with each other. The other thing is that the physical laws are nearly the same but not quite, just enough to allow what seems to you as strange things to occur here."

"Strange things like magic?"

"Precisely!" Lord Perry rambled about the uncertainty principle, including obscure theories on quantum mechanics. Jon nodded as if he understood.

"...So, you can see that this means that people with the proper knowledge can influence reality. Magic, if you will, but really just an extension of physical science."

Jon remembered Gilbert saying how his world was too noisy for magic to work. He noticed Lord Perry was expecting him to say something along the line he understood. "Do electrical devices hinder magic on Earth?"

Lord Perry confirmed that. "Actually, your physical laws didn't allow magic to work as well in any event. But if one believes and knows how to apply one's thoughts properly, magic can be done on your world as well. The magic just works much better on this world."

"This is a bit much for me to understand. You're saying that spells and magic work because you believe it'll work, and when you focus your thoughts, Bingo! There it is?"

"Not quite that simple, but yes. Certain words and phrases cause certain parts of one's brain to focus the necessary energy to bring out the uncertainty principle into a desired state. The use of wands and crystals helps focus those thoughts and direct the energies. When a potion is mixed together, it merely holds the spell or energies as directed by the mind, somewhat like a battery in your world."

"You said the Moon is smaller here. Is this Earth smaller as well?"

"Ah, a good question. This world, we call Domum, is indeed also smaller, about half the size of your Earth and is closer to a smaller sun. The result of all this is that the sun and the moon appear a bit bigger in the sky. The climate is overall about the same as your planet but has fewer extremes; that is, the equator is not as hot, and the poles are not as cold. As far as the geography is concerned, the land masses and features are similar but not exactly the same."

"What about gravity? Shouldn't I be lighter?"

Lord Perry raised an eyebrow, apparently impressed by the question. "Another good question. The short answer is no. When you crossed over your body adopted the physical laws of this universe and thus your weight feels about the same."

Lord Perry continued in his explanation, while Jon did his best to follow his description of multidimensional objects. Lord Perry pointed to the convoluted models of Earth that looked like the model train set up. "This represents the intersection point of one of the gates that Gilbert and you came through. As you can see there are only certain points that can be used to cross over and some of these points are too small for objects as large as a person to go through. For reasons I haven't determined yet, the entry points are like dipoles; that is they allow travel only in one direction."

"Does that mean for me to get back I need to find a gateway that goes in the right direction, is large enough to allow me through and find a crystal that will give me enough magic to make it all happen?" Jon slumped his shoulders. "This could be difficult."

Lord Perry placed a hand on his shoulder. "But quite possible. It can be accomplished with help. I now believe you aren't a con artist out to steal money from Lord Troy Sussex. You seem to be a good man in a bad situation. I will help you find your way home."

"Thank you, Lord Perry. I don't know how to thank you."

"Think nothing of it. I am the King's representative in this region and thus will do my best to help the subjects within it, including those that happen here by chance. If there's anything else I can do for you, just ask."

Jon returned to his room, a suite that included an oversized bed, a bathroom with the gold and marble tub and a walk-in closet. The closet was almost empty, save for a robe. He speculated his room was meant for guests that were wealthy enough to travel with their own necessities, such a change of clothing.

He went to his balcony and leaned on the iron railing that followed the edge of the stone platform. The balcony was nearly the length of room and wide enough to accommodate a set of chairs and a small round table. From his vantage point, he saw the courtyard was enclosed by four other walls of the castle. The green space below had a fountain in the centre with sitting areas spaced around various flower beds.

After breathing in the fresh air, Jon returned to his room, deciding to visit the courtyard below. He followed the now familiar hallways to a marble stairway, with a blue carpet running the length down the centre. He received a few peculiar looks from servants and members of the court.

I wonder if it's because they don't know who I am, or perhaps the way I'm dressed. I must look like a peasant among royalty to them.

Jon found an open doorway to the courtyard and followed a path of irregularly shaped flat stones set in the closely cropped grass. He stopped at the fountain, looking at the finely detailed sculpture of a mermaid and a merman exchanging a kiss as water sprayed over them.

He felt a presence behind him and turned around to see a gnant dressed as a man servant peering at him. The creature swayed on its bare feet, hairy with claws on the six toes.

"Would Massster Jon like refressmentss?"

Jon took a moment to digest the appearance of the gnant and the question. "A cold beer and a sandwich would be nice."

The gnant scurried off, and Jon was under the impression the gnant may have been following him and certainly was aware of who he was. Jon continued his walk around the courtyard, seeing two servants at work in the flower beds. Above the courtyard were the four walls of the castle, each reaching ten floors above him. The top of the castle had a square tooth wall where he saw an occasional guard patrolling the roof.

The gnant returned with his drink and a sandwich on a tray. Jon thanked him but the gnant didn't pay any heed, hurrying off somewhere. Jon took a drink of the ale, finding it of good quality. The sandwich contained a pale cheese, and meat. He wasn't sure what kind of meat it was, deciding ignorance was the best policy as he bit into the sandwich.

After eating, Jon returned to the interior of the castle and ventured to the small library he found earlier. It was vacant, and he poked around the books until he found one written in English, The Elegant Universe by Brian Greene. He carried the book to his room, undressed and climbed into bed to read by candlelight.

As he expected, the reading took his mind off his own problems and at the end of chapter two, he was tired enough to sleep.

———

In the morning Jon had breakfast in one of the large dining rooms, this one on the second floor. Gilbert was there as well, though it appeared not by his choice. He stared at his breakfast, hardly touching it at all. He did manage to consume his ale and on his second glass, finally spoke.

"Uh, well, I guess I owe ye a small apology. I wasn't going to just abandon you, you know…and I, I've decided to go along with you on your quest to help you out."

Jon wasn't an expert on body language but everything about Gilbert screamed of reluctance and not a lot of truth. "Really, Gilbert, why don't you stop trying to con me and tell me what's going on? What happened? Did Lord Perry order you to join me and apologize?" He saw his startled face. "Never mind. It looks like I guessed right. You ought to be ashamed of yourself."

Gilbert threw back his ale. "I may nots be perfect but I'm trying me best I can to help ya. What difference does it make if I'm going with yous on my own or I was told to? I'm going, ain't I?"

"Whatever. When do we leave?" Jon was disappointed in his attitude but not surprised.

"In a day or two. You Americans always want everything now."

It hit him, that nagging hint of a loss of a memory of *something* important. "American..." Jon mumbled and got up, running from the room.

Lord Perry haulted his work in the library. Fortunately, he wasn't prone to be annoyed at just any interruption and listened to Jon's request with a hint of amusement on his lips.

"You see, I was being rather, uh, forward with her. And she then said something like "You remind me of an American..." and I think that may mean she came from the Other-side as well."

"What if she is? She wouldn't be the only missing person from the Other-side that stumbled somehow over here. Remember it's a lot easier to travel from the Other-side to here than the other way around as I explained to you earlier."

"Yes, but...well, I guess I thought if she was also looking for a way back that I could help her."

He smiled and shook his head. "What's her name?"

"Nicole."

"And she is employed where?"

"Magix Inn as a waitress."

"Very well. I'll have someone go down there and see if she wants to be rescued and if the owner is willing to sell her."

"Thank you. I just want to help her."

He stared at him. "You want only to just help her? Nothing more than that?"

The woman assistant did something unusual. She actually smiled at Jon.

"No, I just want to help her. I have a girlfriend back home."

"If you say so." Lord Perry swatted at a fly. "There isn't any law against having more than one acquaintance of the fair sex."

Jon left the room and strode alone down the hallway, mumbling to himself. *Why do they think I've some romantic notion about Nicole? I just want to help her and get back home myself. And see Liz again.* After a moment of reflection, he added another problem. *Nadine. She must be wondering why I haven't contacted her for the past few days. Lord, I hope I can talk to her before she finds out about Liz.*

Jon spent the rest of the day walking around the huge castle. It was odd; the castle didn't look that big when they were walking up to it but inside the hallways seemed to extend forever. The passageways could be confusing if one wasn't paying attention, but it was designed on the grid system, making it easy to navigate. In addition, there were a number of servants and guards that could be asked for help. Jon did see Gilbert during his journeys, a short conversation in one of the hallways showed that he had returned to his old grumpy self, not acting embarrassed about his previous indiscretions.

———

Nicole Keaton tossed the cut-up rabbit pieces into the pot. She wiped her hands on a wet cloth and proceeded to the bar. She didn't see any new customers, checking the closest table if the man hunched over his drink required food or more drink.

"Nicole."

She turned to see the barkeep, William, beckon her to bar entrance. Behind him stood two soldiers.

Now what? She made her way to where he stood. In his right hand he held a short metal rod.

"Is there a problem, sir?"

"Not for you. Lord Perry has decided to purchase you for his service." He used the metal rod to remove her collar. The collar could only be removed by the rod which had a special shaped end that acted like a key.

Nicole was stunned. *Lord Perry wants me?* She suddenly imagined a life in the castle, of comfortable living and good food. She looked at the soldiers. "Did Lord Perry say why he wanted me?"

One of the soldiers answered. "No, just that we're to escort you to the Regis, who will inform you of your duties and position."

There was little more Nicole could do. She knew the King and Lords had a number of slaves to help with the operation of a castle.

Those slaves were not normally purchased from taverns and Nicole wondered why she had been sought out.

———

The trio arrived at Lord Perry's castle and she was ushered to the office of the Regis. She had to wait for him to return to his office, standing with one of the guards.

The Regis entered, taking a long look at her. He spoke in a clipped voice. "Miss Keaton, you are now the property of Lord Perry. You are to finish your slave contract previously held by the Magix Inn by doing duties so designated by myself. Do you understand this?"

"Yes sir, I do."

"I am to offer you an option, which is most unusual. You may join Sir Jon McKinney on his quest."

"A quest?"

"Yes, some sort of quest to obtain a crystal. It involves travel with Lord Perry's appointed guides. You may think about this. In the meantime, you are to be treated as a lady of the court. The guard will take you to the tailor, so you will be dressed appropriately and be given a suite in which to stay."

Nicole wasn't given an opportunity to ask any more questions and was taken to see the tailor. She felt excited to be given a chance to order various clothes, and she took advantage to order clothes that didn't merely drape on her.

Her suite was another surprise for her and as soon the guard left, Nicole waltzed around her room. The closet was a room by itself, although empty. She continued her inspection of the suite, coming across a sunken bathtub. Nicole saw two wood levers by the edge of the tub and quickly deduced it allowed for hot and cold water to fill the tub. *That sure beats using a bucket to fill it.* She saw a silk-like robe hanging on the wall, plus an assortment of clay jars. She smiled as she examined the contents, pouring a liquid of scented oil into the tub as the tub filled with hot water. *Soon I'll be sliding into heaven.*

A knock on the door pulled Nicole back to reality. She opened her eyes, heard a knock again. "Just a minute," she called out.

Nicole hurriedly climbed out of the tub and pulled on the robe over her wet skin. She opened the door to a middle-aged woman of a stern appearance. The short, heavy woman signaled a servant to carry Nicole's new clothes into the room and place them in the closet. The woman frowned as Nicole took a step back into her room.

"I am Lady Rosanne, and you will be reporting to me. These are your clothes as you asked. Your designation at Lord Perry's castle will be a lady of the court. In reality, I have decided you will be best suited as a temporary companion for gentlemen. Is that clear enough for you?"

I'm to be a prostitute. "Yes."

"Good. You beautiful girls have it so easy in life, not having to struggle to gain attention. I will expect you to have proper attire to interest the gentlemen of the court. Lord Perry doesn't believe slave collars are necessary, so you won't be required to wear one. But you are still a slave for the term of your original agreement and if you fail to fulfill your obligations, there will be strong consequences. I trust I'm clear. Good day." She turned and walked away.

I better consider that second option I have.

———

Lord Perry sighed at being disturbed at his desk in the main library when a gnant informed him he had a visitor. "Damn, I shan't get any research done today. He looked over where Nicole stood near the doorway with her hands clasped in front of her. "Nicole, isn't it?" He smiled. "Please, what can I do for you?"

Nicole took a few hesitant steps forward. "Lord Perry, please forgive my intrusion. I was wondering if you would permit me to go on Sir Jon McKinney's quest."

"Of course. Are you sure you prefer that to staying at the castle?"

"Yes. Lady Roseanne informed me I am to be a gentleman's companion. I just don't want to be used that way."

"Very well. To be clear, there's nothing wrong with ladies helping gentlemen in these social activities. However, I will offer you an incentive to go on this quest. Upon the conclusion of Sir Jon's quest I will grant you your freedom."

"Thank you, Lord Perry." *I can be a free woman!*

———

The next morning Jon was summoned during breakfast to come to the main library by one of the gnants, the creature curling its fingers together as it surveyed the remains of Jon's breakfast.

The library hadn't changed much since he was there last; workers were busy retrieving and replacing books as Lord Perry sat at the large table surrounded by books and helpers. Jon marched up to the table as Lord Perry looked up and raised one hand. He returned to making a notation on an open manuscript.

Lord Perry finished with his writing and he returned his attention to Jon. "Alright, Sir Jon McKinney, I've some news for you. I have made arrangements for your upcoming quest—a guide, protection and financial assistance. And I have also obtained the young lady you requested from the Magix Inn."

Jon opened his mouth in surprised. "You did? That, that's wonderful!"

"Which? The arrangement for the quest or the arrival of Miss Nicole Keaton?" He smiled. "Let us presume both, shall we?"

"Yes, of course. Does that mean we can leave soon to get a Voltaire crystal?"

"In a few days. We'll have a meeting this afternoon to discuss the arrangements and requirements of your quest. In the meantime, perhaps you would like to see the young lady. She is waiting in a guest room on the second floor. Reesler will take you to her."

"Thank you, Lord Perry. You have been most kind."

Lord Perry waved off his compliment. "Go. I think you have some explaining to do to Nicole. Reesler, take Sir McKinney up to Tulip Suite D on the second floor."

The gnant led him up the staircase to a suite on the next floor. Jon thanked Reesler, who acted surprised at being thanked, and knocked on the door. The gnant didn't immediately leave, watching as Nicole slowly opened the door. She looked different, her face and hair showing the effects of time spent of having an abundance of clean, hot water.

"Hi, it's me. Do you remember me? I was…"

"Oh, I remember you alright. What's going on here? Why did you ask for me to be brought, or should I say bought, here?"

"Well, would you mind if I came in and explained?"

"Can I trust you? Perhaps I should have that gnant hang around for protection."

"Please, I'm sorry about…"

"Stuff it. Let's hear your story." She turned and walked into the room leaving the door open.

Jon turned to see if the gnant was still there but it was scurrying down the end of the hall. He turned his attention back to Nicole, who was walking away wearing a new, long, soft green skirt and a white blouse. Over the blouse, a matching green corset squeezed in her waist. Unlike the one she wore in the tavern the skirt had only a small slit in it to aid in walking. Jon followed her into the room, closing the door.

The suite was large, even bigger than his room, having a separate bedroom and sitting room. Dozens of tulips bloomed in a large planter box just outside the partially opened window. She walked up to a chair by the window, turned around and put her hands on her hips. The blouse sat at the edge of her shoulders and the scooped neck cut low to reveal part of her bosom. Jon stared for a moment before he continued to walk toward her.

"Oh please, didn't you get a close enough look with your head buried between them?"

"Sorry, I didn't…"

"Forget it. Sit down and tell me what's going on."

"I'm from the Other-side, Earth that is. A few days ago, I was chasing Gilbert who stole something from me. I accidently landed here in Domum. When I saw you, I had too much to drink, and I acted like a real asshole. I'm sorry for that. I promise you that's not really me. I remember you said something that implied you were from Earth, so I asked Lord Perry if I could help you. If I can return to Earth, I'll try to help you get there too."

"So that's it, you decided to have me bought and sent over here."

"Well, I thought you came from the Other-side as well…"

"I did."

"Well, anyway, I thought you'd like to make it back too."

"Did it ever occur to you to ask me first? And why me? There're lots of people who came from the Other-side. You barely knew me and you were mostly drunk when you did."

"You look even better sober."

She gave a half smile at that comment and he continued on with some hope she was relenting a bit.

"I guess I should have checked with you first but things are going so fast. I didn't know if I'd have a chance to ask you. I'm confined to the castle until Lord Perry sends me on this quest to obtain some sort of crystal."

"Hmm. You still haven't answered why me. You just met me once, and you were drunk at that."

"I dunno. I like you and you were nice to me the next day when you didn't have to be."

She sighed. "So, you have been here, what, less than a week? And you're going to journey to Cretal to get a Voltaire Crystal." She shook her head. "Do you have any idea what you're getting yourself into? Do you know anything about magic, demons, wizards, curses, gnants, dragons and other assorted monsters?"

"No, not really. But Lord Perry said he would help me on this quest. I gotta try to get back."

"Is it worth getting yourself killed to do it? And you want me to go along with you as well? What do you want from me?" She crossed her arms in front of her.

"Nothing. If you don't want to come along you don't have to. I'll still try to find a way to help you."

She pursed her lips and stared hard at him, appearing she was trying to come to a conclusion. "I don't think you're lying to me. If that's so, then I'd better come with you just in case there's more trouble than you can handle."

Jon looked at her, trying to keep his eyes off her bosom. "That's great."

"Sure it is. But..." she pointed a finger at him "...I won't be putting up with any of your pawing, understood? I'm pretty handy with a knife and I'll use it to cut something off that'll you'll miss dearly."

"Okay, okay. I know I was wrong before. You can trust me."

"We'll see. Let's go and get something to eat. I'm starving."

Jon led her to one of the smaller dining halls, where one of the gnants brought in soup, sandwiches and refreshments as Jon and Nicole talked.

"So is there someone special on the Other-side that you need to get back to?"

"Well, yes, in a way. But, I'm not sure any more."

She laughed. "What kind of answer is that? Are you married? Getting a divorce?"

He shook his head. "I was seeing someone. But she's not the right one for me. I can see that now. But I met this other girl, her name is Liz, in Ballymiller, the town I was staying in, uh, she's really nice."

"Really? Nice girl, huh? Does she know her new friend is trying to bed another woman when he's drunk?"

"Ouch. Honestly, I don't know what to think. Since I've met Liz, her name is Liz…"

"I gathered that."

"Sorry. Since I met her, I never thought I would even look at another woman, let alone what I did to you, I mean what I tried to do."

"I suppose I should feel honoured then. I managed to lead you astray." She looked amused at his discomfort.

"It seems no matter what I try to say it's going to come out all wrong. For the record, I like you. Also, for the record I won't act like an idiot toward you again. I just want to be your friend."

"Alright. We'll have you on probation for a while." She got up and headed toward the door. "I think I'd like to wander by myself now."

He nodded, waved her goodbye and helped himself to another sandwich and ale.

———

Nicole walked down the hallway, her thoughts racing. *A chance to go back to Earth. Dare even to hope? Does Cindy even remember me?*

Her thoughts drifted back to Earth and her life there. They seemed as distant as a dream. She made her way to the royal tailor who supervised a team of sewers.

A woman looked up from her desk where she was using a piece of charcoal to draw a garment on parchment. Behind her, rolls of cloth were being transformed into uniforms and clothes for the royal court.

"Miss Nicole, is there a problem?" She stood, looking concerned. "I hope we didn't make an error with your garments."

"No, it was perfect. I'm going on a journey and need clothes for travelling."

The woman smiled. "Of course. Tell me what you require, and I will have it made up."

EIGHT

Liz and Sandra met at the Dockers Pub to talk about progress while having lunch.

"Okay, I checked out the power supply and the laser. Uncle Gordon had ordered them but they hadn't been shipped. I'm guessing that's due to him not giving final instructions on how to transport them. They're just sitting in some warehouse."

"How about if we have the laser and power supply shipped here? We could then hook them up somehow. I guess we would need some help to put them together though." She brushed back her hair. Liz found that she was becoming more comfortable with Sandra, although she was rather direct in her opinions, she was friendly, concerned about her brother and had a dry sense of humour.

"You think? How about the entire physics department of Oxford?" She almost giggled at her own thought of a group of scientists clustered in the small castle laboratory. "Sorry, just an image I had. Look, let's take all the notes and information we have and let an expert look at them. See what type of science there's behind this, if any. Uncle Gordon may have been suffering from illusions but regardless there is something strange happening around here."

The two women returned to the castle the next day to collect papers, documents and to take photos of the lab equipment. Liz was able to contact her friends from the university and eventually found a graduate student in the area of physics. He sounded amused by her request and agreed to look at the material if she brought it up to him. Sandra arranged for transportation for both of them to bring the paperwork to where he worked, not wanting to give him an excuse to delay his examination.

———

Tom Markus peered at the two boxes of paper his visitors plunked on his desk. His office, shared with two other graduate students, was hardly big enough for their own work and the new material removed any last space on his desk. Markus was of medium height, a bit on the thin side and sported long, dark, curly hair with an unkempt beard. His red striped shirt was partially unbuttoned as he rose from his chair. The other occupant in the room, a heavyset man, looked up from his desk. 'Tuck' Richards put down his report to watch the proceedings.

"I was under the impression there was only one notebook, not all this." He looked from the boxes to the ladies in front of him, both rather good looking and the younger one was wearing a short skirt. He returned his attention to their faces and tried to look stern about the deception.

The older woman spoke first. "Sorry about the misunderstanding. But most of the material is only here in case you have questions from the notebooks. We didn't know what would be important. We're not the experts that you are, so we brought the whole works."

Liz joined in. "Would you mind just looking at the notebook before deciding if you can't do it?" She gave her best smile at his dubious expression. "Pleeease?"

He rolled his eyes upward at her obvious flirt. "Oh, why not?" He opened the first box and found the notebook. "Okay, come back tomorrow afternoon and I'll let you know if I can do what you want."

"Tell you what, Mr. Markus, how about Liz and I come back around five and take you out to dinner? That way we won't be bothering you at work tomorrow and we'll have a chance to ask you a few questions. Since we're from out of town, how about if you to pick out the best restaurant?"

"You hit his weakness—food." Tuck got up and wandered across the room. "And if you're buying dinner, I'll even help him."

"Thanks, Tuck, for your help in the negotiations." He sighed. "Okay, I'll look at it. No promises."

———

The restaurant was definitely upscale but not the most expensive in the city. After a few drinks were started at the table, Tom cleared his throat and began to recite their findings.

"Actually, I was quite impressed with the mathematics that was used to support his work. And he did apply a proper process to his lab work."

"It was quite easy to follow what he did, fairly well laid out actually." Tuck added his own comment to ensure he deserved to be part of the free dinner.

"Right." Tom gave Tuck a quick glance. "First, the background of, you said it was your boyfriend's uncle? This theory he subscribes to. Not too unusual, plenty of variations of it though. Basically, a multiuniverse and his is based on a superstring model, likely the M theory."

"You're starting on your mumble jumble dialog, Tom. Look, let me a have a go on this." Tuck picked up the leather-bound menu and held it horizontally. "For simplicity assume this is a two-dimensional universe. Now all universes, two or three or otherwise obey certain physical laws, gravity and electromagnetic fields to name a couple. Space-time can also be bent partially due to these physical laws. Thus, the two-dimensional universe is not likely to be flat but rather curved, maybe more in one area than another." He twisted the menu to give it a curved shape. "To someone living on this world, this universe, they don't see it being curved. It looks flat to them because they are subjected to the same physical laws as the rest of the universe. For example, light would bend along the curve and it would appear like a straight line to them. Follow?"

Sandra exchanged looks with Liz, "I think so."

"Good. This menu represented a portion of one two-dimensional universe. But there could be other two-dimensional universes. Let us picture another two-dimensional universe above this one but also curved due to its own physical laws, and then assume its curvature is greater than the first one. Then at some point the two universes must interact, cross at more than one point."

Liz tried to picture one curved menu over the other. "Why more than one point?"

Tom jumped back in. "Because if you extend the menu, the two-dimensional universe enough it will become a circle. If it is curved, and if two circles come in contact so they overlap, there has to be two points, entry and exit. But if we go beyond these two-dimensional universes and to three-dimensional universes, the same thing can happen where two universes overlap. You can't really visualize this since the three-dimensional universes are warped as well."

Tuck put down his glass. "Tom is right but to add to the complication there are up to eleven dimensions according to M theory. So, we could have our three-dimensional universe interacting with another three-dimensional universe that may use three dimensions of which we're unaware."

"But the gist of this is our universe, our world, may have crossed paths with another world. Right?" Sandra directed her question at Tom.

"Right. But there's more. One, the universes are not really touching each other, just sharing an intersection point. Also, the intersection points are slowly moving and may eventually disappear altogether."

The waiter returned to retrieve the menus, ending the science demonstration part. But Liz inquired about the picture they included of the lab and if the equipment worked as Gordon Miller claimed.

Tuck shrugged. "String theory is just a theory, so are multi-universes. Maybe they're right, maybe not. If it's true, then the lab equipment could be valid. Thomas and I studied this stuff most of the afternoon. It was fascinating, his theories and how this equipment was supposed to work. But it was like reading how to make a warp drive on Star Trek. Who knows if his lab equipment actually worked? The equipment was designed for visual only, in other words to see the other universe through the intersection point. But he did have a design to transport an object to the other universe. A little too farfetched to be believable, of course. But whoever this guy was, he was one pretty smart dude. I'd love to discuss his theory with him, real cutting-edge stuff."

"Could someone put his design together with the proper equipment?" Sandra looked from Tom and to Tuck.

Tom shook his head. "Yes, well, with a big team and a large lab.

Not to mention money and time. It's like someone describes on paper how a TV is supposed to work and then trying to assemble it from parts bought from an electronics store."

"What about his findings? He mentioned he saw another world." Liz also wanted to say they saw some strange creatures as well but held back in case they were then regulated to a pair of crazy women.

"Who knows? Might be just his imagination." Tuck looked at Liz, who was leaning forward with her eyes wide open, anticipating something. "People used to see canals on Mars, eyes can play tricks." He took a drink. "Science is about testing theories, checking results and duplicating the results under controlled conditions. We can't just take his word on what happened by a written entry in a notebook."

"But...what if it was true?"

"Then that would be truly amazing. Even if two universes were to intersect, I don't see how there could be a visual interface between the two. The light, the photons would be...Wait."

Tom jumped in. "Calcite crystals are able to split light, changing their angle..."

"...thereby allowing light to slip from one universe to another."

Tom shook his head. "Man, we spend way too much time together."

Sandra grinned at Tom's comment. "So, there might be a way to see another universe."

"Well, I wouldn't bet the house on it." Tuck dragged out the sentence.

"Tell you what, gentlemen. We have the equipment already set up, plus a new and better laser to work with. Are you two interested?"

At first, they refused, then reconsidered, then talked about the logistics of taking time off work, then agreed to think about it again.

The following Friday they took a short flight and used a rented car to arrive at Ballymiller.

Liz was glad that Sandra took care of the expenses. Sandra didn't make her feel awkward about the money. She simply pointed out her brother was worth whatever she could afford and that between her husband and herself, money was not really a problem.

Liz wondered how she became involved so quickly with Jon, deciding it didn't matter why, blaming it on fate. Besides, she wondered, how does one back out of a situation like this? Sandra did ask her on the flight back to Ballymiller if she still wanted to pursue

Jon's disappearance. Sandra suggested to that since she hadn't known him a long time, she wasn't committed to spending all her free time to searching for him.

"But you're welcome to help me, I really mean that."

Liz appraised her carefully. "Thanks. I'm going to stick it out. And I want you to know I appreciate your help as well."

Sandra gave a delayed smile back. "Touché. Sorry, bad choice of words. I get a little possessive about my brother and have a tendency of taking over situations. I'm glad you're not a shrinking violet. I think we'll work fine together."

———

It took all day to unpack the equipment, and another day to hook up the apparatus. After the initial shock of working in a laboratory in a castle, Tuck and Tom laboured hard to get to the point of getting a trial run prepared. Liz and Sandra stayed out of the way, bringing food and were left the task of hauling up a heavy-duty power cord directly from the generator to the lab. Tuck explained there would be less power loss than going through the outlets added to the castle and they would have to pull every bit of wattage from the generator if the experiment was to succeed.

Tom appeared to be the more cautious of the pair, wanting to check at every detail before proceeding, while Tuck was more of a doer, diving into the set up by looking at different pieces. Between the two of them, the project moved ahead in bumps and spurts.

Liz dragged the end of the extension cord into the room. "Okay, boys, here's the power cord. Just plug it into the power box?" Tuck had earlier made a power box that they could tap from to feed the different equipment.

"Huh? Weren't you just here a minute ago at the doorway and I told you just to plug 'er in?"

"No, Sandra and I were busy lugging up this hundred-pound cord. Why? What did you see?"

"I dunno. Out of the corner of my eye I saw someone standing at the doorway. I thought it was you."

"Oh, I should give you a couple of more details about this project. It seems this castle is haunted."

"Haunted? You mean I saw a ghost?"

"No, not exactly." Liz began to explain about the history of Ballymiller and the creatures that inhabit the town. She told him that was why Gordon Miller started the lab; to find out if the creatures came from the other world.

"Lord, I'm not sure what to believe now." Tuck looked at the apparatus set up in front of him. "If that's true this stuff will show us a view of that other world. And it's possible they've already found a means to cross over."

Tom took the extension cord from Liz and plugged it into the power box. "We may have a chance to find out. Assuming dummy here knows how to wire up a simple box. Watch out for the arcs and sparks."

With more than a moment's hesitation, Tom flicked the chrome toggle switch to the 'ON' position. The lights on the control panel, a piece of flat metal with lights and switches on one side and wires trailing out on the other, blinked from red, to yellow and finally to green.

"Looks good," Tom announced. "I'm going to send a low intensity beam for alignment purposes."

A bright red beam shot out from the laser, bouncing, reflecting and disappearing into a variety of mirrors, prisms and crystals in front of it. Tom read out numbers from the panel while Tuck turned dials on a second panel, and carefully twisted some apparatus, causing a mirror to move slightly.

"Good! Lock it there, we have one dot one six. More than close enough." Tom flicked a switch and the bright red light disappeared.

All four of them stared at each other and at the collection of equipment.

Sandra let out a long breath. "Well, I guess the next step will be the big one. When do we do it?"

The consensus was to eat and write what they had done so far, noting time and measurements. Tom took out a camera and recorded the equipment as well as the four of them for posterity, just in case everything did work.

An hour and a half later, the equipment again breathed into life.

Tuck suggested they use a mobile phone camera to view images instead of an eyepiece that Gordon Miller used. He pointed out more than one person on the monitor could see the image and it could also be recorded. The image from the phone was wired to a monitor.

Three of them huddled in front of the monitor as Tom turned the intensity of the laser up. The screen remained blank, with an occasional flurry of snow.

"Nothing's happening." Liz crossed her fingers as she spoke.

"Don't worry yet. There's a threshold that has to be reached, like water pushing against a weak dam. If the theory is right, it'll suddenly come on. I'm slowly turning up the power so we won't overload the system."

As Tom predicted the screen suddenly came into life. The vision was that from the room's window where the apparatus was pointed. It was slightly out of focus, like viewing a hologram in novelty stores. Still it was apparent the scene was not of Ballymiller. The street and buildings were from somewhere, perhaps from a backward place on Earth but not anywhere in the United Kingdom. The people were dressed in odd garments as well, long dresses on women and heavy clothing for the men. Some horses with riders and others pulling a cart could also be seen.

"Do you see Jon anywhere?" Sandra let out a breath long enough to ask the question.

"No, not yet. Let's keep watching though."

After a while, Tom said, "I'm getting a yellow warning light. I better shut this down or the power supply will burn out." Tom hesitated a moment longer, then turned a dial and flicked a switch. "Sorry, if this laser or power supply burns out, we'll lose our chance to do this again for a while."

Liz continued to stare at the monitor. "It's true then, isn't it? Jon's trapped in that other world. How do we get him out?"

"Perhaps the same way I did."

The four turned around in unison to the man in rags standing at the room's doorway. He used one arm to support himself on the door-frame, sporting an untrimmed beard with dark circles around his eyes.

Sandra stared at the figure for a moment and whispered, "Uncle Gordon?"

"In person."

NINE

Gilbert was not looking for any more trouble than he normally got himself into. Unfortunately, it seemed to be searching him out. He kept either to his room or the quieter parts of Lord Perry's castle, not wanting to have the company of Jon or most of the inhabitants. It was during one of his walks that he thought he was being followed, although when he checked behind him the stone hallways were empty.

As usual, Gilbert's feet took him to one of the lounges where superior tasting ale was kept. One of the human servants poured him a tankard and left, leaving Gilbert alone to sit down to drink and eat the fruit and nuts provided. The long room had plenty of windows that allowed sunlight to pour in, keeping the room warm and comfortable. Still, Gilbert let an involuntary shudder pass through him when a gnant entered the lounge. The creature, dressed in a castle servant uniform, rubbed its clawed hands together as it peered at him. It shuffled over to where he sat.

Gilbert slid as far in the cushioned chair as he could and gripped his tankard with both hands. "Go 'way. I don't want nothin' to do with yous."

The gnant stopped just before the table, standing as it swayed side to side. "Perhapsss we havesss ssssomething to offer you for sssome information."

"No, I want don't nothin' from ya. Leave me alone or, or else." Gilbert began to sweat on his forehead.

The gnant grinned, the red forked tongue curling around the yellow teeth. "Tellsss me where Ssssir Jon came from." It held up a gold coin.

Gilbert eyed the gleaming coin. "I, I dunno. We just met a few days ago. That's all I knows, now leaves me alone!"

"Pleassse. Doesss he have the cryssstal key? Yesss?" It reached out with the gold coin.

"I don'ts know what you're talking about. I don't wants your gold."

The gnant curled its fingers around the gold coin and snarled. "You might want to reconsssssider yoursss anssswer next time." It turned and scurried out of the room.

Gilbert sat still for several seconds breathing hard and gulped down his ale.

Gilbert was nervous as he headed down the hall back to his room but that didn't prevent him from speculating on why the gnant was so interested in a crystal key Jon might have. The gnants were interested in power, power usually obtained through magic. The creatures were born in the region of Serius, known for its jungles and sulphur vents, which added to their myth of being the devil's helpers. Males and females were almost identical in appearance, causing gnants often to be referred to as "it" rather than as a gender. Little else was known about them, other than they weren't sociable to humans or even usually to each other.

Despite their antisocial behaviour, gnants were valued as fierce and loyal servants, willing to die in the protection of their master. Unfortunately, sometimes an owner found the gnant's loyalty to be with someone else even after years of service.

Gilbert wasn't sure if the gnant was going to return to him for more information but he was going to make sure he wasn't going to be caught alone with it in the future. The creature may have been acting on its own or under another's influence. He decided he would stay around the more populated areas of the castle. Gilbert also thought he would try to determine just what the crystal key that Jon might be carrying meant.

———

Jon was summoned to meet with Lord Perry, and he followed a servant to a large office. A desk was at one end of the room and a table sat in the middle with a half-dozen chairs around it. The furniture was entirely made out of a dark wood, save for the gold coloured cushions on the chairs. Two men and a woman besides Lord Perry were waiting for him as he entered.

"Sir Jon, I would like you to meet Lady Karla, Sir Keith and Freeman Nathan."

Jon took a seat, and he learned that the three were to join him on his quest.

Sir Keith was to be the group's leader and the guide. He knew the terrain they were to travel, as well as being familiar with the local customs of different regions. He was also to hold the finances necessary to make the journey. Sir Keith was not tall and on the heavy side. He had a full head of red hair but only a thin beard to hide a weak chin. "Good to meet you, Sir Jon. I look forward to our journey together."

Freeman Nathan, bald with a dark brown beard, was the designated protector of the group. The black man stood a few inches above six feet, was broad in the chest with thick limbs and didn't smile as Jon was introduced. He wore light armour that included a red arm band.

Lady Karla stared at Jon as he sat. She seemed perhaps in her mid-thirties and wore long black hair. She sat with her back straight, making her appear to be taller than her five and a half feet. Her slim fingers held a deck of cards just above the table. "So, you are the young man who seeks a path home."

Lord Perry coughed once, and all eyes turned to him. "Sir Jon, please understand, I do not spend money on quests easily. I do have an obligation to take care of Lord Sussex and his needs, but that doesn't mean I'm not going to be prudent when I do so. I want to stress I do trust your intentions. However, I have designated Sir Keith to handle the financial arrangements. He is familiar with the various nuances of the different counties you will be traveling through.

"I hope you and your group won't encounter any danger but Freeman Nathan will be more than adequate protection against the various riff-raff that may be encountered along the way. In addition, he's an excellent cook when you find yourselves spending a night or two in the open.

"Lady Karla is what we call a sensitive. A witch, if you prefer. She'll help you locate crystals of sufficient quality to complete your quest. She will also be able to give warnings of possible trouble during your journey."

Jon took in the faces watching him. Sir Keith seemed to scrutinize him, while Freeman Nathan looked indifferent. Lady Karla peered at him with half open, dark-blue eyes, as if she was just waking up. "Pleased to meet you. Lord Perry, what about Gilbert and Nicole? Are they coming along as well?"

"Yes, yes, of course. Gilbert anyway, Miss Keaton can back out if she desires. These three wanted to meet you before they committed to the task of taking you to Cretal and back. I suspect there will be no objections and will be willing to proceed with you in two days' time."

All three nodded their agreement.

———

Two days later Jon, Gilbert, Nicole and Lord Perry's three hired helpers met downstairs in the foyer of the castle.

Jon looked around and noticed Nicole was watching him before turning away. He caught Gilbert eyeing him as well and to add to his discomfort found Lady Karla had been observing him too. Why the interest in him puzzled him. He touched the sword that hung from his waist. Lord Perry arranged for a far superior one than the rusty one Gilbert gave him earlier. Sir Keith gave him a short lesson on how to use it, as Freeman Nathan was not inclined to spend any additional time with him than was required in his contract.

The initial journey meant leaving through the town toward the east on horseback. The stables were kept in a separate building from the castle and as Jon approached them, the odour gave a good reason why. Nathan kept one hand on the hilt of his large double-bladed sword as they guided their steeds from the castle's private road and onto the main street. Jon was grateful for the meagre amount of riding he had done a few years back but these horses were bigger and more temperamental. Nicole laughed at him as he bounced on the saddle.

"You're going to be sore in the morning."

He gave her nod, rather than tell her he was already feeling the effects of the ride. She was dressed well for the ride into the country. She wore a dark yellow skirt that covered her legs and part of the horse and he guessed that women weren't allowed to wear pants even when riding. She wore a leather bodice over a brown shirt that accented her figure. He noticed that at least she knew how to ride a horse, something he wished he could do better.

Jon had expected the ride to be non-eventful but noted that Council Madoc was viewing them from a vantage point on a balcony from one of the better inns. He also saw the bar waitress, Jessica, hurrying down the street, clutching something in her hand. He was certain she had seen him as well, but she avoided eye contact and quickly disappeared into a shop.

Nathan made one of his infrequent comments to Jon, beckoning him to move his horse to his left side. "Tis probably of no concern but a gnant has been pacing us since we left Lord Perry's castle. Likely just curious what we're up to but stay close to me until we're outside the town just to be sure."

"Okay, but what if he still follows us after that?"

"Then we've got a problem."

Jon looked around for the gnant. He did have an occasional glimpse of it as it darted between people, buildings and horses. Jon eventually gave up trying to determine just where it was, hoping it wasn't going to follow them out of town.

The ride through the town didn't take long, and soon the hard, stone streets gave way to a packed dirt road. Sir Keith led the way followed by Lady Karla, Gilbert, Jon, and Nicole with Freeman Nathan following last. Nicole manoeuvred her horse alongside Jon and paced with him for a few minutes before speaking.

"I want to say thank you for getting me out of the Magix Inn and a chance to go back home. I wasn't too sure what you were up to at first but Lord Perry seems to think you're okay, and well, if you can't trust his opinion, who can you trust?"

Jon heard Gilbert mumble something but ignored him. "That's true. I hope both of us will be able to go home with a bit of luck."

She rewarded him with a smile as their horses walked side by side.

The outer edges of the town consisted of lesser-desired dwellings before giving way to forests of thick trunk trees and heavy vegetation. The forests came within fifty feet or so to the road and stumps showed where the trees had been cut back. One or two small cottages could be spotted set just inside the forests. Jon wondered why someone would choose to live there and asked Nicole.

"They don't want to be disturbed but need to be near the road to do the odd bit of trading. Most of them you wouldn't want to meet, only half human some of them. Others might be witches or warlocks that need some privacy for one reason or another. It's best to leave them alone."

"I didn't plan on knocking on their doors. I was just curious."

"That curiosity could get you in trouble some time."

The road and the journey became uneventful as time slipped by. Jon began to ride his horse easier, moving with the beast, though he knew he was going to be sore later. He felt the stiffness of the ride when they stopped for lunch and groaned when he had to climb back on his horse.

They passed a few travellers along the way heading the opposite direction. Most were small groups, such as themselves, looking as anxious as himself.

One group of three men wearing dark brown heavy cloaks approaching them stopped their mounts, holding one arm underneath the wrap. Sir Keith rose a hand and called a halt thirty paces away from them. "Freeman Nathan, we have need of your presence."

A moment later Nathan moved his horse forward, stopping within a few feet from the new group and addressed them in a loud voice.

"Stand aside I say! We are here under the orders of Lord Perry and I will not tolerate any intrusion onto our space. Move your horses off the road and dismount. Now!" With a flash Nathan raised his broad sword, the blade gleaming in the sunlight.

The three horsemen stared at the large warrior bellowing at them. First one, then the others guided their horses off the road before dismounting. They looked annoyed and sullen but unwilling to test the temperament and skills of Nathan. The red armband told that Nathan was a highly skilled fighter, and more than capable of handling any of them, and likely all three at once. There would be easier victims than this group to rob. Keith led the rest past, and Nathan joined the rear.

The rest of the ride was uneventful, and they stopped for the evening a few hours later. Jon carefully slid off his horse and sat slowly on the ground, realizing as he did, he was close to where Nathan had sat as well.

"You scared off those three men quite well earlier."

"Highway men. No gooders. At least they had the sense to back off when I told them." He spat on the ground. "But I think we have other problems. At least one gnant is still following us."

"The same one?"

"Hard to say. They all look pretty much the same but probably a different one. Maybe they're taking turns to spy on us. The cursed creatures have a way of talking to each other and I might just be seeing a new one each time."

"They use a special voice. High pitched, above human hearing, to communicate." Lady Karla stood in front of them holding a wooden bowl that gave off steam. "Dinner is ready." She turned and walked away to a small grove of trees where she sat down to eat.

Jon went to the fire and scooped rabbit stew into a bowl, taking a piece of dark bread as well. He lumbered toward a tree to sit but Lady Karla signalled Jon to join her. Jon hadn't eaten rabbit before but found the food filling. He sat with her consuming his food when she put down her bowl and turned toward him.

"Do you understand what I do?"

"You're like a psychic or something."

"Hmm, I suppose that will do for now. But let's say I can pick up vibrations around us and that I can interpret those vibrations. You..." She pointed a finger at him. "...are the centre of a lot of vibrations. Gnants are following us and I don't know why the interest. Do you?"

"No."

"Other than Nicole, I don't believe anyone believes you are special in any way. Would you be carrying anything unusual or perhaps hiding something?"

"No, all I got is what you see, these clothes and this thing here." He pulled out the metal and crystal piece that hung from a leather cord around his neck.

She quickly reached out a hand toward him. "Let me see that."

Jon took it off his neck and passed it over to her. "I got it from my uncle, he gave it to me along with a castle. I don't what it is, but it was kept in a wooden box."

She examined the piece carefully, turning it over slowly. "Jon, this is what the gnants are after. And they wouldn't be the only ones. This is one of six segments that are needed to activate the Locus Crystal. This is incredible, very rare and very dangerous." She handed it back to him. "You better hide this from view. Who else knows that you have it?"

"No one, as far as I know. Wait, there was this barmaid, Jessica, who saw it. But I don't know if she knew what it was."

"Don't count on that. From now on keep it out of sight."

"Okay." Jon swallowed hard and looked around. "By the way you mentioned that Nicole found me interesting?"

"Special is the word I used but interesting may be more accurate. You're from another place, have an accent, look okay and are polite. Yes, I suppose she likes you but that should be the least of your concerns right now. Your life is in danger and all you're wondering is if a former serving wench likes you."

———

Jon did not have a good rest. His cloth tent was small, barely large enough for himself and his pack and there were strange sounds during the night. Nathan could be heard walking about the camp looking for any problems but the morning came without incident.

Jon felt tired as he sat on his horse but Nathan, despite not having any rest, looked alert. Nicole didn't seem tired, and she gave him a wave after she mounted her horse. Lady Karla didn't show any facial expression and lifted the hood attached to her dress over her head.

The forest thinned out but still looked formidable to venture into. Fortunately, the road remained in good condition for the horses and remained wide enough to pass the odd traveler. Nathan surprised Jon by pulling up alongside of him.

"Lady Karla has advised me that you may be in additional danger from something you possess. She didn't tell me whether it was something you know or an object of some sort. It don't much matter to me which it is, but I'll watch out for you a bit more. Are you able to use that sword?" Nathan pointed at Jon's sword that hung from the horse's saddle.

"No, not really. Never had to use one before."

Nathan scowled. "Bloody hell." He let out his breath slowly. "Never mind. It ain't your fault. When we stop at camp this evening, I'll give you a few lessons. In the meantime, if we're attacked and you have to use your sword, hold it in front of you and take small swings at the attacker. That will slow them down a bit until I get there to help you."

"Uh, good. Thanks."

Nathan nodded at him and dropped back to the rear, looking deep in thought.

TEN

Gordon Miller sat at the kitchen table drinking tea and eating a sandwich, his hands shaking. Between bites he filled in what happened.

"I hardly know how to begin. My laboratory here was more than just a laboratory. To be sure, the equipment and apparatus functioned as planned. In fact, I was pleasantly surprised by the quality of the images, to the degree that I was able to determine it was of no place on Earth. I saw such things as gargoyles, well I can't be sure it was a gargoyle but it looked similar and then there were these gnome size creatures...I'm sorry. I've lost my train of thought. It's been some time since I've had enough rest and nourishment and it's affecting my thinking. Now, where was I?"

Sandra placed a hand on his shoulder. "Are you sure you still want to talk about this? It would be best if you had a rest."

"No, no. Perhaps later."

"You were talking about your laboratory," Liz added helpfully.

"Oh yes, yes. The creatures in this area and this castle were very interested in what I was doing in the laboratory. I even set up a motion detector for when I was out of the room. Unfortunately, the detector also gave off a noise that frightened them and they destroyed it. I spotted different ones peering into the room from time to time, in particular there was this dreadful looking creature, a hairy human thing with sharp claws and teeth…I'm sorry, I just keep going off topic." He rubbed his cheeks and eyes and peered at the four clustered around him.

"Earlier you said it was more than a lab." This was from Tuck, who was eyeing the remaining sandwiches with interest.

"Oh, of course. I wanted to move to the next stage of my experiments but didn't want interference from these creatures. I wasn't sure what their interest was or even if they just wanted to sabotage what I was trying to do. I continued to use my laboratory but was actually using it as a diversion while I started a new experiment elsewhere. At the toolshed. I noticed the creatures, or at least seemed to, ignored me when I went outside. I created a false wall in a tool shed I built. I suspected they would look inside it out of curiosity, but they would only see the usual tools along the wall. I didn't have to do a lot of work on the experiment itself, basically the setting up of crystals that could work in a resonate pattern. I can give you details later. Though I needed power to run the experiment, it was a simple matter to run a power line from the generator. I was now ready to transport myself to this other world. One of the reasons I chose the back yard was that I didn't wish to appear inside a castle in this other world.

"I filled the generator with fuel, enough that it would stay running for two days. The generator had to supply power for both my transport there and for when I wanted to return. What I also needed was a special crystal when placed in the vicinity of the other crystals that would resonate and create a volume large enough for me to step through. Now I know that these creatures from the other world could come here and go back without any obvious power sources. But I needed power and was restricted to this one location where I hid my crystal array behind the false wall in the tool shed." He stopped speaking, reached into his jacket and produced a flat, oval shaped crystal that reflected a rainbow of colours.

"Beautiful, isn't it? Especially since it helped me return home." He smiled as he turned the crystal in his hand. "It was with some tribulation I planned to step through my portal to the other world. I told no one of my plans as I had become suspicious of certain individuals. They had suddenly become interested in me and my castle in the past few months, and I'm convinced they're not what they seem or claim to be. But enough of that."

Gordon Miller stopped to take another drink of his tea. "After hesitating several times, I wasn't positive what would happen when I stepped through the portal but I took the plunge so to speak. I knew I could return via the same route to home, but it takes time for the generator to rebuild the power supply, perhaps half an hour. Once I stepped through, I had to survive at least that time before I could return home."

"And you ended up in this other world?" Liz prompted him, leaning forward on her chair.

"Yes. I was disoriented initially but soon realized I was in a courtyard of a castle that might belong to someone rather powerful. I made a quick decision to try to leave the immediate area and return later but just as I reached a gate by a stone wall, I was apprehended by some very large guards with these incredible dog-like beasts. Needless to say, I put up little resistance. They took me inside the castle, similar to, but not exactly the same as my own. I was put in a cell. I was getting quite anxious, and decided to hide the crystal. I hid it inside the lining of my jacket. Fortuitously, they did only a cursory check, taking my watch, money, keys and anything else I had in my pockets and missed the crystal.

I was taken in front of some sort of official informed me I was now a subject of Lord Bennett. I was charged with trespassing and was ordered to three months of labour. He assigned me to a work detail, consisting of a guard and seven other workers. A couple of them were women and all of them looked rather downtrodden."

"Was it like prison labour?" Tuck casually reached over and grabbed one of the sandwiches, eliciting raised eyebrows from Liz.

"I can't say. I've never been in prison before. The work wasn't hard, just tending crops for the most part. We would stop at mid-day for a rest if the sun was too strong and generally finished at sundown. We were all bunked together but even with all the time I spent with them I learned little. They were uneducated, superstitious, and mostly kept to themselves. After a few weeks I had a chance to do some work in the courtyard but when I approached the area where I could be transported back, I found it no longer worked. Apparently, the generator ran out of gas and thus there wasn't any power being supplied to the crystal array.

"After my initial disappointment, I decided that I needed only to wait until someone started up the generator again and my crystal array would come back to life. Whenever I had an opportunity, I would go by the courtyard area where the array could send me back. After three months my sentence was up and I applied to continue to work at Lord Bennett's castle. Small cleanup work and landscaping. It was, of course, poor pay but gave me room and board and a chance to stay in proximity to my crystal array.

I cannot describe my relief when one day the transport worked again and here you find me home again." He took a sip of his tea and looked at Sandra.

"But, my dear, I believe I understand Robert is missing now."

Sandra and Liz filled him on the details and he shook his head.

"Terrible, terrible. It is a dangerous place he fell into. Perhaps I'll use that lie down now and when I wake up, I'll try to think of a plan to retrieve him."

———

While Gordon Miller slept, Liz, Sandra and the two men discussed what to do next. The consensus was something had to be done as soon as possible.

"He's my brother. I want to go through this gate, find out what happened to him and try to help him get back."

Liz didn't like the thought of Sandra taking over from her rescue mission. "No, I got him into this mess and I want to get him out. I'll go through the gate first."

"I really think it would be better if I went first. I'm older and more experienced in…"

"Bullshit. Older and more experienced in going to another world? I don't think so. I'm going first because I'm younger and I, I…" She took a deep breath. "Because he's my boyfriend and I have the right to go and find him." *And I think I'm falling in love with him.*

Tuck looked at Tom and then at Liz and Sandra. Tom appeared as perplexed as himself.

Sandra stared at Liz. "Well it's hard to argue against logic like that." She crossed her arms and gave a thin smile. "Okay, if you feel that strongly about it. But let's talk to Uncle Gordon first before we do anything. Maybe we can both go."

Liz realized her fists were clenched. Fortunately, they were held under the table edge but she knew her body posture and face were hostile. "Okay. Sorry, I didn't mean to act so aggressive."

"That's okay. I guess I didn't understand how close you were to my brother."

Liz nodded. "I think we better feed these guys. Tuck's stomach is growling."

Gordon Miller slept until almost dinnertime. When he sat in the living room, he acted as if he had more strength and spoke with more assurance in his voice. He suggested if they were to use his crystal array that they move the apparatus outside the castle backyard, so whoever went through wouldn't be trespassing on Lord Bennett's grounds. "No point in getting caught like myself. Of course, we'll have to move the power line as well but that should be a simple matter with these lads here to help."

Tuck exchanged looks with Tom. "Uh, fine. We'd like to help but we have a couple of questions. Like won't they be waiting for us when anyone tries to cross? Can we send more than one at a time across? How long does it take before we can use the array again?"

Miller shook his head. "Not so fast. I don't think they're waiting or expecting us. At least they didn't seem to give a tinker's damn where I came from. We can't send more than one at a time because of the capacity of the array. Also, to travel through the array you need the crystal and there's only one that has been tuned for this array. I have other crystals but the array has to be tuned for each one. How frequently we use the array going in one direction and then back again depends on the charging cycle. I calculated it to be thirty-seven minutes."

———

Liz watched as Tuck dragged a length of heavy cable over the fence. Tom stood on the other side of the five-foot stone wall and pulled the end to where the crystal array stood. The array consisted of a four by eight-foot sheet of plywood that held dozens of crystals in an oval pattern. A thin gold wire joined the flat hexagon crystals that each, in turn, was mounted on a plastic plate. Each plastic plate was held on by three thumbscrews that allowed for adjusting fine placement and orientation of each crystal. The bottom crystal also had insulated wires that ran to a large metal grey box. It was to the grey box that Tom attached the end of the heavy cable and flipped a simple toggle switch. A pulsing yellow light soon came on at the top.

"It's charging now."

Miller nodded with satisfaction. "Now we wait." He held his crystal in his hand, gently rubbing the surface.

Tuck watched the yellow lamp. It appeared to him it was pulsing faster as the grey box gave off a gentle hum. "How do we calibrate the array?"

"More art than science. When the lamp turns green, I hang this crystal in the middle of the array. I turn the adjusting screws on each crystal until the middle of the array becomes a window to this other world. If the left side of the array is cloudy, then I adjust the right side of the array. It took me a while to understand just how much and which direction to move the crystals."

Sandra turned to Liz. "Are you sure about this?"

Liz nodded. Her own doubts were rising fast. The conviction she felt only yesterday was wavering. Excitement and dread filled her as she fixed her sights on the blinking yellow light.

"You're brave to do this."

"No, I'm scared as hell."

"That just makes you even braver. Remember it's less than an hour that you have to survive. Come back as soon as you can and report what there is. Then we can figure out a game plan for retrieving Jon."

All eyes were fixed as the yellow lamp stopped pulsing and became a steady glow. Then it began to change colour flickering from yellow to green before deciding to stay green.

Miller took his crystal and hung it by a long leather cord from the top of the plywood. Immediately the centre of the plywood changed to a clear image, a faint ghost image of the wood showing a scene of green plants growing in front of a stonewall. He began to adjust the crystals and the edges of the window began to clear up. A dark spot near the middle vanished.

"There, now it's ready." He took the crystal away from the board causing the window to vanish. "Are you quite ready for this?" He turned to Liz and held up the crystal.

"Yes." Her voice came out flat. Then with more assurance, "Absolutely." She took the crystal and hung it around her neck.

"Good, good. Now, did you remember to remove anything metal from yourself and jewellery?"

"Yes." She decided to copy the fashions of the other world the best she could and wore a long-sleeved blouse and a full-length skirt that used a plastic zipper and a button to fasten it. Her sandals used Velcro to secure the straps. Her bra had a metal hook to hold it together. She wasn't keen on going without one and was glad when Miller informed her a slight amount of metal wasn't likely to pose too much of a problem.

She took a deep breath and stepped toward the array, holding the crystal slightly in front of her. The window opened, and she stepped through. A spark flew from the metal hook at the front of her bra, stinging her and then a sizzle in her mouth as a tooth filling reacted to the array. Then she was through, suddenly standing in front of a stone wall. Heat and humidity washed over her and she looked around behind her. There wasn't any sign of the array or of her own world. She released the breath that she had been holding since stepping through the array and took in the strange smelling air.

"Oh, Lord. What have I gotten myself into?"

———

Liz cautiously walked alongside of the stone wall toward what would have been the front of the Miller Castle in her own world. She stopped at a tree that was located at the same spot as the tree on Earth upon which Jon seemed to fall. *This tree is a bit bigger but otherwise looks the same.* She walked around it, looking for a sign Jon had landed nearby. The ground was damp, and she suspected any impressions left on the ground by Jon would have long disappeared. She looked up to where a similar window as the one in the Miller Castle stood. The similarities, to Liz, were uncanny and strange. She turned her attention back to the tree and saw a broken limb. The leaves on the end were still green, testifying the break was recent.

So, he did land on the tree. That means he's probably still alive. But where could he have gone to?

She continued her journey, standing at the edge of a cobbled street, and watched in amazement as horses, people and carts went by. The buildings looked like they belonged in old Europe and the damp air smelled of horses, garbage and stale beer. At first the smell of beer seemed odd until she saw the open windows of the Cobbler Inn. The noise from the inn told a tavern was likely there. She decided to keep to her side of the street, especially since her own dress was a bit different from the rest of the population.

Liz knew it best to just observe without attracting attention to herself. Evening in this new world was approaching, and she wondered what she should do next. She decided that it wouldn't hurt to walk a bit more along the side of the street. Liz still had time to use up before the gate would reopen and more information of this other world would be useful.

To her left was a castle that occupied the same place as the Miller Castle in her own world. She thought that Gordon Miller had enough information on the castle and turned to her right. A brick path went between the street and the brush for about twenty feet before she came across shops. They shared a common roof, and it appeared the front had been modified in the past. The doors to the shops were of different design and size and oddly placed. A second level apparently served as living quarters for the shop owners as well. The windows advertised women's clothing, a seamstress, a bookstore specializing in magic and spells, and a repair shop 'We fix anything, big or small'.

The four stores didn't look busy, though one customer came out of the bookshop and hurried down the street. She wore a long grey skirt with a black shawl over a pale green blouse. Liz watched her disappear around the corner and returned to studying the building. The glass windows had a green tinge to them that distorted images. The oversize yellow bricks weren't completely uniform and depended on cement to fill the gaps.

Liz kept to the edge of the building, as she tried to calculate how long she had been in the other world, deciding she had spent enough time on her sightseeing. She turned to go back to where the crystal array waited.

The brush wasn't thick, and she saw signs that at one time a dwelling stood in the open land but had burnt down, leaving only black timbers as a testament to its existence. She walked along the edge of the stone wall and began to reach for the crystal that hung around her neck.

Suddenly a creature, shorter than herself, leapt at her from behind. Liz fell to the ground and tried to hit the quick moving gnant. It absorbed her blow on its back, yanked the crystal and the cord from her neck, and ran off.

Liz sat on the ground dazed by the sudden attack. It dawned on her she had her way back home stolen. She cursed at the brush where the gnant had vanished and slowly climbed back to her feet. She checked her arm, noticing a red scratch from her elbow to her wrist. Her top was torn slightly at the neck. Other than that, she appeared to have survived the ambush with a minimum of damage, except for the all-important crystal.

Now what do I do?

She decided she had to at least find water and possibly food if she was going to be stranded any length of time. She knew she should avoid the area of the castle where Gordon Miller was caught trespassing. Their prison system, judging by his description, didn't sound like anything she wanted to experience.

She walked on the opposite side of the street and tried to look casual as she peered at the various shops and bars. One older woman, wearing a long blue skirt and a black blouse, stopped by and poked a finger at her.

"Whatcha doing dressed like that here, missy? Did you just fall through from the Other-side?" She laughed and walked away.

Liz watched her departing back and concluded she wasn't to pull off as being one of the locals. She made for one of the side streets and sat on the sidewalk, feeling tired and thirsty.

What else could go wrong here?

She leaned against the stone building behind her, trying to figure what she could do. *Do I try to steal water and a bit of food? Or should I ask for help?*

As the shadows lengthened, Liz heard the footsteps of horses and a carriage. Uniformed guards approached.

Two guards, each wearing dark heavy cloth plus a leather chest protector, preceded two more guards riding on horses. Following them in turn was a guard who rode a carriage carrying a large cage being pulled by a horse. Inside it sat two men.

"Attention, Miss!" The first soldier bellowed at her.

Liz felt her stomach tighten, running would be useless, and she doubted the guards would leave her be on the street.

She stood and waited as a guard took her by her arm. "Do you have means to support yourself?" he asked in a gruff voice.

"No, well, I'm lost. Can you help me?"

"Sorry, Miss. If you don't have a place to sleep, it's to the holding cell you go."

"Please." Liz almost cried as he pulled her to the cage. Not ungently, he pushed her inside and closed the door.

"Best you keep your mouth closed where you're from. It won't do you any good if others learn you're from the Other-side."

ELEVEN

Freeman Nathan, though he preferred just Nathan as he believed the title Freeman just brought attention to the fact he was not of nobility, initially viewed protecting the others a bit of a lark. But with the gnants spying on them and the new information from Lady Karla caused him to rethink what may lie ahead.

Nathan considered it was unfortunate that Jon didn't know how to fight with a sword, but at least the man appeared to be willing to learn. Sir Keith, on the other hand, knew how to use a sword but appeared to be the type that would freeze in battle, if he stayed around at all. He was the sort that did well in contests but didn't have the backbone for battle where rules didn't apply.

The women were not expected to fight, although he guessed Nicole could be a scrapper if it came down to it. Lady Karla wasn't, but she actually appeared to be genuine in her ability to foresee danger.

Gilbert was a different matter. The dwarf acted guilty, suspicious and surly at the same time. He didn't appear to be on the journey on his own accord but rather from orders given by Lord Perry. Nathan didn't trust him, thinking that he may disappear at the first sign of trouble. He had no doubt the dwarf could fight but wasn't sure what side he would be on.

The movement in the forest told of something moving about and while it could be anything, he suspected a gnant was the culprit. The creature by itself was not a danger. They rarely attacked humans in a group and were not inclined to form an alliance themselves. Still it galled him that he was being spied on and he surveyed the forest for a gap. He found an opening that seemed suitable and urged his horse forward, catching up to Sir Keith to advise him on what he planned.

"I'm going to get rid of that nuisance. Keep the others moving and together."

"Fine, but don't be too long. I wasn't hired to babysit this lot."

Nathan had his horse walk slowly along the opening. It was a wide area for the gnant to try to cross and he suspected the creature was at the edge of the previous grove waiting for him to pass before scurrying to the next vantage point. Nathan carefully loaded his two crossbows; one was a smaller version of the other and meant for close fighting. He hung them from his saddle in easy reach. He raised his sword and moved his horse closer to the trees, ready in case the gnant attacked.

It took special training to watch both on his left and right side, one of the many abilities that allowed him to survive and be able to wear the red armband of the elite fighters. His horse was another of his special weapons and it gave an extra bounce in its step to tell him it smelled the gnant close by. He looked carefully along the ground first and then up to where branches in trees with their dark leaves could give refuge. His horse twitched its ears, lifted its head slightly, and Nathan spotted the shadowy shape in the tree, motionless as it hugged a limb.

There you are, you miserable vermin. Let's see what we can get from you.

He nudged his horse away from the tree slowly. He carefully sheathed his sword, freeing his hand to grab his crossbow. In a smooth motion he brought up the crossbow as he twisted in the saddle and fired to the spot he had memorized.

The gnant screeched and fell to the ground with a thud, holding the end of the arrow in its stomach. Nathan had already swung his horse to where his victim lay, writhing on the ground in pain. The gnant saw him and tried to crawl away, but a second arrow tore into his leg, stopping his flight. The gnant screamed in pain.

Nathan slipped off his horse and walked toward it, banishing his sword. "Okay, you rotten piece of hell. Let's have a little talk."

The gnant snarled and tried to roll away, but Nathan kicked it away from the grove of trees.

"Puleesse. Hurtss."

"More of that where it came from." He kicked the terrified creature again. "Tell me why you were spying on us. Who do you report to?"

"Nooo. Cannot."

"Yeah?" He jabbed it with his sword and when it held its hand to protect itself, sliced the skin off one finger. "I can do this for a while. Now talk."

It held the bleeding stump on its hand to his mouth, mumbling his reply.

"Now talk or I'll slice off your devil ears."

"Pay to watch, sssend call. Not know more. Puleesse."

"You're a pathetic excuse for a spy."

"Yesss." The gnant looked horrified as it tried to sit up and pull at the arrows stuck in his body.

"But you're in luck. I'm gonna be nice to you. It's not your fault you're without a soul." He turned as if to walk away but quickly pivoted and with his sword, slicing off its head. "I was going to let you just bleed to death but not even a gnant deserves to be in that much pain before its end."

Nathan rejoined his troop, nodding at Sir Keith. "Tis done, we might have to be a bit more quiet on our journey."

———

Jon sat against a tree during the next lunch break and wasn't surprised when Nicole sat next to him. She kept her horse near him during the journey, exchanging conversation. She ate slowly, nibbling at her food, appearing deep in thought.

"You don't act like you're very hungry. Something wrong?"

She took another small bite. "You said we might be able to go home, back to where we came from. How true is that?"

"I don't know. I'm only going by what Lord Perry said. And others."

"It's just that I'm trying to figure out…let me start again. Back on the Other-side there's a child, her name is Cindy, and a husband, well, actually we only lived together. Eric. Jon, I like you but if I can make it back, I don't want to start another relationship. It wouldn't be right."

"Okay, I got the picture. I have someone special too." His mind drifted first to Liz and then to Nadine. "Maybe we can be friends instead." Jon felt a surge of relief. Another romance was one thing he didn't need.

"I would like that. I know I was giving a different impression earlier, but it looked like I was here to stay. I was trying to make the best of it. Now you've given me hope again after four years in this dreadful place."

"You seem to have survived alright."

She pursed her lips. "Depends how you call it. I was put in their jail as soon as I stumbled into this world. One sleazy jerk bought me and sold me to a tavern. It was horrible, a real low life place. But then I was sold or traded to the bar you found me in, the Magix. I was still in a state of shock but decided I better do what I could or I wouldn't live long. I used my body to get some extra stuff, and I met this warlock who taught me some magic. For favours, I'm sorry to say. I'm not proud of what I had to do, but I did it."

"Hmm, so when I acted like I did that night…"

"I figured you were a nice guy anyway and I've been handled before. I also had this thought you may have some power, power that may help me. I'm good in magic because according to this warlock, I have this gift for getting vibrations from people. I got a good feeling about you."

"That's good to hear. What type of vibrations do you get from this group?" He spread his hand in a semi-circle.

"Some good, some bad. It's complicated to get all the details from them right away. Mostly good. You have something special but I can't discern what it is. But regardless, I think it would be good for us to be friends. You need friends in a place like this."

"How did you come into this world?"

She sighed before speaking. "I was on vacation with Cindy and Eric in Peru and we were on this bus tour. The bus stopped at these old ruins and Eric and Cindy scurried off to explore. I poked around a little and kind of hung around the bus when I saw this little man the size of a doll run from the bus and around to the other side. He was clutching some stuff in his hand like jewellery and his pockets were bulging. I shouted at him to stop and chased after him. I caught up with him just when he was bringing these crystals together and suddenly we both ended up in this world. The little bugger kicked me in the shin and ran off. It wasn't long before I was arrested and put in jail. Now that was a truly horrible place." She shuddered.

"Little crawly things and strange people. I was so glad to get out of there."

"Sounds like you had a rude start here. Those crystals let one go between the worlds. I wonder how they work."

Sir Keith came up to them, leading his horse by the reins. "Time to go. You two can carry on your socializing later." He turned to speak directly to Jon. "Freeman Nathan, and I had a discussion about the gnants that are following us. I've decided that we'll change our route to make it more difficult for those devils to follow us. It will add at least a day to our journey but the gnants will have difficulty following us."

Jon looked over at Nathan who didn't apprear very pleased at all, scowling as he sat on his horse.

Jon was relaxed talking to Nicole now that they were just going to be friends. She seemed more at ease as well and kept chatting away.

"If you watch the sky, you can see dragons sometimes, usually by themselves but sometimes as pairs. I heard that sometimes a family can be seen, two adults with offspring."

Jon was sceptical. "Real dragons? Fire breathing monsters that fly?"

She looked at him, narrowing her eyes. "Yes, dragons. They have these hairy feathers, big wings, can eat anything and as far as fire is concerned, no, not quite like fire. Their breath is powerful, it's like an acid, and hot, it would feel like fire I suppose if it hit you. Probably the result of their high metabolism." She took a deep breath before continuing. "Why do I get the impression you don't believe anything unless it hits you with a hammer?"

"You've had a few years to grow to know this place. I've had only a few days and most of that with my buddy Gilbert, who's not exactly a fountain of truth. I haven't seen any dragons yet and until I do…"

"Have you ever seen my daughter, Cindy?"

"No, of course not."

"Then I suppose you don't think she exists either."

"That's silly, you told me about her."

"Yeah, well I told you about dragons too. I wasn't lying about them either."

"I didn't say you were, just that…"

"Are we friends?"

"Yes."

"Then trust me."

"Sorry, I didn't mean to imply that you were lying about dragons. It just seemed so farfetched."

She softened her expression. "Yeah, I guess you're still finding out this is a different world. I'll tell you more when you're ready."

———

Jon slowed his horse until he was alongside of Nathan. The big man only gave him a side-glance, waiting until Jon spoke first.

"Sir Keith told me we're changing our route to avoid gnants."

Nathan spat on the ground before speaking. "Yeah, he thought it would be safer that way. I have my doubts."

"Why is that?"

Nathan didn't even turn his head to speak. "Because even gnants have too much sense to be going where we're going, that's why."

Nathan continued to look ahead, and Jon took the hint he preferred to be alone. Concerned, Jon moved back up and told Nicole of his short talk with Nathan.

"That doesn't sound good. If Nathan is worried, then it has to be dangerous." Nicole added, "You better learn how to use that sword."

———

Gilbert scowled at Nicole and Jon. It appeared they were enjoying each other's company a little too much as far as he was concerned. He muttered a few thoughts on his opinion of the rest of the travelers as well. Sir Keith's leadership didn't impress him. The man was in front of the rest but didn't seem to pay particular attention to what was around him. It didn't go unnoticed to Gilbert when Nathan talked to Sir Keith briefly and disappeared into the forest. What he did there was open to some speculation but Gilbert guessed it had something to do with gnants. They had been following them when they left town and no doubt were keeping close by for their own reasons. He suspected Nathan may have killed one or more of the gnants but that certainly wouldn't eliminate others from following them. They were tenacious, cunning and quite adept at getting what they wanted. What worried him was the attempt at bribery and not-so-subtle threat the gnant made to him back at Lord Perry's castle.

All of this because that fool Jon thought he saved me. Why couldn't that idiot have just stayed the hell out of the way? It would have been better to leave Jon to fend himself, let him rot in prison and hope no one would have paid any attention about his allegations about saving my life. This is what I gets for trying to help the big oaf.

And do they appreciate it? No! This is putting a serious delay to my own business and the shit I'll get from Harold. Oh, the curse of a dragon's master must be on me.

Gilbert carefully scanned the forest. He didn't see any unusual movement, but gnants were sly on how they monitored humans. Slowly he reached into his backpack and withdrew his canteen, taking a drink in case anyone was observing him. He returned the canteen, pretending to try to stuff the canteen deep inside the backpack and withdrew a small crystal and metal device he hid in the palm of his hand. The object was size of a dollar coin and shaped like the letter 'C' with only a small gap separating the top and bottom portion. The device, known as gnant crier, picked up the high frequency gnant cries and reduced them to the human hearing range. The language was still undecipherable but did allow the user to know gnants were nearby and calling to each. He discreetly attached it to his ear, pretending to scratch his head as he did so. He was aware of Nathan behind him, who was quite observant of any activities within the group. Gilbert tried to appear bored as he listened, hoping for quiet that would indicate they were being left alone.

A minute passed and another. Five minutes later he heard the telling squeal of gnant and a weaker reply. What they said wasn't significant, that they were around and following them was. Gilbert carefully took off the gnant crier and held it in his hand. He waited and returned it to his backpack, doing his water canteen drink method in reverse.

Gilbert considered the implications. The gnants were after something, something important. If it was mere robbery they were after, they would have likely left after Nathan attacked them the first time. Gnants were not known for persistence when danger was involved, at least not for mere money. But power and magic were something gnants wanted very much, something they were willing to take risks to obtain and not be deterred from easily. That meant there was a danger for everyone on this quest to obtain Jon's crystal. Danger that definitely included Gilbert, the one thing Gilbert avoided as much as possible.

The problem was Jon, or rather what Jon had. If he knew more what Jon had perhaps, he could reduce the danger by taking the initiative.

Now what did that devil say? Crystal key. Those gnants think Jon has a crystal key. Couldn't be one of the Pent Keys, those are more legend than real. Maybe one of those Tri Keys, or one of a group that the gnants consider important to their own perverted interests. Now if I's Jon, where would I keeps such a thing?

"Deep in thought, Gilbert?" Nathan's deep voice was barely more than a whisper but carried authority in it.

Gilbert jumped. "Huh? Oh, not at all, not at all. Me was just kind of napping a bit you see. Not much thinking in this ol' noggin." He pointed at his head for emphasis.

Nathan pointed at his backpack. "I see. But I was wondering what you might have in your pack there."

"Me pack? Why just my water canteen and a few personal things, that's all."

"Would you mind if I take a look?"

"I've nothin' to hide. But 'tisn't right to go through another man's belongings, unless he is a criminal. You're not accusing me of anything, are ya?"

Nathan frowned. For a grubby thief, Gilbert was pretty sharp with his words. "No, not at all, Gilbert. But we're on a difficult journey together and it would be nice if one of us wasn't holding onto valuable information that could compromise our safety. Understood?"

"Ah, indeed I do, indeed I do. Perhaps ye can share why you took a little trip by yerself in the trees and what was discovered there then?"

Nathan narrowed his eyes. "That's confidential. I'll tell ya if I deem it important for the rest of you to know."

"Good. Then we understand each other."

Nathan glared at him. "I suppose we do, Gilbert. But remember I work on cause and effect. You cause me problems and there'll be an effect. An unpleasant effect."

Gilbert swallowed hard as Nathan dropped back to the rear. Nathan may make things a bit difficult for him later but he wasn't about to tell him about the gnant crier and the knowledge of gnants being close by. Gilbert was a thief and a trader. If you wanted an item or information from him, there was a price on it. If Nathan wanted to know what Gilbert knew, then he had to make an offer to buy or trade. Gilbert rarely gave anything for free.

Gilbert was prepared when they stopped for the night. He placed himself so that he could observe Jon and watch for any clues about a key crystal that he may have. He noted without surprise Nicole joined him and they sat talking, eating and occasionally laughing. Gilbert found their laughter rather annoying, especially considering the danger they were all in due to the gnants. Still, he leaned back against the tree and almost closed his eyes. Through the small slits in his eyelids, he observed the couple and listened carefully to the snippets of conversation that found their way to his ears. To someone casually looking at Gilbert, it would seem that he was asleep against the tree.

———

Sir Keith picked at his food. He wasn't pleased with Nathan's approach with dealing with the gnant. He had hoped the man would have shown a little more restraint with the creature. Killing the thing was not going to help him finish his mission. He needed answers from it. Tonight, he suspected the gnants would venture close to their camp. He wasn't sure if Nathan would be able protect them all and that would mean Sir Keith himself may have to help in the guard duty. It was not something he liked to do in most circumstances and in this case, there were too many uncontrollable factors. The camp was well enough located, in a clearing that was near the road and a small creek. The tents were located in a semi-circle around a fire. The creek allowed everyone to freshen up, as well as restock their canteens and water jugs. But gnants loved the dark. They enjoyed superior night vision and coupled with sharp claws, teeth and quick reflexes, were formidable opponents. *This camp is not safe by any means.*

Tomorrow they would reach the town of Seilini and would be able to stay in a local inn. The journey through the Drayola Hills would stop the gnants from following for at least a short time and they might lose interest in them. But there was a possibility that the gnants would find them again in Seilini.

Sir Keith walked over to where Nathan stood with a scowl as he watched the surrounding area.

"Freeman Nathan, are we secure for tonight?"

Nathan frowned. "We are."

"Do you need me to take a turn on watch?"

"You? No, I'll be fine." Nathan turned away and studied the woods at the edge of the camp.

"I'm quite capable with a sword if need be." Sir Keith raised his voice.

"I didn't mean to imply you weren't. I just prefer to trust myself alone in matters like this."

"Very well. Just keep in mind the safety of this group is both our responsibility." He turned away, relieved he didn't have to do watch tonight. Still, he was annoyed at Nathan's attitude and the suggestion that he couldn't perform well enough as a guard. Angered, he walked back to his tent by taking a route around the perimeter of the camp. He had made it halfway to his tent when he spotted a movement up ahead in the trees. He quickly withdrew his sword, holding it high.

"Who goes there? Answer me!"

"Tis only I." Lady Karla stepped out from the small trees around the camp area, drawing a dark cape around her shoulders tighter.

"My lady, you shouldn't be out here alone."

"Yes, I know. But I needed some privacy for a minute." She looked down at the ground, appearing to be embarrassed.

"Of course. I was only concerned for your safety. Allow me to escort you to your tent."

She nodded and walked with him, taking a look behind her.

Sir Keith glanced behind him, seeing at a slight movement of leaves. "What was that?"

"Nothing, I assure you. Please, let's go."

Sir Keith nodded but looked concerned.

———

A pair of eyes watched as they made their way back to tents and the fire. The gnant clutched its hands together, twisting her fingers nervously. It was a close call. If the swordsman had spotted her, she would have to attack him to ensure his silence. That was dangerous as humans with swords negated her superior speed and agility. The other option would to be to run. That would leave him with knowledge of her whereabouts and clues why she was there. Satisfied she was no longer at risk, Rattru moved deeper into the forest, meeting with Trruer and Krruent.

The two males stood quietly and listened to her report, clicking approval at her partial success. She kept making eye contact with each male, letting them know she was not going to defer to either one of them. It also prevented one male from feeling outdone by the other. Males did not always tolerate each other's company, often striving to dominate or kill rivals. In this case the cause had taken over individual concerns for a greater good and all were Tyreel Followers.

Females were much more tolerant of the company of other gnants and became the driving force behind the cause. Still it wasn't easy to organize gnants to work cooperatively despite the rewards of success. At one time such prospect of reclaiming their world from humans appeared remote. But several changes had occurred and now the gnants had more than one way to win the battle. Rattru exchanged information with her counterparts, including the death of the young male gnant, Reerrk. It was decided the conditions were right for them to take a gamble against the travelling group of humans.

The gnants were not going to follow the humans through the Drayola Hills. Dragons that lived in the area were only too capable of catching gnants for dinner. Instead, the gnants decided the humans would likely be staying at Seilini the following night and made plans to relocate them in that town by arriving there at a longer, more strenuous but safer route.

———

Seilini was not far from where Jon and the others camped but the journey included tricky climbing and descending as they crossed the Drayola Hills. The rocky hills had little vegetation and not much life other than a few hardy rodents, birds and insects. It was also home of the medium sized Par Dragons who nested in the large caves or on top of the hills. The dragons chose the Drayola Hills for several reasons. The hills were without large predators to endanger their young, the height allowed for easy takeoff and landing and to sunbath for hours. The Par Dragons normally hunted during the evening, using infrared and telescopic vision to spot prey. But if large quarry were to intrude on its territory during the daytime, it could arouse from its slumber to enjoy a meal.

The female dragon awoke first. The noise and smell of the travelling humans stirred her senses. After a moment of considering what and how far away they were, she sent a low rumbling growl at her mate. The smaller male roused quickly, lifting his head to sniff the air. He answered back with his own rumble.

The group dropped to a single line in places as the rock squeezed the sides of the path closer. In other places the path opened to a broad open area with a scattering of rocky pillars. There were a number of paths leading in and out of the open areas, like tributaries to a river but it was easy to cross the hills as long as one kept moving in an east to west direction. The paths criss-crossed each other several times and if there was confusion on which path to take it was a matter of scaling the twelve-foot sides to observe the various paths from above. The top was relatively flat, smoothed over by the almost constant wind and punctuated by the deep grooves where the paths led.

Nathan followed up on the rear. Since entering the hills, he held his sword ready. He had already instructed the others to keep conversation to a minimum and to keep moving forward as quickly as possible; there would be no stoppages in the hills. He had made trips through the Drayola Hills several times before and in all but for one incidence there had never been a problem. But that one time when he was just a teenager remained sharp in his memory.

Nathan had been travelling with two older men when two dragons attacked by pinching them in from the front and rear. Nathan remembered being pushed behind a rock by one of the men as the two older fighters took on the dragons. They screamed as they were hit by the chemical blast that burned their skin, blinding them at the same time. The cries didn't last long, but it was a long time before Nathan slowly emerged from behind the rock. There was little trace of his companions; bits of clothing and blood and a bent sword was all that remained.

Shaken, he made his way through the remaining hills by himself. Later he said a prayer of thanks for sparing his life and to his companions who pushed him to safety and gave up their own lives. He squeezed the handle of his sword tighter as the memory haunted him.

Jon was attentive, looking straight ahead when a deafening shriek exploded over his head. He jumped in the saddle as his horse raised its front legs, almost throwing him to the ground. Jon looked up in time to see a dragon's head dip down toward the path as it flew past. Nicole screamed as a rush of wind pushed down on them. His gaze followed the dragon in the sky, the huge wings lifting it high as it turned around. The dark body had green and red stripes, with the head almost a quarter of its length. A serpent-like tail almost doubled the length of the dragon.

Jon managed to bring his horse under control. Lady Karla fell from her horse but before it had gone far Sir Keith grabbed its reins to halt it. Gilbert meanwhile was hanging grimly to his horse's neck, cursing at the beast to settle down. Nicole slid down from her own horse and dashed to the dazed Lady Karla, helping her to her feet.

Nathan bellowed out, "Get off ya horses and get 'em under control! Now! That dragon is coming back and there's another one in front of us!"

Within seconds everyone had dismounted their horses and turned to face Nathan.

"Now pay attention. That dragon is coming back, and he's gonna stick his ugly head in here for a meal. If you run, you'll find his mate waiting for you on the other end ahead of us."

Sir Keith lost his patient. "What do we do, man? Out with it!" His voice was loud and higher pitched than normal.

"Get a grip on yerself for one thing. For another get out yer bow and arrows. Swords ain't much good against these monsters, you'll never get close enough to use it. Now get behind the horses, when a dragon gives a blast you don't want to be first in line."

Everyone did as they were told. The women held small swords as they crouched behind their nervous horses. Nathan gave Jon a small crossbow. "I can only give you this. It doesn't have a lot of range and that don't give you much time."

The next minutes dragged on as they waited. Then the dragon returned.

It landed with a thud and a blast of air above them, bellowing out its arrival. The horses pranced around in a circle, their reins held by the riders to keep them from bolting. Gilbert and Lady Karla lost control of their horses.

Jon watched as the dragon opened its jaws wide, reaching toward the group. Even with its wings folded, it appeared enormous. A cloud of yellow and red mist poured from its ugly mouth, churning as it drifted to the frightened group. The mist touched on the flank of one of the horses, causing it to rear up and frantically try to escape. The dragon's jaw snapped on empty air but it soon recovered to reach at its next target.

Gilbert found himself suddenly exposed when his horse bolted, and now the dragon's eyes were fixed on him. He gulped, dropped his bow and arrow and ran. The dragon was quicker and closed his jaws on him just as Gilbert leaped to the ground.

Jon watched in horror as the dragon reached for one of the horses. He aimed the crossbow and fired at the huge head but his aim was off and didn't seem to hurt the dragon. The arrows fired by Sir Keith and Nathan had a better effect and some were able to penetrate the tough hide that protected the dragon. It winced at the pain for a moment but wasn't deterred and now plunged toward the frantic Gilbert. Jon felt himself changing, shifting to the warrior his old football coach longed to see more often.

Jon dropped the crossbow, hefted his sword above his head and charged underneath the dragon's head just as it reached Gilbert. The jaws snapped its jaws on Gilbert's backpack. Jon sliced at the lower jaw of the dragon, causing small cuts to appear. He heard the dwarf cry out and repositioned his sword and plunged it upward. The first time the sword penetrated less than an inch, the second time Jon pushed with all of his strength and the sword slid up, up into the jaw to the hilt of the sword. Blood and a yellow liquid spilled out from the opening as Jon worked his sword in back and forth.

The dragon dropped Gilbert and let out a scream of agony, lifting its head up and out of the pathway. Jon almost lost his sword as the dragon pulled away, but he glumly held on as he watched red and yellow liquids cascade down his sword and his arm.

The dragon screamed again as more arrows began to hit its massive head. Suddenly it had enough and took off, its wings beating the air down on them. The acid burn was too much for one horse and it finally broke through the other horses and raced by itself down the path.

Nicole raced to Jon, carrying a canteen of water. "Take off your shirt!"

He stared at her, questioning.

"Take off your shirt. It's got dragon fire on your sleeve! Hurry."

He began to pull off his shirt, but that wasn't fast enough for her. She grabbed at the fabric and yanked at it hard, almost toppling him over as she ripped off his shirt. She took the canteen and poured water over his arm until it was empty.

"I hope we got it in time. Oh dear, it's turning pink in places."

Jon watched as his arm where it was in contact with the sleeve that had been soaked with blood and the yellow liquid turn a blotchy red. It was began to hurt like it was burnt.

"There's not much more I can do here. Can you ride by yourself?"

The pain in his arm was increasing. "I think so. It hurts to move my arm though."

Nathan's voice boomed out. "We better get out of here while we can. Put him on his horse and lead it along if you have to but let's go!"

"One minute, just a few seconds." She held up a finger to Nathan and turned back to Jon without waiting for a reply. She took his hand into hers and closed her eyes. Nicole slowly and quietly spoke out a string of words that he didn't recognize. She didn't even flinch when they heard the roar of a dragon down the pathway.

"There, I think that should help."

Jon looked up when he heard the slow beating of enormous wings and saw the second and larger dragon carrying the horse in its jaws as it flew overhead.

He looked back down on his arm. It was still red, but the pain had almost stopped. He flexed his hand without a problem.

"It hardly hurts anymore."

She held two fists above her head. "Yes! I knew I could do it. I knew it." She was grinning at him.

"Now's our chance. Let's ride out of here as fast as we can. We're short one horse, so Gilbert, double up with Lady Karla." Nathan mounted his own horse and began to crowd them.

Jon took off the necklace that held his Locas Crystal and gave it to Nicole. "Hang on to this and don't let anyone see it, please." Jon remembered his pant pockets had holes in them, not the best place to safeguard the crystal. He didn't trust anyone but Nicole with it.

She stared at it for a moment and slipped it into the top of her blouse. "You better tell me about this later."

They raced as fast as their spooked horses would let them and minutes later broke out of the rock walled pathways into a forest. They maintained a quick pace for the next half an hour and finally slowed to a normal walk. They continually glanced at the sky for a possible return attack of the dragons.

Nathan pulled alongside of Jon. "Not much chance they'll attack soon. The big one is well fed now and her mate, well, I don't think he'll be able to do much for a while. Perhaps ever."

"He's hurt pretty bad?"

Nathan laughed. "That was one of the bravest things I've ever seen. How did you know that was the precise place of the fire gland? You sure got him good."

"I didn't know. I just wanted to save Gilbert. I figured underneath the jaw was the only place I could do damage."

Nathan sat up straighter in his saddle. "My lord. You risked your life on a hunch to save that miserable thief?" He shook his head and gave Jon a rare compliment. "If that be so, then you can ride with me anytime. You have a soldier's blood in your veins."

A few minutes later, Nicole slipped back next to him, inquiring about his arm.

"It doesn't hurt much, but it's still red."

"That was close. The dragon's fire is meant to soften the flesh for easy digestion. If you had not had your shirt on and if we hadn't washed it off with water, your flesh on the arm would have turned to paste. We would've had to cut your arm off to save your life."

He grimaced at the thought. "Thanks for acting so quick. That was another spell you used on my arm."

"Yeah, I was having trouble recalling all the words, so I guessed at a couple of the lines. But it worked, and it looks like your arm's gonna be okay. When we stop in Seilini, I'll pick up some lotion to put on it as well."

The journey through the forest went without incident. The land levelled out, and the trail became a small road that cut through the farmland. The buildings were made with stone and high peaked roofs cut from timber. Encircling the structures stood regular spaced evergreens that looked like a giant picket fence. The trees were also placed around pens and corrals and along the short road that led to the farmhouse.

Sir Keith moved alongside of Jon. "How's your arm doing?"

"Not too bad. It doesn't hurt much but feels a bit numb." He pointed at one of the farms they were passing. "Isn't that an odd place to plant trees? They're planted around buildings and fences."

"The trees help prevent the dragons from landing and the stone buildings are strong enough to withstand them physically"

"I guess that makes sense."

Sir Keith continued his lecture. "Seilini is known as the town of steeples. In nearly every building the roof ends in a point, making the town look as was composed entirely of churches. The peaked roof is a strong deterrent to the dragons. The large wingspread requires the dragons to need plenty of room to manoeuvre and attempt landings. The sharp points of the roof can cause serious damage to the wings. The dragons occasionally fly close to the rooftops but rarely attempt to land or attack."

Jon and the rest of the entourage didn't receive undue attention as they came into town. He slumped in the saddle, too tired to care he was without a shirt.

Sir Keith led the way, cutting through the twisting streets and navigating successfully to the Goodfellow Hotel. The streets of Seilini were narrow for the most part and without sidewalks. They were also rather unclean with bits of garbage lying on the cobbled road.

Nicole wrinkled her nose at the smell of rotting garbage. She called out, "I hope we're not staying in this area, Sir Keith."

"No, we're staying at a hotel further down. Much cleaner, I assure you."

At the end of the business section, Sir Keith pointed to a hotel. "That be the one."

The hotel had a rough stone exterior that rose four stories on a small lot. One building bordering it showed evidence to having suffered fire damage a number of years ago and it appeared to be abandoned. On the other side stood a two-story rooming house that extended to the end of the block. A couple of men sat on front steps smoking pipes and ignored them as they dismounted from their horses. Nathan offered a hand to help Jon down.

Jon fought a moment of dizziness and his legs almost collapsed under him when he tried to stand. A few moments later he recovered and attempted to walk straight as he entered the hotel lobby.

Sir Keith made the arrangements at the front desk for rooms and food. Nathan led the horses with Gilbert's help to a stable behind the hotel, leaving Jon with Nicole and Lady Karla.

Nicole asked, "Lady Karla, why don't you take Jon into the tavern for something to eat and drink? I'm going down the street to get some lotion for his arm."

"I don't normally frequent such places."

"Please. He's weak and needs nourishment to fight the remaining dragon fire in his arm. Sir Keith and the others will get there shortly, and then you can take your leave."

Lady Karla stared at her and at him for a moment. "Very well. These are special circumstances."

The tavern was well lit from the open shutters along one wall. The wavy glass distorted the images from the outside but Jon didn't consider the outside view worth looking at in any event. He collapsed on the first vacant chair he saw.

Lady Karla signalled the barkeep and ordered him to bring bread and cheese immediately, as well as a flagon of wine.

"Eat this now, I'll find out what else they can make here. Take it easy on the wine but it'll certainly be safer to drink than the water here."

Jon nodded and shoved the bread and cheese into his mouth. A bowl of stew was placed in front of him and he spooned the mixture of vegetables and unknown meat into his mouth.

"Jon, what has happened to your necklace with the crystal?"

Jon paused a moment as he lifted the spoon into his mouth. He considered telling her that he gave the necklace to someone without naming Nicole but Lady Karla would quickly be able to surmise that it would be her. And Lady Karla wasn't someone he trusted. He took his time swallowing his spoonful.

"Oh, I just stuffed it into my pocket. It seemed the best place for it." He quickly glanced at her eyes but he didn't get any indication whether she believed him or not. Sometime while he was eating the others joined him. He barely acknowledged them. He stopped to take a drink of the wine and slouched on his chair. The food gave him some strength but now a headache was forming at the base of his skull. He felt hot, hot enough he was sweating on his forehead.

———

Nicole made her way down the street to where they passed earlier on the way to the hotel. She tried to walk confidently, as if she was a free woman but wasn't certain that was the case at all. Lord Perry had purchased her from the Magix Inn but she wasn't clear whether that meant being given her freedom only temporarily while on Jon's quest. Still, she didn't think it would be good to look nervous in a strange town. One thing she was pleased with was that Lord Perry had supplied her with decent clothing, of a quality normally only used by ladies of the court. Several shops sold a variety of goods and more than one might sell her the ingredients she was searching for. She first chose a shop that the owner had at least brushed the garbage away from the front entrance.

The shop was packed with different goods on a mix of shelving and tables. The proprietor, a small middle-aged man with a pronounced limp, greeted her.

"What can we do for you, missy?" His voice crackled as if he was fighting a cold.

"I need griffin oil, ground dustin plant and pie nuts. Just in small quantities."

"Hmm, sounds like you need something for a dragon fire burn. Instead of all that would ya like to have some dragon fire oil instead?"

"You mean they have this stuff made up already?"

"Yeah, we're in dragon territory. It hasn't had a spell put on yet, most prefer to do that themselves but it sure saves the time of mixing the stuff from scratch."

"Please, that would do fine."

He puttered around a table and looked up at a high shelf. "Arr, there's the oil there." He turned toward the curtained doorway at the back. "Czar! Get your lazy carcass out here."

From the back came a small blond-haired gnant. Nicole thought it was probably a young one that had not reached maturity yet because it was without facial hair. As with most gnants it wore dark clothing, an old shirt with patches on its sleeves and pants with too much room for it.

"Yesss masster Russsssell?"

"Be a good fella and get the jar from the top shelf."

The gnant looked up, and scrambled up using small holds on the wall. Russell gave him better direction as he climbed. A few minutes later Nicole took her purchase back to the hotel. She'd noticed Russell and Czar seemed to have a relationship that had an element of respect for each other, which wasn't common between humans and gnants. Czar was not a gnant name, and she suspected Russell had named him himself.

The streets were getting dark, causing Nicole to hurry back. Shadows from the setting sun made details harder to pick out, but she thought she saw movement between buildings. It was a minor relief when she spotted the Goodfellow Hotel and the lit torch at the front door, advertising the hotel and bar was open. As she drew close, she saw Lady Karla come from the direction of the abandoned building and go back into the hotel. *That seemed odd. Lady Karla is not the type to go out for a breath of fresh air, even assuming Seilini does have such a thing.*

———

Jon was trying to stay awake as the conversation from the others circled around him, sipping his wine carefully. He acknowledged the congratulations from Sir Keith and Gilbert on his attack on the dragon. He vaguely heard Sir Keith telling him that he would take care of his sword and pack he had left with his horse. There wasn't much in his pack besides a tent, a shaving blade he had borrowed from Lord Perry's guest room and a soap bar.

Nicole touched him on his good arm, startling him. He wasn't aware she had returned. "We better get you up to your room. Can you walk?"

"Yeah, I think so." He stood up using the table to balance himself and slowly started to walk toward the stairs that led to their third story room. He suddenly stumbled as he passed the open doorway, catching himself on the doorframe.

Nathan stood up to help support Jon. Together Nathan and Nicole both helped Jon go up the stairs. The room held a bed with a straw mattress and without a covering. There was also a small table that held a ceramic pitcher and a single armless wooden chair. Nathan helped ease him on his bed.

"Thanks, Nathan for helping. He's too big for me to carry." She added, "You can go back downstairs, I have to put some stuff on his arm."

Nicole opened the jar from the shop. She spoke words of a simple healing spell on it and sat on the side of the bed to massage the liquid on Jon's arm. He squinted at her, his headache was getting worse and the light in the room was too bright. He was too hot but there didn't appear any relief in the room warm from the afternoon sun.

"You'll feel better when you wake up."

"I hope so. So hot in here. Can you turn down the temperature a little?" He mumbled the last sentence and closed his eyes, falling into a series of broken dreams.

"Sure, I'll get right on it."

———

Jon woke up sometime later from his restless dreams, dreams of dragons, of Liz, of gnants, and of Nadine, Nicole and castles. Sometimes
he was being chased by dragons, in some he was chasing women.
Some dreams were better than others.

When he woke up, he felt different. The fever had broken. But
there was something else odd as well. It took a moment for him to
understand what it was.

TWELVE

The cell wasn't crowded, although Liz stayed near one wall by herself. The others were resigned to their situation, except for one rather well-dressed young man who yelled and cursed at infrequent intervals. Liz studied him. Besides his better clothes, he appeared well groomed, save for a shadow on his face. *He has the classic Greek look to him. He would be good-looking if he wasn't acting like a madman.*

Their prison consisted of stone walls, a single window set high on one wall with iron bars to prevent possible escape and a door made of thick wood with a square opening in the centre. The rest of the room consisted of a small table made of thick wood, bits of straw covering the floor and a few darting mice. The air smelled musty and dust particles floated in the air.

After an hour a servant accompanied by two heavily armed guards placed water and bread on the table in the centre of the room. Most of the inmates quickly consumed what was available. They tore the loaves of bread with their hands and passed around the container of water with a wooden ladle. Liz took a piece of bread and gingerly tried the water.

She looked at the others. Besides the well-dressed young man, there was a middle-aged man who sat close to his—she presumed—wife, and an elderly man who appeared to be sleeping. The other four inmates

147

were women. Three were about her age plus another close to middle age. She studied the middle-aged couple. They acted worried as they held hands without speaking. Their clothes indicated they weren't entirely without means but obviously not rich.

The three women near her age nervously engaged in a low conversation. Their dress was poor, looking like borrowed garments that ill fitted. The other woman sat looking annoyed but better dressed. Liz thought she dressed a bit on the revealing side. Cautiously, Liz slowly moved where she leaned against a wall. When the woman noticed her, she asked her what was happening.

"Not much. In an hour or a day, we'll be taken in front of the judge. He'll send us to prison, work camp or whatever." The woman finally acknowledged her. "First time?"

"Yeah."

"Don't sweat it. Better than having to live off the streets. You get two meals and a dry bed."

"What am I being charged with?"

The woman gave her an odd look. "Living off the streets and not havin' a place to live."

Liz took in that bit of information. It sounded like she was being charged with vagrancy. She believed she was dressed well enough and if she explained she was merely lost, maybe she would be let off by the judge.

Two hours later, a servant and three guards summoned them to the door. The guards were well armed and stood a head above anyone else in the room. Only the angry young man was not intimidated by them, pushing ahead of the rest with his fists clenched.

They were marched down a corridor that led past several rooms, some of which were smaller versions of the cell she had been placed in. Their journey took them to a large room that served as the courtroom. The guards pushed them toward the back where they sat on wooden benches. Another group, consisting mostly of men, was already present. The young man started to announce his innocence again but was quickly made quiet by a guard who used his gloved hand to smack him on the side of his head. The man grunted in surprise and gave the guard a look of disdain, but finally kept silent.

They sat there and waited and waited some more before a judge entered through a side door. The judge was an older, heavy man with thinning hair and sat at a front desk with two other officials. He wore a blue robe with a high collar, while the two other officials wore green ones with a more subdued collar. It appeared to be a random choice, but the guard pointed at one of the young women and she rose to stand before the judge.

One of the green robed officials wrote a comment on a large notebook.

"Name." The voice was monotone.

She whispered a name that Liz couldn't hear from the back.

"You are charged without having monies to sustain oneself and using the public streets as a place to live. Do you have anything to say before sentencing?"

The woman meekly shook her head.

The judge leaned forward. "You're still young, there's still a chance for you to upgrade yourself. One year as kitchen help in Lord Bennett's Castle."

The young woman barely nodded her head and was led out by a servant. Liz saw her face, looking relieved at her sentence.

Another was brought forward, and another. Some tried to bargain their way out but to no avail. Sentences ranged from a year of work in Lord Bennett's castle to five years in a labour camp. Some were sent to a side room where their services could be purchased. Those sent there were considered more fortunate as they were given not only a place to live but also a small payment for work. The contracts normally ran between two to ten years, though occasionally the inmate could bargain for a slightly better deal in terms of pay and time.

Liz watched with a bit more interest when the older couple was brought forward.

After taking their names, the green robed official asked if there was any explanation they wished to give for their vagrancy.

The man took a deep breath and in a quiet voice spoke of their ordeal. "We just common folk, farming near Oldsder. We bring in chickens and grain by wagon to sell when two highwaymen jump in front of us and take our horse and wagon. We were too far to walk back home, so we headed here to earn enough to go back but we got caught by Lord Bennett's soldiers."

The judge seemed interested in the answer and leaned forward. "Did you explain the nature of the circumstances to the soldiers?"

"Aye, your honour. But they not interested."

"Hmm. I believe in what you have said. This institution is not interested in punishing victims of crimes. Prosecutor, see that these two are given a decent meal and an escort back to their farm. In addition, I want the soldiers who arrested these peasants to report to me this evening."

The couple thanked him profusely, which gave Liz some hope she would get a reprieve as well.

Next up was the well-dressed young man who shrugged off attempts of one guard to lead him to the front.

The green robed official looked up with a smirk on his face. "Name?"

"You know bloody hell who I am." He glared at the official. "I am Sir Anthony Graham, son of Lord Kevin Graham."

"Sir Anthony, you are charged without having a place to live and without means to support yourself. Do you have anything to say in your defence?"

"My father will clear this up if you contact him and I suggest you do that immediately before you get yourself in serious trouble. My family is powerful and..."

The judge held up his hand. "Enough. Your father has contacted the court and has informed us that he's tired of your gambling, drinking and womanizing. He stated that he would not interfere with any sentence we find just." The judge paused to look at the stunned face of Graham. "You, sir, are a disgrace to nobility and deserve to be treated no better than a common drunk. However, out of respect to your father and his contributions to the court, we will be lenient." He let his words sink in to the now quiet Graham. "You will be turned over to the Labour House. I'm sure they can find you a prospective employer."

Graham was led to a side door where he turned once more to glare at everyone in the courtroom. The guard escorting him gave him a hard shove, obviously not impressed by Sir Anthony's former status.

The next prisoner was a man who was charged with theft, apparently stealing a knife from a weaponry shop.

The judge shook his head. "This court takes a dim view of those who would take items that do not belong to themselves. Forty lashes, and if you are ever brought here on a similar charge, the punishment will double."

The man was dragged out of the courtroom crying out for mercy before he was silenced to a blow to the head by one of the guards.

Liz was somewhat shocked at the punishment. *Obviously, crime here could have severe consequences. If forty lashes for a simple theft is considered just, I would hate to see the judgment on more serious crimes.*

A young woman was brought forth on a charge of public mischief. The green robed official informed the judge she was seen trespassing on Sir Charles Rigor's land and refused to halt when he ordered her to do so. She in fact made an unladylike gesture and ran off. Fortunately, he was able to give a good description to the guards who found her hiding in a tavern.

"Do you have anything to say in your defence?"

"I'm sorry, sir. I made a mistake in crossing his property but I was in a hurry and I didn't see no harm in it. I am also sorry I raised my finger at him but he did call me a very nasty name."

"One has to show more restraint than that when dealing with men and ladies of high rank. As far as trespassing is concerned, how much of a hurry could you have been if you were caught in a tavern? Not the best place for young ladies." The judge paused to massage his chin as he thought. "You need to learn your place in society and what is proper behaviour. I will have you assigned to the Labour House. Good luck to you."

The woman bowed her head and looked up. "Thank you, sir."

Liz wondered just what the Labour House was as the woman was led to a side door.

Several more prisoners were dealt with in the quick justice system. Without lawyers present the prisoner had one chance to explain his or her actions before sentence. Liz considered the court system. *It seems you're assumed guilty unless you have a very good explanation.*

Liz was finally pointed at and she made her way to the front of the court.

"Name?" The green robed official queried her.

"Liz O'Doul."

"Two names? Very well. You are charged with being without means to support yourself and being without a place to live. Do you have anything to say in your defence?"

"Yes, I do. I do have a place to live but it's not here and I just can't get there right now. And usually I have money but I didn't bring any with me and this is just a horrible mistake. You see…"

"Enough. May I make the assumption you came from the Other-side by mistake?"

"Yes, I suppose you might call it that. You see this…"

"Please, I don't need to hear your life story." The judge held up his hand as he spoke. "Coming here from the Other-side without permission is also a crime but I will be tolerant with you because of your ignorance."

Liz didn't appreciate being called ignorant but on the other hand if it helped her cause, she could accept that. "Thank you, sir. I didn't mean to be here."

"Of course not. But now you are stuck here, and we are stuck with you. The best place might be a labour camp to keep you out of trouble, but I doubt you would survive there long. You're not built strongly. Therefore, I shall send you to the Labour House and I hope that you will learn enough of our world not to appear here again in this court."

A guard came by and grabbed her arm and began to pull her to a side door. "Thank you, sir," she added quickly. Someday she might be back in front of him and she thought she might as well be courteous.

The Labour House was not what she expected, although in truth she didn't know what to expect. Liz was taken with the others destined for the Labour House, including the angry Anthony Graham. Each of the ten prisoners had a metal cuff attached to their right wrist. The metal cuff, locked by use of a bolt, had a large ring attached to it. A chain was passed through the ring, with the chain secured to first and last prisoners' cuff. Four guards escorted the group down another corridor, outside to a courtyard, through another set of doors and after a short journey inside they arrived at the Labour House.

The rectangular area was large and partitioned off in various rooms. The first area they arrived at was the cleansing room. Liz looked at the square stone bath, wrinkling her nose at the humid air as the chain and cuffs were removed.

An older, heavy-set woman, called out. "Alright, everyone takes off yer garments and scrub yourself clean." She clapped her hands. "Move it! We ain't putting up with you lot any longer than we have to."

Liz followed the others in removing her clothes. The woman in charge went over to her, picking up her bra.

"Ain't that something. Pockets for yer boobs." She laughed in a cackling voice. "Ye must be from the Other-side. Well, ye won't have need of these clothes no more."

Liz removed her panties reluctantly and slowly made her way to the communal bath. She took a rag from a pail filled with soapy water she quickly immersed herself in the warm water. Liz scanned the others in the water but they weren't taking any heed of her. She watched Graham, now understanding why he acted so angry. *His own father has rejected him, sending him to the Labour House.* She noticed he didn't seem to care he was naked in front of the others but switched between sulking and glaring at the rest.

Under shouts of "scrub harder and wash yer hair too" Liz quickly washed herself, wanting to get out of the bath as soon as possible. Graham was given more leeway and was more or less ignored as they washed.

When they were judged suitably clean, they were all ordered out, and each given a thin towel to dry themselves. As she was drying herself Liz notice the water was being drained out and a new supply of water was added for the next group.

They were led naked to a cell, given a well-used white robe to wear and left with tea and sandwiches.

Liz put on the white robe quickly, tying the cloth belt to close the front. The material was light and didn't hide her figure. The other women were slower in putting on theirs and Graham sat with his folded on his lap for a full minute before slowly putting it on, his head cast downward.

Liz found herself hungry and rapidly consumed her sandwich and tea.

One of the women came over to her and handed over her sandwich. "I'm not hungry, you can have mine." The dark-haired girl watched her intently as she passed over the sandwich. "You look hungry."

"Thanks." Liz took the sandwich, feeling she was eating a little too quickly. "My name is Liz."

"Juleen. Are you really from the Other-side?"

Liz spent a moment drinking her tea before answering. "Yes, I suppose I am. That is, if the Other-side is what I think you mean."

Juleen asked a few questions about Liz's world but didn't have a chance to inquire too much before the cell door opened. A guard beckoned them to follow.

The hallway led to another room that was enclosed by three walls and a heavy blue curtain. A second guard drew back the curtain revealing a stage. Beyond the stage were rows of seats, approximately a quarter filled.

The white robed prisoners, seven women and three men kept silent after the guard gave them fair warning by shoving a young woman to the floor that had leaned against a wall. "And there'll be no noise from the rest of you fools either. Understand?" The heavyset guard had a black beard and hair that flowed out from under his helmet, looking menacing without even trying.

Several prisoners nodded. Liz reacted to the woman on the floor and offered her a hand as she tried to stand up. She heard the rest of the prisoners gasp and she saw the scowling face of the guard. She immediately guessed she broke some taboo in helping up the woman.

The guard took a half step toward her and the others parted before him. Liz wondered what she could do. It didn't seem speaking in her defence was an option. Liz did the only thing that came to her mind. She gave her best pickup smile, the one that had worked well on men in the past.

He stopped in his tracks, giving her a perplexed look. Then he shook his head at her and returned to where he was standing.

Liz felt her heart pounding in her chest and tried to relax.

After ten minutes of waiting, Liz noticed a well-dressed woman walk into the auditorium and sit near the front. Her dress was layered of different fabrics, dark yellow followed by a pale green with lace separating the colours. In addition, she wore small white gloves and carried a white handbag.

A servant girl and a guard, dressed differently than the ones she had seen, accompanied her. A leather vest, high leather boots and shoulder protectors supplemented the guard's dark blue uniform. The servant girl wore a simple light-yellow skirt and a white peasant blouse.

A male servant offered her a goblet on a tray. She accepted the offered refreshment, and the servant bowed before backing away.

Time passed, and another guard entered and pointed at Graham. "You, out there."

Graham was losing his defiance and merely walked out to the stage. He stopped at the centre and faced the rest of the auditorium.

Liz watched the lady whisper to her guard an instruction, and he immediately stepped forward to the front where a clerk sat at a table with pen and paper.

The clerk rose to his feet. "Lady Monique Rosemore requests the subject to disrobe."

Graham looked shocked.

A guard standing on the stage uncoiled a whip. "You heard. Disrobe."

Graham closed his eyes momentarily as if steeling up his nerves. He undid his belt and took off his robe.

The clerk snapped out another command. "Walk around in a circle."

To the laughter from the audience Graham did as he was ordered, coming to a stop after completing the task. Liz felt sorry for him, not because he was naked but due to the laughter from those seated. She admired his body. Besides his strong chest and arms, flat stomach, he had other assets she found interesting. *Nice ass and his assets will make women happy.*

The clerk stood up again. "Any bids for the subject?"

There was silence as Lady Monique whispered another instruction to the guard, who quickly signalled the clerk with a hand signal.

The clerk nodded. "We have a bid of one fern. Are there any other bids?" He did a brief scan of the audience. "Sold. Subject is sold for one fern."

There was a howl of laughter from the crowd as Graham was led to the far side of the stage.

The guard who had pushed the young woman down and had started a threatening action against Liz, looked at the rest of prisoners. "Yer all in luck. Lady Monique's lookin' for a girl as well."

Several women raised their hands and moved to the front, hoping to be picked. Liz wondered if she should do the same as several women pushed in front of her.

The guard snarled at their behaviour. "You, you, and you." He pointed at the women, picking what he considered the best of the lot. The rest slumped their shoulders. "And where's the cute one who smiled?"

Liz stepped forward to the middle.

"You can go too." He gave her a grin, showing off broken teeth.

The four women walked in a single file on stage, separating themselves by several steps. The clerk stood up and yelled instructions.

"Ladies, walk with yer head up. Five steps...turn around and back the other way."

Liz remembered her mother giving her advice when she was fifteen. *Lizzy, a lady walks with poise, her head up and with small steps on a narrow path. Remember, don't walk as if you're pushing a wheelbarrow.*

The clerk looked at Lady Monique, who whispered to her guard again. The guard relayed the message with more hand signals.

"Number two and four, your services are not required at this time. Please return to the waiting area."

Liz and the remaining girl stood on the stage.

"Disrobe." The clerk yelled the next set of orders.

Liz took a deep breath. She considered she didn't have a lot of options. The other girl had already slipped off her robe and Liz followed suit.

"Turn around."

Liz obeyed and looked at her rival. She was a bit taller but their figures were about the same. The other was also pulling back on her shoulders to help emphasis her figure. Liz didn't believe that would have much effect on Lady Monique and remained relaxed in her posture.

"You, tell why you wish to work for Lady Monique." The clerk pointed at the other woman.

"'Cause she's the best to work for. I promises to work hard and be obedient. Please, Lady Monique, you won't be disappointed in me."

The clerk pointed at Liz. "Speak your reasons."

"Look, I don't know who you are. I just arrived here. I don't even know what I'm supposed to do if I work for you but I'll do my best."

Lady Monique smiled and spoke up, her voice light but it carried across the auditorium. "You sound educated, Miss. You also have a hint of rebelliousness in your voice. I like that. Clerk, I'll bid ten ferns for her."

The clerk looked around the room. "We have a bid of ten ferns for the subject. Any challenges? Sold for ten ferns."

Liz was led off the stage with mixed emotions at being purchased by Lady Monique, not sure what work she would be required to do.

Another clerk had her sign a form before she was allowed to accompany Lady Monique's guard. She stood on the opposite of a small desk and read what she was about to sign.

"Hurry up, I don't have all day." The clerk didn't have any other paper work in front of him and she wondered if the clerk had anything else to do. She decided to keep the thought to herself.

The form was a legal document, she surmised, that required her to provide whatever services Lord Dungan Rosemore decided was fair in exchange for room and board, plus twelve ferns per month. The contract was for four years. Rather one sided, she concluded. Still it was better than being in prison or some labour camp and being naked in front of the clerk and the leering guard hastened her decision. She took the quill pen and scrawled out her signature.

"Hmph. Fancy that, she can spell her own name in writing." The clerk spoke to the guard. "Looks like an educated bitch that had a fall from grace."

Liz crossed her arms, not appreciating his words or the tone of his voice. The guard reacted a little different though and handed her a blue robe to wear. He also kept his eyes averted, and she felt less self-conscious when she finished putting on the robe.

The guard escorted her outside, and she carefully made her way across broken rock and weeds to a waiting carriage. The guard offered a hand to assist her step up. Graham was already sitting in the carriage, wearing a similar blue robe, clutching his hands in front of him with his head hanging down.

A guard rode on the outside of the coach at the back leaving them alone in their journey.

"Are you okay?"

He glanced up at her and shook his head, resuming his posture of staring at the floor. "I can't believe my father did this to me. Casting me out and allowing me to be sold. What did I do to deserve this fate?"

"Did he say anything to you? Did you two have a fight?"

"Oh, well, he did say I was a disgrace to the family and if I couldn't be more like my brothers, then he wouldn't put up with me. He's said that before and nothing ever happened but last night he had two guards throw me out into the street. Without a furling in my pocket." He clenched his fist and stared at her. "Why did he disown me? Why won't my mother help me?"

Liz shrugged. "Do your brothers get along with him?"

"Oh, yeah. The apples of his eye. All three of them were given their own land."

"Well, it could be he wants you learn something first before getting your own land.

Graham perked up. "You think so? Maybe he'll buy out my contract and give me my own land as a way of an apology."

Liz closed her eyes and thought Graham heard only what he wanted to hear. "What's this lord of the castle like?"

"Lord Dungan Rosemore. Okay, I guess. Older guy. Lady Monique is his second wife. My father knows them quite well. They treat their subjects better than most."

Their coach stopped at a large castle after almost an hour's ride. The guard pointed at a side door of the castle. "Miss, go to those doors and ask for Miss Nora." He turned to Graham. "You, report to the stables."

"The stables!"

"Right. Are you hard of hearing or just stupid?"

Graham's face turned red, and he clenched his fists. He appeared ready to take a step toward the guard.

Liz grabbed his forearm with her hand. "Stop, don't be a fool. Do what he tells you to do and you won't get in any more trouble."

The guard smirked and crossed his arms. "Better listen to your little lady."

"Alright, I will. But just remember I was once Sir Graham and someday I'll earn that title again. Then we'll have a little talk." He strode away to the stables, leaving the guard looking a little less smug.

Liz was ushered into a side door. Miss Nora, a tall brunette with a slim figure, beckoned her to follow her. Liz guessed Nora was in her early forties and had an officious presence about her.

"The Rosemore Castle has over fifty servants, including three gnants to oversee its operation. Your primary job, and it's a most important one, is to act as a hostess for our guests. You will be given other assignments and work to do in the future but for now I want you to concentrate on this one." Nora lectured as she led Liz down a tunnel to the servant's quarters.

Liz was pleased to find she had her own room, though it had space for only a single narrow bed and dresser. A washbasin sat on the wide window ledge.

"The bathroom is down the hall. Breakfast will be served one-half hour after the wake-up bell and is on the main floor of the servant quarters. You have been given three skirts, three blouses, two pairs of shoes and one formal dress. It is your responsibility that they remain in good repair and clean at all times. Only garments that have shown signs of long term wear will be replaced, otherwise the replacement will come out of your salary."

Liz listened as Nora expanded on the various rules and regulations, not asking many questions as Nora covered almost all areas. Liz sat on her bed after Nora left and sighed, wondering how so much had happened to her in such a short time. She suddenly started to cry, unable to stop torrent of tears from her eyes.

Will I ever see Jon again? Am I going to be stuck here as a servant for the rest of my life?

THIRTEEN

The room was dim, lit only by a single lantern that cast a yellow light as it sat on the table. Jon's head still hurt, and he slowly moved to look around. The window had the shutters closed but the cracks in the wood indicated it was dark outside as well.

His head was being soothed by something wet and cold. Another wet, cold sensation was around his neck. He turned to his left and saw Nicole, noting that she was holding a wet cloth in her hand.

"How're you feeling?"

"Better." He touched the wet rag on his head. "I must have been really out of it."

"You were." She picked up the rag from his neck and replaced it with the cloth she was holding. "But the worse is over, you're gonna be alright."

"Thanks." He was still a little warm, but the cold cloths were doing a good job of keeping him comfortable enough. He looked down on his arm, the one hit by dragon fire. From the yellow light it seemed normal and there was only a slight warm feel to the skin. Then he looked down. "Hey, I'm naked."

"That was me. You were complaining about the heat, so I decided to help cool you off by taking your clothes off."

"Alright, but could I have my pants back now?" He struggled up on his elbows but the effort to do more wasn't there.

"No, they're still wet. I had some time while watching you, so I washed them. They really needed it." She gently pushed him on his chest to get him to lie back down. "I hung them outside the window to dry. They'll be okay in the morning."

"What time is it now? What do I do in the meantime?"

"It's around midnight. I would suggest rest until morning. Unless you want to go to the tavern like that." She grinned at him.

"Hardly."

"Do you want me to stay here and keep putting cold rags on your head or do you think you'll be okay by yourself?"

"I think I can manage to do that by myself." He yawned. "I guess do need to sleep some more."

"I would think so. By the way Liz must be quite a girlfriend."

"Why?"

"You talk in your sleep. And I would say they must have been interesting dreams as well." She covered her grin with her fingers. "Goodnight." She closed the door behind her after blowing out the lantern.

Jon wasn't sure just what she meant by interesting dreams but felt vaguely embarrassed by this latest revelation, deciding he wouldn't pursue the conversation in the morning.

––––––

The knock on the door woke him. Light was streaming through the shutters where the wood had split.

"Just a minute." He scrambled out of bed and opened the door slightly, standing behind it.

"It's only me. Can you make it downstairs for breakfast?"

Jon recognized Nicole's voice. "Yeah, sure. You said my clothes are hung out the window?"

"That's right. We'll also get you a shirt from town after we eat."

Jon opened the window to retrieve his clothing. He saw only the street below, his clothes, other than his sandals, were nowhere to be seen.

This isn't good.

He looked around the room for anything that would cover him. There wasn't much in the room other than the pitcher and with ice water inside it. Around the pitcher was broken pieces of pottery, the same type it was made of. He sighed, there wasn't much he could do but wait for help.

A few minutes passed before Nicole knocked on his door again. "You okay in there?"

"Yeah, but my clothes are missing."

"You're kidding." She opened the door and walked in, ignoring his startled look. She strode to the window, looking down to the street. "Isn't that odd? I attached them to this rail. Not even a wind could've blown them off."

Jon wondered what to do. To try to cover himself up now would seem silly after last night. And he didn't think he could pull off the nonchalant look either. He felt too self-conscious to do anything. He did push the door slightly closed in case anyone else came walking by. He stood with his hands by his side as she stared at him.

"I'll get you some pants and a shirt from the shops downtown. In the meantime, I'll send up some food for you to eat unless you prefer to go downstairs. I'm sure they wouldn't mind if I explained what happened." She grinned.

He smiled at her joke. He was starting to feel less uncomfortable standing naked in front of her. "Yeah, right, that would cause a reaction. I think Lady Karla would have a heart attack. No, best send up the food."

She continued stare at him and he was glad she was making eye contact.

"There's broken pottery. What happened there?"

She glanced at the table. "Oh, that." She shrugged. "I was trying the spell to make ice water. After a few tries I managed to turn water into ice. Unfortunately, I turned all the water into ice and it burst the pitcher." She took a deep breath, appearing there was something else she wanted to say. "I better get going. People will be wondering why I'm spending so much time in the room of a naked man." She laughed. "See you later."

Jon closed the door after she left. He passed the time looking out the window and noticed scratch marks on the shutters, as if something was trying to break in. A few minutes passed again before Sir Keith brought up his breakfast, much to Jon's relief. He had visions of Lady Karla bursting in instead, screaming at the sight of him and causing him more problems.

Sir Keith did not seem to notice or be bothered by his nudity and stayed while Jon ate. "I must say when word went around the tavern last night about your battle with the dragon, a lot of people wanted to meet you and many were concerned about your injuries. There will be a few watching to see if only one dragon flies the evening skies in the next week. If so, then you'll have earned the title Sir Jon, the dragon slayer. Lord Perry, in any event will no doubt give you the gold seal of a dragon fighter."

"Really?"

"Yes, indeed. That seal isn't taken lightly and will open many doors for you. Well, eat up, I'll see you downstairs later."

Sir Keith left the door open, and Jon began to wonder if he was the only one bothered by his lack of clothing. Jon pushed the door closed and sat on the bed, walked to the window and looked out at the view below. He repeated his bed sitting and window viewing when there was a tap on his door.

"It's me again." Nicole carried his new clothes into the room and placed them on the bed. "Here you go. I got them on the large side, so they should fit."

"Thanks, I feel a prisoner in this room." He picked up the shirt and the pants. "They look big enough. Thanks." He noticed she hadn't made an effort to leave, and he quickly pulled on the pants and shirt. Both were a combination of heavy cloth with leather in areas where the most wear would occur.

Nicole appraised the new clothes. "They actually look better than the ones you were wearing before."

They left the room and went downstairs. The innkeeper waved at him and shouted a greeting. Outside of the hotel his horse and pack were waiting for him and he noticed Gilbert now had his own horse. The new horse was smaller and older than the rest but wouldn't have a problem carrying Gilbert's weight. Nathan moved his horse up by Jon's.

"Look what I found by the stables." He handed Jon his pants, torn to rags. "Looks like the work of gnants to me. I hope they didn't find what they were searching for." He waited for Jon to answer.

"No, there was nothing of value in those pants."

"Good. Keep secure whatever they were after. If I can be of assistance in that regard, let me know."

They followed in a single line out of town with Sir Keith leading the way. The town ended abruptly with farm land stretching out before them. The road was in good condition, the lack of rain in the past few days had allowed the road to stay firm. They stopped late in the afternoon for a break, bypassing lunch due to their late start from Seilini. Nathan and Sir Keith decided they would push until the evening when they should arrive at Horsbridge.

Nicole sat close to Jon during the break. It seemed she had something on her mind and wanted to talk to him but Gilbert came up to them.

"Pardon the intrusion but I'd like to say, that is, thank ya for what you did the other day."

Jon didn't reply, figuring he wasn't going to make it easy on the dwarf who had tried to avoid his responsibilities earlier.

Gilbert swallowed. "I guess you saved me life. I just wanted to say thanks."

"Does that mean you're in my debt again?"

The dwarf closed his eyes as if in pain. "We can ask Council Madoc if you like. I'm not sure if I can owe two lives at the same time to you."

"Relax. Don't worry about it, you can buy me a pint in the next pub."

Gilbert brightened up. "Sure, sure. We can share a few laughs. That would be good, yes indeed." He walked away as if a load was lifted off his shoulders.

"You let that weasel off too easy you know."

"Ah, he isn't so bad. Just needs to be shown the right way."

"It would take a pretty good map to do that."

"Probably."

She took a deep breath. "Jon, remember when I said you talk in your sleep?"

"Uh, yeah."

"Well, of course you were just dreaming, so it doesn't mean much or anything at all, but sometimes dreams can tell a person something. Like their subconscious sees something and can only tell you through dreams."

"Okay, I understand that." *Lord, did I say something stupid?* "Are you trying to tell me I called out your name as well and if I did, I'm sure..."

"No, not that. Well, you did say something about me but that wasn't what I want to talk to you about. You were talking about Nadine and how she was turning into a gnant. It sounded like a really bad dream, like you were trapped in a room with her and you screamed out 'You're turning back into a gnant! You're a gnant.' It sounded like you were horrified. Then you suddenly stopped. I thought you may want to know. Probably means nothing." She brushed back her hair with her hand. "Just something to think about, I guess."

Jon considered what she said. Nadine was slim, short but with long fingers and toes, a full mouth and wide-set eyes. She had an odd walk as well but she explained that was due to a hip injury that was still healing. Jon could see vague similarities between her and a gnant as one was morphed into the other but to him, she was definitely human. *My mind must have been playing tricks with me.*

"I think it was just a bad dream."

"Okay, just wanted to tell you."

"What did I say about you?"

She grinned. "Oh, I think that I better keep that to myself."

"That's not fair!" He pointed his finger at her.

"Doesn't matter, I'm not telling."

The journey resumed with Jon thinking about what Nicole said. He tried to picture Nadine as a gnant, but really couldn't see many similarities. He thought it was odd that the dream decided to combine the two images, not wanting to believe she could be a gnant in disguise.

But didn't Uncle Gordon warn me about those who were not what they seemed to be? Another world, dragons, magic. I guess I'm ready to believe almost anything.

His thoughts were disturbed when a hawk-sized bird swooped down and attacked something in the bushes. There was a sudden snarl and a porcupine like creature but without the quills and sporting a large tail with spikes ran out. It turned around in a circle and fell on its side. The furry body twitched a few times and lay still as the bird approached its kill to feed. The bird was ugly, looking like a large headed vulture. Then Jon noticed it had four legs as well as a set of leather like wings.

He moved his horse up to Gilbert.

"What the hell is that thing?" He pointed at the four-legged bird.

"Oh, that. It's called a devil bird or a volvcris. They're a type of dragon, only small."

"There's more than one type of dragon?"

"Oh sure. There're lupus dragons, they're dog-size and hunt in packs. Then there's patiri dragons, they be bigger still but usually hunt by themselves. The dragon that attacked us was called a par dragon, and then there's a couple that don't fly. A small thing called a lacerta and a big one called a tantus. But the biggest and meanest dragon is the fornido dragon. Lives high on a mountain or cliffs."

"So, all these dragons can shoot this acid like fire?"

"For sure. The only reason these dragons haven't killed everything is that they're on the slow side and most of their prey can run away before getting a blast of dragon fire."

Jon thanked Gilbert and dropped back. A whole collection of different dragons was not a good thought.

Horsbridge was slightly larger than Seilini. The streets were wider, though still without sidewalks, and ran in straighter lines. Like the former town Seilini, it sported buildings with sharp roofs but also included towers where large crossbows were mounted as a weapon against the dragons.

Once again Sir Keith seemed to have a hotel in mind and led them to one that was at least on the quality of the Goodfellow.

"Here we are, the best hotel in this town." Sir Keith beamed as he pointed at their next place to rest.

The Elite Hotel didn't quite live up to its name. At one time the furnishings and the interior might have been of high quality but those days were long past. They stood in the lobby, save for Gilbert and Nathan, who tended the horses, and looked around. Sir Keith frowned and turned to the others.

"My apologies. The premises here were much better the last time I was here, though that was a number of years ago. Shall we search for other accommodations?"

"It'll be fine. I've been in worse," Nicole answered.

Lady Karla smirked. "Maybe for some of us. However, it's late and I suppose this will have to do."

Jon shrugged. He was tired and figured any place would be good as long as it had a bed but he was surprised at the sharp comment made by Lady Karla at Nicole.

The group met in the tavern to eat later that evening, the food simple but filling. Lady Karla ate quietly and then excused herself, claiming she was tired. Jon was tired as well but was easily convinced to stay and share drinks with the others.

Gilbert proclaimed loudly that Jon was his good friend and told the barmaid to bring him a mug of their finest ale. In truth there were only two types of ale available in the bar and the more expensive type was already being served at their table. The other part of Gilbert's generosity was diminished somewhat by the fact Sir Keith was paying for all lodging, food and drink from monies advanced by Lord Perry. However, Gilbert made a great show of making sure Jon was never without a mug of ale in front of him.

Nicole sat next to Jon at the table and laughed at Gilbert's antics. The dwarf was getting drunk but was in good spirits and was telling off-colour jokes. Nathan drank his ale and seemed to enjoy the conversation for a change. He took his normal guard duty less seriously and enjoyed several ales during the evening. He didn't stop looking around the near empty room but there was little to suggest there was any danger tonight.

Sir Keith, however, appeared annoyed with the crude banter and quietly drank his wine. He scowled when Gilbert stood on his chair and proclaimed Sir Jon, the great dragon slayer. Still, he didn't leave, apparently thinking there was little else to do in the small town and it was too early to retire.

Gilbert leaned toward Jon and nudged him with his elbow. "Hey, are yous and Nicole sharing a room together? She's a nice dish."

Jon shook his head. "No, we're just friends and we're not sharing a room together tonight."

"Be better friends, that what I'd do."

"Gilbert, I have a girlfriend back home."

"Hey, why drink one tankard when you can have a bunch?"

Jon laughed. "And you're an expert on that, aren't you?"

"There's only so much ale in a barrel, drink what you can while you can." Gilbert took another drink and waved the barmaid to bring more ale. "Do you still have that charm of yours? The times on your wrist?"

"Yeah, but it doesn't do much good here."

"True, different world. Do you have other charms from the Otherside?"

"No, why?"

"Oh, just wondering. Me heard rumours that you have a crystal of some sort. They's can be dangerous to those who have them. Wouldn't want anything to 'appen to me friend, that's all. Or to anyone you may have given it to."

Jon eyes flicked to Nicole for a moment but she was ignoring their conversation. "No, don't worry Gilbert. No crystals around here."

"Oh, that be good, that be good." Gilbert shouted, "Hey wench, get me friend another ale and be quick about it." He now knew Jon did have a crystal and the quick glance to Nicole told him she was holding on to it for him. The next question was what type was it and what should he do about it.

———

Lady Karla carefully opened the front door and walked to the end of the block, just far enough away from any prying eyes and ears. She waited for only a minute when she saw him shuffle up close to her.

"It wassssn't there."

"That wasn't my fault. He did have it. But after he fought the dragon, he lost his shirt. When I checked it wasn't around his neck."

"Lossst it?"

"I don't know. I don't think so. He must have hidden it somewhere else."

The gnant swayed, and it worked its fingers together. "You find out, quick."

"It's not that easy. I'll try to find out."

"Deal! You make deal."

"I know, I know. But some things take time."

"No times. Quick or else." The gnant first shuffled and suddenly disappeared into the night.

Lady Karla shuddered in the cool air. The deal she made with the gnants wasn't working to plan and if she didn't do something soon, she wouldn't have a long life. She quietly slipped back into the hotel and went to her room, not noticing Sir Keith had observed her return from a vantage point in the tavern.

———

Jon held up his hand, "No, I've had enough to drink. I better go to bed before I fall asleep here." He stood. "I'll see everyone in the morning."

Gilbert tilted back his tankard. "That be okay. More for me." He looked over at Sir Keith. "Did ja ever hear 'bout the time a maiden and a knight found a magic bottle of rum?"

Nicole hurried after Jon. "Wait for me. I don't know if I can take another of Gilbert's jokes."

"They are rather crude."

"Crude I can handle but his are on another level." When they reached the stairs she asked in a low voice, "What about this crystal you gave me? I need to know what this is. I can sense it's powerful."

"It was given to me as a rare necklace when I was on Earth. When I ended up here, Lady Karla told me to keep it a secret."

"So why give it to me and not her?"

"I don't trust her."

"Me neither." She pulled at his arm, taking him into her room. "Please understand, this crystal may be dangerous. Some of them are highly sought after and you better be careful who does know about it."

"I know. I think it's best you give it back to me now. I don't want you to be in any danger."

She patted her chest. "It's safe here. No one knows I have it or can see it."

"I'd be worried about you with it."

"I can handle myself. Besides you can protect me when we're on the road."

"Alright, thanks."

He slipped out of her room and to his own across the narrow hallway.

Nathan wasn't surprised to see Jon step out of her room. *Those two have a thing for each other. At least they're discreet about it.*

FOURTEEN

The road out of Horsbridge degenerated into little more than a trail. Sir Keith called a halt around lunchtime that coincided with a stoppage in the light drizzle. Jon, like the others, eventually had put on an oiled cape. The leather garment was saturated with oil that made an effective barrier to the rain but was heavy.

Sir Keith announced when they stopped for lunch it was unlikely they would reach the next town by evening and therefore they would set up camp just before sunset.

"Sorry if the conditions will be a bit damp, but the rain has slowed us down some and the next village, a hole called Marshland, doesn't have decent accommodations in any event. Freeman Nathan will try to obtain a deer or other game for dinner tonight so we won't be suffering unduly."

"Great, overcooked venison served on mud. No ale 'nd no serving wenches to pinch." Gilbert spat on the ground and walked away.

Nicole winced and leaned into Jon, whispering into his ears. "I can't imagine why he's still single, such a gentleman."

"He does have character."

"C'mon, walk with me." She crossed her arms to ward of the chill in the air.

Jon walked with her down toward the trail.

"What's up?"

"You tell me." She held out the crystal necklace to him. "This thing has an energy of sorts. Why do you have it? Where 'cha get it from?"

Jon elaborated on what he had told her earlier. "My uncle gave it to me, in a will. He said it was special but I honestly don't understand why."

"If you look at its shape, you can tell it's meant to be locked into something else, like another crystal. I was told by this warlock, the one who taught me magic, that there're certain crystals like that."

"What do they do?"

"Well, they're different ones. Usually there's just three crystals that can be joined together and when the bond is made, they make available certain powers, such as the ability to fly or make one invisible.

Some of them are very old, maybe thousands of years. I heard of some that require five crystals, but some crystals are missing. I think what you have here is one of those."

Jon peered at the crystal. It did have a hook like portion that could be to be joined to something else. "How do these things supposedly work?"

"If you look real close at the crystal, you'll see a kind of thin gold wire and a little black dot in the middle."

Jon squinted at the crystal. Now that she had mentioned it, he did see a thin gold wire from one end to the other and a tiny spot near the middle.

"I guess when all the crystals are joined together, they make a circuit of some sort and then they suddenly have all this power. Latent stored energy is what this warlock said."

"Do we know what this particular crystal does?"

"Not me. Unfortunately, Lady Karla may be the best choice there."

"You don't like her?"

"It's not just that. I have a sensitivity to people and I get a very bad feeling about her."

"Great, there goes my short list."

———

Sir Keith eyed Nicole and Jon as they returned. Jon had told him they were just friends, but he wasn't so sure about that. It was just one more complication in this journey to Cretal, a trip that was supposed to be just routine. He would be more at ease if Nathan wasn't acting like they were about to be attacked every minute and if Lady Karla wasn't acting like she was hiding a secret.

"No," Sir Keith said aloud, "there is more to this quest than meets the eye. Lord Perry couldn't have known all the facts or he would've given me more than just Nathan as a protector. I wish knew more about this lot." He saw Gilbert scowling as he sat by the small fire. "At least it's easy to figure out where he's coming from, anything he can get his grubby fingers on."

The rest of the journey saw the end of the rain and emergence of the sun. Progress was still slow due to the muddy trail they followed, and Sir Keith called a halt in the early evening to make camp.

Nathan disappeared for an hour and returned with a small animal hung over his shoulders. He dropped the still warm body, a medium-dog sized plant eater called a dorse, near Gilbert.

"You might as well earn your keep. You and Lady Karla can prepare it while I start a fire."

"Since when do ya get to start giving orders?"

"Then I'll give you a suggestion instead. Someone, and that would be me, has to protect this group. Do as I say and I'll try to make sure no mishap happens to you."

Gilbert matched Nathan's stare for several seconds and took out his knife. He tossed it a short distance in the air and caught it by the handle. "Then I best be preparing this doe."

Nathan frowned. Gilbert, even when he lost a confrontation, didn't entirely back down. He understood the threat Gilbert implied with the tossing of a knife. That show of defiance made Nathan warier of Gilbert and moved him up a notch in respect. He turned away, almost bumping into Lady Karla.

"What's this nonsense about me having to help prepare an animal for dinner? I am a lady, not a mere servant. I've never done anything like this before."

"Well, Lady Karla, this journey is proving to be more troublesome than first anticipated and we all have to do a little extra."

"You really can't force me to do this. Lord Perry mentioned nothing about doing menial labour."

"As I pointed out, the situation seems to have changed. We need everyone to do a little more." He crossed his massive arms, peering down at her.

She took a half step back, frowning. "Very well. I am willing to be accommodating."

Nathan walked away and noticed Sir Keith was standing by the horses, making sure they had food and water after securing them to some bushes. He waited until Sir Keith had seen him and walked up to him. "My apologies if it seemed I was usurping your authority."

"Not at all. It's good to see those two doing work for a change. Although there may be hell to pay when we get back, depending on Lady Karla's influence on Lord Perry."

"So be it. It won't be the first nor likely the last time Lord Perry had words with me." He saw Jon finish setting up Nicole's tent. "Sir Jon!" he bellowed. "Come. It's time to learn more of the art of sword fights."

Jon followed Nathan to a small clearing near their camp. Nathan used his sword to slice off two branches from one of the trees. He shaved the branches into sticks and gave one to Jon.

"We can use these as swords. They may hurt a bit but at least we won't have serious injuries."

Jon held his wood sword vertically, waiting to see what Nathan would do. He didn't expect the strong attack that Nathan used. It took only three swings and an elbow from Nathan to send Jon to the ground.

Nathan stood over him. "You just died. Never hold your sword straight up in the air. That won't provide any defence." He held out a hand and helped Jon to his feet. "Now I best show you how to stand."

Jon followed his instructions and did much better in the next series of combats but still "died".

Jon was glad when dinner was finally ready. He was sweating and tired with multiple bruises on his arms and body from the wooden sticks Nathan had used for their practice.

"You learn well. Not bad at all for someone new."

"Thanks. I didn't know there was that much to it."

"Oh, there's more. Lots more. But you're getting the hang of it."

Jon ate slowly, feeling the stiffness in his arms.

"Bit sore?" Nicole sat next to him by her tent.

"Yeah. It's like training camp when I played football."

"You did well. Nathan really knows how to fight. He has that red armband. That means he's an elite fighter and would have done damage to anyone. You're fortunate to have him as a teacher."

"Yeah, I feel very lucky."

———

The evening was cool, and the group sat around the fire quietly, enjoying its warmth except for Nathan who sat a distance away. The fire made it harder for his eyes to adjust to the dark and Nathan needed to be observant of any small movements in the bushes. He chose a spot just behind the tents so they blocked the campfire.

Nathan had learned how to watch with part of his mind while he almost went into a dream state. If his eyes saw a movement, and they missed very little, then his whole being jumped to alert. It was this ability to be diligent while resting that allowed him to guard all night and still be able to function the following day.

There was little movement as dusk came and the night followed. The moon gave a soft light that was sufficient for him to catch small movements in the trees beyond. In the early part of the evening he saw a dark cloud of bats just above the treetops silhouetted by the glow of the sun after it disappeared below the horizon. A pack of lucus dragons of perhaps eight wheeled above the trees and turned toward the camp. The fire attracted them and they circled above for a full minute before moving on. A group of humans were not a preferred prey for them and it was easier to find creatures with less resistance. A single person might have been in danger if the dragons were hungry enough but the pack was a family and rarely attacked prey that provided a risk.

A few hours later a herd of trumpeters, a distant relative of elephants, but much smaller and with fine brown hair covering their hides moved through the forest. These, more than the lucus dragons, caused a minor concern to Nathan if they decided to cross through their camp. They weren't easily deterred from their desired path and could damage the tents and cause the horses to panic. Fortunately, they preferred to stay among the trees rather than the open area where they camped.

Nathan moved occasionally to make sure his limbs didn't get stiff from the cool damp air. The fire had dwindled to glowing embers, but he still avoided putting it within his line of sight. The others, he assumed, had gone to their tents as he no longer heard the quiet voices from the campfire. His ears picked up the sounds of sleep. Quiet breathing, not so quiet breathing and, early on, the mutterings of Gilbert. Gilbert, he noticed, could curse almost as well in his sleep as he did awake. Jon called out a name or two as well but for the most part was quiet.

In the hours between midnight and sunrise Nathan heard the sound of branches swaying and the rustle of leaves. He watched among the trees but didn't see anything unusual.

"Gnants, probably," he muttered to himself. He knew killing one wasn't going to stop them from their spying but he hoped that at least they would keep their distance. He pulled out his crossbow and loaded an arrow and walked along the perimeter of the camp. He listened for the slightest noise as he peered into the darkness of the forest. He kept his back to the campsite and walked backward to the tents. Nothing broke the silence or moved in the dark shadows.

Nathan started to relax when he heard a sound, a sound that he identified after a fraction of a moment. He whirled around with his crossbow raised and stared at the tents. Someone had just drawn a string that secured the tent flaps closed but now there was only silence.

He wondered if it could have been something like a gnant trying to enter the tent but confirmed in his own mind that it sounded more like the flap being closed rather than being opened.

After a few minutes he uneasily lowered his crossbow, watching the area. He considered what may have transpired at the tents and a wry smile came across his lips as he thought, *Ah, Sir Jon may have doing a bit of visiting with Nicole on the sly. They claim they're just friends but I think there's more to it than that. I suppose he's trying to protect her reputation by visiting when everyone else is asleep. Sir Keith heard she was little more than a common serving wench but she doesn't present herself like one, nor does she speak like one.*

Nathan let his thoughts drift away and presently found a spot on the ground to his liking. He sat with his eyes carefully surveying the area while the rest of his mind relaxed.

Morning came and while Sir Keith and Nicole prepared a breakfast of yesterday's warmed up dinner, Nathan took a few minutes to sleep. Twenty minutes later he arose refreshed and made a check around the campsite. There weren't any obvious signs of the gnants but that was to be expected as they were careful about revealing themselves.

Sir Jon and Nicole busied themselves in rolling up the tents. Jon noticed Lady Karla acted withdrawn and nervous, giving little back in his attempt at conversation. He walked with Nicole to the campfire and took reheated breakfast.

Nicole favoured him with a smile. "Good morning."

"Good morning to you, too. Does this stuff taste any better than yesterday?"

"If you use enough salt. Tea?"

"Sure. Sleep okay?"

"Yeah, for the most part. Say, you didn't come into my tent last night, did you?"

"No. Was I supposed to?"

She shook her head. "You wish. It's just that my stuff was messed up in the tent, like someone was searching for something."

"And you thought it was me? What would I be looking for?"

"Well, I thought that you came into my tent, realized that would be a bad thing to do and left but messed things up in the process."

He stared at her wondering what to say and they both burst out laughing.

"Okay, so we both have one-track minds. But be a gentleman and don't try to take advantage of me."

"Fine, I'll be a gentleman. But who messed up your tent?"

The question remained unresolved and neither of them wanted to bring up their concerns to Nathan or Sir Keith. The journey to Marshland was uneventful and the town itself was, as Sir Keith indicated, nothing to be excited about. They entered the town near noon with the sun beating down hard enough to cause even the flies to stay in the shade. Grey brick was a common building material with the roofs made of timber, some of them with points on the end as a defence against dragons. The people of Marshland, for the most part wore old dirty clothes, moving about as if life had seeped out of them. "This town's been cursed," Gilbert spoke to no one in particular.

Jon had to agree with him. If there was a single redeeming feature of the town, it had yet to reveal itself. He wasn't sure what hotel Sir Keith had in mind for them but camping out in the open last night may have been better than what was available here.

Sir Keith led the group as usual and made the way to a small tavern at the edge of downtown, such as it was. The commerce area consisted largely of a general store, a physician/veterinarian clinic, a few open food market vendors, a church and a spell shop.

With a bit of reluctance Jon dismounted from his horse and

followed the rest into the tavern. He wasn't surprised by the dark interior or by the older wooden furniture. But the barkeep and his daughter were friendly and quickly prepared food and drink. Jon exchanged looks with Nicole who gave a bit of a shrug that she had seen worse and sat down at one of the tables. Gilbert wasted little time in downing two pints of ale and annoying the waitress with his hands that kept reaching out when she came close.

Lady Karla took a glass of wine and reluctantly ordered some food. She looked around the room with a bit of disdain and leaned away from the waitress when she served the wine as if incidental contact with her would cause contamination.

When the food arrived, Sir Keith had a smirk on his face as each member of the party tried the food and found it rather good, much to their surprise.

"Now, is there any question I know where good food is served? Regardless of the town we visit?"

"There is something to be said for atmosphere, Sir Keith. Or in the case of this town, perhaps too much," Lady Karla replied in a flat voice.

Sir Keith barely glanced at her. "So be it. The food is good, service is fine and the company, for the most part, is pleasant." He held up his mug in an uncharacteristic display of comradeship. "To us and Sir Jon's great quest!"

All joined in, though Lady Karla barely touched her cup to her lips. Gilbert more than made up her effort. He attacked the food and ale with great enthusiasm. Nathan ate well but took only a single pint of ale, reluctantly turning down a refill.

"I must keep a sharp head as we still have some traveling to do."

They left the town of Marshland immediately after their lunch. The next town on their route was Stone Retreat, originally settled by a wealthy lord who used it as a hunting lodge. Eventually others decided to invest in the area as well, including those who saw an opportunity to help reap the benefits of the lifestyles of the well-to-do. For those who couldn't afford to have their own residence built, there were several expensive hotels that would cater to the semi-wealthy.

Dusk came by the time they reached the outskirts of the town and they had to halt in front of a guarded entrance to the town. The two guards seemed more symbolic than posing a strong deterrent but Sir Keith took them seriously and explained they were on a mission commissioned by Lord Perry of great importance. Within a minute they were waved through, entering onto a wide brick street.

The buildings on the side of the street were large and usually protected by a stone wall. Traffic was brisk as they moved past streets and avenues, encountering well-dressed riders on horses and several carriages. Above the streets stood oil-fed torches on stone towers, spaced close enough to light up the streets during the evenings. Potted plants and flowers sat on the raised sidewalks as well as the occasional statue and fountain.

Jon, Nicole, Gilbert and Nathan looked around in wonder at the sights while Lady Karla and Sir Keith seemed to take it in stride.

One castle had a stone wall that was open in the middle and fitted with a cage. The cage, over thirty feet long and ten feet deep, was secured by a close-fitting white bars. Behind the cage paced three locus dragons.

"Is that safe? Can't the dragons spray fire through the bars?" Jon stared at the agitated dragons that occasionally tried to fly but were rebuffed by the eight-foot ceiling.

Gilbert spat on the ground. "Na, the bastards removed their glands. They can't even soften up their own food properly to eat it. It has to be pounded into mash first."

"A bit cruel, isn't it?"

"A bit? I've no love of dragons but these rich jerks are torturing these things. They be better dead."

Jon was surprised at Gilbert's attitude toward the dragons. There was a side to him he hadn't seen before. "What are those white bars made from?"

"Stonewood. Comes from a tree that turns itself into stone as it grows. The inside of the limbs has a bit of wood in it but it covers itself with stone. It's done by magic. Some wizard puts a spell on a plant and then it grows that way."

"Why don't they use iron bars instead?"

Gilbert considered him a moment before speaking. "Iron, any metal for that matter, is 'pensive'. Also, that much iron would disrupt magic spells in the area so that stuff is avoided. Iron, more so than any other metal, can stop magic spells. You not paying enough 'tention to what's around you."

"Huh? I just asked…"

"I knows, I knows. But better to think out the answer than to ask. I may not always be around to help ya."

Jon fell silent. First Gilbert sounded like he cared about how the dragons were treated and now he sounded like a kindly mentor than the ale guzzling, serving wench pinching and ill-tempered dwarf he came to know.

Jon looked at the sights as they made around the broad avenues. A pair of gargoyles sat on either side of a stone gate of a seven-story rectangular building. The creatures were the size of a large dog and had a chain securing a hind leg to a post.

"Those gargoyles have a metal chain attached to their legs Gilbert."

"Aye. The metal will help prevent a simple spell from making the gargoyles ineffective in protecting the property." Gilbert pointed across the street. "That building is three stories high and has two floors underground. Another behind us is six stories high and has one under it."

"Oh."

He pointed at another building. "That one is seven stories high. So how many floors under it?"

"How should I know? Wait. There has to be a pattern, Right?"

Gilbert nodded.

Jon thought of the other buildings, their height and the underground levels. "Four stories underground. That would make eleven. All those buildings have floors in prime numbers."

Gilbert raised his eyebrows. "That was quick. Took me a week to figure that out. Magic doesn't like numbers that can't be divided. Part of the castle's defence."

Sir Keith led the way to a small castle that was protected by two guards dressed in red holding spears.

The castle, High Park Lodge, boasted several lounges where the outside could be seen that surrounded Stone Retreat, making it easy to survey the land and plan a hunt.

Jon's group was given half a floor to themselves. The rooms were all large, and each had a separate sitting area and washroom. Each room was also connected to its neighbour via a double set of doors. Jon found himself a neighbour to Nicole and Sir Keith.

"I think these accommodations will more than make up for the hardship we had in the past couple of days." Sir Keith sat in one of the large armchairs that grouped around a fireplace in Jon's sitting room. He munched on an apple from a fruit bowl that rested on a dark wood table and between mouthfuls, hooked a thumb toward the door that led to a room next door. "Besides, it may allow you and Nicole to have a discreet evening together. I arranged for her room to be next to yours." He gave Jon a wink.

Jon waved a hand in front of him. "No, it's not…" A knock on the inter-room door interrupted his protest.

"Jon? It's me, Nicole. Can I come in?"

Sir Keith stood. "Right. I'll see you downstairs later for dinner. Should be good with all the game around here." He quietly closed the main door behind him.

Jon opened the side door that allowed Nicole to enter.

"Hi, what's up?"

She grabbed his arm. "There was a gnant in my room!"

"Okay, but doesn't this hotel use gnants as part of the staff?"

"Yeah, it was dressed as if it worked here but what was it doing in my room? It just leered at me and rubbed its hands together, said something and left the room."

"Well, do you want me to complain or something to the management?"

"No, I don't want you to do anything. I'm just scared, that's all."

"I can see that. Let's make sure your door is locked tonight. And the window shutters closed."

"Alright." She looked up at him. "Would you mind if I stayed with you tonight? Only to sleep, nothing else."

Jon's mind shifted into high gear. *Nicole wants to sleep with me. Only to sleep?*

"Sure, that would be fine," *And let the rumour mill about us really get going.*

He had no doubt that somehow someone would find out they shared a room together and, however platonic it might be it, make for interesting gossip.

———

Dinner was the best they had on their journey so far. Jon chowed down on the dinner with vigor. It consisted of several choices placed on the long table he shared with others in his group. He took a selection of different meat, later finding one of them was a dragon. He shrugged. He hadn't developed his size by being a fussy eater. The vegetables were not fresh but quite edible. Their flavour was enhanced by a yellow sauce and Jon was impressed enough to take seconds.

He finished off the meal with dessert, a pudding with a sprinkle of sugar.

Jon relaxed with a glass of wine, noting it had considerably more flavour than what he'd had at previous stops. After his second glass, he followed Sir Keith's lead and announced he was going to retire for the evening. Lady Karla had already disappeared after dinner, presumably to go to bed and Nathan had departed to inquire from the hotel manager what dangers may be in tomorrow's route.

After Jon had reached his room, a knock on the adjoining door indicated Nicole wanted to enter.

He opened the door. "Hi."

"Hi." She eyed the bed. "I don't mind sharing the bed with you. I trust you'll keep your hands off me."

"I will. I promise."

"Good. I really don't want to sleep alone here. Those gnants scare me."

"I understand."

"It's too warm to sleep in all my clothes, just so you know why I'm taking off my skirt." She removed her leather bodice, took off her skirt, and climbed into bed. She stared at him. "I don't expect you to wear all your clothes, either. We can share this bed and be adults. Right?"

"Right." Jon took off his shirt and kicked off his sandals. "I better leave my pants on." *Either that or sleep naked next to her. That would not be good.*

"If you prefer. I've seen you naked already, so it's not a big deal."

Jon lifted the cover to the bed. *Maybe it's not a big deal to you, but it is to me.*

Jon rested on his back, staring at the dark ceiling. He heard the steady breathing of Nicole. She'd turned her back to him and after a minute of leg twitching, rolled to face him. Her breathing increased in its depth and a hand moved to rest on his chest.

I'm glad she's asleep. I hope I can fall asleep as well.

FIFTEEN

Liz took her turn at the crowded mirror and sink in the women's common washroom. She greeted a couple of her new friends, an older servant named Rita, and Roxy, a young maid. Rita was a tall brunette who laughed easily, while Roxy was a redhead who was worried how she would ever get a man while working twelve hours a day.

Liz learned from others that she had a highly coveted job. Unlike many of the servant jobs she didn't have to start work at six in the morning, allowing her to sleep in and have breakfast in a less packed dining hall. She also had more free time during the day between the arrivals of guests to do as she pleased. Liz was given more attractive clothes than her counterparts elsewhere working for Lord Rosemore. The fabric had a finer cut to them and her blouses had a scoop neck versus the high collar for the maids. As Rita pointed out, she had to be pleasant to the eye for the guests to the castle.

It had only been a week since she was given employment at the Rosemore Castle but Earth already seemed far away and she had gotten used to a routine, developing a friendship with a few of the other workers. The days were often long but not necessarily hard, and several times during the day Liz was able to enjoy a cup of tea with one of them or have some idle chat.

This morning she had some free time and chose to visit Anthony

Graham at the stables. She found him shirtless and sweating as he tossed hay bales into a corner of the stable.

"Hey Tony, how's it going?"

He looked up and leaned on a pitchfork. "Alright. But the name is Anthony."

"Too stuffy. I like Tony better."

"How would you like it if I changed your name?"

"To what? Is there a shorter name than Liz?"

He laughed. "Good point. What brings you out here? Don't tell me another break."

"I'm just efficient at my work."

He shook his head and tossed the pitchfork into a bale, leaving the fork standing up. "Come over here, I want to show you Nellie."

He led her to the back of the stables where a large black horse stood, eyeing them as she ate.

"Isn't she great?"

Liz nodded. She slowly approached the horse and stroked her head. "Are you going to get to ride her?"

"Hmm, well the stable master said he'll think about letting me. Big maybe."

"Have you apologized yet for that argument you had with him a few days ago?"

"No, he was in the wrong…"

"You're just being stubborn, Tony. Say you're sorry to him for what you said. Unless you don't want to ride Nellie."

He frowned. "I guess you have a point. Say, do you want to go for a tea tonight?"

"Can't, I have to wash clothes."

"This is the second time you've turned me down. Are you playing hard to get?"

"No, it's not that. Tomorrow, after dinner I can go. But just tea and it's not a date, understand?"

He grinned. "Sure, Liz. Tomorrow it is."

"Okay, I'll meet you in front of the stables an hour after sundown."

The next day Liz met Tony in front of the stables. She took a bit of teasing from her friend Karie about meeting with him, hinting she could do worse than going out with a son of Lord Graham. Tony had changed into cleaner clothes and was waiting for her when she arrived.

"Forgive me if I still smell like a horse. I scrubbed as much as I could, but I suspect it didn't completely vanish."

Liz laughed. "You smell fine. Besides, I like the smell of horses."

They walked down the street with Liz content to let Tony lead the way. He claimed he knew of a teashop that was nice inside but not expensive. Both of them were without much money, although she was being paid twelve ferns versus his six ferns a week.

The teashop was located on a side street that served as an open market for fruit and vegetables during the day. The street was almost deserted with people usually going to or from the small lone tavern. Tony showed he had been taught manners as he escorted her to a table by the window and pulled out the chair for her to sit. The small room held only five square tables with four non-identical chairs each. The floor, like the furniture, was made of wood and showed signs of heavy use. A heavyset woman, looking she was nearing her sixth decade, still appeared energetic as she approached the table.

Tony smiled at her. "Just two cups and a pot of tea, Harriet."

She appeared surprised for a moment. "Sir Anthony, is that you?"

"Yes, it is. And I'm sorry to say I don't have the title of Sir any longer. You may just call me Tony if you like." He gave Liz a grin.

"Oh, very good, sir. Won't be but a minute." She walked away, looking unsettled.

"Good woman. I used to come here for tea and a bite after a night of drinking. She put up with some rather bad behaviour I'm afraid to say."

"That drinking got you into a bit of trouble, did it?"

"No doubt about it. I can tell you it feels good not to wake up half drunk with a hangover, which I used to do more often than not. And the work in the stables makes me feel good. I guess I didn't realize how much I love being around horses, something I did as a child a long time ago."

"So, something good is coming out of working for Lord Rosemore."

"I suppose so. But enough of my fall from grace. Tell me about how you ended here. You're obviously a lady of education."

"Thank you. It's a bit complicated." She proceeded to tell him of

Jon disappearing and her resolve to try to find him and her own misadventure in getting arrested.

"Your boyfriend was chasing this dwarf, who in turn stole something from you? What did he steal that made this guy risk his life?"

Liz covered her face with her hands. "My underwear. Don't say anything. It's embarrassing enough."

He laughed. "Your underwear? Well, I hope the dwarf wasn't planning to wear it."

She crossed her arms, trying to keep herself from grinning. "Enough about my knickers."

"Okay, okay. What did this dwarf look like?"

She described him as she remembered, including his way of talking.

"Ah, that sounds like Gilbert. Well known for his way of doing business. I've had a couple of pints with him in the past."

"You did? Do you know how to get a hold of him? He'd know what happened to Jon."

"What? Help you find Jon when I have designs on you myself? What a dreadful thought." He laughed.

"Stop it. I'm serious." She started to blush.

"I know. I lost a lot of my friends since my arrest but I'll do what I can. I can't promise much."

"Try, please."

"Absolutely. For you I'll try my best."

———

The next couple of days were routine for Liz, other than she kept hoping Tony could help her find Gilbert and, by extension, Jon. The usual stream of visitors came through the front doors, including a gentleman named Council Madoc. The first time Liz met him she quickly presented him to Lord Rosemore. The following day she was required to entertain him first. It wasn't unusual for guests to wait until Lord Rosemore could have time in his schedule to see them, even with an appointment made earlier.

Council Madoc selected a small glass of wine while she sat with a cup of tea in the drawing room. He soon began to ask questions about her status and where she came from.

She gave an abbreviated description of how she ended up at Lord Rosemore's castle, including the fact she was looking for her boyfriend.

"Quite an adventure. And it must be quite a fellow for you to go chasing after him into a new world. You were very brave to do so."

"Thanks, but I haven't found him yet. It's hard to do any searching while working here."

"Hmm, that is a dilemma. Perhaps I could watch out for him during my travels. What does he look like and what is his name?" Council Madoc stood up with Liz when she received a signal from a maid that Lord Rosemore was able to see him.

"Well, he's quite big, has lots of dark hair, blue eyes and has an American accent."

"Oh, well, that should help, I'll watch out..."

"And his name is Jon McKinney."

Council Madoc froze in mid step. "Jon McKinney? Do you know if he was with a dwarf named Gilbert?"

"Yes, that was the name of that miserable dwarf who stole...never mind. You know where Jon is?" She held her breath.

"I might have some information. Tonight, I will send a carriage for you and we can have a discussion. Until then." He strode off to Lord Rosemore's office upstairs, leaving Liz excited and curious how Madoc would happen to know of Jon's whereabouts.

———

Liz was nervous as she waited just inside the two massive front doors. Nora had already informed her earlier in the afternoon that Council Madoc had requested that she be made available for a dinner consultation. Because of the esteem Council Madoc commanded the request was immediately granted, and the outing was not going to count against one of the two evenings a week she was allowed outside Lord Rosemore's castle.

Presently the door servant answered the door and a black-cloaked carriage driver stood with his hands behind his back.

"Council Madoc is here to see a Miss Liz O'Doul. Please inform her that his carriage awaits her." He gave a quick nod and disappeared.

Liz sprang forward to the door, smoothing out her best dress as she did so. Council Madoc was standing by the open door and smiled broadly as she approached.

"Ah, Miss O'Doul, you do look lovely this evening. Thank you for agreeing to our meeting."

Liz mumbled a reply and disappeared outside to the waiting silver and black carriage pulled by two black horses. She glanced back at the castle and saw several servants eyeing her departure. Apparently, rumours were rampant after her date with Anthony Graham, and now with Council Madoc they were wondering what a simple hostess could be up to.

The carriage travelled for several minutes before beginning an uphill journey to an area where street lamps were lit at the corners of the blocks. Council Madoc answered her questions on the various buildings and sights they passed, content to allow her to stare out the curtained window. Several other carriages were parked along the broad street and Council Madoc's carriage stopped in one of the free spots.

A guard stood at the doorway of the stone building but moved aside at their approach. A servant bowed and led them past a curtained doorway into the restaurant. The tables were placed at a generous distance from each other. Most of them had guests enjoying dinner and a few of them looked up as they passed, acknowledging Council Madoc. Their table was set at the back and enjoyed an open window that overlooked a flower garden. A series of lanterns hanging from trees lit the surrounding area and the yellow light gave an exotic appearance to the garden.

After Liz had a few minutes to enjoy the sight and smell of the garden Council Madoc waved at a waiter, who came over to recite the current menu. He poured two glasses of a dark red wine and stood off to the side to give them time to make a meal selection.

Madoc chose venison while Liz decided the chicken was a better choice. After Liz sampled the wine, she declared it much better than the product she had with evening meals at Lord Rosemore's.

Council Madoc chuckled. "I do hope so. There is a bit of a cost difference." His tone changed. "I suppose we should discuss some business at hand. First, perhaps I should clarify who I am and what I do for a living."

"I was told that you collect and sell information."

He held back his reply when the waiter came to serve their first dishes. "That is correct, although I like to think of it as a little more sophisticated than that. I use various means to obtain information and analyse it. My clients are usually kings, lords or various people of high influence and they depend on me to be accurate. You see, the various lords usually make an alliance with each other to prevent war. In this city alone, there are six lords of high standing and an equal number of lower status."

"I thought Lord Bennett ruled here. The city's name is Horstof?"

"Horstruff. Lord Bennett does the administration for the city with the support of the majority of the lords. That could change, depending on alliances and on King Charles' favour."

"King Charles? Where does he live?"

"His kingdom contains several counties, and he resides in what on Earth would be Wales. Of course, being king depends on the support of the lords as well. You can see it can be all rather complicated on who is planning what and with whom. When we add gnants and other creatures into the mix, it can get very messy indeed. That is where I come in."

"Since you know so much, why aren't you a lord?"

He laughed. "Because I can't. Lords are lords usually through birth or marriage and the majority of the lords must also support any appointment. Occasionally a nobleman can be promoted, but that is rare and I would never be raised to that position of power."

"May I ask why?"

"Of course. I would have too much influence then. The other lords are cognizant of my knowledge and that I'm also a warlock. Magic still brings fear to the lords."

Liz sat up straighter. "A warlock?"

"You seem surprised. Don't be, magic is fairly common on this world. A warlock on Domum doesn't mean the same on Earth. Here it means a person using magic who doesn't belong to the witches' guild." He took a long drink of his wine. "But let us move the discussion on to your boyfriend. My business is based on honesty. What I tell my clients is always the truth and I expect the same from those who sell me information. Thus, what I have to say about Sir Jon is the truth as I know it and in return, I ask you to answer any question you are able to. Agreed?"

"Yes, if you can help me find Jon."

"I didn't say that exactly but the information I have could help you with your search."

"Okay, what can you tell me?"

"Your boyfriend is currently going under the name of Sir Jon McKinney. No one has seriously challenged his adoption of the title Sir and is not likely to do so. He is currently in a part of this world that would correspond with Earth's southern France and is on a quest with several others to help him. Jon is searching for a Voltaire crystal that he requires to be able to return to Earth."

"Who is with him on this quest?"

"Gilbert is one, the dwarf who got him into trouble in the first place. There is Nathan, one of the freelance soldiers who serves as the group's protector. In addition, a sensitive named Lady Karla, though I'm not certain of her status now. The guide and leader is Sir Keith. He fancies himself as an explorer and an adventurer but is limited in experience. And there is also Nicole Keaton, a former barmaid."

"What's she doing on this journey?"

"Let us say that Jon and she have become friends, and he has decided to help her to return to Earth."

"What? Just how good a friend is she?" Liz crossed her arms, dropping her fork on her plate with a clatter.

"I'm not privy to all the details but as far as I know it has been a platonic relationship."

"It better be. I go chasing after him to another world and if he's been doing anything that doesn't fall under the guidelines of friendship, he'd better sleep with one eye open."

"Try not to jump to conclusions. I'm sure I don't know all the facts concerning them."

"Hmmp. He had better be careful, that's all he needs to know." She pushed at her potatoes with her fork. "How long is this journey going to take? Is it dangerous?"

"Another week at least before they can get back. And there is danger from gnants. They are under the assumption Jon has a rare crystal. Do you know anything about it?"

"Not really. I saw a crystal around his neck tied by a leather string. It was an odd shaped, like a twisted tube. Kind of had a bluish tinge to it."

"Where did he get it from?"

"His uncle left it to him in a will. I understand it's supposed to be important."

"And the uncle's name?"

"Gordon Miller, he's the owner of the Miller castle. It corresponds to Lord Bennett's castle here."

Council Madoc rolled his eyes upward. "Of course, I should have deduced that earlier. No matter, it does explain a lot, like why gnants are trying to kill him."

"They're trying to kill him? We've got to help him!"

"Lower your voice. There isn't much I can do and you're certainly in a poor position to lend assistance. Rest assured he can take care of himself."

"Jon isn't much of a fighter."

"No? Apparently, he has killed a large dragon and has been given the title of Sir Jon, the dragon slayer. That sounds like a fighter to me."

"Jon killed a dragon? Wow, I never would have guessed. That's so brave." She sat back on her chair, barely breathing.

Council Madoc shook his head. "You have a tendency to overreact to news, my dear. Care for some dessert? They make a lovely orange cake here."

Liz was eventually returned to Lord Rosemore's castle. She felt better knowing Jon was all right and begged Madoc to keep her updated on Jon's progress. The morning came too early after her late night and one wine goblet too many.

She tried to ward off questions from Rita and Roxy, claiming there wasn't much to tell.

Rita wasn't giving in. "Come on, tell us what Council Madoc wanted. What did he ask you? It had to be something important."

"Oh, it was nothing, really. But he did tell me something about Jon."

"What?"

"He killed a dragon, a big one. And now they call him Sir Jon, the dragon slayer. Isn't that wonderful?"

Roxy laughed. "Wonderful for him anyway. He's got his pick of the ladies now."

Liz stared at her two friends. Maybe they were just teasing me about him and other women. Maybe.

———

"Lady Monique wants to see you. I'm to take over while you're gone."

Liz acknowledged the brunette, looking cheerful as she entered the reception room. Liz considered the girl was likely happy to take over her job, being one of the most sought-after positions for the women servants. "Okay. Is she in her sitting room?"

"No, I believe you will find her in the new solar room."

Liz knew her way well enough around the castle, often escorting visitors to various parts of the castle. She hadn't been in the solar room before and only knew it had been extensively remodeled last year. The new larger room had become a favourite place for the Rosemore family.

A guard stood at the entrance of the solar room, blocking her path.

"Lady Monique requests my presence."

He turned and opened the heavy wood door. Liz entered, looking at bright sunlight that entered into the room. One wall featured multiple sheets of distorted glass, allowing the sun to warm and brighten the room. Lady Monique rested on a lounging chair, her bare legs exposed from the open gown. The top was closed, but Liz could see bare skin between the halves.

"You wished to see me, Lady Monique."

"Yes, please sit." She gestured to one of the silk upholstered armchairs.

Liz sat as Lady Monique changed her position on the lounge, placing her bare feet on the floor. Her gown remained opened over her legs. "I do enjoy this room. I have a bath on the other side of the room in which I occasionally indulge. Other times I like to relax in the sun. The reason for the guard at the door is that I enjoy sunbathing in the nude. Does that shock you?"

"No, not at all."

"But you're from the Other-side so I suspect you've seen many things that aren't common here."

"True."

"Good. I placed you as hostess for a few reasons. You're smart, speak well and perhaps most important of all, very pretty."

"Thank you, I understand."

"To be clear, I was looking for a new hostess when I purchased you at the Labour House. I was also there at the request of Lady Luanda Graham to purchase her son. She is quite worried about him and knew I would ensure he would be taken care of. I understand you are good friends with him and there is some romance between you two."

"I am his friend but there isn't any romance."

"No? A handsome, educated man like him doesn't attract you? Do you like only women?"

"Oh, no. I do like men. But I have someone else."

"I see. But you're not married or otherwise committed?"

"No."

"Then I don't see the problem if you like him." She stood. "Come with me. I have a special task for you." Lady Monique walked to a wardrobe. She slipped off her gown, standing nude as she removed a dress from a section. She stepped into the dress and turned to Liz. "Would you please tie me up at the back?"

"Of course, Lady Monique." She pulled on the string ties that drew in the sides of the green and yellow flowered dress.

"A bit tighter. I need to show that I still have a figure."

"I'm sure you attract attention whatever you wear."

Lady Monique laughed. "Yes, and partly because I don't like wearing undergarments unless I have to." She put on a pair of shoes and beckoned Liz to follow her. "I'm known to have a shameful side. Fortunately, Lord Dungan does not discourage my adventures."

They left the solar room, making their way to the third level.

"I want to inquire if Anthony is doing well and if you perceive if he is having any difficulties."

"He seems to be doing well after the initial shock of being told to work in the stables. He said he enjoys working with horses and not being drunk all the time."

"That's good to hear. I'll pass that on to Lady Luanda."

They entered a large room and Liz immediately noticed the smell of paint. An older man with a beard, standing slightly stooped as he worked, looked up.

"Lady Monique, is this our new subject?" He spoke in a raspy voice.

"Yes, she is." Lady Monique turned to her. "Please disrobe. Sir Winston will be painting you."

"Disrobe? He's going to paint me in the nude?"

"Correct. Do you have a strong moral objection to this?"

"No, I was just surprised." Liz took off her garments, leaving them folded on a chair. She was instructed to lie on her side on a bench, the wood seating worn smooth with age. One hand supported her head, and the other reached down to her lower stomach.

Lady Monique gazed at Liz. "Tell me, do most women remove most of their hair down there?"

"Uh, yes. It's not uncommon, anyway."

"I like the look. I may have to consider that for myself. After you're finished, here you may return to your usual position. Sir Winston may require more than one visit from you."

Liz tried to relax as much as possible as Sir Winston worked on the canvas. He didn't talk much, occasionally stepping closer to her to obtain a different view.

"Okay, let's take a tea break."

He took off his smock, covered with colourful marks of paint. "Let us sit near the window. I get tired of looking at the walls in front of me."

Liz walked over to the balcony that provided most of the light for the studio. A round table with three chairs stood to the side.

"Sit down. I'll get us some tea." He tottered over to the fireplace and retrieved a pail. A few minutes later he poured water into a small pot on the table. "We wait a bit for the leaves to soak." He produced a flask and poured a yellow liquid into two tiny cups. "This be whisky."

He plumped down on the chair. "You warm enough? I can get you a blanket."

Liz realized she wasn't uncomfortable nude in front of him. "No, I'm fine. Do you know why Lady Monique wants a painting of me?"

"Ah, there be a lot of paintings in the castle. I've done many of the paintings that are placed on the walls of the castle. Lots of landscapes. Some dragons and war scenes and a few paintings of women. Some of them are partially undressed. But Lady Monique likes nudes done for her private rooms. I have done a few for her, including a couple of the lady herself. These paintings are hung in the boudoir and in the master bedroom. I believe your painting will be given to Lord Dungan as a gift. Perhaps it will be placed in his study. There are rumours that she enjoys men and ladies. So be it. I hold her in the highest regard. She allows me much freedom in my paintings."

Liz sipped at the whisky, finding the drink strong. She was glad when the tea was ready and could wash down the taste. The whisky did warm her up and helped her relax.

"We need to do some more painting. Not too much. We will finish tomorrow."

Liz resumed her position on the bench. *This is actually exciting. A nude painting of me.*

———

The brunette reluctantly gave up her spot near the entrance area of the castle when Liz returned. "It was nice to stand around here and see all the important gentlemen and ladies come and go. I guess it's back to work for me now."

Liz checked to make sure the refreshment bar was filled and checked with the doorman to inquire if any guests were expected.

"No, Miss Liz. I believe it to be a quiet night."

"Thanks, I think I'll go for a walk. I'll be back in a bit." She knew the doorman, an older gentleman, would simply usher any guest to the sitting room. She thanked him and went for a walk down a hallway. The hallway led to an exit and from there a small walk took her to the stables.

She entered the open doors of the stable and stopped to watch Anthony Graham. He was tossing hay with a pitchfork from the ground floor to an upper loft. He was shirtless and his back gleamed with sweat.

"Tony."

He turned around and tossed away the pitchfork when he saw her. He smiled and made his way to her.

"How are you doing, Liz?"

"I'm not working as hard as you, that's for sure."

He laughed. "Yes, but strangely enough I'm enjoying it. My muscles ache but it's good to be doing honest labour."

"I can see you've been working out." She looked at his chest, his muscles giving his shoulders a definition of strength.

"What's new with you? I'm afraid to say not much is happening in the stables."

"Hmm. Well, don't go broadcasting this but I posed for a painting for Lady Rosemore."

"One thing at a time. What is broadcasting?"

She laughed. "Sorry. It's an Earth expression. It means telling everyone."

"Ah, I understand. Why shouldn't I tell anyone you posed for a painting?"

"Because I was naked at the time. Somewhere in the castle a picture of me in the nude is going to be hung."

"Wow, I would love to see that."

"I'm sure you would but it's not going to happen."

"You do love to tease, don't you?"

"Only those I like."

"Will you come for a ride with me? I'm allowed to take the horses out for exercise. I want to show you the sights of the town."

"I don't know. I haven't ridden much. In fact, the last time I was on a horse was when I was in grade school."

"I promise I'll put you on a nice, slow horse."

"I have to get back to the front doors. I'll think about the horse ride."

SIXTEEN

Jon woke up just as the sun rose above the horizon, casting a reddish glow in the room. He looked across at Nicole sleeping quietly on her side facing him. He decided he wasn't going to sleep anymore and might as well get out of bed after spending most of the night tossing and turning.

He tried to be quiet as he used the washroom. He also made use of the razor he took from Lord Perry's guest room, carefully trimming away his beard. With only a couple of minor cuts, he finished and made his way downstairs.

Breakfast in the dining room was a quiet affair, and he shared the large room with only a few other people. He ate quietly and tried to think of what he should be doing next. Somehow his quest had gotten away from his control. He was sure Sir Keith was still heading toward Cretal as fast as possible but now with the problem with gnants his confidence was wavering that they would reach there.

He ordered two glasses of orange juice from a waiter and took them back up to his room.

Nicole opened her eyes as he closed the door. She yawned and sat up in bed, mumbling good morning. She took the orange juice glass gratefully. "Thanks. Boy, I had a great sleep for a change, didn't you?"

"It was alright. Nicole, tell me more about gnants. All I know about them is that they're supposed to be half demon creatures. What do they want? Just the crystal?"

"Well, to tell the truth I don't know all the details myself. But from what I understand they're native to this world and humans showed up afterward. They're not too common around here because they prefer warmer and more humid areas. As we journey to Cretal you'll see more and more of them.

"They don't like being around humans or each other very much, not too social at all. They're good in magic. They have a natural ability to use it but don't flaunt it much as far as I can tell. They love crystals and steal as many as they can, but what for its hard to say.

"As I said they don't like people much and they barely tolerate us. They would like it if the lot of us would go back to our world. Fortunately, they're not well organized and lost a couple of skirmishes with humans in the far past. That's about it, except they have their own language but can learn English well enough."

"Okay, thanks. I wish I knew more about this world. I'm going for a stroll. See you later."

"Okay. While you do that, I'm going to do something I've been wanting to do since I arrived here."

———

Jon walked around the area of the High Park Lodge after Nicole announced she was going to take a long, hot bath. He knew he didn't need to see Nicole taking a bath after spending the night with her. The temptation would be rather strong.

The brick streets were clean and the people walking along them, for the most part, seemed to be strolling along in their Sunday best. He reminded himself this was like a holiday resort for the rich on his own world.

It certainly looked well maintained with an abundance of flowering plants, small ponds set off from main walks in small parks and fountains. Jon remembered Gilbert telling him all he had to do was just look around and there would be evidence of magic. Stone Retreat could have been created by normal engineering methods he supposed, but more likely there was a lot of magic used to build and maintain it.

His feet carried him toward the downtown area. Merchants had opened their shops, and some were standing on the sidewalks to greet prospective customers. He noticed the sidewalk was clear of additional tables shopkeepers normally put out, apparently the local laws forbid such unsightly obstructions. Down the street, a small cluster of people grouped around a roped off area and Jon decided to investigate.

He stayed in the background and listened to an announcement that Lord Batten and his family had generously donated the construction of a new fountain for Stone Retreat. Polite applause issued forth and two black-cloaked men stepped near the edge of the restraining rope. They first stared at the open area where the fountain was to be constructed and turned their attention to an artist drawing of the finished work. The ten-foot fountain was to have a pair of water nymphs playing underneath a small waterfall. The whole fountain was to be made out of two types of stone, a light grey rock for the fountain and a dark yellow for the nymphs.

There was a hush from the gathered crowd, as if they were watching a long putt at a golf tournament. At first little happened and then a cloud of white smoke started to form in the centre of the roped off area. It began to turn darker in some areas as it expanded in volume, coiling around itself and solidifying for a brief moment. Gradually, the outline of the fountain began to appear, appearing solid for a second before misting into smoke again. The fountain slowly pulsed into solid form, a weak yellow light emanating from within the structure.

Jon noticed the temperature had dropped during the creation of the fountain with cool air swirling around him. Several of the others had crossed their arms to ward off the chill.

The black-cloaked magicians had now focused their attention on the almost solid fountain, throwing their outstretched hands at the form.

Jon heard a sudden crack, like the snap of a whip coming from the center of the fountain, and the crowd burst into applause. Water poured down on the nymphs in a fountain that looked like it had been there for years.

The magicians gasped for air and quietly walked away. The speaker heaped more praise on Lord Batten.

Jon stood in awe of what he just saw. He had to admit there wasn't a shadow of doubt that this world used magic. How he wasn't sure, but he couldn't deny it any longer.

Jon took a different route back to the hotel. The temperature continued to rise, and he decided to have a drink at one of the taverns before he returned to the hotel. He walked through the main entrance and was surprised that a large foyer separated the pub from where one could check one's coat. He turned toward the pub when he felt a hand restrain his arm.

"Excuse me sir. Your name and title would be?"

Jon appraised the tall man in a white shirt and black pants, looking like a maître d'. "I would be Sir Jon McKinney. And who would you be?" Jon squared himself in front of the smaller built man.

The maître d's face went pale. "Sir, Sir Jon McKinney? The dragon slayer?"

"The one and same."

"Oh, a thousand pardons Sir McKinney. I hadn't known, do please forgive my clumsiness." He turned toward the pub. "Noreen!"

A moment later a young woman dressed in a green dress appeared at the door. "Yes sir?"

"This is Sir Jon McKinney, the dragon slayer. Show him to our best table and the house will buy anything he desires. Understood?"

"Yes, sir." She smiled and curtsied before leading Jon to a table on the second level by an open window, looking out to the open forests beyond Stone Retreat.

The ale was the best he had since Lord Perry's castle and his tankard never came close to being emptied before being replaced. Food arrived soon after he ordered it, and Noreen was never more than five steps away in case he required anything. He was surprised at the attention he received for being a dragon slayer.

When Jon returned to the hotel, he was partially drunk but in a very good mood. Nicole was in the lobby drinking tea when she spotted him entering the front doors.

She put her hands on her hips and shook her head. "Typical man. Free time on his hands and he goes out drinking. Do you need to lie down or do you want to eat lunch?"

"Neither. I ate already. Where's the rest?"

"I haven't kept track. Lady Karla disappeared early this morning according to Gilbert. And Gilbert was later caught trying to steal hotel silverware. Sir Keith managed to smooth out that and has been mapping out our next route in his room.

Nathan was also looking for you to give some more sword fighting lessons. You might find him in the dining lounge."

"Great. More pain."

"By the way you are now known as the dragon slayer. That dragon you injured saving Gilbert succumbed to its injuries. Congratulations." She took a deep breath, looking partially annoyed and pleased with him at the same time.

"Thanks. I better go and look for Nathan."

―――――

Nathan was just finishing his lunch when Jon sat across from him.

"Sorry, I didn't know you planned another lesson. I've had a few ales already."

"You've been hanging around with Gilbert too much. Still the lessons will be good, one doesn't get to choose when one gets attacked and you can't always be at a hundred percent."

Jon groaned inwardly.

―――――

Two hours later Jon limped into his room and fell face first on the bed. The wooden swords used in practice didn't cut but left welts and bruises instead.

No matter what Jon tried he couldn't do much damage on Nathan. The big man moved with amazing grace and agility, defending Jon's attacks and returning them with several blows each time. Still Nathan praised him, telling him he had improved considerably since the first lesson.

A half hour later Jon rolled slowly onto his back and used a trembling arm to push himself in a sitting position. He pulled off his shirt and looked at the red marks on his chest. He shook his head. *A tiger has fewer stripes than this.*

Nicole walked in from her own room using the connected doorway. Without knocking, he noted.

"Hi, how are you feeling? Nathan really gave you a lesson, did he?"

"I had him crying for mercy."

She laughed. "Want me to draw you a bath?"

"I dunno. I think I just want to sit here."

"You smell of beer and sweat. You need a bath and besides the hot water will ease the bruises." She walked to the bathroom and turned on the water, calling out to him. "I'll make up some ointment as well while you soak."

Jon used his feet to kick off his sandals and gradually walked to the bathroom. She stood there testing the water.

"Okay, I don't think it's too hot for you. Aren't you going to take off your pants first?"

He looked at her and the bath. "A gentleman doesn't walk unclothed in front of a lady."

She laughed. "Oh, I see we have both been given a promotion." She walked out of the bathroom, leaving Jon alone with his pain.

The hot water, after he got used to it did seem to ease the pain. This was especially true on his back where he'd landed too many times after Nathan's counter attacks. The marble stone used in the tub held the heat of the water a long time, and he didn't need to add much hot water to maintain the temperature. He closed his eyes, enjoying the warmth of the water as it eased away his aches. He was startled when Nicole waltzed into the bathroom again, apparently not concerned about his need for modesty.

"Here, I bought you some tea. I put some whisky in it as well. Feeling any better?"

"Yeah, a bit better." He massaged the bar of soap again, trying to supply the surface with bubbles but the water dissipated the foam.

"Good. I went to a shop and picked up some stuff for those welts. I'll rub it on when you're finished in here."

"Just leave the stuff here. I'll put it on later myself."

"Don't be silly. How can you reach your back?" She put her hands on her hips. "You may be the first man I ever met who didn't want me to give him a massage. Stop being so damn shy and let me help you. So you're naked. I've seen a lot of naked men before. It's no big deal." Nicole walked out, leaving Jon to wonder if Nicole could have been a nurse.

The water had finished its healing effects and Jon climbed out of the tub, using what passed for a towel on Domum to dry himself. He heard Nicole call out from the bedroom.

"Wrap the towel around you and I'll use that cream."

The towel barely circled his waist, and he held the ends together with one hand. He entered the bedroom and Nicole pointed at the bed. "Okay, lie down." She held a ceramic jar in her hands.

He rested on the bed on his stomach. Moments later Nicole rubbed the cream on his back. The cream was initially cool on his skin but Nicole's hands warmed up the lotion as she applied it. To his dismay, she ignored the boundary of his towel, going past the top portion. He wasn't sure just what was in the ointment and wondered if Nicole put some magic in it, but it did work wonders. "Thanks, that feels good."

"You're welcome. In some ways, I'm just along on this quest as a passenger. So, I'm glad to help out any way I can, including taking care of injuries. Please don't act funny when I try to help you."

"Alright." She finished his back, massaging some ointment on the back of his right thigh. "Turn around. I'll put some cream on your chest."

Jon twisted around, using his hand to ensure the towel covered him. Nicole worked on his chest as she sat on the edge of the bed.

"Those marks look pretty sore."

"Believe me, they are." He closed his eyes, enjoying the touch of her hands.

"That should help." She stopped massaging and rested a hand on his chest. "I was glad to do it."

"Thanks." He opened his eyes, watching her leave the room.

Jon checked the towel. It had a definite lift to it. *I hope she didn't notice that.* He rolled off the bed and dressed, suddenly feeling hungry. The main floor contained the main dining room, but he choose a smaller lounge on the third floor. He picked a table near the balcony and looked out at the forest that covered the surrounding hills like a blanket. The meat was venison and he could taste the gaminess. The rest of the food, turnips and corn, tasted fine. He washed down the dinner with wine. The pain had largely disappeared from his sword lesson from Nathan and he thought a walk would help. That walk ended up in a lounge on the main floor, where he found Sir Keith and Gilbert.

Sir Keith inquired how he was feeling. "I saw part of the lesson Nathan was giving you. He certainly wasn't holding back on his blows. You must still be hurting."

"No, not too bad."

Gilbert added, "Drink more ale. That always helps with any problem."

Jon laughed. "Or creates them." He finished his ale and announced he was going to turn in. "I think my body needs a bit more recovery time that I won't get drinking in here."

He didn't want to stay out too late, knowing Sir Keith wanted to leave at daybreak. Still it was long past dark by the time he made it to his room, only to find Nicole sleeping in his bed.

He sighed and quietly undressed, determined to try to forget she was sleeping right next to him. He found it too warm in his room and opening the shutter didn't have much effect. The outside air was warm and without movement. He left his pants on, although they were uncomfortable to sleep in. Unlike the others on the journey, he didn't have spare clothes. He asked Sir Keith about purchasing additional clothing but was told Stone Retreat was an expensive place to purchase any goods.

He closed his eyes and almost instantly fell asleep, not waking until he heard Sir Keith pounding on his door as a wake-up call. He called out, "I'm awake."

The room was still dark, and he noticed his arm was under Nicole's neck with her facing him. She stirred after his shout and her hand briefly stroked his chest.

She groaned. "Why do we have to get up when it's still dark?"

Jon yawned. "I guess it's because we have a long way to travel today." He waited, not wanting to move his trapped arm until she was ready to rise.

Nicole pressed a hand against his ribs and slid out of bed. She lit a lantern sitting on a table and made her way to her room carrying her clothes, save for the top she was wearing that covered her to her hips. "See you downstairs."

Jon looked at her leave, admiring her legs. *This sleeping arrangement is getting a tad frustrating.*

———

Jon ate breakfast, sitting across from Nicole who chatted away about the weather, food and the hotel's furnishings. Occasionally he nodded or spoke a word or two but for the most part just listened to her ramble on. Jon waved at Gilbert, who was consuming his second ale, and at Nathan. Nathan was eating a large mound of food but he took a moment to acknowledge him.

Sir Keith walked into the dining lounge and approached Jon and Nicole at their table. "Have either of you seen Lady Karla?"

After the others confirmed they had not seen her, Sir Keith elaborated. "I knocked on her door twice. The first time she didn't respond I assumed she needed a bit more shut-eye. However, she has not answered the second call, and I am worried."

Nicole asked, "Did you check inside her room?"

"No, I am a gentleman and would not enter a lady's chamber without an invitation."

Gilbert laughed. "Ye be waiting a longs time."

Nicole gave Gilbert a sharp look. "I suggest we go up to her room right now. I'll enter first if you feel that's proper."

All of them, including the burping Gilbert, followed Sir Keith to Lady Karla's room. Once again, he thumped on her door and called out.

"Let's go in." Nicole pulled on the door latch and pushed open the door.

Lady Karla lay on the floor face down, her arms and legs sprawled about her. Her long nightgown was torn in several places. Nicole rushed to her, turning her over. Blood seeped from her forehead, cheek and a gash on her forearm.

"She's breathing. Let's get her onto her bed."

Lady Karla suffered from several cuts and bruises as well as a gouge in her back. Sir Keith hurried out of the room and summoned the healer the hotel had available for guests.

Nicole stayed with the healer, an older, thin woman. The men were ushered outside of the room.

Sir Keith paced the up and down the hallway. Jon tried to reassure him, "I'm sure she'll be all right. The healer will help with her injuries and she was regaining consciousness when we left the room."

"I do hope she'll be all right. Lady Karla is not used to the physical exertion of our trip and these injuries will take a lot out of her."

Nathan sighed. "No point in all of us waiting here. I shall go and check on our horses and see if I can obtain some dry provisions for later."

"I needs a beer." Gilbert walked away, leaving Jon and the anxious Sir Keith to wait.

The door opened, and the healer gave them a word of caution. "She is fine but will need bed rest."

Sir Keith rushed in. "Lady Karla, how are you faring?"

"Better now. Thank you for getting a healer for me." Lady Karla sat with two pillows behind her. The blanket was drawn up to her neck, and her nightgown folded at the foot of the bed.

"You are most welcome. What happened, if I may ask?"

"I was attacked by…by, I don't know."

Nicole asked, "Did you see anything?"

"No, it was dark."

"Was anything stolen?"

"I don't know. I'm very tired. I do wish to be left alone for a while.

Sir Keith answered, "Of course. We will withdraw immediately."

They left Lady Karla to rest with Sir Keith suggesting they meet in his room to discuss the situation.

Jon agreed. "I'll get Gilbert and Nathan."

After Jon left, Sir Keith spoke to Nicole. "I didn't think it was appropriate to badger Lady Karla with your questions. The poor woman was attacked and was still in a state of shock. In the future, you need to recognize your station and not treat Lady Karla as if you were equal status with her."

"I was merely asking for information to help identify who and why she was attacked."

"That may well be but if your attitude prevails, I will make a report to Lord Perry concerning your behaviour. You are still a slave."

Nicole seethed but decided against rebuffing his statement.

"One other thing, I am quite aware of your night time relationship with Sir Jon. I have no objections to this, other than to tell you to be discreet. He is known as Sir Jon, the dragon slayer and has a reputation to uphold."

Nicole's jaw dropped. *His reputation! What about mine you pompous moron?*

When they reached his room, he gallantly opened the door and allowed her to enter first. "I believe our discussion on these matters are over and there will be no need to mention them to the others. Wine?" He walked to where a cabinet held a flagon of wine and several cups.

"Please." *I suppose he'd think it would be proper if I curtsy in front of his presence.* She noted the room was considerably larger than Jon's and her own and with more amenities. Jon and Gilbert arrived and Sir Keith addressed them. "This is a most unfortunate and unexpected situation. I cannot think of any reason why Lady Karla was attacked so viciously." He squeezed his hand into a fist, shaking it a moment before continuing. "We have a problem and it now appears Lady Karla will not be available for travel for some time. I suggest we're unable to delay our journey that long and set forth without her."

Nathan crossed his arms as he sat back in an armchair. "What about the crystals? Wasn't she supposed to pick out the best type? I can't think of any other reason we need her."

Nicole responded. "I can inspect crystals to some degree. I'm not as good as Lady Karla in knowledge but I can sense different crystals. We could also hire someone with knowledge of crystals when we arrive there."

Gilbert jumped from the chair he was sitting in. "Looks, I'm sure we cans make it to Cretal and beyond without her. We finds crystals as well. But can anyone figure out whys she was attacked? It looked to me to be the work of gnants and I thinks they left her for dead. What did she have that they wanted?"

Nicole added, "I tried to ask her what happened but she said she didn't know anything." She saw Sir Keith stare at her but carried on. "That attack happened for a reason. That looked like a Gnant attack and they always have reasons for doing something like that."

Nathan nodded. "Gilbert's right. That attack may not be random. She had, or knew something, they wanted. Did they get it? One thing is Lady Karla isn't being very cooperative, she knows more than she's telling."

Sir Keith acted surprised. "Please, we should not speculate on her virtue. I believe the consensus is we carry on to Cretal without Lady Karla."

Jon listened to the discussion without speaking, the group arriving to the same conclusion as he did. He did agree there was something odd with Lady Karla's refusal to provide any information on the attack. Someone or something had hit her on the face and her arms showed signs she'd protected herself and therefore she had to have seen the attacker. Still she had declined comment on the attack, leaving Jon to wonder what she was hiding.

Sir Keith exited from the room to see about arrangements for Lady Karla's care. "I believe she should stay at the hotel in Stone Retreat to rest. When we return, we can aid her return to Lord Perry's castle."

Nicole turned to Jon and whispered, "Stay here. I'm going to have a little talk with that witch."

———

Nicole entered Lady Karla's room after knocking.

"I want to check on you and ask you a couple of questions."

"I don't want to talk right now."

"I understand. That was quite an ordeal." She poured Lady Karla a glass of juice from a ceramic pitcher sitting on the night table. "Are you from the Other-side originally? I was."

She took the orange juice and nodded. "A long time ago."

"I wish I could go back, I miss my little girl and husband. Is there family for you back there?"

Lady Karla swallowed and looked down. "Not that I remember. I arrived here as an infant or so my mother told me."

Nicole nodded and snapped a question at her. "Did you make a deal with the gnants to try to get back to the Other-side?"

She shook her head. "No, don't be ridiculous. I know enough magic to accomplish that myself, if I desire." Lady Karla tried to retreat in the bed, looking down and away from Nicole.

"Gnants tore apart Jon's clothing looking for a crystal. Only Jon, myself and you knew about the crystal. You had to have told them that Jon has a certain crystal. You were the only one who could have. What did they promise you?" Nicole jabbed a finger at Lady Karla.

She glared at Nicole. "Nothing you would understand, you simpleton."

"Try me."

"Power, enough magic that I could do anything." She squeezed her fists. "Enough magic I could be young again, travel back and forth to Earth as many times as I wanted, to make gold out of wood. But you'll never understand that will you? You have your ignorant youth, your nights with Jon. What does someone like you comprehend of needs, of the mystery, of the arts?"

"I'll tell you what I do understand in my ignorance, we all want something. But you sold out the others to gain something for yourself. Look in the mirror and see what you've bought yourself. Bitch."

Lady Karla winced. "I only told them." Her voice sounded strained, and she stopped to compose herself. "About the crystal, not how to get it." A tear ran down her cheek and she wiped it away with her hand.

"What's so damn special about the crystal?"

Lady Karla took a deep breath and slowly released it as she spoke, starig at a distant wall. "He has one of the six crystals that make up the Locas Crystal."

"Locas Crystal? Is that the one that makes a person invisible?"

"No, you're thinking of the Lerue Crystal. The Locas Crystal, when all the segments are joined together make the owner invincible, irresistible. It's like having a force about you."

"Who has the other segments?"

"The gnants have two, according to rumour. Lord Holdstock has two others kept in a safe place, assuming he hasn't forgotten where he's put them, the old fool. But where the last one is, no one knows."

Nicole got up to leave. "I'll warn Jon about the crystal."

"The gnants thought I lied to them about where the crystal was. That's why they attacked me."

"You're lucky they left you alive."

"I suppose so. I almost rather be dead." She touched the scar that ran along her cheek. "Please, I beg you. Don't tell the others what I've done."

"I'll think about it."

The two women stared at each other for several seconds before Lady Karla looked away. Nicole left the room, almost slamming the door behind her.

The road from Stone Retreat was excellent for the first few miles, and they met several travellers going toward the city. The other travellers often were in carriages to make their journey easier and the riding parties were much better equipped. The road branched out continuously and after several forks in the road it developed into more of a trail than a road.

Nicole took the opportunity to inform Jon what she had learned from Lady Karla as they rode together.

"I didn't think she was the type to sell out."

"Jon, you have a lot to learn about people. She rarely sat or talked to the others. She considered herself apart from our group and no doubt thought herself as superior. And resentful, didn't you notice that about her?"

"Well, now that you mentioned it. But still putting the rest of us in danger. I dunno, she must have been desperate I guess."

"If you had a chance to go back home by informing a gnant one of us had a treasure, would you do it?"

Jon pursed his lips and replied. "No, not if it put the others in danger. Thinking only for yourself causes problems."

She smiled. "I'm pleased to hear you say that."

———

Gilbert carefully slipped the gnant crier by his ear and listened for a few minutes. He shook his head as he replaced the device back into his backpack. The gnants he noted were especially noisy as the morning ended and there were several of them talking at once. He would have to be on alert for an attack, in particular at night.

Sir Keith called a stop for lunch and the rations were excellent, leftovers from their stay at Stone Retreat. Gilbert joined Nicole and Jon for lunch, not talking much himself but listening carefully to what they had to say. Nathan came up to Jon as he finished up his meal and informed him with the problems they were having lately, he thought another practice session with swords would be in order.

"Damn, I'm barely healed from the last round," he said to himself after Nathan had walked away.

Nicole touched his arm. "You need the practice, Jon, it could save your life."

"Yeah, that might be true but just once I would like to beat him."

"Just keep trying. With luck you might. He's an elite fighter, you know."

Gilbert chimed in. "You'll never win using his rules."

"What do you mean, Gilbert? What other rules are there?"

"Simple. He teaches you only part what he knows, but he still knows more. If you wanna win, you gotta use something he don'ts knows. Theres hasta be something you learns at the Other-side that you cans use."

"I didn't fight back at home and certainly no sword fights."

"Alls the same, you musta learns something back there you can use. Just gotta think it out."

Jon thought about what Gilbert said as the three of them made their way to the clearing where Nathan waited with his wooden swords carved out from the local tree branches.

Gilbert and Nicole sat down to watch as Jon and Nathan began the practice.

"Sword up higher, Jon! You're inviting an overhead smash. And keep your feet planted when you swing your sword, no power if you're not stable."

Jon nodded at Nathan's instruction. There was so much to learn about sword fighting and the technique was more difficult than he first guessed. It reminded him of his football coach yelling out constantly what do during practice. Jon remembered Gilbert saying he must know something from his time on the Other-side.

Whump! Jon found himself on his side from a quick blow to his knee and then to his shoulder. Nathan did so smoothly that it almost appeared to be one motion but actually involved several rotations of the sword to complete the manoeuvre.

Jon got up and resumed his stance, thinking about football and what he knew. Jon lowered his sword, squaring it in front of himself. Nathan saw the opening and as Jon expected, used an over the head hit. Usually Jon would back away from Nathan's blow or roll on the ground to avoid being hit. This time Jon kept his sword in front of him to protect his head and stepped up inside Nathan's swing.

Low man wins. Jon remembered hearing the voice of his coach yelling out to those working on blocking, a reference to whoever managed to get underneath his opponent's shoulder pads would usually win the battle. Jon planted his shoulder into the rib cage of Nathan and the bigger man grunted with surprise as his feet left the ground. He landed solidly on his back.

He stared up in surprise. "Where in hell did you learn that?"

"Football."

"Nicely done. I have to remember that one."

Jon glanced at Nicole, who clapped her hands together enthusiastically, and at Gilbert, who merely nodded.

Jon tried to think of other football techniques he knew and surprised Nathan on one or two moves. He didn't knock Nathan down again and landed on the ground several times himself. Still, he was pleased with his one knockdown and Nathan clapped him on the back with congratulations.

"You've learned quick, Jon."

"Thanks. You've taught me a lot."

"Aye. But I think you now know enough to handle yourself." He lowered his voice as he glanced in the direction of Sir Keith preparing his horse. "In fact, I'll wager you're a better fighter now than Sir Keith, so there's no need for more lessons. We might start hurting each other."

Nicole gave Jon a hug and a kiss on his cheek for his solitary victory.

"I'll bet it's the first time he's been knocked down in years."

. . .

Sir Keith clapped his hands to announce it was time to start off again. Jon slowly mounted his horse and followed the others back on the trail.

They rode without incident until an attack by a pair of tantus dragons. The flightless predators paced them first, moving noisily among the trees. The dragon's bodies were slightly longer than a horse with their tail almost doubling their length. They stood closer to the ground on their thick straight legs while a small set of wings twitched uselessly. The tantus dragons had evolved to live on the ground as their wings gradually shrunk.

Nathan called for the others to stay close to each other and moved his own horse to the front. One dragon increased its pace, running ahead to cut them off in front while the other moved behind them. Nathan yelled at Sir Keith to keep the group moving and charged ahead. As he approached the lead dragon, he fired his crossbow before he was in the range of the dragon's acid breath. The dragon roared in pain as two arrows pierced its hide, sending a cloud of acid at Nathan. Nathan moved his horse back to be safe as it rapidly dispersed before reaching him. Nathan fired another arrow at the dragon and it now retreated into the forest deciding to wait for easier prey.

The second dragon snorted at the rest of the group but decided if its partner was retreating, it would do so as well.

"Do dragons attack often like that here?" Jon found himself talking to Gilbert who had pulled his horse up to ride in the middle since the attack.

"Occasionally. Dragons don't 'tack people much. They must've been hungry."

"But these dragons were like those other ones, the large par dragons, and tried to attack from the front and rear. Is that how dragons usually attack?"

"No, just those types. The rest usually attacks in a pack, except for the fornido dragon. Big thing, hunts alone." Gilbert scanned the sky.

"What are you looking at, Gilbert?"

"Nothin'. Just looking."

Jon sighed. "Come on, Gilbert, does everything have to be a big secret?"

"Alright, alright. I'm looking for devil birds. They usually show up after tantus dragons attack, wantin' an easy meal. They won't do much to us but they spook the horses and sometimes shoot a bit of fire."

"Devil birds, they're those small ones that fly in flocks?"

"Yeah." Gilbert lowered his voice. "Tonight, be prepared. Gnants are around us." Gilbert let his horse drop behind before Jon could continue the conversation.

The camp was set up near a small stream and later, after starting a fire, Nathan disappeared to hunt, returning with rabbit sized creatures..

The game wasn't the only thing Nathan was looking for. There was something else in the forest that was calling for his attention and he casually turned back toward the camp with his hand gripping his cross-bow. He took two steps, twisted to his right and fired high into the trees. A screech answered back as a dark body fell from a branch. Nathan wasn't finished as he continued his turn and fired a second shot behind him. This time there wasn't an accompanying cry as the arrow found its mark, but the result was much the same as a second gnant fell

Nathan was concerned the gnants he killed might be part of a larger group gathering together. The climate was warm and more suited for gnants so it was possible they merely lived in the area. Nathan decided tonight he had to be better prepared. He started two more campfires at each end of the tents as well as the original centre fire.

Sir Keith nodded his approval. "That should render attacks from the sides less feasible."

"Yeah, but if they're out, there they'll still attack."

Sir Keith pointed at Gilbert's tent set away from the rest. "Is that going to be a problem?"

Nathan shook his head. "I don't know what the dwarf is up to at times but he sure as hell wouldn't put his neck in danger for any reason. He can stay there if he wants to."

"He's sure spending a long time inside that tent. Do you think he's up to something?"

"Probably, but it's not my concern."

It was later than normal when everyone, save for Nathan, turned in. The evening hadn't provided much relief from the daytime heat and Jon was too warm as he undressed inside his tent. He remembered Gilbert's warning about gnants and kept his sword close as he slowly drifted off to sleep.

———

Nathan sat as usual with his back to the fire when he spotted a movement at the edge of the forest. He stood quickly with his sword raised, his short-range crossbow dangling from his hip. In a few seconds he saw several gnants running toward him. He shouted out a warning at the tents and reached for his crossbow.

Nicole sleep was disturbed by Nathan's shouting. She opened her eyes, seeing the canvas cover of her tent give off a soft glow from the campfires. Shadows flicker across the top when suddenly a dark shape landed on the tent. Nicole heard the sound of the cloth being cut open. Suddenly a gaunt fell through the opening.

Nicole sat up, screaming.

"Quiet human. Where isss the cryaaatal?"

———

A gnant named Ryeel entered the small human's tent, thinking he may have the easiest of the tasks. The dwarf had his chance to divulge information and now was to be killed. The dwarf was smaller and slower than the gnant and Ryeel didn't expect much of a challenge.

The first indication there was a problem was when he lowered his head inside the tent, finding it too dark. Ryeel surmised the dwarf had cast a spell that absorbed light. Still, the gnant could make out a mound where the dwarf slept and leaped with claws and knife extended. He landed on the soft pile, only to discover the pile of clothing and a blanket was an illusion, another magic spell. Ryeel, spun around, finding the dwarf had been behind him. He was too late to react, as a knife pierce his chest. He looked down in surprise and in the dark could see his blood gushing out as he collapsed to the ground.

———

Nathan had his hands full with two gnants attacking him. He managed to kill another with his crossbow as they charged him and now tried to cover his rear and front at the same time by backing toward a tree to use as a shield. He spotted Sir Keith, wearing only breeches, struggling against the lone gnant attacking him. *That fight is not going well for Sir Keith.*

. . .

Sir Keith was tired and puffing heavily as he wielded his sword. His left arm was bleeding and hurt from a deep knife wound. He hoped Nathan could come to help but the chance of that appeared remote. The sword became heavy in his arm as the gnant made quick movements with a knife.

———

Jon heard Nathan's shouted a warning and reached for his sword just as the gnant slipped through a tear in his tent. He sat up, watching the gnant turn a knife in his hand when he heard Nicole scream.

Jon lashed out with his sword at the gnant, cutting it along its legs as it raised the knife. As the gnant stumbled, Jon plunged his sword into its chest, killing it instantly when a second gnant jumped on him.

Jon rolled on his knees and flipped the gnant onto its back. There wasn't enough room to swing his sword as the gnant raised his knife. Jon dropped his sword and closed his fist, punching the gnant on the jaw. Jon heard the clack of teeth as the jaw closed violently and the creature lay limp on the ground. He jumped up and dashed outside his tent spotting two forms against the side of Nicole's tent. Jon didn't hesitate and threw himself at both figures, causing the tent to collapse under his weight. He heard Nicole scream again and decided the sound came from his right. He began to pound the other body with his fists until it stopped moving.

"Nicole! Are you okay?"

"I'm, I'm fine."

He helped her out of the tent and looked around, seeing Sir Keith struggling and almost ready to fall down from the fast moving gnant. "Hang on, Sir Keith!"

The gnant looked at Jon and decided to retreat, leaving an exhausted Sir Keith holding his damaged arm as he knelt to one knee. Jon returned to his tent to grab his sword.

Nathan was battling two gnants, when suddenly one fell face forward on the ground with a knife sticking out of its back. The other gnant was startled when its companion fell. It looked toward the tents where Jon was running with his sword raised. It turned and ran.

Nathan looked at Jon first and at Gilbert, who was casually approaching him. "Thanks, Gilbert, nice throw."

"Tis nothing, glad to help."

They gathered around Nicole's tent and checked inside but the gnant Jon had pummelled had disappeared. Nicole stood wearing just her blouse as Nathan and Jon inspected Jon's tent. Inside his tent they found an unconscious gnant and dragged him to the fire after tying his hands and legs.

"Here are your pants."

Jon turned to Nicole's voice, seeing her hold his pants.

"Oh, I forgot I wasn't wearing any." He quickly put them on.

She laughed. "I didn't forget. I better take care of Sir Keith's wounds."

"When that devil wakes up, we'll have a little talk with him." Nathan threw some water on its face but it remained still.

A half hour later the gnant stirred.

Nathan poked it with his sword. "Come on. We need some answers."

It looked up bewildered and confused.

"What were you looking for? Why did you attack us?"

It remained mute. Jon noticed it had a streak of white hair on its head and assumed the creature must be showing the sign of old age.

Nathan kicked him on his leg. "Speak, damn it!"

"Cryssstal. Only look for cryssstal." It looked at the crystal hanging on Jon's bare chest.

"Why? What's so important about a damn crystal?"

"Don't know, jusst told to find it."

"It's not telling everything it knows." Sir Keith spoke.

Nathan poked him with his sword. "Tell me more. I can do some slicing if you don't talk."

"Nooo, I not know more. Puleeze." It tried to squirm away.

"If you don't know anything more, then we don't need you alive, do we?"

It became frantic as it wiggled on the ground. "Puleeze let Rzet go. I do no more harm."

"I can guarantee that. You sure you know nothing more?"

The gnant squeezed his eyes shut and tried to roll away. Nathan raised his sword.

"Don't." Jon raised his hand in front of Nathan in a sudden move.

Nathan froze with his sword held high. "Don't? Why not? It can't help us any more."

"Yeah, but it can't hurt us any more either. We could just let it go."

Nathan looked surprised and amused. "It tried to kill you. You really want this thing wandering around us?"

Rzet open his eyes. "I do no more harm. Let go pleasse."

Jon dropped his hands down to his side. "To defend ourselves is one thing but to kill him while tied up like that is wrong. It's like murder."

Nathan shook his head. "It's up to you, but I'd just as soon have one less gnant to worry about."

Sir Keith spoke up. "If you don't kill it, it could come back to attack you. They're just animals, not human."

Nathan stared at Sir Keith for a moment and sheathed his sword. "You do what you want, Sir Jon. Just make sure this thing stays away from us."

Sir Keith stood and walked away, calling out, "Be very careful, Sir Jon. These creatures are not to be trusted."

Jon looked between Nicole and Gilbert and then at the quivering Rzet. "Nicole?"

"I don't know. It seems cruel to kill it. Just make sure it stays away."

"Can you look at its jaw? It looks swollen from where I hit it."

Nicole bent down and gingerly touched the gnant's jaw, the gnant staying still as she reached out her hand. "It's not broken, it should be okay in a day or two."

"Gilbert, what do you think? Let it go?"

"Always nice to have a second chance I say. I think you make the right choice."

"Well, Rzet, are you going to leave us alone from now on?"

"Oh, yesss sssir, I promisssess."

Jon cut the rope holding the gnant's legs and wrists. It quickly jumped to its feet. "I leave you alone, no more trouble." It began to run off to the forest and stopped, turning around. "Rzet not forget life favour." It sprinted toward the trees, disappearing a moment later.

Jon walked back to his tent with Nicole following close behind. "We better fix your tent."

"Don't bother, I'm not sleeping in there alone tonight." She entered Jon's tent. "Don't act so surprised, you're the one who wrecked my tent and let that gnant go." She softened her expression. "By the way, thank you for saving me." She kissed him on the lips. "You're my hero."

Later, Jon lay with eyes open, though not out of concern from another gnant attack. He fingered the crystal that hung from his neck and understood everyone knew he had it now, wondering if that would change things on the journey. Nicole was curled next him and he gazed at her, thinking about the kiss.

How would I ever explain this to Liz? And what about Nadine? What if she was really a gnant? What does it mean to the chance of returning to Earth again? It took a long time for Jon to fall asleep and soon after that it was morning.

SEVENTEEN

The forest changed, growing denser and taller as Jon and the others travelled. When the sun began its downward journey in the afternoon, they soon found themselves in dark shadows as the top of the trees cut off the sunlight. Noises from the forest varied from birdcalls to growls and a few screeches. The horses shied several times, seeing or hearing things that escaped the attention of the riders. The riders subconsciously kept their horses closer together, talking only quietly along the gloomy path.

"What is this place?" Liz looked around carefully, gripping her reins tightly.

"It's called the Dark Green Forest," Sir Keith supplied. "Quite an old and established forest."

Gilbert spat. "Dark Green? More like dark soul. It also goes by the name of the Devil's Woods. Those trees grow by magic and they get so close together ye can barely squeeze by them. All sorts of strange creatures live there, some of them made up by magic, I tell you."

"Superstitious nonsense."

"Yeah? I tell ye, Sir Keith, if you to walk a hundred yards into that forest, we'd never see you again. And I'll tell you another thing, you won't see a dead tree in there, nor any fallen branches. Those trees grow forever and never die."

"Rubbish!"

"Bet you a gold fern you can't bring me a dead branch longer than your forearm."

Sir Keith looked nervous. "So you say, but you don't have a gold fern to back up your bet."

Nathan finally ran out of patience. "Enough. Can we let this argument lie still for now? I for one don't relish being on this trail at dark. We could be victims of magical creatures or just plain dragons. I suggest we stop at the next inn for safety reasons. Agreed?"

The others nodded and voiced their approval. Sir Keith urged his horse on faster. "There should be an inn about a mile or so up ahead. It should be as good as any."

The Green Inn stood three stories high and access was through a small gate set in high stone walls. Jon noticed iron spikes along the walls and he asked Gilbert, "I thought iron wasn't that common?"

"It ain't. But this is the centre of some strong magic and someone went to a lot of trouble to keep out magic. Wouldn't do to have a werewolf coming through the front door."

"Werewolf? You mean there…?"

"Yes, yes. I don't know how or who did it, but these woods are cursed. Take my word for it even if Sir Keith won't."

Jon noticed the trouble Nathan had pulling the skittish horses one at a time to the stables and had his hand on the hilt of his sword as he headed to the inn's front doors.

The Green Inn's windows were small and recessed from the outside face. The roof had a high peak with a row of iron spikes at the top. The innkeeper appeared, a short man with a full head of white hair. He walked over to the counter, slightly bent over. He coughed twice and surveyed the group in front of him.

"We have a few guests tonight, Irene," he called out. 'Irene' didn't appear.

Sir Keith looked around dubiously. "See here, innkeeper, we need five…" He stopped and regarded Nicole and Jon. Jon nodded vigorously, and Sir Keith continued. "…that is five rooms for tonight with meals and bath."

"Very good, sir. That'll be twenty-five ferns."

"Twenty-five ferns! For this accommodation? This is outrageous."

"Yes, sir, of course. The next inn is only about four miles up the road. Of course, their rates may not be any less than ours."

Sir Keith slapped his hand at the counter. "You seem to have us in a bind. But I warn you, I'll not soon forget this robbery."

"Yes sir. So, it will be only one night then?"

The downstairs was used mainly for dining and to provide living quarters for the innkeeper. Jon and the others trooped upstairs to the second level to wash up and returned to the main floor to dine. Jon and Nicole had neighbouring rooms, while the others' rooms were across the hall. Jon noticed his room had strong wooden shutters that included a notice requesting that the shutters be secured after dark. It seemed the Jon's group were the only residents at the Green Inn.

The dining hall featured a long table that could hold fourteen guests and an oversized fireplace on one wall. Above the fireplace, the head of a wild boar provided an interesting choice of decoration. The plain wooden chairs were of a mixed type and the table followed the design criteria with a different pattern on the plates. Various bowls and plates held the dinner served for the night. The innkeeper was nowhere to be seen even after Sir Keith called out for him.

"That thief is not around so we might as well commence with the meal."

A large slab of meat sat in a pan. Nathan attempted to cut the dark meat with a knife only to find it tough as it oozed blood from its centre.

"I don't know what animal it came from, dragon tail I suspect, but it sure hasn't been fully cooked. The flesh has an odd appearance to it, as if the creature was diseased. I suggest we leave this alone unless your stomach is a great deal stronger than mine and eat the chicken instead."

The chicken was better, although burnt in a few places. Nicole barely touched her portion and chose to fill up on the vegetables instead. "These carrots are odd looking, aren't they? Like they aren't exactly round and they're kind of twisted."

Gilbert commented, "Everything is odd about this place."

She nodded. "I can't explain it but I sense a strangeness, an evil here. Bad vibrations. It gives me the creeps."

Sir Keith shook his head. "You see what your talk has done, Gilbert? Now you got her imagination working too."

"It's not my imagination, Sir Keith. I can sense these things. Gilbert's right about magic being used around here."

"Maybe some, but…"

"You have your knife on ye?" Gilbert asked.

Sir Keith nodded.

Gilbert pointed his finger at him. "Pull it out and feel the blade then."

Sir Keith drew out his knife and touched the blade with his fingers. He quickly withdrew them.

"Blade's warm and vibrating, ain't it?"

Sir Keith reluctantly nodded.

"Now do you believe me about this place?" Gilbert crossed his arms.

Jon looked between Sir Keith and Nicole. "I don't get it."

Nicole answered. "The knife is made of steel, which has iron in it. Iron tries to repel magic and when it's placed in a field of strong magic, it vibrates from the energy and gets warm, sometimes hot depending on the amount of iron and the strength of the magic. This inn and the surrounding woods are not a good place to be."

Sir Keith stood up. "Gilbert was right about the magic around here. I'm man enough to admit I was wrong to scoff at his suggestion. I suggest we turn in early and leave at first light."

Jon expected Gilbert to look smug, but he merely appeared nervous.

The innkeeper showed up just as Sir Keith was leaving the table. "Was the meal satisfactory, sir?"

"No, it most certainly was not. Where did you learn to cook? That meat was almost raw."

"Oh, please sir, don't speak like that. Irene would have a fit if she heard you talk that way. She is very sensitive to such words."

"Well, whoever she is, she had better learn to cook better than that." Sir Keith stomped off, leaving the innkeeper upset.

"Oh dear, oh dear. I better talk to her before she gets too upset." He hurried off, calling out her name.

Nathan stood up then. "I think I'll turn in as well, tomorrow will come soon enough and I may need to be alert during our last leg through the woods."

Jon and Nicole waited as Gilbert finished off another goblet of wine. He was annoyed the inn didn't keep ale on hand, the small quantity they did had gone bad and he had to revert to the wine. When he finished, they headed back upstairs to their rooms.

———

Jon bid goodnight to Nicole and entered his room. He closed the shutters and secured them. He took off his shirt, feeling too warm.

He was barely asleep when the rattle of the shutters woke him up. The wind was strong, and he listened to its howl before turning over to ignore the sound. The low rumble of thunder started, increasing in volume. A crack of lightning caused light to spray through the shutters. Rain followed immediately, adding to the noise as it beat on the shutters.

The clamour of the storm continued, at times slowing down only to return with new vigor. He heard sounds in the hallway, a woman's voice yelling and a thumping on a door. A man's voice called out as well, calling her by name. "Irene, you mustn't..."

Then the thunder drowned him out. Another voice and the running of footsteps down the hallway. Jon rolled out of bed and reached the door as he picked up his sword hanging on a clothes hook.

In the gloomy hallway lit by a few candles, he saw Sir Keith step back toward him. Nathan stood a few feet from him on Jon's other side. A dozen feet away he saw the innkeeper call out to a woman holding a butcher knife as she approached the flustered Sir Keith. Irene stood taller than her husband and was heavier built. Her complexion was pale, almost to the point of being transparent. The most remarkable thing about her was a large knife that protruded from her chest. She screamed at Sir Keith as she advanced.

"How dare you criticize my cooking, you worthless fool! I'll show you what I can do to men like you!"

Nathan calmly stepped forward and sliced the air with his sword at her. "Freeze there, lady, or I shall be forced to do you harm."

Jon wondered how much more harm she could suffer with a knife in her heart but decided it wasn't time to bring up such details. She stopped where his sword pointed and promptly vanished.

"You see, I told you she would be upset. Now I better go and try to calm her down. I'll tell her that you said you were sorry." The innkeeper hurried away.

Sir Keith looked like he was about to faint.

Nathan sheathed his sword. "I don't know about the rest of you but that was one odd ghost. She doesn't know she's dead yet, and neither does her husband."

"It's the magic. It won't let the soul rest proper." Gilbert stood behind Nathan. He gave a long pause. "I ain't scared of much but that was almost enough to make me wet myself. It's going to be tough sleeping after that."

"I agree. I don't relish the thought of sleeping and being awakened by that ghost." Nicole eyed Jon.

Nathan opined, "We can't all crowd together in one room. I can rest with one eye open, so I suggest…"

Once again Jon found himself sharing a bed with Nicole, which he considered rather pleasant circumstances if it wasn't for the snoring and mutterings of Gilbert who slept on the floor next to him. This time he slept with his sword by his side. An oil lamp flickered on in the room, attracting suicide prone insects that fluttered above it. Sir Keith and Nathan shared another room across the hall and Jon hoped dawn would come soon so he could get some rest on his horse.

The storm had finally passed, and he closed his eyes to try to relax when the shutters banged as something tried to enter the room. The creature on the other side of the shutters screeched in frustration. Nicole screamed in fright. Jon yelled in agony as she dug her nails into his chest.

Gilbert jumped up and began to wave his sword yelling, "Gets away froms me, gets aways from me!"

Nathan and Sir Keith rushed into the room with their swords banishing.

"What's happening, man?" demanded Nathan.

The creature thumped the shutters again and clawed at the wood before giving up and leaving.

Jon rubbed at the red scratches on his chest as he sat up. He hooked a thumb at the window. "That."

Nicole looked at his chest. "Oops, sorry. I got startled."

Gilbert seemed to have woken up from his dream state and dropped his sword-wielding arm down. "Woman, you've got to learn to control yerself. I thought the devil himself was attacking us."

Nathan shook his head and headed back to his room with Sir Keith following.

Jon dropped his head back on his pillow. Nicole curled up next to him with her head on his shoulder and whispered in his ear. "I'm truly sorry about that. I think I also hit you with my knee."

"It's alright. You just caught me off guard, that's all."

The conversation ended there and Jon listened to her breathing over the mutterings of Gilbert until morning came.

Jon limped downstairs from the bruise in his thigh for breakfast. The innkeeper avoided them as much as possible, placing the eggs, bread, cheese and ham on the table and hurrying away.

Jon waited with Nicole while the others retrieved the horses at the front of the inn. She abruptly went back inside and Jon followed her, wondering what she was doing.

"Innkeeper!" She yelled at the front counter.

A minute later he appeared. "Yes, Miss?"

"You're dead, aren't you?"

He stared at her for a moment and nodded.

"You and your wife were murdered?"

"Aye. And this cursed place will give us no rest. When I have enough ferns, I'll be able to pay for a wizard to remove the dark magic long enough for us to leave this world."

"How long has it been?"

"We have been in between for over a year now."

"How much do you have now?"

"One hundred and six ferns, Miss. Not nearly enough."

"Okay, do you have any gold of any sort around here?"

"No. Wait, Irene's wedding band."

"That'll work. Look, I know a little magic. If I can lift this curse long enough for you to pass on, may I have those ferns?"

"Yes, yes. Anything you want is yours. We no longer have a need for anything."

"Jon, wait outside please."

Jon stood outside with the rest. They wondered what was going to happen, if anything.

The inn changed, the stone walls seemed to be encased in mist. Moments later the mist vanished. A chill in the air descended upon them. Jon held his breath as he stepped toward the front doors.

"Nicole, are you okay?" He reached the front doors just as Nicole opened them and stepped outside, holding up a cloth bag of coins.

"It's done. They're free."

As they rode out past the gate, Nicole jumped at the chance to explain what she did. "The curse was strong, it had to be to cover the whole woods but it could be broken for a short time easily in small areas. It's like lighting a candle in a fog, it burns out a small area where it's lit but can't do much to the whole thing."

"Very good, Nicole, but rather than talk I would like to make good time to get out these woods." Sir Keith increased the speed of his horse and the others followed suit.

They didn't stop for lunch and continued to ride as hard as the horses would permit without getting too tired. At mid-afternoon the woods suddenly changed. The height of the trees dropped, and they became less packed together. Sir Keith soon dropped the pace and conferred with Nathan. After a short discussion, Sir Keith announced they would stop only long enough to water the horses and refill their own canteens. "After that if we proceed at a moderate pace, we will reach Thorsgate where we can spend the night."

———

Thorsgate was a border city that marked the end of what Sir Keith considered the civilized part of Domum. King Charles ruled what on Earth would be Western Europe, which covered almost a quarter of the landmass on Domum. North America was almost non-existent, South America much smaller, and while Asia and India existed in smaller versions, Australia wasn't much larger than most Pacific Ocean Islands.

King Raphael, on the neighbouring county was inclined to allow a greater use of magic, permitting several wizards to increase their powers to what King Charles considered dangerous levels.

Thorsgate made use of white marble on many of its buildings that gave the city a clean and sophisticated appearance. The streets were wide, making it easy for Sir Keith to lead the rest to a hotel he had previously decided on.

The hotel also made use of the white marble on the outside but used a darker style inside. Sir Keith motioned to Jon to join him at the front counter.

"I don't mean to pry into your private affairs, sir, but almost every night Nicole and yourself have shared a room or bed through various circumstances. I hope you don't think I'm being too forward but I have assigned the two of you one room. It will save us a bit of money as well. I had to pay a fair bit to ensure Lady Karla was taken care of in her extended stay at Stone Retreat. It was an expense I had not planned on."

"Oh no, you see…"

"Besides saving on costs it will afford Miss Nicole security as well. She seems to be frightened about spending the night alone and I believe the most practical solution is for the two of you is to use one room. I think we will all sleep better if Miss Nicole is not feeling anxious."

"Yes, but I doubt…"

"I have already discussed the issue with her and she is in agreement."

Jon couldn't find a counter argument and reluctantly agreed. It was not that he minded Nicole's company, but he knew it would be difficult to explain such reasoning to Liz, or Nadine for that matter. *If they find out.*

After dinner, Jon spent some time in the bar before going up to his room. Nicole had taken a bath and was brushing her hair when he entered. She wore only a white silk camisole and a short petticoat.

"Nicole, I'm not entirely sure with this arrangement of us sharing a room."

"Because of your girlfriend?"

"Yeah."

"Well, when she was still your girlfriend, you made a rather strong advance to me and later insisted on buying my freedom. The end result is I ended up on this perilous journey with you." She turned and pointed a finger at him. "And now you're having to live with the consequences of those actions which is being my protector, and that includes days and nights. I nursed you back to health from a dragon attack and now I want you to make sure I'm not endangered from some gnant. If you're worried about what your girlfriend might say I'll even talk to her on your behalf and tell her you acted like a gentleman." She continued to brush her hair.

"I can tell her myself."

"Fine. Just don't try to squirm out of your responsibilities." She stopped brushing her hair for a minute and turned to smile at him. "Of course, if you really feel you can't keep your hands to yourself you can sleep on the floor."

Jon was a bit mystified how he ended up in sharing a room with Nicole and wasn't sure if she was annoyed at him or not. He saw that she had removed her petticoat and wore just her camisole to bed. She rested on her side, putting an elbow on the bed so her hand could support her head.

Jon took off his shirt and approached the bed.

"Take your pants off too. It's warm in here and when you sleep, you generate too much heat as it is. You'll sweat and I don't like that. I've seen you naked before so it's nothing to be alarmed about."

Jon turned to his side, trying to give himself a degree of modesty. His pants dropped and his penis rose. He quickly climbed into bed and pulled the blanket up to his chest. He knew she had seen his involuntary reaction when he removed his pants.

"Would you object if I put my head on your shoulder? It makes me feel safe and this pillow is useless."

"Sure."

He stared at the ceiling, his heart thumping as Nicole rested next to him. Her head twisted slightly and she kissed his neck.

"Your skin tastes salty."

"I guess."

Jon froze as her hand stroked his chest, followed by a second kiss at his collar bone.

"I think you're a very brave man." Her leg moved over his thighs.

"Thanks." He gulped.

Her hand slid down his chest, his stomach, and enclosed his erection. "I don't think you're going to go to sleep for a while."

"No, I guess not."

Jon knew he wasn't able to resist and struggled with her on who was going to be on top. It was the most pleasant contest he had ever had, eventually deciding he would let her have her way.

She collapsed on his chest, moaning, "That was too long between fucks."

Jon wasn't sure what to do and stroked her back.

She sighed and kissed him on the mouth. "Thanks, I really needed that."

Jon nodded. *Me too.*

Nicole took her time getting off him and went to the washroom. Jon slowly sat at the edge of the bed, regaining his energy.

Nicole returned to the bed. "You're okay with what happened, aren't you?"

"I'm fine, all good."

"Alright. I don't want to lose you as a friend."

I think we're more than friends now.

Jon fell asleep quickly after that. Nicole snuggled up to him, with a leg sprawled over his. Her warm breath relaxed him and he had one of the best sleeps in days.

He woke up with Nicole already dressed. She noticed he was awake and walked over the bed next to him.

"You're awake." She bent down and gave him a kiss.

"Yeah. I had a good sleep. No gnants or ghosts to fight in the middle of the night."

"I see you have your sword ready in any case." She touched the blanket where his erection was pressing against the fabric. "See you downstairs."

———

Jon went downstairs and joined Nicole and Gilbert for breakfast. Nicole was actually laughing at one of Gilbert's jokes and Jon concluded she must be in good spirits to enjoy Gilbert's company.

"Good morning, Sir Jon. Have a good sleep?"

Jon eyed Gilbert suspiciously. "Yeah, I guess so. Did you?"

"I dids. I just wonderings how your sleep was with Nicole taking half your bed."

Jon laughed. "I'm not telling you what may or not may have happened last night."

"Does anyone else want more ale before we leave?" Gilbert slid off his chair and headed toward the bar.

Nicole and Jon passed on his offer and finished their tea instead.

"You talked in your sleep again last night. You mentioned Liz a couple of times. It doesn't bother me. I understand what the situation is."

"I was just dreaming, Nicole, I didn't mean to…"

She waved a hand at him. "Jon, I like you. Really like you and don't mind sharing some space with you. Men are men sometimes when it comes to women and let's leave it at that. But when, like last night, you dreamt about her it could mean a couple of things."

"Such as?"

"You might have dreamed about her because you miss her. Or…"

"Or?"

"Or she has made it to Domum and you're feeling her vibrations."

"I'm not sensitive to such things."

"But I am, and you're next to me in a relaxed state when such perceptions are greatest. I just want you to be aware there could be some other factors in your quest to return to Earth."

———

After travelling a few hours, Jon was surprised when they came to an eight-foot wall made out of stonewood. The branches twisted among each other, like a giant hedge without leaves. The grey was occasionally punctuated by green twigs showing that the plant was still alive but slowly changing into stone.

They travelled parallel to the wall for a mile before they came to a gate patrolled by a small group of bored guards.

Sir Keith talked to the guard in charge for several minutes, debating on the charge for entry. Nathan sat back quietly for several minutes and moved forward.

"What's the problem here, Sir Keith?"

"This sergeant wants twenty bronze ferns to enter their county. I'm trying to convince him to be more reasonable."

"What! Twenty ferns! You must be joking." Nathan dropped from his horse and strode to the gate. His dark face was without a smile and his hand rested on the hilt of his sword.

The guard moved a half step back from Nathan. "It's the going rate." But his voice lacked conviction.

"This group is under a mission ordered by Lord Perry. I'm ordered to protect them from danger and thieves and I consider these toll charges nothin' but robbery. Am I making myself clear?"

The guard looked up at Nathan, who stood a full head higher and was broader at the chest. He also took in the armband that signified him as an elite fighter and took a long swallow. "Well..." He turned back at the other guards who were listening but not offering him any support, standing well off from the confrontation. "Hmm, you said you were under orders from Lord Perry?"

"That is so."

"Well then we don't wish to impede anyone under the direction of Lord Perry." He straightened up and turned to face the others. "Allow these travellers to pass, men, they are under orders of Lord Perry himself."

After they had rode out of earshot, Jon heard Nathan laugh.

"It's amazing how fast those useless guards can back up when they're met with a challenge."

"What would you've done if he hadn't backed down?"

"Well, let's just say I would've been surprised by his foolishness."

After a full hour of riding, Sir Keith called for a short rest and for a short meeting while the horses grazed.

"We have reached a critical part of our journey. We are just a few hours away from Paderno City and it is by far the largest city on our quest. Besides the inherent danger of a large city, we are also in a region that has the highest population of gnants. I trust we all understand what that may mean."

"But we'll be staying in inns, won't we?"

"Yes, Nicole. But as we have learned, no place is entirely safe. You will also notice magic is much more prevalent here. Any questions?"

They shook their heads and soon they were riding toward Paderno City. The road they followed was joined by other roads and traffic increased steadily as they journeyed. Gnants were seen on the road as well but the creatures seemed to ignore them.

On top of a rise on the road they came across upon Paderno City, its white buildings glistening in the sunlight as it sat nestled in a valley. The large buildings supported towers sporting unique geometric designs. The wide boulevards were lined with an abundance of trees and flowered plants. Jon took in the sight, his vision sweeping from the city to the high hills covered in snow.

"Nicole, why is there snow on those hills? It could hardly be cold enough for snow to be here."

"Paderno City is made up almost entirely by magic, a lot of strong magic. But magic is mostly the transference of energy and though they try to be careful on how they apply their spells, there's an occasional loss of power that has to be made up somewhere. That comes from the energy in the hills, a loss of heat and therefore snow and ice."

"So energy is borrowed from there to give to the city. Why doesn't the snow melt anyway after a while?"

"They keep drawing on the energy. Ice is the easiest spell to do because all you have to do is pull energy from the water and put it somewhere, anywhere." She followed his gaze downward. "It sure makes a pretty sight, doesn't it?"

"Hmm. It looks artificial like Disneyland."

"Trust me, Disneyland is more real than this place. You're going to see some strange things down there."

EIGHTEEN

"Come on, I know you can sneak away for an hour. Nora won't care as long as you get your work done and you do that."

Liz stared at Tony as he held the reins of the two horses. "I'm not really dressed for horseback riding."

"It's not a day trip, just a ride up to Shake's Point and back. I'll have you back for lunch, I promise."

"I'll ask Nora first. I just can't disappear like that." Liz returned to the castle and sought out Nora. She found her in one of the libraries, this one located on the second floor. The Rosemore Castle didn't have one large library but rather four small libraries on separate floors.

"Miss Nora, may I have a moment of your time to make a request?"

Nora stopped reading a manuscript she was studying. Liz understood she had an interest in the original families that crossed over from Earth to Domum, trying to determine her own connection to them. "Of course. What is it?"

"May I have a few hours to travel with Anthony Graham on a horse ride? I will be back by lunch time."

Nora smiled. "You have been seeing him fairly often. Fortunately, you have done superior work as a hostess, and Lady Monique was very pleased with the painting done of you. Thus, I will grant you the rest of the day off. Be back by dinner time."

"Thank you very much." Liz grinned.

"Are you aware of Anthony and his reputation toward ladies?"

"Yes, I am."

"Alright. Don't get yourself pregnant. That would change your employment."

Great. I wonder if the pill works on Domum.

She went to the kitchen, obtaining bread, cheese and ham. One of the kitchen workers, a tireless woman named Elsie, wrapped the food in a cheese cloth.

"There you be, dear. Now you go and enjoy your lunch with your man. I assume it is with a man."

"It is."

"I'm sorry. I didn't mean to pry. I suggest you take a flagon of wine with you." She opened a door to a side cupboard and gave Liz a clay bottle. "Here, this should make the lunch better."

Liz thanked her and returned to the stables. She showed Anthony the lunch and wine. "And Nora gave me the rest of the afternoon off. So, wasn't that smart of me to ask her rather than try to sneak off?"

"Yes, that's great news." He took a length of rope and wrapped it around the cheese cloth and the flagon of wine. He left a length of rope and used it to tie to the saddle of his horse, a large brown stallion. "This will make it a more pleasant ride."

Tony walked to a stall and returned with a reddish-brown mare. "I think this will be to your liking. She won't give you any difficulties."

"Good. Please help me up. Skirts are not best for riding in."

While the skirt wasn't tight, she still had to pull it up to her knees to swing her leg over the saddle. She noticed Tony eyeing her exposed leg. "Hey, get on your own horse. Haven't you seen a woman's leg before?"

"Sorry, didn't mean to stare. It's just that... well, it's been a long time and..."

"Enough details. Apology accepted but understand I'm not taking a ride to make out with you."

"Yeah."

"We're friends, nothing more. I have a boyfriend, remember?"

"Of course, m'lady. Can't a man enjoy the sight and company of a beautiful woman without getting chastised for it? My eyes sometimes can't help themselves, that's all."

She laughed. "Okay, your eyes are forgiven then."

Liz tried to adjust to riding her horse and eventually learned to move with the motion. Fortunately, with Anthony leading the way, the pace was reasonable. The ride took almost an hour, coming to an end near the edge of town. The horses easily climbed a hill and when they reached the top, they dismounted their horses.

Liz looked down at the town below.

"It seems rather quaint from here."

"Perhaps, depending on what you call quaint." Athony helped her from her horse.

She walked over to the tree lined hill, seeing a river and the buildings clustered around it.

He put an arm around her waist and pointed out different parts of the town below them.

"That be the old section of town and over there's where my brother Michael lives. My parents' castle is behind those hills there. That big one is Lord Perry's."

"Who is Lord Perry?"

"King Charles rules our land but because he is so far away, he appoints one of the lords to be his administrator and act on his behalf. Lord Perry is his designated representative."

"Does that mean Lord Perry controls everything? I thought Lord Bennett, or at least his castle, was where they had the jails and court."

"True. Lord Perry delegates some duties to other lords. I will attempt to explain. Lord Perry is the ruler in this area. That rule is subject to the support from King Charles and the other lords here. If he didn't have the support of the other lords, then King Charles would appoint another lord who has more support."

"Does that mean another lord could take over?"

"Yes, but unlikely. Lord Perry enjoys the support of the more powerful lords. Having said that, Lord Bennett is hungry to increase his holdings and influence. Lord Perry gave him the authority to run the court and prison but that may have not been enough to satisfy him. One other thing, Lord Bennett is quite mad. A lunatic."

"That's not good." She felt Anthony pull her tighter. "What about the other lords?"

"My father has a strong influence due to his wealth, but he does not seek more power. Lord Sussex is an interesting man. He tried to induce a spell on himself to keep his youth. It worked, but only if he remains within the castle perimeter." He laughed.

"That's very sad." Liz laughed with him.

"There's more. The man is a sex maniac. He loves women and keeps a bunch of them as sex slaves. He dresses them half-naked and, well, let me put this way. His lust is almost insatiable."

"Wow, so he lives alone with his sex slaves and can't leave the castle. He must get lonely, all the same."

"A nice type of loneliness, just him and his beautiful women. He does have parties at his castle and they are well attended. In fact, his invitations to his galas are most sought after."

"I suppose you've been to one of his parties."

"Yes, of course. One doesn't turn down an invitation to such an event."

Liz pointed at the downtown area of the town.

"This is fascinating. I can see how the town is laid out and how it follows the hills and the curve of the river."

"Speaking of curves." He used his arm around her waist to turn her in a new direction. "If you look straight between those two hills you can just make out the tower of Dina."

Liz wasn't sure if 'speaking of curves' was a reference to the tower or to her waist. His arm went around her but didn't press. "The Tower of Dina. Is it that white thing?"

"Yeah. Lord Alexandra commissioned these wizards to build the highest tower in the land so his mistress could see anywhere she wanted. After they were finished, he only gave them half of their agreed-on price because he said the tower wasn't high enough. He also claimed it wasn't white enough."

"It sure looks white."

"He wanted it so white that it would glisten like virgin snow, which was open to interpretation. The wizards were so angry that the next day they came back and caused the tower to twist."

"They weren't inside were they?"

"No, the wizards to their credit, informed a servant of their intentions so no one was hurt. Although they were offered full payment to undo their damage, they refused. So, the tower stands useless, the stairs squeezed so tight that only a cat can pass through it."

She placed her arm around his waist and gave him a short squeeze.

He turned her, lowered his head and when she didn't resist, kissed her.

Liz responded, wrapping an arm around his neck. The kiss lingered. "Best we have something to eat now."

Anthony placed the wine and cheesecloth on the grass and untied the rope holding it together.

Liz complained, "I didn't bring any cups for the wine." She sat on the ground next to Anthony and reached for a piece of cheese.

"Then we drink from the bottle."

Between the bites of the bread, cheese and ham they shared the flagon of wine.

"That wine is a bit strong, either that or I'm not used to drinking anymore."

Anthony chuckled. "I'm afraid to say I've had too much practice with drinking. One of my many bad habits."

"And what would be some of your other bad habits?"

"Unable to resist pretty girls." He leaned into her, kissing her.

Liz went down on her back, his weight pinning her. She returned his kiss while his hand slid up her ribcage. She gasped as his kisses worked downward to her neck.

"Anthony, you mustn't."

He ignored her whisper and continued to plant kisses lower on her neck. His fingers opened the top button of her blouse. "I don't want to stop."

She moaned, "I'm not sure what I want. This feels good, but…"

"How about if I take away your objections so you can enjoy our time together?"

"And how do you propose to do that?"

"Hold your hands together."

Liz complied and watched as he took the rope that held the cheesecloth together. He quickly circled her wrists with the rope and did a quick tie.

"Hey."

Anthony pulled her tied wrists above her head. "There, now you can say you were unable to resist."

Liz giggled. "So that's your solution. Tying me up."

He didn't answer. He used one hand to hold her wrists and the other hand to undo the buttons of her blouse as he kissed her chest.

Liz groaned. The buttons were undone, exposing the tunic she wore underneath. The light fabric covered only her front, using straps to secure it around her neck and back.

His hands slid over the cloth, massaging her breasts. As Liz took in deep breaths of air he began to fumble with the closure of her skirt.

"Please. I cannot resist you. But this is too fast. Please stop."

Anthony paused, and she saw understanding in his face.

"I will not push you further."

"Thank you." She noticed the erection deforming his pants. "Sorry."

"There will be other opportunities." He smiled. "I hope."

"Perhaps. We'll see."

"Come, let us rest a bit and finish off the wine." He helped her up, and they moved to a tree to sit against. She sat between his legs, leaning into him.

"You still have my hands tied and my top is open."

"It will remain so until it is time to leave."

She giggled. "Yes, sir." She felt his member press on her back. "Thank you for stopping. That meant a lot to me."

"It is only right to stop if the lady requests so. A gentleman can always look forward to another occasion, while a scoundrel can only look forward to disrespect."

"Well said."

"Besides, now that I know you like to be secured prior to love-making it gives me a few ideas for the future."

"Oh, don't be so sure of yourself. Maybe I just pretended to like to be tied up so I could see what you would do."

He laughed out loud. "Women lie about when they tell lies."

She tried to elbow him in the stomach as she laughed. As he stroked her sides under the blouse, Liz reached for the wine.

"Do you need your wrists untied to drink the wine?"

"No, I think I can manage." She used her fingers on both hands to tilt the bottle to her mouth.

Anthony took the bottle from her, taking a long drink.

"This is nice. Drinking wine in the sun and relaxing." His hands moved under her tunic, cupping her breasts. She sighed and closed her eyes. "I thought you had agreed to stop."

He pulled his hands away. "Sorry, I just couldn't resist. You are so beautiful."

"You're forgiven." She took another drink of wine and he took the flagon from her, draining the rest of the wine.

"Perhaps it is best we get back." She saw the sun had dropped near the horizon.

"True, m'lady, I wouldn't want you to be late." He helped her stand, untied her wrists and insisted on doing up her blouse. "I undid the buttons, I will redo them."

―――――

They rode back to Lord Rosemore's castle, the horses willing to run and Liz had to slow her mount down to a safer speed. Tony jumped off his horse first and then helped her down, placing his hands on her waist and slowly lowered her to the ground.

"Thanks for riding with me." He quickly kissed her on the lips. "Another ride sometime?"

The kiss reminded her of what he wanted from her. "Tony, you have to remember that I'm on Domum to find Jon." Her hands were still on his shoulders and his hands on her waist.

"Of course, of course. That was just a little peck for being my friend."

"Okay." She broke free from his grasp. "Thanks for the ride. I had a good time being with you. And not just the making out."

Liz figured there were spies everywhere. At lunchtime Roxie questioned where they rode to and if there was anything going on.

"No, we're just friends."

"But you kissed him and he sure is happy out there."

"He kissed me. I didn't know he was going to do that."

Roxy wasn't letting her off the hook. "You didn't exactly resist him from what I heard."

"What was I supposed to do? Slap him? Tony and I spent time together and we have an understanding where we are with each other." *I hope.*

"Tony? You mean Anthony. He doesn't like being called Tony, and you sure could do worse than hooking up with him. Someday he'll be a lord."

"Whatever." She took a deep breath and knew her next question was going to cause more teasing. "I want to ask something personal and please no snide remarks. How do women here prevent getting pregnant?"

Roxy put her hands on her hips, grinning. "Okay, no snide remarks and it's good that you asked. A single woman with a child doesn't have it easy here. There's an older maid, Catrina, here who does some magic. She will make up a potion for a couple of ferns. I'll take you to her tomorrow."

"Thanks."

———

Liz sat at the breakfast table when Roxy came up to her from behind, touching her shoulder.

"Come on, finish up. I'll take you to Catrina."

Liz gathered up her plate and tea cup, carrying them to a table set at the back. "Okay, what does this potion do? Anything bad from it?"

"It's safe. Lots of women use it. It tastes like a spicy licorice root tea."

Liz followed her to the second level. She appreciated Roxy not making a big deal about her seeking protection and taking time to show her where Catrina was located.

Unlike some castles, as Liz heard, the Rosemore Castle allowed their staff flexibility in their duties as long as the work was done satisfactorily. Liz, on occasion, covered for one of the servants if they needed time for a personal nature and the favour was reciprocated.

Catrina was repairing garments worn by the Rosemores and other higher-ranking individuals at the Rosemore Castle. Her room was a converted bedroom and featured plenty of light from the open balcony. She looked up from the mound of fabric on the table, sitting with a curved wood needle and coloured thread. The room was dominated by tables, various garments and rolls of cloth. Liz noticed Catrina didn't mind the interruption. The short, stout woman greeted them warmly.

A few minutes later Liz explained what she wanted and Catrina produced a clay cup, filling it from a flagon she kept under a table.

"I made this up just last night." She seemed pleased at her statement as if she had anticipated Liz's visit.

"How does it work?" Liz peered at the dark liquid and tried to sniff it.

"Magic, dear. You drink it and you won't get in the family way for three full moons."

"Three moons?"

"On the night after the third full moon the potion loses its magic. Then you better see me quick again. Two ferns please."

Liz swallowed the liquid. *I've tasted worse shooters in the bar.* She passed over two ferns, a pair of small coins with a hole in the centre, thanked Catrina and hoped the potion worked as advertised.

———

Liz met Tony at the stables just after dinner a few days later, a little reluctantly given the teasing she received from her friends. He had been after her for another ride and she agreed after first turning him down for another excursion.

The day was hot and Liz was glad for the cooler air the evening brought as they made their way down the cobble streets. He made her laugh when he told her of the mishaps that happened when he became drunk along with his friends.

"Good grief, did you really punch the horse in the mouth?"

"I swear I heard that horse call me a name. Or so I thought at the time." He laughed with her.

"It's a good thing you can't drink as much as you used to."

"True. I miss having the odd pint now and then but it's nice not waking up with a hangover six days a week."

"Six days a week?"

"I wasn't totally irresponsible. I left one day to be respectable."

He helped her again from her horse when they returned to the stables this time and she didn't mind when he sought another kiss from her, returning his kiss with one of her own.

"Thanks for the ride."

"Liz, I would like to spend more time with you."

"I know." She looked down and back up at him. "I truly enjoy your company. But I came here to find my boyfriend, Jon. It would be very complicated if we were to get involved. Understand?"

"I do. I also understand something else." He put his hands on her waist, holding her tight. "We don't know where life will take us or how long we have. I don't wish to worry you but your friend, Jon, is on a very dangerous journey. Life is uncertain here. Sometimes we have to ensure we live without regrets. All I mean to say is that there's nothing wrong in enjoying moments of pleasure."

"Okay. I understand what you're saying." She gave him a final kiss, disappearing past the front door.

———

A few days later she agreed on another ride with him. She sought Nora's permission as the ride would take most of the afternoon.

"Of course. It's good to make sure Anthony is socializing and not isolating himself in the stables. Lady Luanda Graham has been requesting about his well-being. I think it is good that you're spending time with him."

———

"Where are we off to this time?" Liz placed a hand on Tony's shoulder as he helped her on the saddle.

"I thought we could cross the river, and I'd show you a different view of Horstruff."

"Okay, lead the way." She noticed he had packed provisions for a lunch, including a flagon that likely carried wine. She wondered what she would do if he pushed to have his way with her. She eyed the rope holding the food together. *Maybe he'll tie my hands together again.*

They rode across a stone bridge. Liz relaxed and enjoy the sights of the town. The other side of the river wasn't as well developed, and he found a grassy area to enjoy their lunch.

"We have to watch out a bit more for dragons and gargoyles. They avoid towns and people, but they will show up here. Don't be afraid, I will keep you safe."

She helped him unroll the cloth holding the food and took a drink of wine.

They tore off pieces of bread, cheese and dried meat. Suddenly the horses began to act up. Tony stood quickly, eyeing the nearby forest.

"Quick, get on your horse. Gargoyles."

Tony hurried to his horse and pulled out a sword from the saddle. He hollered at the two creatures approaching them.

Liz thought the gargoyles resembled pigs with wings in body style

242

but with a long, hairy tail. A set of wings flapped as they trotted toward the food. The faces had a dog like snout, fangs and bat like ears. The gargoyles stopped in their approach when Tony stepped between them and the remains of their lunch. He held the sword up high, the blade gleaming in the sunlight.

"Get!"

The gargoyles stopped, staring at him as they drooled. Their wings began to flap harder. The horses became more agitated.

"Tony, get on your horse and let's get out of here."

Tony yelled and ran toward the creatures. They howled at him, refusing to give up their ground. They flapped their wings and began a slow advance.

Tony swore and sprinted to his horse, quickly climbing on the saddle. "They want our lunch more than I'm willing to fight for it. Let's get out of here." Liz and the horses didn't need any more encouragement.

Tony complained, "I guess that might be it for lunch. Damn, I'm hungry too."

Liz laughed. "We get attacked by those two monsters and all you think about is food."

"Honestly, with you close by I'm not just thinking about food."

"Thanks, but I think I've had enough adventure today. Let's go back to the castle and eat there."

Tony led the way back to Lord Rosemore's castle, helping her off the horse when they arrived at the stables.

Liz went inside the castle with him to eat in the staff dining room. She wondered if Tony suspected that if the gargoyles hadn't interrupted them, she was willing to let him have his way with her. *Nothing happened and I still feel like I'm betraying Jon. I have needs and I don't know when, or if, I'll see Jon again This is frustrating*

————

Later that afternoon Liz ventured outside to the stables.

"Tony?" Liz called out as she entered the stable.

"Around the back." Tony yelled from rear of the stable.

Liz walked the length of the stable, admiring the horses as she breathed in the heavy air.

She opened the rear door and saw him working on a bridle, the black leather straps hanging from the table where he a set of tools. He was shirtless, and she watched his muscles move as he twisted at a piece of metal.

He stopped working. "I'm repairing some bridle pieces. What's up? Are you wanting another ride?"

Liz grinned. "No, although I do enjoy that. Actually, that's what I want to talk to you about. I like you as a man and I don't regret our excursions. I need to be honest with you and I hope you understand. I came here to this world to search for Jon. I love him and I don't want you to believe what we have is anything more than friends"

"And if you never find this Jon person? Then what?"

"I believe I will. I have to believe I will. I know I'm a slave here who has to work until my contract is concluded. But I won't lose hope. So, to be clear, Jon is the one I'm here for. I don't want to lose you as a friend. You have saved my sanity with our time together."

"Okay, I understand. I shall be your friend and perhaps more than that during our excursions." He raised his eyebrows.

Liz laughed. "On Earth we call that friends with benefits."

Tony considered what she said and suddenly laughed. "Oh, I get it now. Benefits. Tell me, can those benefits also include the use of rope and a bit of spanking?"

She wagged her finger at him. "Very dangerous benefits."

"I understand. But if Jon cannot be found, perhaps you'll consider me more than just a friend with benefits."

I do already. "We'll see. Now I best get back to work."

NINETEEN

The party, according to Nora, was to be a small one, only about fifty people and was a celebration to mark the occasion of a new-born granddaughter of the Rosemore's. A small band of string and horn instruments played in the corner of the large ballroom while servants walked around with trays of drinks and hors-d'oeuvres. Liz wore her best dress and circulated among the guests, making sure everyone was enjoying the festivity. Her own yellow gown had simple lines with a deep scooped neck and was unassuming compared to those worn by the other ladies. The dresses were usually layered with the fabric billowing out below the waist and several women sported matching hats or scarves. The men wore dark suits with cloaks, some of them holding canes.

Liz was enjoying the party, a nice change from her usual evenings at the castle when Lady Monique approached her with an older, anxious woman by her side.

"Liz, this is Lady Luanda Graham. I told her you had befriended Anthony, and she's curious about your perception of him." She smiled warmly at Lady Luanda and walked away.

Liz stood quietly. The older woman spent a few seconds appraising her before speaking.

"I'm trying to find out how my son is doing. I've heard reports that he's well, much better than I expected. But my sources may be only telling me what I want to hear. Please tell me the truth. How do you see Anthony?"

"He's always very polite to me. I see him quite a bit during my quiet times here and well, he's a lot of fun to be with. He loves horses, and he took me riding a few times. And Tony has a great sense of humour. He makes me laugh a lot."

"Tony?"

"Uh, I told him I thought Anthony was a bit stuffy. He didn't seem to mind a nickname."

"Oh, but Anthony is named after his grandfather. I thought it was a special name, not stuffy."

"I didn't mean to offend you, Lady Luanda. My sincere apologies."

"That's alright, dear. If Anthony doesn't mind, then I have no objections. But Anthony, Tony, has been nice to you?"

"Lady Luanda, Tony is polite to everyone and has been a perfect gentleman to me. You have raised a very fine son."

She grabbed Liz's arm. "Thank you, thank you for saying that. I'm going to talk to my husband about this. I want him to know how he has changed."

———

Two days had passed when Tony burst through the front door and grabbed Liz by the waist and spun her around.

"I'm a free man! My father has purchased my freedom and is going to give me my own land. You're looking at Lord Anthony Graham the second, or at least very soon."

She grinned back at him. "That's terrific, Lord Tony. You deserve it."

"I got more great news. You're going to be given your freedom too. I insisted my parents do that for you."

"But I don't understand."

"My parents think we're romantically involved."

"But we're not." She watched him turn away. "You did set them straight, didn't you?"

"Well, not exactly. I did tell them we're good friends but they may have misunderstood."

"Tony, I don't know what I have to say to you to make you understand."

He grinned sheepishly at her.

"Oh, what's the use? My freedom, huh? That means I can go search for Jon." His grin disappeared.

———

Liz arrived at the Graham Castle with Tony in a carriage. Despite wearing servant clothes, she was treated with respect by the staff. A hostess took her to the third level of the castle where she was given a large suite.

"We will have clothes for you brought up shortly. In the meantime, if there is anything at all that we can do to make you comfortable, please notify us immediately." She pointed at a cord hanging near the doorway.

"Thank you." Liz noticed the servants appeared to be much more formal than those at the Rosemore Castle. "I think I'll just relax for the time being."

Liz considered that with Tony preoccupied with his return to the family castle, it would be best if she didn't wander about the castle still wearing servant clothes.

Her windows didn't offer much of a view other than the grounds beyond and she began to doze off when a knock caused her to jump.

Two servants were there when she opened the door, with one carrying an armful of clothes. The first servant, a tall, thin woman, asked, "Do you desire help to dress?"

Liz shook her head. "I can manage just fine."

"Very good, Lady Liz. Dinner will be served at sunset. Your presence is desired." The two servants bowed and left.

Very stuffy. I'll bet there aren't any paintings of nude women hanging on any walls here. She smiled. *I suppose it wouldn't be proper for me to offer my services in that regard here.*

———

Liz tried on two of the dresses, placing them back in the closet and found a third more to her liking. All the dresses offered more coverage than she thought was necessary and decided the underwear and a petticoat was protecting her virtue a bit too much. Still, she layered on the garments, including a heavy bodice where she wished she did have help in tying the back laces.

She ventured from her room, wanting to see what the castle Tony grew up in looked like. She noticed paintings, full of colour but largely of battle scenes. A few portraits of distinguished men were also placed in prominent places in the high hallways, and she found only one lone painting of a woman. *Everyone fully dressed and looking very proper. Boring. They could use some nude paintings here.* She smiled at the thought of her nude painting hanging on the walls.

When she passed any servant, they paused at what they were doing and acknowledged her. She decided she liked the informal ways of the Rosemore Castle much more to her liking. She saw two gnants as well, wearing poor fitting clothes.

The castle, as much as she could tell, was larger than the Rosemore Castle. Several rooms she came across were the size of ballrooms, including one that served as a library.

She was interrupted on her exploring by a servant who indicated that it was time for dinner. She followed the older man walking with a pronounced limp.

"May I ask how you hurt your leg?"

"Of course, Lady Liz. It 'taint no secret. I hurt it in a journey many years ago to deliver supplies. Those demons attacked us. We killed one, but the rest stole our cargo."

"Demons?"

"Gnants. One and be the same."

"I'm sorry you were injured so."

"Thank you but I'm used to it now." He stopped at a double set of doors. "Here be the dining room."

Liz slowly entered the room. The table could seat sixteen but currently held five people. She recognized Lady Luanda, Lord Kevin, and Tony. The two others were both men, dressed as noble men. As she approached all the men stood with Tony moving behind an empty chair next to his own.

Am I supposed to curtsy? Instead she stopped just before the head of the table where Lord Kevin stood and gave a small bow of her head.

"Lord Kevin, Lady Luanda, thank you for the invitation for dinner."

She continued to where Tony stood and allowed him to seat her.

She heard Lady Luanda whisper to her husband, "See, I told you she had proper manners."

Various servings were placed on her plate and she was quite aware how others were observing her. She took small bites and was careful how she held her utensils. She took a glance at the plate of Lady Luanda and saw how she left a small portion on her plate after each serving. She decided to copy her example but knew her mother would be annoyed for wasting food. She noticed speaking was done only in low voices and not often. Tony gave her a whispered hello and informed her the two other men present were the ones who did much of the minor decision making for Lord Kevin.

After the last course, Lord Kevin cleared his throat. "Lady Liz, I have been told you met my son while in the employ at the Rosemore Castle."

"Yes, Lord Kevin. We were both working there."

"I see. Could you tell me the circumstances which led to you being there? I have noticed you show the signs of a formal upbringing which is not common on those employed as servants."

"Kevin! That is a bit blunt," Lady Luanda stared at her husband.

"My apologies if I offended but I find being direct is the best way to avoid misunderstandings."

"No offence taken. The truth is I came from the Other-side. I was unprepared for being on this world and ended up in the Labour House where Lady Monique purchased my services. That is where I met To…Anthony. She turned and gave Tony a smile.

"Shall I assume on the Other-side you came from an upper-class family? Perhaps comparably to our position here?"

How do I answer that? I doubt he would be impressed with my folk's little home. "It's hard to draw parallels between our two worlds. My parents own a home, don't have to work and they have always supported me in my pursuits to better myself."

Lord Kevin nodded, stroking his chin. "Anthony has told me you have need to contact someone who is from the Other-side as well. He didn't say who but implied this Sir Jon is an acquaintance of yours that you have an obligation to help." He stared at Liz, waiting for an answer.

"Yes, that wouldn't be incorrect to say." *Which means not exactly the truth either.*

"Very well. My son still has to prove to me he has some growing up

249

to do and one method would be to lead an expedition to help you find your friend."

"Thank you. That would be wonderful. I'm grateful for your support on this."

———

After the meal Liz walked with Tony down one of the hallways, reminding her of the size of subway tunnels. "So, I'm pursuing an acquaintance, am I?"

"It was a situation of one thing leading to another. The only way he would buy out your services to Lord Rosemore was if I implied we had a serious relationship."

"How serious?"

"I'm officially courting you. That is, if we find our company mutually agreeable, then we become engaged."

"That's not going to happen. My friend, Jon, remember?"

"How could I forget that?"

"Good. I truly like you—a lot—but I need to find Jon. Okay?"

"Okay. There is one more minor detail."

"And that would be?"

"Father has told me in no uncertain terms I had better find a wife and start producing heirs soon."

"And if you don't find a girl to marry?"

"I'll be cut off from the family in terms of financing. I'd be on my own. It cannot be just any woman. It has to be from a family that has land holdings and where the woman has been raised properly."

"I see. Your parents found me acceptable in that regard?"

"You have manners, good health and speak well. His questions at the dinner table were partly to determine that you came from a family of influence."

"Your father seems to place status over character, if I may say so."

"You are correct. He has high ideals that aren't always consistent with reality. As you can guess, my father and I don't see eye to eye on a lot of things."

"That much is obvious." *And your mother tempers that.* "When do we leave to search for Jon?"

"In the morning. I would love to spend the night with you but my father would not approve of that until we are at least engaged."

"I think it's just as well. I don't want the benefits to outweigh the friendship part."

———

The following morning after breakfast Liz was surprised to find eight horsemen wearing uniforms of guards, two horses without riders, a carriage and two wagons. Each wagon was piled high with supplies and required two horses each to pull it. In all, she guessed there were close to twenty people to join them on their trip.

"Is all of this necessary?"

"Likely not, but when doing anything under the Graham name it must be done with a certain amount of flourish and pomp." Tony assisted her into climbing into the carriage.

"At least we can ride in comfort there."

"The truth is these carriages are anything but comfortable to sit in during journeys on roads outside the town. However, we can converse in some manner as we ride."

The train of horses, carriages and wagons caused a reaction from the town folk and many of them waved at their carriage. Liz waved back.

Tony laughed. "It is not common for those in carriages to wave back but no harm in doing so."

"I guess riding in this carriage is better than sitting somewhere wondering how Jon is doing. Besides, I'm sure I'll be safe with you and your bodyguards."

"My father's elite guards are more than just bodyguards. They're also..."

"Whatever, it's nice to have them along." She gave him a smile. "And you as well."

"Thanks, I was starting to wonder if you'd preferred to go alone in search of this Sir Jon."

"Look, this Sir Jon is the one I'm in love with. But you are my friend, my best friend in this whole world. I want you to go with me and not just for protection but because I really enjoy your company."

"Fair enough. You did a lot to help me and I'm grateful for that."

———

For Liz there was something of interest on almost every part of the journey. Tony told her of various trees and plants that made up the great forests and as well as some the creatures that inhabit them.

"They're several types of dragons but not all of them fly. They're the main predators here. As far as game is concerned, humans imported deer, lamb, cattle and what have you before the Great Gate was closed. There're also omnivorous eaters such as gargoyles that we saw. I think they may be related to dragons, or so I've been told."

"Is there any danger of being attacked by dragons?"

"Well, some. But that's why we have the elite guards with us. They can handle just about anything. Besides, we're not going all that far."

"Stone Retreat. You said we could meet Jon there."

"It seems the best place to meet, a half way point. I have sent messengers ahead to tell him to expect you there."

"How will we know he gets the message?"

"In this world nothing is certain. But the messenger service is quite good if one pays enough."

"And thank you for taking care of that as well."

"Don't mention it. Expenses are not a problem for me now."

She relaxed as their carriage rolled down the bumpy road. It was hard to believe she was going to see Jon again, and she wondered if she was ever going to go back to Earth. It didn't matter. Her goal was to find Jon, and it seemed she was going to do that. Unless that girl he was travelling with had sunk her hooks into him. She thought of Tony. *I guess I'm not on the high horse here. I gave into temptation rather easily with him.*

Late in the afternoon they stopped for the night. Liz found she ached as she stood next to the carriage. *That was not a comfortable ride. I think a horse would have been better.* She watched as the crew started a large campfire, made tents and took care of the horses. The tent Tony and herself were to stay in was a large affair that consisted of a main sleeping area, a smaller room for dressing and a small area to use as a toilet.

She looked inside the tent. *One bed.*

Liz heard the dinner bell and stepped outside. Tony was waiting for her under an awning where a table and two chairs were placed. He helped her sit and shortly after servants brought plates and food and drink.

Between bites she commented, "I noticed only one bed in the tent."

"Yes. I could have brought a second bed and tent but that would have been an extra burden for the horses. I thought we could share the bed if you have no objections. Otherwise, I can sleep in a cot."

"Yes, I'm sure you were concerned about the burden on the horses." She smiled. "We can share the bed, but that's all."

————

Once the sun set, Liz and Tony retreated to inside their tent. A pair of lanterns kept the inside well lit.

Servants quickly set up a small table with chairs inside the tent, leaving a pair of goblets and a flagon of wine.

Liz accepted a wine from Tony. "At least there aren't many bugs inside the tent."

"True. Are you hungry? I can have some snacks made up for you."

"No, I'm quite full." She sipped at her wine, with the bed close by and in her thoughts.

"Do you wish for me to call for one of the servants to help you dress for bed?"

Liz laughed. "I think I can take off my own clothes." She went to the wardrobe, a cloth covered closet that held her selection of garments. She pulled out a long nightgown. *This to be just about the least sexy nightwear I've ever seen.*

Tony spoke. "I will have a drink outside the tent. I believe that will allow you sufficient time to change."

She put on the nightgown and climbed into the bed. The mattress was soft and sagged in the middle. She waited and Tony returned from his drink.

He didn't have the same qualms about changing in front of her. She watched him strip naked, with his back turned toward her, and slip on a nightshirt. Tony turned off the lanterns and joined her in bed.

He pressed against her as the bed sagged in the middle. "Sorry, it seems we have limited space here."

"That's okay. I'll just sleep on my side." She gave him a quick kiss goodnight and rolled over, facing the outside of the bed. Shortly later she noticed his arm cover her as he spooned her.

She closed her eyes and began to drift off. There was a pressure on her ass. *Damn, I hope he doesn't expect to get anything tonight. I thought I made that quite clear.* She pretended to sleep, hoping he wouldn't try to push past her weak defences. She felt a kiss at the back of her neck but nothing more. She fell asleep.

———

Liz woke up to a soft glow in the tent from the morning sun. She lifted her head to see Tony getting dressed. Her head dropped back on the pillow. *I better get up too. It'll probably be another long day of travel.*

Liz dressed and left the tent to find a small table had been set for breakfast for Tony and herself. As they drank tea and ate, workers took down the tents and other gear. The cooks continued to cook breakfast for the rest of the staff that journeyed with them.

"Sorry we had to camp out last night but Seilini is too far to travel in one day. Of course, Seilini doesn't have the best accommodation either but I'll try to keep you comfortable."

"Comfortable? Tony, this isn't exactly roughing it you know. We're being served breakfast by servants in the middle of nowhere. That tent is bigger than my first apartment back home and the bed is softer than the one at Lord Rosemore's."

"Yes, well, you're my responsibility now and I want to make sure you're at ease during the trip."

Liz relaxed as the staff efficiently repacked the camp on the wagons. She watched Tony as he talked to two workers and continued his walk to their carriage. As he passed by a female servant, he gave her a pat on her behind.

She quickly turned around, her frown turning into a grin as she recognized him.

I can see where his reputation as a womanizer came from.

———

Liz found the journey interesting, but she didn't notice any danger that Tony warned her about. "It seems pretty safe on this road. I guess the elite guards help keep robbers away."

"They do. Highway men, dragons and other dangers would be there if we weren't traveling with protection."

"I'm sure you're right. I haven't seen a dragon yet other than that small one you pointed out to me earlier that hid in the forest."

"You'll see some eventually that are a lot bigger than that. It is best to avoid them if at all possible. Notice those farm houses and barns with spiked roofs?"

She looked where he pointed.

"Those are meant to discourage dragons from attacking but every year some farm is left in ruins from those damn beasts. They get hungry enough they assail the cattle and people. Sometimes the dragon dies but usually the farm is left in ruins. It's a tough way to eke out a living, raising livestock here."

The journey was uneventful and their conversation light. Liz did consider mentioning that if he was serious about finding a wife, he would have to learn to control his urges every time he saw a pretty woman. *He's doing me a big favour in helping me reach Jon and I shouldn't criticize him right now.*

A few hours later they arrived at Seilini. Liz considered Horstuff was more appealing for a medieval town. Seilini had narrower streets, and both the buildings and the inhabitants looked worn down.

They stayed the night in Seilini, taking over two floors of the Luscious Inn. Any guests currently staying on those floors were told firmly they had to relocate to another part of the hotel. The inn was only four stories high but covered a large area. In addition, the inn supported a large stable for the horses. Immediately after they moved in, the cooks went into town to purchase fresh produce and meat. When they returned they took over the kitchen. The staff at the inn was pushed off to the side from their normal work and spent the time sitting in the inn's tavern, drinking in the corner. They weren't too upset as they would also be allowed to enjoy the food the cooks prepared.

Tony took a small drink from his tankard, tasting the liquid carefully. "Not too bad, not bad at all."

"Don't enjoy it too much. You only get two pints."

"Hey, I can handle more than that."

"I'm sure you can. But you don't want to fall into your old habits again, do you?"

"No, but…"

"No buts." Liz took a drink of her own ale. "And if the waitress brings you an extra ale by mistake, I'll just have to drink it for you." She grinned at him. "So there."

"You know you could drive a man to drink with your attitude."

She laughed. "I'm assuming I'll have my own room tonight."

He sighed. "Yes, I thought you'd want that."

"Tony, if we're to share a bed tonight, I *know* what would happen. I'm not pretending what we did in Horstruff didn't happen but now that I'm on my way to see Jon I can't have you as more than a friend."

He nodded. "So, the benefits are gone." He gave a smile.

"Gone, but never forgotten."

Liz went up to her room, leaving Tony to sip a final tankard in the tavern. She gave him a kiss on the lips but quickly broke it off when his hand touched her waist. The bed was not comfortable and her thoughts kept returning to when she would see Jon again. Eventually she dozed off, dreaming of Jon fighting a dragon to save her.

They left as early as was possible for a large entourage the next morning. The inn was glad for the business that Sir Anthony brought, although slightly annoyed how Sir Anthony took control over much of the inn.

Liz didn't sense any danger as they travelled down the road. Travellers along the road they came across quickly moved to the side to allow them to pass.

The danger of attacks by dragons never materialized, the creatures apparently preferred to attack only single travellers or small groups. Liz did see several of the large par dragons fly overhead and the carriage was buzzed once by volvcris dragons. One flapped past the carriage window, causing her to scream and elicited laughter from those around her.

They stopped for lunch, which involved much work for the staff to build a fire, cook dinner and set a table and chairs. It gave Liz a chance to stretch her legs and Tony joined her.

"Perhaps in another day or two, you'll see Jon again."

"Yes, I'm so looking forward to it."

"That is good. I am happy for you and glad to assist you on this expedition. But a selfish part of me hopes he doesn't show up and I'll have you for myself."

"Tony…"

"I know, I know. But I thought it best that I be honest with you now so if I act less than gracious when I meet him, you'll understand."

She reached for his hand, giving it a squeeze. *How did I end up with two men I could spend the rest of my life with?*

Lunch was a hot meal and Liz had to refuse some dishes. *Too many calories at breakfast, lunch and dinner. And for exercise I sit in that bouncy carriage.*

Their journey resumed, and at mid-afternoon Tony suddenly pointed to a grey and brown structure on the horizon.

"There be Stone Retreat, Liz."

She leaned across where he sat next to her, peering out the carriage window. She grinned, "I wonder if Jon is there already?"

He rested a hand on her back, "One can always hope."

TWENTY

Lord Bennett hurled his goblet against the far wall. It bounced, spraying the red wine across the wall and floor. "What do you mean he doesn't have it?" He yelled at the quivering gnant as a guard stood behind it, holding a knife at its throat. There was little the gnant could do with its hands bound behind its back.

"He hidess it. Then he hasss it later but we fail attack."

"You and your kind are worthless. Absolutely useless!" Lord Bennett paced the room, his purple robe blossoming out behind him. A lean man of average height, he displayed agitated energy, causing his ninety-two-year-old face to be creased with anger even at sleep. Magic kept him younger, perhaps at his mid-fifties, but he needed stronger magic to halt ageing completely.

"So, he has it now...he'll have reached Paderno City by now, staying overnight before going on to Cretal where they will buy whatever crystals they're searching for." Lord Bennett thought out loud. "From Paderno City to Cretal is at least a five-hour journey and they will need time to do business in Cretal, so they will undoubtedly spend overnight in Cretal before turning back. There're only two inns they'll consider staying in, the Rose and the Garland." He gave a small smile. "I want you gnants to attack him in Cretal at whichever inn they use. Kill them all and return that crystal to me. You gnants think you know magic. Well, if you screw this mission up, I'll show all of you a lesson in the arts."

The gnant scurried out of the castle, bleeding at neck and ear where the guard had nicked her with his knife. Rattru rubbed her wrists from where the ropes dug into her skin.

She was glad to leave the castle grounds and headed to the open field next to the castle grounds. She passed the blackened timbers of the church that had burnt down years before and the spot where Liz had entered Domum. She continued on to where the forest had reclaimed part of the vacant lot and river bank. A few minutes later, several other gnants joined her.

"/What did Lord Bennett tell you?\"

"/He said he was the ruler and that if the gnants didn't follow his orders he would order all humans to eliminate us.\"

"/He can do that to us? He has that power?\"

"/I do not know. He has lied to us before. He has no honour.\"

"/Correct. Can we risk that he is lying again?\"

Rattru was quiet as she considered the possibility Lord Bennett's threat was a lie. "/Too great a risk for gnants. He ordered us to kill the travelling humans and to obtain the crystal for him. I say we kill humans and take crystal. Then decide what to do with it.\"

The gnants approved of her suggestion and they dispersed into the woods. After ten minutes, Laquil crept out of a hiding spot and hurried as fast a gnome could to sell his information.

———

Lord Perry sat heavily in the chair behind his massive desk. The cushions sagged under his weight as he viewed Council Madoc. "Now is this security really necessary or are you just trying to hype up the sale of your latest gossip?" Council Madoc had insisted on an isolated room and that no one, especially gnants, be allowed in, even next to the room.

Council Madoc sighed. "I do not deal in gossip. Lord Perry, have I ever given you information that was either wrong or not helpful?"

"You have a point. Tell me what is of such great import this time."

"Please have a bit of patience with me. I had to follow quite a trail of facts to find what could be a most unpleasant conclusion." He took a drink of his wine before continuing. "Sir Jon and the rest of the assemblage you sent to Cretal to obtain a crystal are in grave danger. I interviewed a young lady named Liz O'Doul, who happens to be a girlfriend of Sir Jon. She is, of course, also from the Other-side and is here to search for him. She informed me that Sir Jon actually has the missing link to the Locas crystal."

"What? But that crystal's location has been unknown for centuries!"

"Yes, it was in the castle on Earth that corresponds to Lord Bennett's. And Lord Bennett has at least one himself. After I found out Sir Jon had a missing link to the Locas crystal, it became obvious the two missing links would be at either end of a gateway.

"Lord Bennett found out Sir Jon had the crystal from a barmaid who saw it on him."

"Not Nicole Keaton?"

"No, a different one."

"He seems to meet a lot of bar maids."

"Indeed. But to add to the problem, Lady Karla has apparently told the gnants he has the crystal as well. I assume they offered her some sort of payment for that information. The gnants failed to find the crystal and punished Lady Karla for failing to keep up her end of the bargain."

"I heard that she has been hurt quite badly. I didn't know how."

"Lord Perry, I have also found out that Lord Holdstum has been less than diligent in caring for the two Locas crystals in his possession. I have come to the conclusion that Lord Bennett now has them."

"That power hungry warlock has three links!"

Madoc shook his head. "Worse. He approached the gnants, actually their Adepts, and told them his own link had suddenly come to life by itself, glowing with light. He suggested that they bring their link close to with his own to see if it activated the other links. They agreed, and with magic and subterfuge, he took their crystals, killing many gnants in the process."

"The Adepts were angry at his deception and were willing to attack Lord Bennett and his castle but he threatened them with extinction unless they followed his orders, claiming he was the ruler of all humans."

"He is a madman."

"True. And what is also true is that he plans to usurp King Charles and be crowned king himself."

Lord Perry sat back, digesting the information. "Why are you telling me this? You have no loyalty to me or any other lord. What do you obtain by telling me this? Do you want payment for this information? Speak."

"I ask nothing in return. However, if Lord Bennett becomes king, my life becomes risky indeed. There might not be room for another warlock of his strength in his kingdom. Also, quite frankly, I do not want to see another human-gnant war which would be the outcome if he has his way. But the biggest danger is that if he joins all the links of the Locas crystal together he may unleash powers, he cannot control. Earth and Domum may be joined together by a permanent gate, a rift that cannot be closed."

"What would you have me do?"

"Lord Perry, I know you dislike politics and the alliances one has to join to keep the balance of power. But it is now time for you to talk to the other lords about stopping Lord Bennett before it's too late."

"I shall consider your request. But you know a cynical man might think you were trying to arrange a situation where Lord Bennett was to lose his status as a lord. And correct me if I am wrong but he was the one who led the vote against you receiving the title of a lord and the resulting privileges. With him gone, you would stand to reap some substantial benefits."

"That isn't why I came to you with this information."

"So you say. But it does beg the question of who gains the most and who loses the most under your suggestions and if all the facts are known."

"Then it comes down to whether you trust me or not." Council Madoc stood up. "Lord Perry, if it would make your decision easier, I'm willing to go to the Other-side and never return to Domum. That way you can put whatever gains I may make out of the equation. But I beg of you, please act quickly to stop Lord Bennett. Before it's too late."

———

Lord Perry sat a long time at his desk after Council Madoc had left. He tapped his fingers along the wood of the desk. As Council Madoc had pointed out, it came down whether he believed him or not. As far as going to the Other-side in exile, that may have been an empty gesture.

If Lord Bennett does indeed take over as king, then that would be the safest place for him. If Lord Bennett is defeated in battle, there was nothing to prevent him from returning to Domum at a later date.

Lord Perry came to a decision. He stood up and walked briskly out of the room. "Reesler! I want to see you now!"

TWENTY-ONE

Paderno City was indeed filled with mystery, as Nicole claimed. Jon thought he saw ghosts walking about but Nicole informed him they were real people using magic to cast projections of themselves to move about the city. The projections couldn't touch objects but could relay sights and sounds to their owners.

"Almost every building here is made from magic. If you go inside some palaces here, you'll find they're actually bigger on the inside than the outside. Rather disorientating if you go in one door and out another. And in some paintings, the scenes actually change as you watch. Like a horse will move from one end of the frame to another."

"Then it disappears from the painting?"

"No, it comes back on the other side again."

A black and silver clad man on a horse called out as he passed them. "Message for Sir Jon McKinney. Message for Sir Jon McKinney."

"Jon! That's you!"

Jon reacted quickly and caught up with the rider.

"You have a message for me?"

The rider scrutinized him for several seconds. "Yes, the message reads; Liz O'Doul has reached Domum and awaits you at Stone Retreat. She will be staying at the Kosture Inn."

Jon froze, his jaw slack.

Nicole fluttered her hand at the messenger. "Go. He understands what you told him. You can delete the spell now."

"Liz is here!"

"I heard."

"She's at Stone Retreat!"

"I heard that too. Come on, let's catch up to the others and let them know what's going on."

The five arrived at a hotel and Sir Keith frowned at the price per room at the medium class facility.

"There won't be anything cheaper here unless we want to drop to the lower end of accommodation. We have a choice, our separate rooms in far less than prime conditions or we can share two rooms here." He looked first at Nicole and next at Nathan. "That likely means Gilbert, Nathan and myself in one room with Nicole and Sir Jon in the other."

Nicole spoke up first. "It's safer if we share rooms. Besides, the food will be better here I assume."

Nathan shrugged. "Fine with me."

Gilbert thought he had a better suggestion. "I says we takes turns sleeping with the girl. Everyone happy that way."

Nicole had a flash of anger on her face as she spoke. "I'm not the girl everyone gets to sleep with, you moron." She whacked him on the back of his head. "What kind of woman do you think I am?"

She glared at him as he picked up his hat.

"Oh, I think you as a nice lady. Very nice lady. Me jaw talk before I think. Sorry."

She whacked him on the back of his head again. "Next time I won't be such a nice lady." She turned and walked into the hotel.

Nathan laughed. "Well, I guess that issue is settled. Gilbert, Gilbert, Gilbert. You do say the damnedest things at times."

Gilbert spat on the ground. "Women."

The five sat around a large circular table drinking wine or ale while their food was being prepared, deciding to order half a pig that they could divide among themselves along with a mix of roasted vegetables.

Jon questioned Nicole on how the messenger knew where to find him.

"They use a simple spell, but it has unique characteristics."

Gilbert piped up. "Spell can find person only if a person using it don't get a direct benefit from finding you. Nicole couldn't use a spell to finds ya fer instance, 'cause she knows ya and would gain from finding you."

Nicole nodded. "Messengers get paid whether they find their subject or not; therefore, they don't benefit from finding you. If a person doesn't want to be found then the spell won't work either."

The meal arrived, and Nathan used a knife to carve up the meat to the various plates. Jon learned a lot more about magic and spells during the meal as the other members told tales of one magic spell or another. They also talked about crystals, and Jon asked about the bright light that lit up the sky from one of the towers.

Sir Keith explained, "You see the common folk here speak of the crystals as being alive or dead but what they really mean is if the crystal has latent energy or not. The crystal that shines here, and the one around your neck as well, had energy placed in it during its formation. Gradually over time, the force is spent and the crystal dies. But in the case of that tower crystal that force can last centuries. Someday it will stop shining but not in our lifetime."

"Is there a way to stop the crystal from shining? I mean besides breaking it."

"Well, one could join it with an annul crystal and the two would cancel each other out. But never break or destroy a live crystal; it would suddenly release all of its stored power and the result would be disastrous. For example, if you were to destroy the crystal around your neck, the explosion would level several blocks in all directions."

Jon waited with Gilbert, drinking ale, after the others and Nicole had gone up to their rooms. Jon decided he should give her some time to get ready for bed first.

"Yous lucky. Nicole likes you lots."

"Yeah, I guess so. But my heart really is with Liz."

"I see why, nice body, big boobs."

Jon laughed. "Appearance is one thing alright. But we clicked personality wise too."

"So what happens when Liz shows up? Nicole and her get along?" Gilbert gave a toothy grin.

"Gilbert, you have an evil mind. No, when Liz shows up, I spend my time with her."

"Hey, then Nicole free. You put in a good word for ol' Gilbert?"

"I think you better put in your own good word. Don't you have a girlfriend back home?"

"I does. But there be a saying. If your love is further away than a day, then ye can play."

"You know…" Jon's words were interrupted by the appearance of a gnant that wandered around the almost empty room and came toward their table, stopping a few feet away.

Jon noticed the hair blemish on its head. "Hey, are you that gnant that attacked us a few nights ago?" He quietly rested his hand on his sword.

"True. I am Rzet. You give me a life. I now return life." He shuffled closer. "Adeptsss order to kill you all in Cretal when you sleep. Do not stay the night in Cretal or you die." Rzet looked left and right and began to back away.

"Wait." Jon stole a glance at Gilbert who was trying to disappear in his chair. "Come back here."

The gnant hesitated.

"Sit down and have some food. I want to ask you something."

The gnant licked its lips, showing off its yellow pointed teeth. He quickly jumped up on a chair and reached for slices of pork. Gilbert gasped and grabbed his tankard of ale with both hands.

"Rzet, what's so damn important about this crystal that we'd be killed for it? Like I know it's important but to murder for it?"

"Lord Bennett hasss five linksss, want lassst one. Orders gnantsss to get it from you, kill all humansss around you." Rzet jammed several hunks of pork into his mouth.

"Lord Bennett ordered that? I find that hard to believe."

Gilbert gulped his ale and then spoke. "I belief it. Lord Bennett is a power hungry warlock. But I still don'ts trust any gnant. He may be saying this to lead us to a trap."

"Nonsense. Why would he have to say anything to lead us to a trap? We don't know what they're planning one way or another. I think he's more trustworthy than Lord Bennett."

"We isss. I not want to kill humansss. Just follow ordersss."

"If he gets all the crystals…that's dangerous, isn't it?"

Gilbert answered, "Lord Bennett would kill alls the gnants and then anyones he don't like. I says to you, Lord Bennett make a worse friend than enemy."

"He say he order all humans to kill gnantsss if we don't listen to him and follow orders."

"Listen Rzet, he doesn't command all humans. He sure as hell doesn't command us, does he? He lied to you."

"You ssspeak truth. He lied." The gnant grabbed another piece of pork and jumped down. "Rzet go now. Beware when in Cretal."

Jon looked at the back of the disappearing gnant. "Well, things are getting interesting."

"Yous right there. Gnant warning us, makes sense now. If Lord Bennett has all the other crystal links, he has a chance for a lot of power if he gets the last one from you."

"We better decide what to do in the morning. I'm going to bed, see you in the morning."

"Sure, you gots Nicole waiting for you. I have Sir Keith and Nathan. Wanna trade?"

"If I did, Nicole would clobber both of us."

———

Jon woke alone on the bed and after his eyes adjusted to the morning light of the room, he spotted Nicole fastening the buttons on her dress near a mirror.

"Good morning, Nicole."

She turned and glanced at him. "Morning yourself. You stayed up late last night."

He yawned and swung his legs off the bed. "Couple of things happened. I'll tell you and the rest at breakfast."

"Did you get drunk with Gilbert?"

"No, why?"

"'Cause you slept on top of the covers. You took off your shirt but not your pants."

"I waited until I thought you were already in bed before I came into the room and decided I should sleep on top of the covers because…."

"To protect my virtue?" She grinned at him.

"In a way."

"That's a little late. But thanks for the thought. See you at breakfast."

Jon washed up and joined the others in the dining room. He, with the animated support of Gilbert, described the warning the gnant gave him last night.

Nathan frowned. "A gnant warned you not to go to Cretal?"

"More like not to stay there overnight."

Sir Keith shook his head. "You can't trust a gnant."

"I believe this one." Jon looked at Nicole and Gilbert for support. Gilbert nodded while Nicole gave a non-committal shrug.

Nathan took another piece of bread, and with his mouth full, mumbled, "If Sir Jon believes that gnant, then let us follow his wishes." He swallowed his mouthful of bread. "Let us travel to Sevenor first. We can obtain the Mood Figurines there and stay there overnight. Cretal is just a short journey from there. We get a Voltaire crystal and hightail it out of there. Agreed?"

The road to Sevenor was well traveled, with the dirt and rock pathway hard packed. Sir Keith led the way and found they made excellent time, arriving at Sevenor sooner than was expected. There was no doubt they were being watched on their travel. Gilbert finally informed the rest of the group of his ability to detect gnant cries.

"Theys makings lots of noise." Gilbert eyed the trees suspiciously.

"I expect they're following us rather closely. There isn't much we can do about it. I, for one, think it's best we stay on the road and move as swiftly as possible to Cretal."

They reached the fork in the road that would take them to Sevenor, rather than Cretal, and turned south.

Gilbert called out to Nathan, "Gnants getting mores excited."

"That is not unexpected. I saw a couple of them try to follow us but they're not prepared for our change in direction."

An hour passed and Gilbert used his gnant crier to inform the group that they were still present but the gnants were not as prevalent.

"I bets they's surprised we going to Sevenor instead of Cretal. They don't know what to do nows." Gilbert stuffed his gnant crier back into his pack. "That gnant maybe tell truth."

Jon nodded. "The gnants don't seem to like surprises, or at least don't react quickly to new situations."

"Agreed. But we still better be on watch for an attack." Nathan swivelled in his saddle and looked around. "Those creatures can strike at a moment's notice. We best not underestimate them."

Sevenor was a clean but drab town. The most popular stone was grey and the building designs were basic square blocks. Sir Keith led them to the market place and Nicole discovered several shops that sold Mood Figurines. She examined several in the different shops.

"This one."

Jon approached her. "Why? How can you tell the difference between them?"

She didn't answer but continued to examine the crystal sculpture, an abstract art form that was supposed to represent two bodies intertwined together.

Jon was about to repeat his question when he felt a change in himself, a stirring in his loins. As his hand reached for Nicole, Jon suddenly realized what he was doing and stopped.

"Do you feel it too?" Nicole turned and looked at him. "It's a slow but steady force that works on people nearby." She held the crystal away from her and approached the clerk.

Jon was surprised a crystal could cause a change in people that way but didn't doubt its ability to do what it claimed. He watched as Nicole bargained for it, countering an offer to the initial price. She also purchased a special cloth that had a spell placed on it to counter the Mood Figurines powers. She wrapped the crystal carefully in it and gave it to Sir Keith to carry.

Sir Keith appeared puzzled that he was given the object to care for. "Why are you giving this to me to carry?"

"I can trust you to take good care of it..." she shot a quick glance toward Gilbert. "...and it's a bit bulky for me to carry. Please?"

"Very well, Nicole. You can trust me to safeguard it."

Nicole turned to Jon when Sir Keith was out of an earshot. "I didn't need any more temptation from that thing. Last night was hard enough with us sharing a bed. It was a good thing that you left your pants on, that's all I'll say for now. If you're going to meet up with Liz soon, it's best we respect boundaries. I didn't want to push our luck by having it close by."

"Good point. I have to tell you, sleeping next to you made those pants rather uncomfortable."

She laughed. "Good, because I ended up having rather interesting thoughts."

Sir Keith led the way down a maze of similar streets, arriving at a large hotel. "The inn was originally a castle for a minor lord. I think it'll provide us with superior protection than other accommodation. We can obtain rooms on the second floor and they can be made quite secure from the outside by shutters. I believe this is the best we can do under the circumstances."

They carried their belongings up to the second level of the hotel. Sir Keith didn't ask Nicole and Jon if they wanted to share a room, merely indicating which room would be theirs.

"You can rest up but I suggest we get together for dinner. Safety in numbers."

Nicole opened the door. "It's bigger than the other hotel rooms we stayed in."

"It is." He walked over to one of windows. "At least we'll get some fresh air in here tonight."

"Look, I don't want to be critical but you really need a second set of clothes. Why don't you wash up and I'll pick up something new for you to wear?"

"I don't have money to purchase clothing."

"That's okay. New, clean clothes is as much for my benefit as it for you." She grinned. "You smell."

Jon took a bath while Nicole was gone and tried to wash off most of the dirt from his clothes. By the time he was finished cleaning up, Nicole returned with a new shit and pants.

"Thanks. That's really nice of you."

"No worries."

The thumping on the door interrupted them. "Dinner downstairs." Gilbert yelled.

The former lord's castle had a single long table in which a dozen guests sat around to enjoy dragon tail, pork and yams. After dinner, Nicole, Gilbert, and Sir Keith moved to a separate lounge to drink. The lounge had several chairs loosely grouped around the fireplace set in the middle of the room.

Jon sat with Nathan after dinner in the dining hall, discussing when they should leave and just how soon they should arrive at Cretal.

"It's not far, perhaps a three-hour ride. We won't stop there other than to buy your crystal and to grab some provisions to eat along the road. With luck we can arrive at Paderno City before twilight."

Two hours later, Sir Keith decided to take a walk around the inn's courtyard before turning in. Gilbert was starting to fall asleep in his chair, occasionally waking up from his snooze long enough to take another drink.

Jon waited another half hour and woke up Gilbert, helping the dwarf stagger to his room that he shared with Sir Keith.

Nicole was still awake when he entered his own room. He checked the shutters that Nicole had locked. He undressed and tried to wrap the towel around his waist.

Nicole turned on her side toward him. "I'm wondering how long that towel will stay on." She laughed.

"Why is it so damn warm in here?"

"Shutters closed, no air movement. Don't worry, I think I can hold myself back from attacking you."

"Good night." Jon quickly pull the sheet over him.

———

The following morning Jon stretched as he sat on his horse and considered he had slept well enough for a change. He saw Nicole at breakfast and she simply gave him a wink.

The air felt heavy, and he suspected it was going to be another hot, humid day. Most of the others were tired as well and there was little conversation. Gilbert slumped in his saddle moaning about his head while Nathan was the lone person looking alert as he trailed behind the others.

A few hours along the road, the entourage stopped for lunch and to stretch their legs. Sir Keith was nervous and paced around their small campsite, while Gilbert covered his head with his blanket.

Sir Keith approached Nicole and Jon. "Nathan has heated up a small lunch for us. Now remember, our plan is for Nicole and myself to go to the market in Cretal while the others wait at a local tavern. If gnants or spies were watching, it's likely their interests will be on Jon and his Locus Crystal. That leaves Nicole free to find the right Voltaire crystal. I'll provide protection and help negotiate payment for the crystal."

Nicole nodded. She wasn't certain exactly what would be the right crystal and how much it would be worth. She could tell if the crystal was working and its strength to some degree, but knew she would have to depend on the honesty of the merchant as well. If she obtained the wrong crystal, the whole trip was for naught. She and Jon might never get another chance to return to Earth. *No pressure at all.*

———

Sir Keith led the way to the market, again showing an uncanny ability to know where he was going even in a town he had never been in before.

"Quite logical, actually." He spoke to Jon after being asked how he knew where the main market was located. "The market of any town is normally in the oldest part that's near a river. There's almost always a church steeple near the centre one can see from a distance that provides a guide as well. The first thing most settlers do is to build homes right by the river, then a church and finally a market of some sort. Eventually, more homes and buildings surround these earlier parts but if one understands how the town grew, then finding the market area is easy. Ah, here we are."

Nicole peered at the cobbled streets that twisted and turned. Shops crowded along the sides as people moved about in a slow pace. She turned to Jon. "I see the Sea Maiden's Dragon tavern. Let's meet there after I find the crystal."

"Okay. Are you sure you'll be okay by yourself?"

"Sir Keith will be with me."

"I know, but I'm not confident he can offer you much protection."

"If you or Nathan were to accompany me, that would raise suspicion among the gnants and whoever else is searching for Jon's crystal."

"I suppose so. I have to say I'm not happy about you doing this but we don't have a choice."

"Don't worry. I'll be fine."

———

Nicole started her search by entering into the shops. She eventually began to converse with a woman selling an assortment of rugs and baskets. She responded to Nicole's inquiry of Voltaire crystals by reminding her they were illegal to sell but several shops a block past the church would discreetly sell them.

"How do I know what quality they are?"

"You don't. The merchants don't always know either. They buy them on chance as well. The crystals are all alive, but who knows what they are supposed to do unless you try them? And they don't work here, only near gateways. The nearest gateway is in Horstruff."

Nicole thanked her, going past the church to another set of shops clustered together. "Sir Keith, we may have to buy more than one to be assured we do get one that works."

"You may be right there. I might be able to buy two." When she opened the door of the first shop, she saw a wide arrangement of crystals.

Sir Keith whispered to her. "Perhaps he may have one."

Nicole nodded and returned the greeting from the shopkeeper. The man was old, stooped at his thin shoulders as he eyed them. Liver spots decorated his bald head as he leaned on the small counter in front of him.

"Anything in particular you're longing for?" He rubbed his left hand with his right.

Nicole approached the counter as she surveyed the various crystals and abruptly stopped. "No thanks, just looking." She led the surprised Sir Keith out the door.

"You didn't ask him about the crystals?" he challenged her after they left the small shop.

"No. He was dishonest. I could tell and wouldn't trust him to sell us a true Voltaire crystal."

"Oh." That was the extent of his reply as he followed her into the next shop.

The next shop was larger than the first and featured a middle-aged clerk who was missing his left arm. A gnant was also there, and the two were rearranging crystal and wooden sculptures on a shelf. The clerk was not overweight but had a large waist that contrasted with his thin legs and arm. His dark hair was long and only partially combed.

The gnant stopped working as well as the clerk and it was the gnant that spoke. "Good day."

Nicole was caught staring at the clerk, but quickly recovered and spoke to the gnant. "Good day. We're interested in Voltaire crystals. Do you have any?"

"Not legal them."

"I know, but I heard that you may have a source."

The gnant looked at the clerk who in turn stared at her and Sir Keith. The clerk gave a small nod.

"True. We may help." The gnant reached behind a small table and produced three cube shaped crystals with one corner shaved flat. Each was the size of a fist and had a faint green colour to them.

"We have three."

Nicole touched them under the watchful eye of the gnant and the clerk.

"Which one is best? Do you know?"

"No. Do not know."

"How much are they?"

"Two gold fernsss each."

Nicole heard Sir Keith draw in his breath. She touched each crystal again and stared intently at the clerk and the gnant.

"Too much. How about a gold and a half?"

The clerk and the gnant exchanged sign language.

"Not enough."

"How much can we afford?" Nicole turned to Sir Keith. She didn't bother to whisper, knowing the gnant would be able to overhear any whisper easily.

"I have just over three gold ferns to pay for the crystals. I hadn't expected them to cost so much."

Nicole reflected that they also hadn't expected to put Lady Karla up in a most expensive resort while she healed from her injuries. Less money for a lot of things she concluded. "Give them to me please."

He handed over the gleaming metal coins.

She placed them on the counter and produced a small leather bag, dumping the contents beside them.

"There, that's all we have. I want all three crystals or I go elsewhere."

The gnant and the clerk exchanged looks and began their sign language. The clerk pushed the coins around and quickly calculated how much was spilled on the counter.

"Deal. Joe think you pretty. Like you."

The mute Joe gave Nicole a smile that she returned as the gnant scooped up the coins and placed the crystals on a cloth, wrapping them up.

As they walked away from the shop and back to the pub to meet up with the others, Sir Keith complimented Nicole on her negotiations. "Well done, well done."

"I think it helped that Joe liked me."

"He did at that. Your womanly charms certainly were an asset."

"That gnant seemed to work quite well with him."

"Yes. I have never heard of a gnant using sign language before. And he was quite friendly as well. The gnants here are more numerous than at Horstuff and seem to act much better."

They met up with Jon, Nathan and Gilbert at the pub. Gilbert had recovered from his hangover sufficiently to be drinking ale again while the other two decided to drink tea and eat bread and cheese. Jon was delighted with their success in obtaining three Voltaire crystals after Nicole explained that the odds were at least one of them may work.

After Nicole and Sir Keith had a quick bite to eat and tea to drink, they headed back on the road to Paderno City.

TWENTY-TWO

Lord Perry clasped his hands together as he rested them on his desk in the library. Several people watched with interest as well as two gnants who stood along a far wall. On the opposite side of the desk sat two gnants, Reesler, and an Adept named Rxwer.

"I want to make this as clear as possible and I'm allowing others to listen to what I have to say so that no one can claim we are making a private deal only to help myself." He paused, knowing he had the attention of everyone in the room. "Reesler, I'm disappointed that you didn't come to me with concerns or information on what Lord Bennett was up to, coercing others to do his work. However, we can't change what has happened so let's put that behind us."

Reesler had shrunk into his seat when Lord Perry first mentioned his name but now began to resume his normal sitting position. His chair was a foot behind the Adept's chair toward the table and he continually licked his lips with his forked tongue.

Lord Perry turned his attention to Rxwer. "Adept Rxwer, you and the other gnants have a decision to make. If you continue to work with Lord Bennett and offer him support of any kind, then I'll have to make the assumption all gnants are my enemy and will be dealt with accordingly. I say to you now that you must back out of the dispute between humans and allow us to settle our differences without your interference. Please understand I'm not asking you to support our side. I have no wish to see gnants fighting humans on any circumstances and risk any war between our races.

"I have been in contact with the other Lords in this area and have received support from most of them if I choose to battle with Lord Bennett. I have issued him an ultimatum that he is to step down from his position as administrator of Horstruff County and to notify King Charles of such. He is to halt all hostilities as well. So far he has not responded to my demands."

Lord Perry took a long drink of his wine and pointed a finger at Rexer. "I need to have your answer in one hour if gnants are going to withdraw from this conflict. If you cannot give an answer within that time frame, I will assume you have decided to side with Lord Bennett."

"Difficult to anssswer for all. Need time."

"One hour. Find a way."

———

Lord Bennett scowled at the messenger. "He dares to challenge my authority? Tell Lord Perry if he wants a fight then he shall have one!"

The messenger nodded rapidly as he bowed and backed out of the room.

Lord Bennett jammed a knife into a table that held maps and his notes, the blade and handle quivering from the blow. He stomped around the room for several minutes and called out to the closed door for his assistants. "Smythe! Bryan! Get in here now!"

The two men hurried into the room and stood a safe distance from Lord Bennett.

"I have to move quickly now. Is Sir Jon still travelling toward Paderno City?"

Sir Smythe nodded vigorously. "Yes, yes, Lord Bennett. Sir Jon and his group are heading there according to our informants."

"Then they're likely going to Stone Retreat where that injured woman is staying. Is Sir Jon still spending time with that wench?"

"Yes, Lord Bennett."

"Make arrangements at the stables. I need to get to Stone Retreat as soon as possible."

"How many guards do you wish to attend with you?" Sir Bryan finally found his courage to speak.

"Whoever is available to leave in ten minutes but I don't want the security of the castle compromised."

Fifteen minutes later Lord Bennett left his castle with a dozen men on horseback. They travelled light, pushing the horses at a fast pace.

———

Council Madoc watched from a hotel balcony, leaning on the stone rail and shook his head. He turned back into his room where a woman with long red hair sat on a bed with the bed cover drawn up to her waist.

"Are you coming back to bed?"

He tossed his black robe onto a chair already covered with her clothing. "Unfortunately, no, Katherine. It appears another situation or rather one that continues from a previous problem is developing." He paused to stare at her bare top. "Most unfortunate." He began to dress.

"Shall I leave then?"

"No hurry. I hope to return in a couple of days. Perhaps you won't mind waiting for my return."

"Am I to be a kept woman then?" She spoke with a smile on her red lips.

He laughed. "If that's what it takes to have you on my return." He reached into his pocket and tossed her two gold coins. "The room is paid for. Stay here if you like until my return."

Council Madoc made haste downstairs and quickly summoned his driver and carriage. When the carriage arrived, he called out to the driver instructions where to travel as he entered the cab.

A dozen minutes later the carriage dropped him off just past Lord Bennett's Castle and Council Madoc made long quick strides in the open field next to it, pulling out a small crystal as he did so. He muttered a few phrases as he walked and suddenly disappeared.

———

For Tuck, Sandra, Tom, and Gordon Miller, it was indeed anxious minutes, then hours and finally days. Tuck and Tom wanted to calibrate the array to another crystal and go in search of Liz. Sandra and Gordon Miller wanted to wait one more day, reasoning that if one of them should cross through the array using a new crystal, then Liz wouldn't be able to return. Gordon thought she may be under arrest but not in danger, and they should be patient for a bit longer. The how much longer developed into another debate.

"I'm getting hungry. Anyone for frozen pizza?"

"I think you ate the last one last night, Tuck."

Tuck looked at Tom in disbelief. "There was two in the freezer yesterday. What happened to them?"

Sandra got up from the couch. "I'll see what's in the kitchen. You guys should stop eating four meals a day." She headed to the kitchen when she heard the heavy doorknocker at the front entrance. "Don't worry. I got it." She called out to the others who hadn't made any move to get up.

She opened the door revealing a tall man dressed in black, his clothing looking odd with a cape around his shoulders.

"Good day, madam. My name is Council Madoc and I'm here regarding news concerning Sir Jon and a lady named Liz." He gave a short bow of his head.

Sandra stood there in shock for a few seconds and stepped to the side to allow him in. "You better come in and explain this to the others."

"I thank thee." He marched into the room to the surprised looks of Tom and Tuck. Gordon Miller, however, stood up and pointed a finger at him.

"You again!"

It took several minutes to calm Miller down who accused Council Madoc of trying to steal things from the castle.

"Please sir, I am not a thief. I was searching for items located here but I would not take anything without permission."

"Humph."

Miller wasn't entirely satisfied. Council Madoc had come more than once to the castle asking questions about its age, previous owners and if any artifacts were found inside. Miller had also found Council Madoc snooping around the back yard once and threatened him with a cricket bat.

"Let's drop the hostilities for the time being. You said you had information about my brother and Liz."

Council Madoc appraised her for a moment, apparently surprised at Jon being her brother. "It's a rather complicated undertaking Sir Jon has embarked on but I will give you a quick description of what has happened."

Tucks stomach growled a few times as Council Madoc described what Jon and Liz had gone through.

Tom summarized what Council Madoc told them. "It doesn't seem like there's a huge problem then. Jon and Liz will meet up at Stone Retreat and then head back here and slip back to Earth using that crystal."

Council Madoc nodded. "That would be correct, except Sir Jon has taken a Locas crystal with him to Domum from the castle here. And there's lots of interest in that crystal, in particular from Lord Bennett who is desperate to obtain it."

"What the heck is a Locus crystal?" Sandra glanced over at Tuck who was taking a staring at the kitchen entrance.

Council Madoc described the Locus crystal and its power. "Lord Bennett believes he can control Domum and proclaim himself king this way. Unfortunately, there's also a danger that may also open a gateway between our two worlds. I believe it was the Locus crystal that opened the original gateway thousands of years ago between our worlds."

"So my brother and Liz are in danger?"

"I'm afraid so."

Tom leaned forward in his chair. "And where do we fit in this scenario? Why did you come to us?"

"This is a difficult situation for you. You have to believe me and trust me. Unfortunately, you don't have the luxury of time to decide." Council Madoc sighed and raised his eyebrows. "I need your help to stop Lord Bennett. The fact that stopping him helps you is only incidental to my own plans. Given that, however, we can work together and if at all possible, I will try to save Sir Jon and Liz from harm."

Sandra began to get impatient and stood up. "What do we have to do to help you?"

"Lord Bennett has headed to confront your brother in Stone Retreat. He will arrive there well before I can hope to if I go the same route he does." He paused for a moment. "I'm requesting that you provide me with transportation to the southern part of this island that corresponds where Stone Retreat is located."

"And how would that help you?"

"Well, miss, I am a warlock and I possess enough magic even in this world to be able to slip back into Domum from there. Unlike others I don't have to be near the vicinity of a gateway to go between worlds. I could then be at Stone Retreat at the same time as Lord Bennett."

While Council Madoc waited alone in the kitchen, the others discussed whether to help him travel to the south of England.

Gordon Miller listened for several minutes before he spoke. "To tell you the truth, I'm not certain if he's telling us everything or not. But he did come to my door more than once and probably could've overpowered me easily enough to get what he wanted. But he didn't and walked away when I told him to leave. I vote that we do as he asked and take him on his trip. We all want to do something besides waiting and this is as good as a chance we'll get."

———

Sandra paid for a small rented van that they squeezed into. She was surprised how relaxed Council Madoc appeared during the journey, though he continually stared out the windows as they drove and clutched the armrest for security. Tom was taking his turn driving with Council Madoc sitting in the passenger seat. Tuck and Sandra shared the rear seat. He answered questions from the others and asked several himself as they made their way south.

"So, if this Bennett character gets all these crystals together then there's a gateway between Earth and Domum?"

Council Madoc looked at Tuck before answering. "I suspect that would happen but it could be worse."

"How so?"

"Lord Bennett would have enormous power, so much so that he wouldn't care or be worried about any damage he was doing. But the problem is much worse than Earth being joined by a gateway to Domum. You see there may be also other worlds, no, there are other worlds. Worlds that have other creatures such as goblins, leprechauns and fairies that could invade our worlds."

"That could be ugly."

"True. But I must be careful here because it's only a rumour...have you wondered where the souls of the dead go?"

Tuck was taken back at the question but Sandra jumped in with her answer. "You mean like heaven or hell?"

"Yes, that is one thought. Another is that the souls travel to another of these worlds that hide in the other dimensions. It might be where heaven and hell is located. What if those crystals open a gateway to them? The thought gives me some concern."

TWENTY-THREE

The road to Paderno City was busy, though Jon and the rest found the travel uneventful.

Jon was anxious to carry on to Stone Retreat as fast as possible and asked Sir Keith if they had to stay at Paderno City overnight.

"Why don't we keep going until dark and camp somewhere? It would save us money and get us back faster."

"I suppose that's possible. The gnants may be looking for us in Paderno City. If we camp instead, that may confuse them. I believe camping may be as safe as staying in a hotel and a great deal cheaper. If the others have no serious objection, then we can bypass Paderno City."

The others agreed to carry on, and Sir Keith led them on a road that skirted the outside perimeter of the city. They continued to ride for another three hours, stopping a few miles before the wall that was made of stonewood.

Nicole helped prepare dinner with Nathan while the rest set up the tents. The tents were set close to one another for the sake of security.

Jon ate quickly, going for a second helping of the stew.

Nicole watched him dig into his second portion. "Hungry, are we?"

"Yeah. Just don't tell me what mysterious animal I'm eating."

"I won't, other than it's from Nathan's hunting skills." She pointed at the tents. "It wasn't necessary for you set up my tent. I'm not convinced there isn't any danger, so I'm sleeping with you."

"I thought you'd say that, but I didn't want you to think I was just assuming you would."

"Thanks, but you're still my protector." She leaned over and gave him a kiss on his cheek.

Sir Keith stood, addressing the group. "We'll be leaving at first light and suggest we don't spend too long around the fire.

Gilbert grumbled, "No ale to drinks, or women to pinch theirs bottoms. Might as well go to me bed."

Nathan laughed. "Gilbert, you must have lived a charmed life that some woman hasn't murdered you yet. I shall patrol the area before turning in."

Sir Keith joined Jon where he sat on the ground, watching the fire.

"It seems to me, if you don't mind my speaking about it, that you're in a bit of situation. Clearly, Lady Nicole has deep feelings for you, all the while you're to meet your lady friend. Have you a plan on how you're going to handle it when you see her again?"

"I honestly don't know."

"Someone's heart is going be denied. May I offer a small bit of advice?"

"Sure."

"Be honest with yourself first. Whichever lady you decide to pursue, make sure it is for the right reason and not out of obligation."

"Thank you, Sir Keith. I'm not sure of anything right now. I hope when I see Liz, I'll know the answer."

Sir Keith stood and placed a hand on Jon's shoulder. "Sleep well."

Gilbert used his knife to whittle a piece of wood. "Ah, Sir Jon, me advice is you have two women. Tell them you wants them to get along, if yous knows whats I means."

Jon laughed. "Yeah, in a perfect fantasy world." He went to his tent and undressed. He lifted the blanket, lying next to Nicole on his back. She took his arm and stretched it out, placing her head on his shoulder. Her leg moved on top of his.

"That's better."

He felt her bare skin against his. *How the hell am I going to be able to fall asleep like this? I've got to think of something other than sex right now. Two, four, eight, sixteen, thirty-two, sixty-four...*

Jon ate his breakfast with his eyes half closed.

"I see you're still a bit tired." Nicole sipped at her tea.

"Yeah, I didn't fall asleep right away."

"Sorry, I guess I had something to do with that."

"That's alright. The tea will help."

Nathan kicked at the remains of the campfire. "Time to roll." He looked at Jon. "You look like you could sleep in your saddle."

"Yeah, I was thinking too much last night."

Nathan handed him yellow root. "Here, chew on this."

Jon took the offered root. "What is it?"

"It's something I use to keep awake."

Jon stretched and climbed on his horse. He tried chewing on the root, absorbing the bitter flavours. *Tastes awful. I hope it works. What I really need is strong coffee.*

Shortly later, Jon moved his horse next to Nathan's. "Thanks for whatever that was you gave me. It worked great."

"You're welcome. After me, we need you to protect our group. If you're not at your best, I'd hate to have to rely on the others for their fighting expertise."

They reached a gate that allowed them to pass through the stonewood wall. There was a different set of guards at the crossing of the wall than the last time. The head of the guards, a tall thin man with a no-nonsense demeanour, insisted on a nominal sum for passing through.

Sir Keith tried to avoid the fee by declaring they were on a special mission by the order of Lord Perry.

"I don't give a tinker's damn if you are on a mission from Lord Perry or God himself. One bronze fern per person. If you cannot afford that, then you can earn it by brushing down our horses." He hooked a thumb at a half-dozen horses grazing.

"Your price is fair, unlike the last one who patrolled here." Sir Keith opened his leather purse and gave him five coins.

"Oh, you mean Douglas. Alas, he seems to be in a spot of trouble for some minor indiscretions."

Sir Keith led them within a mile of the Devil's Woods where he called a halt. "I suggest we camp here rather than trying to find accommodation in these woods again. The woods are too long for us to try to get to the other side before dark is upon us and as Gilbert pointed out they aren't safe to be in after the sun goes down."

The camp was set up similar as before, with the tents placed close to one another. This time Jon didn't waste the effort in setting up Nicole's tent.

The fire burned well enough but Gilbert pointed out the influence of the Devil's Woods was still prevalent. "Sees how the night air swallows up the light. You walks too far aways from here, and yous barely see the fire."

Jon wasn't sure if he believed him but decided there was little reason to find out. *All I want out of tonight is a good sleep.*

Jon and the others turned in shortly after dinner. He heard Gilbert in the next tent, grumbling about something.

Nicole whispered. "Sound travels really well here. Too bad, that means we can't do what I want to do with you." She gave him a kiss. "Sleep well."

The area around the Devil's Woods were consistent with the last time they went through. Later that night a thunderstorm developed. The rain that fell was not as heavy as in the Devil's Woods itself but was cold, chilling the air rapidly. The tent was too warm when Jon went to bed but during the storm, he drew up the blanket around Nicole and himself. A continuous roll of thunder accompanied by several flashes of lightning disturbed their sleep. Jon heard Gilbert call out in his sleep and the horses acted agitated as well.

Nicole shifted in her sleep but stayed pressed against him.

"Who goes there?!" Sir Keith called out from his tent.

Nathan returned his question. "Tis nothing, Sir Keith, just lupus dragons coming close to our camp. They were just curious and have disappeared. It's a pity the rain has put out our campfire."

Jon listened to the conversation and to Gilbert calling out. A cool wind blew at the tents, pushing past the flaps. He heard Nicole quietly speak.

"Jon? You awake?"

"Yeah. You scared?"

"A little. How do you manage to stay so warm?"

"Lots of body mass I guess."

Nicole turned on her side away from him. "Put your arm around me."

Jon turned on his side, spooning her. He felt her feet press against his legs and wiggle her back as she snuggled closer to him.

"That's better. Nice and warm."

The thunder boomed again, but he realized he didn't care. *I can't change where I am, so I might as well enjoy a warm body next to me.*

Jon woke up before her and untangled his arms from around her. He struggled to put on his clothes in the small tent before going outside. Nathan had the fire going once more and had made some tea with biscuits for breakfast.

"Mornin', Sir Jon. Sleep okay?"

There was a hint of a smile on the big man's face.

"Morning. Not bad, considering the storm last night." He poured tea for himself. "Nicole was scared from the storm."

"She has a reason to be, I suppose. But she's in love with you even though you don't see it. You could do worse, you know."

"I know, but I have someone waiting for me. If there wasn't…"

Nathan held up his hand. "Say no more. I understand." Nathan took a small stick and tossed it on the fire. "You know, when we started this journey, I didn't know anything about you. I thought you were just a big, clumsy oaf. But you sure have proven me wrong. You learned how to fight, showed courage where other men would've turned tail and haven't taken advantage of Nicole when it would have been easy to do so. You have honour, Sir Jon."

"Thank you. I…"

"Didn't mean to put you on the spot. Let's wake the others, shall we?"

They made good time through the Devil's Woods, drawing on the horses' nervous energy to move along the trail at a brisk pace. The towering forest again hid most of the sun and most of the ride was done in the shadows along the narrow road except for a few hours close to noon. They didn't stop to eat lunch, but instead waited until they had made it to the other side of the woods and still rode for over an hour before stopping to rest.

"I'm glad we made it through that without incident." Sir Keith mopped his brow with a cloth. "I must say that I didn't relish the thought of spending another night there."

Nathan had started a fire and began to roast several rabbits he'd shot earlier. Jon helped him skin them reluctantly.

"I think I'll never be much of a hunter, Nathan. I don't like killing anything and preparing them is not much to my taste."

Nathan lowered his voice as he replied. "I know what you mean. But a man's gotta do what has to be done to survive. I remember a few nights ago when you insisted on sparing that gnant's life."

"Rzet."

"That was the right thing to do. Sir Keith said they were nothing but animals. That got me to thinking, a little soul searching. I had nothing but contempt for gnants before, but after Rzet came back to warn us and I've heard of other stories as well about gnants acting civilized. I guess what I'm saying is that I see them different now." He looked at Jon. "Now don't go spreading rumours ol' Nathan is getting soft in the head. I'm just a little more understanding now."

"I wouldn't dare."

After the break they rode for another hour, trying to get out of the range of the peculiar weather that hung over the Devil's Woods. According to Gilbert, thunderstorms were a common occurrence at night over the woods and areas close to it could expect to have some rainfall that accompanied it.

The camp was set in a larger clearing and close to a stream.

Gilbert walked around with his gnant crier but reported there was only one gnant in the area and even it didn't seem too close to them. Gilbert eyed the crystal that hung from Jon's neck. The warm air had caused both Jon and Nathan to take off their shirts. Gilbert felt too warm, but preferred to leave his on, not wanting to have to explain the mixture of scars and tattoos that covered his back and chest. There was also the concern that if Nicole were to inspect one of the tattoos on his chest, she might understand what the magic symbols mean. The crystal continued to attract his attention. He had tried to steal it from Nicole several nights back by sneaking in her tent but couldn't locate it.

But now he wasn't sure if it would be wise for anyone to have it. Valuable, yes. But it could mean death to anyone carrying it, even if they were only planning to sell it.

"Whatcha thinking about, Gilbert?"

Gilbert tooked at the plate offered by Nicole. She held her own plate of potatoes and rabbit. "Thanks. Nothin' much, just idle thoughts."

She sat down next to him. "Can I ask you something?"

"Of course, but I haveta warn ya that I just want a good night's sleep."

She laughed. "You're awful. No, I was wondering what this girl Liz looks like. We'll be meeting her tomorrow and I was a little curious."

"She okay lookin'. Blonde hair, big boobs, small waist. About your height."

"I see. She and Jon close?"

"I not know. Only see them together once." He licked some food from his fingers. "You want to know if you stand a chance with Jon?"

"No, I was just asking because…"

"I knows, I knows. But Jon, he loyal. Even if you be the better girl for him, Jon stay with Liz. Sorry."

Nicole shrugged. "I guess I knew that too." She sighed.

"No need to fret, Nicole. Gilbert here is still available. But yous gotta be nicer to me in the future."

Nicole laughed as she picked up the empty plates. "Thanks, Gilbert. And thanks for listening." She walked back to the fire where Sir Keith was telling Jon a story on how he had to battle several soldiers at once. Jon appeared dubious but listened carefully to Sir Keith's supposed fighting skills. *I guess Sir Keith and I have something in common. We're both trying to impress Jon and he politely carries on.*

"Jon, I need to wash some stuff in the stream. Will you come with me?" She held a blanket wrapped around something.

"Sure." He stood. "I better go with her to be on the safe side."

They reached the stream and Nicole followed the bank a short distance.

"Jon, we both need our sleep tonight. You're naked with a hard on and I keep thinking about it. Neither one of us are doing ourselves any good by feeling this way each night."

"What do you suggest? Separate tents?"

"No, I want to sleep with you and not by myself." She took off her top and tunic underneath. "I'm getting naked and I want you to join me." She took off her skirt.

"You want to have sex here?" Jon took off his shirt.

"We'll never be able to do it in the tent with everyone so damn close." She pulled at the closure of his pants. "Come on, hurry up."

Jon hurried.

———

Sir Keith noticed Jon and Nicole returning.

"Ah, good. They managed to clean those clothes without incident."

Gilbert laughed. "Oh, if you believes that, thens I is of royalty."

———

Jon helped make breakfast, greeting the others as they approached the campfire.

Nicole took her tea and stood next to him. "You look happy."

"More like I finally got a good night's sleep." He lowered his voice. "Thanks for taking me to the stream yesterday. That really made a difference."

"That helped me too. I think we both can relax a bit more now."

The trail they were using widened, joined by other trails, and became a road. The road had other travelers as well, increasing in numbers. As evening approached, Jon pointed out the grey outline of Stone Retreat.

"I can see it! Stone Retreat!"

Nicole frowned, keeping her thoughts to herself. *Great. This is where I lose Jon to a woman I never met. It's not fair.*

TWENTY-FOUR

Liz had trouble believing the size of her suite and bedroom in the Kosture Inn. Tony didn't act overly thrilled by the luxury of the rooms at the Stone Retreat hotel but was pleased that she found it exciting.

"It's so big, like there're chairs everywhere. My bed is big enough to sleep a whole family."

"If you like this type of thing, then all you have to do is hang around with me."

"Only hang around with you?"

He smiled. "A close hanging around."

"Ah, there's the catch. How about we go and get something to eat?"

Liz ate her supper and relaxed with Tony, drinking wine in a lounge overlooking hotel gardens.

"This is nice, a bit like a place Council Madoc took me to back in Horstruff. This is bigger though."

"Everything is bigger out here, no restrictions on size with all that land around here."

A waiter, wearing a black and gold ensemble, interrupted their conversation. "Beg your forgiveness sir, madam. There are some travelers in the hotel lobby looking for a Liz O'Doul. Would…"

Liz jumped up. "That must be Jon!" She ran out of the lounge.

Tony turned to the waiter. "It seems she might be happy to see him." He placed a few coins on the table and walked after her.

By the time Tony arrived in the lobby, Liz was still hugging and kissing Jon. There was several others close by and were watching, partly amused and partly embarrassed by the show of affection. As Tony approach, they broke apart, though still with their arms around each other.

"Liz, I want you to meet Sir Keith, the leader of our group." Sir Keith gave a short bow and kissed her hand.

"Nathan, our protector and who struggled to show me how to use a sword."

"He's too modest, Miss. It's good to meet you."

"You have already met Gilbert, who has been kind enough to aid us in my quest."

Gilbert stood a bit back from the rest and raised one hand in a small wave. "Uh, good to meets yous again."

She stared at him but was still happy from finding Jon again. "Nice to see you too, Gilbert."

"And this is Nicole. My good friend who has been a lot of help to us on our journey."

The two women stared at each other and seconds ticked by as they slowly smiled and murmured, "Good to meet you."

Liz turned and pulled Tony closer by the hand. "Everyone, this is Tony, *my* friend who was kind enough to bring me to Stone Retreat."

Tony nodded at everyone and gave Nicole a second look.

"Tony is it now? It's been a while, Anthony."

"You're looking…" He paused, searching for the right word. "Well. Very well indeed."

Jon was surprised. "You know her?"

"Lots of men…" Gilbert's reply was silenced by a quick whack on the shoulder by Nathan.

"Anthony, Tony, we have known each other for a couple of years. You're looking well yourself."

The group elected to go back to the lounge, save for Sir Keith, who wanted to check on Lady Karla staying at High Park Lodge.

Liz sat next to Jon and held his hand occasionally as they talked to the others about their adventures. Nicole sat with Tony across from them with Gilbert and Nathan sitting at the ends of the table. Gilbert nervously sat back as far as he could in his chair, holding his tankard of ale in front of him.

Jon gave a brief description of what happened after he fell out of the Miller Castle window with Gilbert. Liz told him how she ended up in Domum and her adventures.

"And you became Sir Jon, the dragon slayer? Wow! That's even more impressive than being a football player. Were you scared? You didn't get hurt?"

He laughed. "I was scared alright. And I did get hurt a bit."

"He's being modest. He charged the dragon without fear to save Gilbert here." Nathan nodded across the table at Gilbert, who gave an embarrassed grin. "And he got hurt in the battle too. And if it wasn't for Nicole here…"

"I nursed him back to health. He had dragon fire on his arm and was pretty sick."

Jon suddenly asked, "So, you say Uncle Gordon is alive and well? Then I guess I don't own a castle after all." He took a quick drink of his ale.

Liz glanced at Nicole before looking back at Jon, "But you own my heart instead. Fair trade?"

He answered by giving her a kiss.

"I need to go to the ladies' room. Nicole, could you show me where it is?"

The two women left the table, leaving Jon feeling a perplexed.

"You have a fine lady there, Jon."

"Thank you. And thank you for bringing her here. That was kind of you."

"My pleasure. She helped me a great deal getting my head turned around."

"Good. Nicole, have you met her before?"

"Yes, in my days as a drunkard. She was a barmaid then."

"Lord Perry bought out her contract with the bar. She's also from Earth and hopes to return there. She's a fine lady and has been my friend as well."

"I'll have to admit she does look fine. Lord Perry, you say? That would make her a lady of the court then."

The ladies returned to the table. Liz was still smiling at Jon. He supposed Nicole hadn't said too many bad things about him. After another round of drinks, Jon and Liz excused themselves, going upstairs to her room.

"Nicole said that you called out my name while you were sick."

"I guess I did. I don't remember much."

"Hmm. She also said other than the first time when you met her you acted like a gentleman and kept your hands to yourself. That was true? Or was she protecting you?"

"I acted like a boor the first time I met her when I was drunk. It was stupid of me. Liz, I need to confess that there was a time when I didn't believe I would see you again."

"Stop. Nicole told me all I *want* to know. To set the record straight, I didn't know if I'd ever see you again. You were *with* Nicole. I was *with* Tony. We were both in a difficult situation. We didn't know if we would ever meet again. What happened then is in the past. Now it's just you and me. Right?"

"Right. You're with me again and that's all that matters." He looked around her room. "Pretty swanky."

"It's nice. You must try out the bed."

He helped her undo her top with the laces tied at the back. "Good grief, that's a lot of clothing."

She laughed, "Yes, and the joy of getting dressed in the morning." She tugged the last of her garments off and watched him take off his shirt, and then his pants. "That's it? No underwear?"

"I didn't have any money to buy clothes. Nicole actually bought these for me."

"Okay, I don't mind at all. Now let's get you and that sword of yours into my bed."

———

Gilbert started to sing some obscure fighting song and had to be hushed by Nicole. Tony and she were getting along rather well and comparing notes on what was going on in Horscruff. Nathan added a few comments of his own.

When Gilbert started to fall asleep in his chair, Nathan announced he had enough as well. He helped Gilbert out of the lounge.

That left Nicole and Tony alone to talk, nursing their wine long into the night.

"Allow me to escort you to your room, Lady Nicole."

"Thank you, that would be nice."

They climbed the steps to the third floor.

"Tony, I have to say I really like the change in you. When I knew you before you didn't show much restraint in what you said or did."

"Thank you. Liz helped me as I mentioned, but there's something to be said for being sober too."

Nicole laughed. "There is that, I suppose." She stopped walking. "My room."

"Would it be too forward of me to call on you for breakfast?"

"That would be fine."

"If you prefer, I can have breakfast delivered to your room and we can dine together privately."

"That would be wonderful." She gave him a kiss on the cheek. "Until tomorrow."

Nicole slowly closed her door and sprang into action. *I've got to clean my clothes. In my room? What do I wear?* She took off her clothes, checking at each garment for dirt. Her suite contained a sink and a bathtub and she used both to wash the dirt off her small selection of clothes.

Okay, not bad. Mostly clean, and they should be dry in the morning. Okay, I guess I'll sleep in my camisole tonight.

———

Sir Keith sat with Lady Karla in her sitting room at the High Park Lodge. He had taken a room in the Kosture Inn, a smaller less extravagant lodging than Lady Karla enjoyed.

"I suppose I should move to less expensive accommodations now that you and the others have returned to Stone Retreat."

"Ah, yes, well we should be staying together. And, unfortunately, the cost of this suite is a little beyond what we have budgeted for. I am glad that you seem to have fully recovered from your injuries."

"Thank you. But I will have a scar on my cheek as a memory of that attack." She touched her cheek with her hand.

"Really? I hadn't noticed any mark at all."

"Sir Keith, you're such a gentleman." She turned away from him and looked at the floor. "Even more so after what I did, I'm so ashamed of my behaviour."

"Come, come now. None of us are perfect and we all can be tempted at times. You are forgiven for a momentary loss in judgement."

"If that be the case... Sir Keith, may I be so bold as to call you just Keith?"

Sir Keith leaned forward and touched her hand gently with his fingertips. "I think I would enjoy that very much."

"Keith, perhaps when I move to my new quarters, we can have adjoining rooms. For safety reasons, of course. If danger comes, I would so appreciate knowing a brave man is close by."

Sir Keith arranged for Lady Karla's belongings to be relocated to the new room. He further insisted on using a carriage to transport her, rather than have her walk.

Lady Karla inspected her new room with Sir Keith nervously watching her reaction. "Keith, this may be a smaller room but I love the décor. I believe this may be an upgrade to my previous accommodation."

"That is wonderful to hear."

"Now, there are two things I must insist on. One, is that we share a nightcap. The other is that the doors between our rooms be kept open. That is in case I am in need of your strong presence."

Sir Keith face went flush. "Of course."

Sir Keith felt obligated to dip into his own funds to pay for a flagon of wine to be brought up to the room. He didn't think it was appropriate to use the dwindling funds for such an indulgence.

Lady Karla listened intently as Sir Keith described parts of the journey without her. "The gnants attacked, but they were surprised by our resiliency. I was clad only in my underwear and suffered a knife wound but refused to let either of the two gnants that attacked me to win the day. With Sir Jon busy protecting Nicole, I had to step up my game, so to speak."

"How very brave of you. That must have been a sight. You, almost naked, wielding a sword to protect the others."

Sir Keith stiffened his shoulders. "When called upon, a true man must make sure his efforts are full and without fear for himself."

"Oh, Keith, you make my heart beat faster." She finished her wine. "Now I am worn-out. This has been a most trying day."

He stood. "I will take my leave. But fear not, I shall be in the next room.

———

"Keith." Lady Karla called out the following morning. "Keith."

Sir Keith sprinted into the room, clad in his underwear while holding his sword in front of him. "What is the matter?" He looked around the room, not seeing any danger.

Lady Karla sat up in bed, revealing a lacy gown. "Keith, I have just had a most dreadful vision."

He hurried to her bedside, "My dear, Karla. How may I be of assistance?"

"You must warn the others. Lord Bennett is coming here to attack. He is after Sir Jon's crystal and has brought armed men to take it by force."

He held a finger in the air. "Fear not. I shall inform the others immediately."

Sir Keith returned to his room and quickly dressed. He hurried to where Jon and Liz were sharing a room and pounded on the door. "Sir Jon! Sir Jon!"

———

Jon woke up at the same time as Liz by a thumping on the door followed by Sir Keith's shouts. He struggled to put on his pants as he ran to the door. "Just a moment, for crying out loud." He flung open the door.

Sir Keith spoke. "Lady Karla has a vision of impeding danger. It seems Lord Bennett has arrived here at Stone Retreat with the purpose of doing you harm and taking your crystal."

"Where are the others?"

"I don't know. I came here first."

"Okay, I'll get dressed. In the meantime, inform the others to meet downstairs in the main dining hall."

Jon turned to Liz, who was getting dressed. "We have a problem."

"I heard." She tossed him his shirt. "We better hurry."

They arrived downstairs. Nathan had already been up and had finished breakfast. Gilbert slumped in a chair, still recovering from last night's celebration. Sir Keith and Lady Karla stood off the side, close together. Liz glared at Gilbert, who made an effort to sit up.

Nathan spoke, "Gilbert is a bit under the weather, but he's here. Sir Anthony has gone to get Nicole."

Liz replied, "What're we going to do? We have to protect Jon from that madman."

"Relax, Lady Liz. Nathan and the rest of us are used to handling difficult situations. We will formulate a plan." Sir Keith placed his hand on his sword and straightened his back.

Nathan rolled his eyes.

Sir Anthony ran into the dining room, "They have taken Nicole!" He sported a cut on his cheek and a bruise on his forehead. "Lord Bennett's men have her. I caught up with them as they were dragging her down the hall. Unfortunately, I wasn't up to the task to handling four of them. I decided to retreat and warn you what happened rather than to get myself killed. Sorry, I wanted to do more..."

Nathan cut him off. "You did the right thing. At least this way we know what happened."

Jon began to get anxious. "Where did they take her? What're we going to do?"

Nathan asked, "Does anyone have a thought on where they would've taken her?"

Sir Keith stepped forward to the centre of the group. "I presume Lord Bennett wishes to have Sir Jon's crystal, and rather than risk a direct assault on him, he has decided to take Nicole as a hostage. This means two things. One, Lord Bennett does not enjoy the full complement of his troops or the support of the authorities at Stone Retreat. Two, Lady Nicole has not been harmed yet or she wouldn't be any good as a hostage."

"Do you have any idea where she was taken?"

"Yes, I do. Logically I believe he would've taken her to Lookout

Point Inn, a place I know he has stayed in the past and thusly be familiar with the layout. In addition, it affords a fine view of the surrounding area and would allow him a vantage point of the area for any hostile troops. I would suggest he would have taken her to the terrace on the roof of the inn."

Jon asked, "Where is Lookout Point?"

"Adjacent to this hotel. That would make it less of a challenge to take Nicole to where they are holding up."

"Then we should head over there." Jon took a half step toward the exit.

Nathan held out his arm. "Hold on, Sir Jon, we don't know what we are fighting here. Let's not just rush into battle."

"We just can't do nothing!"

Liz held a hand on his arm and felt his muscle tense. "Jon. Listen to reason. We all want to save Nicole but getting ourselves killed isn't the way to do it."

Jon began to get impatient, almost shouting his words. "Then what the hell do we do?"

"I believe I have an answer to that problem." Council Madoc stood at the entrance of the dining room. He strode across the floor, his royal blue cape lifting off his black jacket.

They all turned in unison to face Council Madoc.

"Sir Jon, I see Lady Elizabeth has managed to locate you." He gave a thin smile. "There are several developments that you are not aware of. Lord Bennett is making a desperate bid to obtain the remaining Locus crystal that Sir Jon has. He will stop at nothing to obtain it. Lord Perry has declared a challenge to Lord Bennett's role as administrator. To that end he has formed a new alliance with the several other lords to usurp those who would support Lord Bennett's authority. He has petitioned King Charles that Lord Bennett be considered hostile to his rule and be stripped of his rank of a lord."

"Bravo for Lord Perry!" Sir Keith acted pleased at the news. "That Lord Bennett is truly a scoundrel."

"Indeed. Lord Perry has ordered that gnants stay out of this present struggle for command and they have apparently decided to obey.

Lord Bennett has brought with him only a small armed force with him here, leaving the majority of his troops to protect his castle. That castle is under siege and will fall by nightfall, either by force or by surrender depending on the results of today at Stone Retreat."

"So, is it up to us to defeat Lord Bennett's troops?" Nathan spoke quickly, appearing ready to do battle as he reached for his sword.

"Yes, but with help. I have spoken to the local authorities at Stone Retreat and convinced them that they must support Lord Perry in this matter. They have pledged their local force, plus several of the Lords visiting here have offered some of their own troops. All they requested is that we avoid a fight that would cause damage to the properties here. They also asked who was the leader that their men would fight under." He spoke directly to Nathan. "I informed them that Sir Nathan would be leading them in battle."

"But...but I'm not of that title."

"You will be when I inform Lord Perry of your role in defeating Lord Bennett. I did not wish to ask the lords to place their men in anyone underneath that rank. Sir Keith, Sir Anthony, I respect both of you for what you are able to do but none of us are fighting men. This battle may need the skills and reputation of a soldier to assure peace."

Both Sir Keith and Sir Anthony nodded.

"Lord Bennett is on the roof of Lookout Point Inn. He has Lady Nicole with him with only a few soldiers with him. The majority of his force is in the lobby of the inn with Sir Nathan's troops waiting outside. I suggest we go now. He has demanded the remaining Locus Crystal be yielded to him in exchange for Lady Nicole's life."

Several flags of the different lords flew among the troops outside Lookout Point Inn. Nathan and Jon walked through them and entered the inn and a murmuring arose among the men as they made ready for battle. Sir Keith, Tony and Liz waited outside the perimeter of the men.

Nathan didn't draw his sword as he advanced to Lord Bennett's men. The forty men faced him and a heavily armed soldier stepped forward. At a head higher than most men, wearing a heavy woven leather vest, Sir Richard looked formidable with his red beard and hair. He held a large double-bladed sword in his right hand and a spiked shield in his left.

"Sir Richard."

"Freeman Nathan."

"This is a difficult situation."

"Indeed. Are you the leader of the troops outside?"

"I am. You are outnumbered."

"We will put up a strong fight and if God is willing, be victorious."

"You are a brave man, Sir Richard, and a damn good fighter. But you didn't live this long by being a fool."

"As you say."

"If we must fight, it will be us that will battle first." He paused to allow Sir Richard the opportunity to nod his acknowledgement. "You will give me a good fight but surely you know the odds are against you that you will see the evening sun."

"That may be so but if you insist on a fight, I'll give you one."

"I don't insist but for the sake of the men that you lead, I ask that you surrender. I assure you no harm will come to thee and that your record as an honest soldier will assist you gaining another post."

"Lord Bennett will have my head if I surrender for any reason."

"You haven't heard? Lord Bennett has lost his castle and his title of lord is going to be revoked by King Charles. He's in such a desperate situation that he has taken to kidnapping a young lady to save himself."

Sir Richard frowned as his men behind him began to murmur among themselves. "I have heard rumours to that effect."

"They are not rumours. Do what's honourable for your men, don't make them die in a doomed cause led by a selfish man who has lost his title."

Jon watched as he stood just behind Nathan. Sir Richard squeezed his eyes shut and slowly exhaled as he contemplated the circumstances.

———

Sir Nathan opened the front doors to the inn and stood on the stone steps. He raised his voice to reach all those gathered around. "Lord Bennett's troops have surrendered. There will be no battle." He waited until cheers died down. "I have promised there'll be no punishment for them and that they may go as free men."

The cheer rose again, and the troops began to disperse.

Nathan turned to Jon. "Get Sir Keith and Sir Anthony. And Gilbert, if he's willing. We still have to rescue Lady Nicole."

Jon asked Liz to wait at the inn for him. "It might be dangerous around here."

"Hey, I travelled all…"

"Please, no arguments. Unless you've suddenly learned how to fight with a sword, I want you where you'll be safe."

"Alright. But be careful. No heroics."

Gilbert lagged around the others as they climbed the steps of Lockout Point Inn.

A deep rumbling sound came from the sky and Jon looked up, expecting to see dark clouds forming. Instead he saw the dark outline of a large dragon. He watched it as it circled Stone Retreat.

"Oh, it's the mother of hell." Gilbert pointed at the high figure. "Lord Bennett musta called it. A fornido dragon."

"Fornido dragon?"

"A bit rare to see but that is the largest dragon of them all. Lives by itself most of the time. Cunning creature, lives close to two hundred years." Sir Keith watched it circle as it called out once more. "They normally stay away from large human settlements, preferring easier prey. But Lord Bennett may be using a device, known as a fire-caller, to bring it here. To what end I'm not sure."

Jon fingered the crystal hanging from his neck. "Whatever his plan, I'm sure he still wants this." He took it off his neck. "Council Madoc, would you protect this, please? I cannot risk it falling into Lord Bennett's hands."

Council Madoc nodded. "A wise decision. I know where to keep it safe." He took the crystal and took three steps away from the others before turning around. "I will make sure it cannot fall into Lord Bennett's hands."

Jon watched him stride toward a waiting horse and carriage.

"I say it's time to rescue Lady Nicole." Sir Keith gave Lady Karla a quick kiss and walked to the Lookout Point Inn.

Nathan, Jon and finally Gilbert followed.

Jon looked at Sir Anthony marching away. "Where's he going, Gilbert?"

"I dunno. Says something abouts needing another weapon."

The roof terrace of the inn was five floors up and accessed by a series of broad stone stairs. Nathan sprinted the stairs seemingly without effort. Jon kept up until the last set of steps but Sir Keith and Gilbert were left far behind. The terrace sported potted trees and plants among the tables and chairs that covered an area of half a foot-ball field. Along the border of the terrace, a small fence helped prevent patrons from accidentally falling over the edge to the forest below. A series of poles were also set at regular intervals that served two purposes. First, lanterns were hung to give a soft light during the evenings and two, the sharp ends of the poles helped dissuade dragons from trying to land and eat the guests.

When they arrived at the top floor and entered onto the roof, Jon saw overturned table and chairs. Most of the poles were knocked down. Part of the fence was damaged and missing along the border. Lord Bennett was at the far corner of the terrace kicking at a potted plant. His two assistants, Smythe and Bryan stood nervously a short distance away.

Nathan and Jon exchanged looks.

"This is a little odd, Nathan."

"I agree."

Sir Nathan continued to advance with Jon a step behind him, still trying to catch his breath. "I see Nicole." He pointed to a spot behind Lord Bennett, just as the dragon rumbled a growl again, circling closer to the terrace.

Nicole stood with her wrists tied together and above her head with a length of rope that was attached to one of the poles that remained standing. Her torn camisole hung by one strap from her shoulder. Thin, red stripes marked her body. When she saw Nathan and Jon, she struggled to free herself. "Jon, help me!"

"That bastard!" Jon started to walk toward her but Nathan grabbed him by his shirt, stopping him in his tracks.

"That's not the way to do it. Let's approach slowly but with confidence and see if we can free her without a fight. A fight could also excite that dragon into attacking."

Lord Bennett saw them approach as the dragon dove within a hundred yards of the rooftop before soaring away. Jon froze as he watched it. The creature was huge, over fifty feet in length including a long serpent tail. He caught a glimpse of yellow, brown and blue colors on the reptilian skin.

Nathan didn't lose his stride and called out to Lord Bennett and his two assistants. "We have come to free the lady. Stay where you are and you won't get hurt."

Smythe and Bryan looked from Lord Bennett to Nathan and Jon. They slowly began to distance themselves from Lord Bennett and crept toward the exit.

Lord Bennett didn't seem to notice or care. He took a leg from a broken table and hurled it at Nathan. "Don't tell me what to do, you fool." He screamed at them, spittle flying from his mouth.

Jon was shocked at Lord Bennett's appearance. With his eyes wide open, a flushed face and hair that sat like a mop on top of his head. Lord Bennett looked like a madman.

"Do you want a fight? I'll give you a damn fight!" Lord Bennett screamed and threw a simple wood chair in their direction. He walked toward them and began to wave his sword at them.

Sir Nathan held his own sword steady as he slowly advanced. "Lord Bennett, we don't have to do this."

Lord Bennett laughed. "You're right there, Nathan." He began to chant out a phrase, calling out Nathan's name as he did so.

Jon watched as Nathan walked slower, his feet suddenly unsteady and he fell to the ground.

"Nathan! Are you alright?"

Lord Bennett continued to advance toward him.

"You see, I still have my powers. A warrior is no match against the spells." He waved his sword at Jon. "And now I'll have that crystal. Hand it to me or I'll take it."

Jon looked at the still form of Nathan and at the struggling Nicole. *If Lord Bennett were to find out I don't have the crystal, he might decide to kill them right now. I need to delay him until Sir Keith and Gilbert can come to help or I can think of something else.*

"I don't have time to waste." Lord Bennett began to chant out a spell.

"...his name being Sir Jon McKinney.

Weaken before me such that ye can no longer stand.

I command my power over thee."

Jon felt weak and could hardly keep his eyes open. He fell to the ground, his arms and legs barely moving. *My muscles aren't responding. He can kill me without a fight. There must be something. Come on, Jon...My name isn't Sir Jon. I'm Robert McKinney. My name is Robert, Robert, Robert.* An arm moved, then a leg. The spell wavered, losing its strength.

Lord Bennett stepped toward him, grinning. "I will now take that crystal and put an end to your miserable life."

Jon suddenly rolled on his back, raising his sword that moments ago was limp in his hand. He thrust it forward into the midsection of Lord Bennett.

"How?" Lord Bennett staggered backward as blood seeped out of chest. "How?" He fell on his back, his legs shaking uncontrollably as he tried to lift up his head. His whole body arched suddenly, and he lay still.

Jon lifted himself to his knees as the rest of his muscles responded. He stood still for several seconds and heard Nicole call out his name.

"Jon, Jon! The dragon!"

He looked at her and at the far edge where the beast had landed. It held its head high and a giant tongue tasted the air. The head lowered, carefully scanning the area before fixing its yellow eyes on first her and then on him. Jon moved slowly away from Nicole, deciding if it were to attack it might be satisfied with just him and leave her alone. The dragon's head shifted as it watched him move to the edge of the terrace.

Jon heard a noise behind him, and he expected to see Sir Keith and Gilbert. Instead he saw Tony on a black horse galloping across the terrace, knocking over one of the few remaining tables in the process. With a swing of his sword he cut the top of the rope holding Nicole and pulled her on her stomach over his horse. The horse did a quick pivot and charged back toward the exit.

The dragon roared his disapproval. Jon wanted to cover his ears against the thunder. Instead he shook Nathan by the shoulder, noticing he was starting to wake up.

"Nathan, the dragon, it's attacking!"

Nathan looked up. "Damn." He slowly began to stand up with help from Jon.

Jon watched in horror as the dragon gave chase to the horse, sending broken tables and chairs scattering in its wake. It took only a few steps for the dragon to cover the distance where Jon stood and two more to where the horse and riders disappeared through the set of open double doors. The dragon jammed its head through the doorway and stood there, trying to decide if it was worthwhile to pursue its prey down the set of stairs.

Jon was relieved that Nicole so far had been saved but now there was the immediate problem of the dragon looking for other food. He saw a potted tree a few feet away from the edge of the terrace.

"Nathan, help me push this tree on its side. Hurry!"

Nathan was rapidly regaining his strength; the spell that sapped him of his strength died with Lord Bennett. He joined Jon in pushing the tree over until the top half hung over the edge of the inn's perimeter.

"Grab onto a branch and hang over the side. The dragon may not see us." Jon locked his fingers on a branch and dangled above the ground five stories below. Nathan did the same as the dragon backed out of the stairwell and searched for other prey.

Smythe and Bryan were not so quick or fortunate as Jon and Nathan. Bryan let out a petrified scream as the dragon snapped Smythe in half and engulfed him in its huge jaws. Bryan fell to the ground and covered his face as the dragon let out a blast of dragon fire. He rolled on the ground in agony until the dragon snatched him in its maw as well, silencing his screams. The dragon scanned the terrace once more and saw nothing edible moving. It walked over to the body of Lord Bennett and grabbed him in his front claw. Satisfied with its haul, it leaped into air. The wings caused a windstorm on the terrace as it lifted off. Jon and Nathan glumly held on to the tree branch before deciding it was safe to climb back to the terrace.

———

Nicole thought she would never be able to catch her breath. Her stomach was being pounded by each step the horse took down the stone steps. It had been a frightening several hours since Lord Bennett and his men forced their way into her room and dragged her by the rope around her wrists to the terrace. She tried to fight the men but one merely slapped her head, telling her not resist or make a noise. In the hallway she saw Tony.

He didn't have a sword with him and was not a match for the four men kidnapping her.

She was carried to the Lookout Point Inn, the guards annoyed with her resistance at trying to make her walk. There wasn't anyone to offer her help in the deserted hotel and she was taken to the terrace. Lord Bennett was angry, blaming her for helping to hide the Locus Crystal.

After she was tied to one of the light towers, he used a thin branch cut from one of the trees to whip her.

Nicole thought she was going to die when the dragon appeared and was ready for such a fate when Tony suddenly appeared on a horse. Now she was being bounced on a horse, not sure where she was going.

Tony placed one hand on the small of her back to help stop her from sliding off. After what seemed an eternity, Tony stopped his horse.

"I think we're safe now, the dragon hasn't followed us. Are you all right, Nicole?"

"Yes, if I could only breathe."

Tony jumped down from his horse and quickly pulled her from the saddle. He took his knife and cut the rope that was still holding her wrists. Nicole rubbed her wrists and wrapped her arms around his neck and hugged him.

"Thank you, thank you, thank you." She blubbered out.

"You're welcome, my Lady."

Nicole planted a kiss on his cheek. "But we have to go back and help Jon and Nathan."

"Not we. I'll go back."

"I can fight. Just give me a sword."

Tony jumped back on his horse. "Dressed like that? No, Nicole, I didn't rescue you to put you back in danger."

Nicole covered her breasts. "Okay, you have a point."

"Who goes…" There was a pause as the speaker caught his breath. "…there? Answer at once."

"Tis I, Sir Keith. I have Nicole here. Could you look after her while I go back to the roof?"

Sir Keith, red faced and his chest heaving, appeared from around the corner of the staircase. A moment later Gilbert followed.

"Damn stairs! What bloody idiot made these steps so high?"

Sir Keith answered, "Yes, I would be honoured to protect Lady Nicole." He took out his sword and held it unsteadily in his hand.

Nicole was still frustrated that she wasn't able to return to help Jon and pointed a finger at Gilbert. "Gilbert, just what're you going to do?"

Gilbert closed his eyes, as if in pain. "Sir Anthony, might there be room on that horse for me? Me friend Jon may need help."

"There is. But where we'll be going is dangerous."

"Aye, I know." Gilbert slowly extended his hand for Tony to pull him up. "But I owe him me life and I must give what I have to help him. Tis only right."

Nicole watched them climb back up the stairs on the horse. "Be careful!" She shouted at their backs.

"They're brave men to return to fight that dragon. I wish I was in better shape so I could join them." He sighed. "I guess we better go back downstairs."

"Can't we wait for them here?"

"My lady, that could be dangerous and you're not really dressed for being out in public." He extended his arm for her to hold.

"Oh, damn it to hell anyway." She slipped one hand on his arm. "Do you think you could get me something to put on?"

"I'm not sure where…"

"Take off your shirt and give it to me."

"My shirt?"

"I'm damn near naked! Give me your damn shirt or I'll rip it off you."

———

Nathan and Jon surveyed the wreckage of the terrace when they heard the clatter of hoofs on the stone steps. A moment later Tony and arrived on his horse with Gilbert sitting in front of him, waving his sword.

Nathan raised one hand. "It's over. The dragon is gone and Lord Bennett is dead."

Gilbert replaced his sword back into its sheath. "Too bad, I's was spoiling for a good fight."

Jon laughed. "The only thing I'm spoiling for is a cold beer." He spoke to Tony. "How is Nicole? Is she badly injured?"

"I had to convince her she couldn't come back here to help save you. Almost naked, no weapon, and she was willing to charge back up here. I think she's alright."

Jon and Nathan followed the horse downstairs. In the lobby there was a sparse crowd that had ventured back into the hotel, mostly soldiers. They gave him a loud cheer as he entered.

"Jon!" Liz ran to him, giving him a big hug and kiss.

Jon received congratulations from Sir Keith. "Well done, sir. Well done. We certainly showed them."

Lady Karla had a hand on his arm as he stood bare chested, still holding a sword. "All of you were so brave." She looked at Sir Keith.

"You, Nathan and Tony saved my life." Nicole had tears running down her cheeks. She put her arms around Jon's neck, kissing him on the lips.

Liz frowned, watching the shirt she wore rise up to her cheeks during her long hug to Jon. *Okay, that's enough of a thank you.*

Nicole then gave Nathan a hug and a kiss on the cheek. The big man appeared uncomfortable with hands floating around her back without touching.

Nathan spoke. "I suggest we retire to our rooms and get a change of clothes. We can meet later for a celebration dinner and drinks." She spoke to Nicole. "I suspect you have some injuries that need to be taken care off."

Liz saw the red marks on Nicole's legs and softened her attitude toward her. *Those look painful.* "Can I help you with anything? You had quite an ordeal."

"Thanks. Actually, just some company to my room. My heart is still pounding."

"Allow me to accompany you." Sir Anthony stepped forward.

"That would be wonderful."

———

The normally staid lounge was noisy at Kosture Inn. Gentlemen insisted on buying drinks for Jon and all those who sat his table. Gilbert stood on the table and tried to sing a ballad of the great fight with Lord Bennett, using crude words that verged on the outrageous. Jon laughed at his lyrics as he sat with one arm draped around Liz. Nicole sat next to him on his other side, followed by Tony who sat next to her at the head of the table. Sir Keith was reserved but happy with Lady Karla by his side and while not drinking much, was still enjoying the festivities. Sir Nathan sat at the other end of the table and was getting drunk, though he wasn't being loud.

Jon was relieved that everyone survived the confrontation with Lord Bennett. He glanced over at Nicole. He noted that Tony and she seemed to be getting along rather well. He was also thankful that so far Liz, and himself had come to an understanding that what happened on Domum before they found each other was of no importance.

Sometime tomorrow they were to head back to Horscruff, meet with Lord Perry and find out if any of the three Voltaire Crystals Nicole had obtained could return them to Earth. Jon was curious what became of the Locas Crystals that Sir Bennett had, if they disappeared with him when the dragon took away his body or if they remained hidden somewhere. He also wondered about the whereabouts of Council Madoc and his own crystal.

Jon took another drink of his ale and decided problems such as that should be pondered with a clear head.

———

Jon, Tony, Liz and Nicole shared a carriage on the way to Seilini, enduring the bumpy ride. Occasionally, Jon and Liz rode their horses, finding the saddle more comfortable. It also gave them an opportunity to have a private conversation. Tony and Nicole didn't have the same flexibility, as Tony was expected to remain in the carriage.

"You certainly look the part of a warrior now. I never would've thought that when we first met."

"I guess it was forced upon me. I still don't like fighting."

"That's good to hear. But I do like you in these medieval clothes."

"Thanks."

"And the fact I know you're not wearing any underwear makes it even more interesting." She laughed.

Jon protested. "It's certainly not by my choice."

"I don't care. It does make easier for you to get ready for action when we stop tonight."

"Unlike you with your layers of clothes."

"No kidding. I'm roasting in these clothes. I wish I could strip down to a bikini."

"You could start a new fashion trend here." He laughed.

"Oh, sure. I'll end up being arrested for indecent exposure."

Nathan listened to Jon and Liz talk, laugh and enjoy each other's company. *It must be nice to have a companion. I can't complain. I'm going to be promoted to a Sir.*

———

When they reached Seilini, they moved into the Luscious Inn. Once more they took over two floors. Nicole turned down Tony's offer to share a room.

"Tony, I like you very much. But I'm not going to reward you for helping to save my life by going to bed with you. Perhaps when we get to know each other better."

He sighed. "I respect your wishes."

After dinner, the group retired to the lounge. Gilbert sang as he drank, inventing words to songs he couldn't remember.

Lady Karla quietly spoke to Sir Keith. "I cannot put up with this uncouth behaviour any longer. I believe I will go to my room now. I don't mean to impose but would you be so kind as to bring me wine to drink in my room? It is unseemly for a lady to be carrying drinks out of a lounge."

"Of course."

"Please give me a few minutes to prepare for bed."

Sir Keith nervously finished his ale. He bid Jon and the others goodnight and went to the bar to request a flagon of wine and two cups. He made his way to Lady Karla's room, tapping on the door.

"Enter."

Sir Keith saw Lady Karla was in bed, resting against a pillow at the headboard. A single candle in a glass container on a bedside table gave a warm glow to her.

"Thank you for bringing me a nightcap."

Sir Keith sat at edge of the bed, talking of the tumultuous time they had rescuing Nicole from Lord Bennett.

"I must say my pulse raced a bit when I saw you shirtless, practically carrying that barmaid downstairs."

"Now, Karla, she is a former barmaid."

"Perhaps, but she certainly didn't seem embarrassed being half naked in front of the others. I mean, I'm a bit exposed being in my bed wearing just this thin nightgown but at least I'm not in a public place." She pressed a hand against her lace top. "What do you think of this Liz person?"

"I don't know much about her. Sir Jon seems very taken with her."

"Yes, that may be due to her figure. I wasn't too impressed by her show of public affection for Sir Jon. She needs to learn there is a time and place for such things."

"I quite agree."

"For example, since we are alone here, I would say it is quite permissible to exchange a kiss with each other." She put down her wine cup. "The wine seems to have gone to my head."

Sir Keith assisted her to slide down under the covers. He bent down and gave her a gentle kiss on the lips. "Until tomorrow."

———

Tony took charge of paying for the hotel accommodations. The large number of people in his charge made travel slow, and he called a halt late afternoon to set up camp.

He approached Nicole. "We have a minor shortage of sleeping tents. There are a few possibilities we can consider."

"I can sleep in the tent I used before."

He shook his head. "No, you are no longer a common woman. It would raise eyebrows if you were to sleep in such a small tent. We can take one of the large tents that sleep six of the servants and have them double up in the smaller tents."

"That's not fair or very nice to the servants."

"True. We could share my tent. I could have a cot set up in the tent so we would have separate beds."

"One tent, separate beds. I guess that may work."

"Good, I'll make the arrangements." He walked away.

Nicole climbed into bed while Tony waited outside, enjoying an ale by the campfire. The lanterns gave a soft yellow light, and she relaxed into the pillow of the huge bed. *What a huge bed to go camping with.* She looked at the cot. *That looks uncomfortable.*

The tent front flap opened and Tony entered. He greeted her and began to undress.

Nicole watched him in the flickering light.

He didn't turn away from her, and simply undressed. For a moment she stared at his naked body until he pulled on the night shirt. Tony turned off the lantern and stretched on the cot. She heard it creak from his weight and his movements of trying to get comfortable.

"Tony, this is silly. This bed is big enough to share. Just stay on your half."

"Are you sure?"

"No, so you better hurry."

She noticed the mattress sagged in the middle and she ended up rolling next to him. She rolled on her side, facing away from him. Then she flipped around, facing him.

"Tony?"

"Yes."

"Can I cuddle up next to you? I don't want to have sex with you tonight but I do like being close to you."

He moved his arm around her, pulling her closer.

"Just so you know, I'm no longer a bar maid. I consider myself a lady of the court."

"Of course."

"That means you must treat me with respect and not just have a good time with me."

"I understand. I would be appreciative of the chance to engage you in courtship."

"That would be nice." She sighed and quickly fell asleep.

When she woke in the morning, Tony was already gone. She climbed out bed and dressed. Breakfast was waiting for her outside the tent on a small table. She saw everyone was hurrying about, getting ready for the trip to Horstruff. *Time to go home.*

TWENTY-FIVE

Nicole rode in the carriage with Tony, stepping outside when it was time for a lunch break. Nicole sought out Jon's company.

"Hi Liz. Can I borrow Jon for a bit? I want to ask for his advice."

"Sure, as long as it isn't on fashion. He's a bit hopeless on that topic."

They walked away from the main group.

"What's up?"

"You said you could take me back to Earth. I know that depends on the crystals working, but I felt them. I think they'll work."

"I hope so. What's the problem?"

"Earth. Full disclosure time. Eric, my man on Earth, is a bit of a brute. I was ready to pack it in with him before I ended up here. Cindy is his daughter. She's not mine, but I cared for her. If I was to return to Earth, I suspect they would have moved on. I don't think I could go back into their lives.

Here on Domum, with my new free woman status, I think I can have a pretty good life. I know some magic, which will be handy. Tony promised to help me get settled down, although I'm not sure of any long-term plans with him.

"So, I'm not sure. Do I go back to Earth which I don't know anymore, or stay in this medieval world that I do know?"

"I believe you could have a good life on Earth or on Domum. You're smart and resourceful. I think the question is, in five years, where do you see yourself? What do you want to be?"

"Hmm. I do kind of like living in a castle." She laughed.

"If you do stay here, perhaps you can travel to Earth sometime later. Learn a bit more magic and do a world jump."

"That's a thought. Thanks. I wanted your thoughts on it."

———

Lord Perry sat with Jon and Liz in one of his study rooms. He sat back in his large chair enjoying a drink of ale.

On the other side of his desk, Liz drank a glass of wine while Jon joined Lord Perry in drinking ale.

"I wanted to talk to Jon and ask him his perceptions of what happened on his quest, but I certainly have no objections to this wonderful young lady joining us." He grinned at Liz. "First, to confirm what I assume you already know, I'm the administrator of Horscruff. There are some details to take care of, for example, if I should retain Lord Bennett's castle as the location of jails and work camps. No matter, that's not why I've asked you here." He took another drink of his ale. "You see, I have a few questions concerning the relationship of Sir Anthony and Lady Nicole. Lord Graham is concerned about her past experience."

"Her past experience!" Liz almost stood up from her chair before Jon held a restraining hand. "Wasn't he a stable hand and before that a drunk and a womanizer? And they're judging her? What a load of BS."

"Liz, calm down. He was just asking…"

"I know exactly what he was asking. Why is it that she has to be pure while he can screw around and do what he wants?"

Lord Perry held out his hands with the palms facing her. "Please, please you have made your point to me. I'm friends with Graham family and will attempt to convey your thoughts the best I can." Lord Perry sighed.

Jon spoke. "The Grahams have nothing to be concerned about. I've spent a lot of time with Nicole, Lady Nicole that is, and she's a brave and virtuous young lady. Tony is lucky to have her interest."

"Thank you. I'll try to pass those sentiments along as well." He took a moment to gather his thoughts. "I have some unease about

Lady Karla. Sir Keith has given his endorsement concerning her involvement with the gnants and thought it was because she was acting under undue pressure. I was wondering if you saw the situation differently."

"She sold out to them, gave them information that caused danger for the rest of us. She did seem to be repentant afterward, if that means anything. Nicole's a good judge of character, uses vibrations or something, you may want to ask her opinion."

"Very well, I may do that. I understand Gilbert behaved himself for the most part and has essentially fulfilled his obligations to you."

"That's true. I've actually grown to enjoy his company a bit."

"Remarkable. Sir Keith mentioned to me that you also apparently befriended one gnant."

"Yeah, Rzet."

"Rzet. That's good. Humans and gnants will have to find a way to get along, eventually. That pretty much covers what I wanted to ask you except for the disappearance of Council Madoc. He seems to have vanished. That in itself isn't unusual; he's often disappeared for weeks at an end. But, apparently, he has the Locas Crystal."

"Yes, but I thought he could be trusted. He can be, can't he?"

"I've asked myself that question on more than one occasion." He sighed. "Council Madoc is a powerful warlock, and he does have ambition. But I don't believe he would use that crystal for his own gains. Having said that, I really don't know what he's doing with it."

"The other five crystals are lost, right?"

"Well, I think we can presume they disappeared with Lord Bennett, so that may mean that they're in that dragon's stomach. It wouldn't be easy to get those crystal."

"Unless one was a warlock."

Lord Perry nodded. "Unless one was a warlock. One thing that Council Madoc said to me as he was trying to convince me to oppose Lord Bennett was that it came down to if I trusted him. I did and I don't often make mistakes in judging people."

"I hope you're right this time as well. Are we still scheduled to return to Earth after lunch?"

"Oh yes, yes. Anytime you want actually. I thought you might enjoy a final celebration meal here first. It's also the best opportunity to give you the title Sir Jon, the dragon slayer."

Liz squeezed his hand and grinned at him.

"You're to give Nathan a title as well?"

"Yes, indeed. I will make him a sir as well and ask if he wants permanent employ within my castle. I believe he'll accept. I've also decided to pardon Lady Karla and Gilbert of past indiscretions."

"Is there any job you could give Gilbert? I'm sure if he had steady pay, he'd stop all those schemes he tries. He has a girlfriend in town and maybe..."

"I'll see what I can do." Lord Perry laughed and shook his head. "You want help everyone you know?"

"When I can. I have a favour to ask. I have the Mood Figurine that needs to be given to Lord Sussex."

"Yes, I can take care of it." Lord Perry smiled. "I don't believe you would have much use for its power."

———

Jon walked arm and arm with Liz to what used to be Lord Bennett's castle. Close behind them Nicole and Tony followed along with a host of others, including Sir Keith with Lady Karla, Gilbert and Donna and finally Nathan.

Jon shook hands with Sir Nathan first and the big man clasped him on the shoulder as well.

"If you ever get yourself in a spot of trouble, just send the word and I'll be there to help you."

"Thanks. Hopefully my life will be a bit quieter for a while."

Gilbert had a grin on his face as he said goodbye. He was still holding a tankard of ale from the celebration lunch. "'Tis been a grand adventure we've been on. Perhaps me ands Donna will gives you a visit sometimes."

"That would be great, Gilbert." He gave Donna a hug as well, with Gilbert watching carefully.

Sir Keith gave him a warm handshake, telling him to come for a visit sometime. Lady Karla offered her hand to him and gave him a prediction. "We'll be seeing you again, I'm certain of that. Take care in the meantime."

Tony and Jon eyed each other first before shaking hands. "Take good care of Liz, she's a treasure."

"I shall. And don't let Nicole go, you'll never find another like her."

He held out a hand to Nicole, but she ignored that, wrapping her arms around his neck and planting a kiss on his lips. "Don't you dare forget me."

"As if that's possible. I hope you can make it to Earth someday to visit."

"I'm hope so too. Magic and crystals are not guarantees of being able to travel between worlds."

Jon turned to his side where he saw Liz give Tony a kiss on his lips as well, perhaps a quarter of a second longer than Nicole's kiss to him. She glanced quickly at Nicole and returned to Jon, gripping his hand.

Jon took the Voltaire crystal and twisted the top half as he held the base. A spark jumped momentarily in the centre but then the crystal remained quiet. Jon frowned. "I guess this one doesn't work. Let's try the next."

This time the crystal shot a bright blue light between the halves. Jon watched the crowd around them fade and disappear into a white haze. When the white haze disappeared, Jon found they were standing on a rocky embankment far above a white-water river. The river didn't look like it belonged in Horstruff or in Ballymiller.

"Where are we, Jon?"

"I don't have a clue. This doesn't look like any place I know of."

"Perhaps it's Earth but in South America or someplace."

"Yeah, you could be right."

The roar from the thirty-foot lizard silenced his reply. The creature resembled a crocodile but stood high above the ground on its four legs. The tail appeared slimmer, but the head was oversized to its huge body. From forty feet away, it fixed its yellow eyes on Jon and Liz.

Jon almost dropped the crystal but recovered and gave it another twist. Again, a mist enveloped them and when it cleared, they were standing back in Domum.

"You're back! Decided you liked it better here after all?" Nicole grinned.

"We just got a helluva scare. Damn crystal took us to where this monster roared at us. I'm just glad we got back here and not some other place."

Gilbert shuffled forward. "Some of thems crystals do that. Not many. It's just another world, nothin' to worries abouts."

"We can try this last crystal then?"

"Sures. Bound to work. Three the charms, as they say."

Jon tried the last crystal. The spark between the two halves was strong and after the white mist evaporated, they found themselves home, standing in front of the Miller Castle.

He looked at the crystals in his hand. One of them had broken in three pieces, *I guess we can't use those to return to Domum, These are done.*

After spending a minute checking to make sure everything not only looked familiar, but also in fact was home, they went to the front door and walked in.

"Hey anybody, we're home!"

The first person to come from the living room to greet them was Sandra, followed closely by Council Madoc and Gordon Miller. Staying well at the back were Tom and Tuck.

"Jon! And Liz!" Sandra gave Jon a hug first and then Liz. "God, we didn't know what to do or think when Liz disappeared. Fortunately, Council Madoc showed up and informed us you were both alive and likely quite safe." She put her hands on her hips. "You could have phoned you know."

Jon laughed. "Didn't have money for a payphone."

Gordon Miller shook Jon's hand and Liz's. "Welcome home. Quite the adventure you must have had."

Everyone retired to the living room and Council Madoc informed Jon that he had left Domum to ensure Lord Bennett would not be able to steal the crystal.

"There are always some doubt when it comes to the outcome of battles. After some consideration, I decided the safest place was to return to Earth with it. If Lord Bennett won the battle, he still would be without the final crystal. Having it here would provide the highest level of safety. I also made a commitment to live on Earth, in exchange for Lord Perry's opposing Lord Bennett's grab for power."

"Sir Gordon has been kind enough to offer me accommodation at his castle, if I should have to remain on Earth."

Sandra watched Jon and Liz as they sat together in one of the loveseats, still holding hands. "We have also been infested with gnants and other creatures since you have left. Council Madoc has assured us they'll cause us no harm but they still give me a fright every time I see one."

"The gnants are just very curious what's transpiring in the battle between Lord Perry and Lord Bennett. I explained to Sandra and the others they're just trying to figure out the new order of things and believed this castle may have an influence on it. I spoke to one of the gnants and requested they kept their visits to a minimum and not to enter bedrooms unannounced. That seems to have reduced some screaming."

"I didn't scream that much." Sandra said.

Tuck pointed a finger at Tom. "I think he was referring to him."

"However, now that Jon and Liz have made it back safely, I think it best that the gateway you made between the two worlds be closed and the technology be hidden. Domum wouldn't last long from even mild interference from Earth."

Jon looked at the others in the room. "I agree. Domum must have a chance to exist on its own."

Liz nodded, followed by Sandra and Gordon. Tuck and Tom sighed heavily and agreed as well.

"You would know best. But damn, the discovery of the century."

Tuck patted his friend's shoulder. "We may have to go back to doing real work instead. Hey, anyone for pizza?"

Jon sat alone in his bedroom and made a phone call. The others continued celebrating their return by ordering a pizza to go with the beer.

Nadine answered on the third ring.

"Nadine, it's me, Jon."

"I know." Her voice was quiet, without emotion. "I am glad you made it made it back alive."

"Thanks. I met someone."

"That is good." She paused a moment and then continued. "Best of luck to you. I am leaving Boston. It is too cool and dry here."

"I see. Are you from Domum?"

"Yes. I was a gnant. Now I am not. I suppose I consider myself human. I am sorry I wasn't honest with you before. I was under the direction of the Adepts, my superiors. I like you as a human, Jon, but I know it would not have worked well between us."

"Where are you going to go?"

"South. Maybe Florida. I know it is warm there and better for my body."

"You have enough money?"

"Yes. I have gold."

"If you need any help, just call me."

"Thank you for your offer. Someday I might."

Jon said goodbye and reflected on his adventure to Domum, glad he had made it back to Earth.

"I wonder if I'll ever go back there?" He mused, not knowing events on Domum were already settling his fate.

The End

ABOUT THE AUTHOR

For a few years I wanted to try my hand at writing but too many obstacles prevented me from having the time to do so; three boys and a darling wife that loved home renovations to be more specific. Now the boys have "grown up" and left home I have time to do a bit more what I want to do, such as writing.

My other interests include wine, reading, astronomy, photography and convincing my wife that our home is actually fine the way it is. I have actually lost that battle. She wants our deck replaced; apparently rotten boards isn't considered safe anymore.

www.jhwear.com

 twitter.com/JH_Wear

ALSO BY JH WEAR:

Novels
A Taste Of Murder
Play Dead
Witches and Warriors
Shadows And Sensations

———

Castle Series
#2 The Return To Domum (coming soon!)
#3 The New King (coming soon!)